"Where's my dad?" The words were slurred, but comprehensible.

"Relax, Iris. It's okay," Cynthia whispered, caressing the girl's forehead tenderly with her fingers. "Your dad's outside with your mom and the doctors. You're in Ellis Hospital. I'm Cynthia, your nurse. Do you know what made you sick?"

Iris seemed to focus briefly on Cynthia, then closed her eyes, dramatically going from pale to dusky. "Mick Jagger. He tried . . . kill me. He wants . . ."

Adele and Cynthia exchanged glances. The girl was delirious.

Within a second or two, Iris stopped breathing. . . . Adele felt for the girl's carotid pulse. Pulling the teen's head back so the neck was flexed, she inserted a plastic airway between Iris's teeth. Adele said a silent prayer, pressed the soft mask of the ambu bag tightly over the girl's nose and mouth, and pushed air into the young, compliant lungs. . . .

By Echo Heron
Published by The Ballantine Publishing Group:

INTENSIVE CARE
MERCY
CONDITION CRITICAL
PULSE
TENDING LIVES
PANIC

PANIC

Echo Heron

IVY BOOKS • NEW YORK

This book contains an excerpt from *Paradox* by Echo Heron. This excerpt has been set for this edition only and may not reflect the final content of the forthcoming edition.

An Ivy Book
Published by The Ballantine Publishing Group
Copyright © 1998 by Echo Heron

Excerpt from *Paradox* by Echo Heron copyright © 1998 by Echo Heron.

www.randomhouse.com

Library of Congress Catalog Card Number: 98-92890

ISBN 0-8041-1458-7

Manufactured in the United States of America

First Edition: August 1998

10 9 8 7 6 5 4 3 2 1

ACKNOWLEDGMENTS

For their technical advice, continued friendship and support, I wish to thank:

First and foremost, Ken Holmes, Coroner—for his encouragement and persistent support, and all his forensic and law enforcement advice;

Tom H. Stevens—for his expertise in things biochemical;

As always—Thomas Meadoff—the "Most Competent and Thorough" M.D. around, for his medical advice;

Frank Langben—for taking the time to help with the on-line research;

J. Patrick Heron, Esq.—for his caring support and the legal advice;

Jane and Glen Justice—for always taking me in no questions asked; Storm Salato Deputy—for driving with her demanding, bratty little sister across country without once attempting to strangle her; Petula and Glen Dvorak-Justice—for providing a voice for Mirek; Kellie Moore and Scott Jones—this nomad's moving experts; SDB, for the Heimlich maneuver in Los Angeles and the brainstorming in the storm in Detroit;

Catherine Barnes, Art Coolidge, Elinor and Franco Mazzucchelli, Simon Heron, Mary C. Bianchi, Kelly J. Pratt, Madeline Weber, and Chere Burke—for their continued friendship and love.

DEDICATION

For Mooshie—a.k.a. Moo Shoo Pork with Pancakes:

My constant companion, familiar, monitor ornament, and keyboard walker. So many years of your little dances between me and the screen, and you've never once hit the delete key.

ONE

THE FRECKLE-FACED TEEN TAPPED HER FINGERS against the crystals hanging from the antique lamp. Rainbows of light jitterbugged over the walls of her father's study. Home from boarding school for less than a week, and already Iris Hersh missed London and her friends at St. Theresa's. Perhaps, she thought, she should have gone on the summer holiday bike tour through France instead.

She rested her chin in her hand and shrugged. No big deal. She'd go on the bike tour next summer; this year she had other obligations. *Somebody* on the home front had to help her father during his campaign for state senator. With all the time her mother was spending on the dumb renovation of the study and the library, she was useless to him.

Fromer, her father's campaign manager, focused too much on the business end of things and not enough on the social aspects of the political realm—anyone who'd advise her father to refuse an invitation to speak at the California League of Women Voters annual conference in favor of attending an NRA convention, wasn't exactly experiencing reality on a regular basis.

She hadn't liked Samuel Fromer from the moment she met him. Why her father had settled on such a dweeb for a manager was beyond her. The way he looked at women, including her and her mother, was "politically incorrect," she said aloud, mimicking sticking her finger down her throat.

Iris hunted for a handkerchief in the pocket of her brushed silk culottes. She sneezed, said "Euew," and blew

1

her nose. That stupid geek of a man who'd sat next to her in first class from London. He'd hacked and coughed all over her for the whole trip. Whatever germs he'd blown her way had been virile—she'd been fighting off a cold ever since with massive doses of vitamin C.

Momentarily a brightly colored image of millions of germs—fresh out of the body of the Geek Host—invading her innocent orifices, made her want to spit into her already damp handkerchief. Grimacing, she restrained herself. As the daughter of a state senator, she would have to maintain a pose of refinement and breeding.

The ongoing low-grade headache and the drippy nose were a minor worry—as long as she wasn't sick for the fund-raiser dinner. It was, her father assured her, one of the more important events in his campaign—a make or break event. She had to be up front and center for him, doing as much as she could to tell people that he *was* the best candidate for the job. She wanted to know his platforms and his issues backward and forward, so she could spout them off with conviction whenever asked.

The teen put away the handkerchief and picked at her cuticles. A vague sense of frustration and boredom plagued her. It wasn't like she didn't have every possible toy at her disposal: there was the wall-sized TV screen and an unlimited access to videos, or the computer with all the bells and whistles. Or, she could taxi to her father's campaign headquarters and help send out flyers or whatever it was one running for office sent out. She could play tennis, or ask her mother for a ride to Village Mall to meet her friends and shop.

She had plenty of friends who wanted to see her and hear all about London and the latest European styles and what the English girls were like. Mostly they would want to know about the English boys. Were they handsome? Were they sexy? Did they have sex the same way American boys did?

Still encumbered with her virginity at fifteen, she would have to make up some stories. Then again, she could repeat one of the hundreds of detailed stories she'd heard from the other girls at school. The Brits, it seemed to her, were oversexed in general. The English boys were way more aggressive than American boys, and the English girls were promiscuous beyond belief. It both shocked and fascinated her the way they all had sex so casually, and with so many different people. She was spellbound when they talked about it, describing the various acts and positions, blow-by-blow—so to speak. It was, she rationalized, part of her formal education.

She smiled. She couldn't wait to shock her friends with details of the scandal that took place in the first semester between a fourth-level girl and one of the headmistresses. Of course the incident had been hushed up and the guilty parties dismissed at once, but the stories had gone through St. Theresa's like flames up a dry Christmas tree. The older girls would not talk about it around her, mistakenly thinking she was too young and naive to understand. Iris rolled her eyes. She wasn't too young or innocent, nor was she stupid. Not with an IQ of 130. Did they think she wouldn't *know* about girls who . . . who did those things together?

Getting up from the desk, she idly strolled over to the samples of marble tiles Hannah had left behind for her parents' approval. She chose an Italian beige tile, veined with dark pink and maroon, and set it to the side. For the trim, she chose the maroon.

Hannah Sandell, besides being a famous interior designer, was her parents' latest obsession. Over the years, her parents had displayed a pattern when forging friendships. They would suddenly take up with a certain couple or individual, make fast friends, and then, over the course of a year, drop them slowly but surely.

Hannah had been her mother's college roommate from a hundred years ago. Tall, blond, and blue-eyed, the woman whom everyone in her parents' social circle called the "White Swan" was, in Iris's opinion, beautiful and mysterious. One thing was for sure, the White Swan knew everything there was to know about fashion and style. Her makeup, the way she dressed, her jewelry—was the latest and the best.

She looked out over the manicured yard toward the greenhouse. Her mother knew nothing about fashion, and cared even less. She hoped Hannah would have some influence on Mimi, not only on her expensive, albeit tasteless, wardrobe, but in bringing some focus into Mimi's life.

Most days, her mother spent her time talking on the phone with friends, reading insipid novels, leafing through clothing catalogs (though never buying anything), and, once in a while—to the annoyance of the women who worked there—trying to make herself useful as a file clerk in her husband's plastic surgery office.

Then there was Mimi's habit of getting jazzed about something and then never following through. The last pursuit, in a long line of brief interests, had been gardening. Initially motivated, Mimi purchased the most expensive gardening equipment one could find, along with half a library of landscaping and horticulture books. She'd even hired a gardener to come twice a week to tutor her in the art.

Within two weeks, she'd canceled the gardener; the gardening tools were left out in the rain to rust alongside the muddy patches of unplanted raw earth; and the books went into boxes that were eventually put into storage, never to be seen again. Eventually, Gordon hired a landscaper to come in and clean up the mess.

It had been the same with the book she was going to write about Taco their cat (since deceased), learning French, or how to play the piano, the framing and matting project, not to mention the computer fiasco. There was a list as long as her memory, and an excuse from Mimi for every unfinished undertaking.

Now there was Hannah and this redecorating venture. She hoped Hannah was one friend they would not be so quick to let go; the idea of a long-term family friend as socially aware and sophisticated as Hannah appealed to her. It certainly wouldn't hurt her father's campaign, either. Iris hoped

Hannah would do a complete makeover on her parents' lives, let alone their house and Mimi's wardrobe.

The grandfather clock in the corner, one of the many pieces of tacky furniture Hannah had thankfully marked for removal to storage, chimed one. Through the glass of the greenhouse, she could see her mother and Hannah moving around, repotting the young datura plants Mimi loved so much. While she watched, both women suddenly burst out laughing. The sound of their laughter made her smile.

She stretched, then rolled her neck. She would make lemonade and bring it to them. Maybe she could talk them into telling her more stories about when they were crazy college students doing jockstrap raids on boys' dorms.

Hannah smiled as Iris sipped a thimbleful of the cabernet she'd bought for dinner. "Like it?" she asked.

Iris rolled the wine slowly over her tongue and decided she really did. "Yes. Very much. What is it?"

"It's a nineteen-eighty private stock cabernet from the Phelps Vineyards. How about you, Gordon? Like it?"

Gordon Hersh tasted the wine and imperceptibly shrugged. Wine was wine. Knowing good wine from Manischewitz had never been one of his strong suits, but he'd faked his way through enough wine tastings to know the lingo. He held his glass to the light, then sniffed the wine.

"Very nice. Good clarity, a lovely bouquet. Full and rich . . . almost velvety. . . ." He saw his daughter roll her eyes and laughed at himself. "Oh hell, I don't know, Hannah. It's too dry for my taste. Give me a good German beer any day, although I'm sure my grandfather would roll over in his mass grave at Dachau if he heard me say that."

Mimi shot her husband a disapproving glance and stirred a second packet of artificial sweetener into her tea.

"You really should try some of this, Mimi," Gordon encouraged. "A little red wine is good for you."

"And suffer with a headache all night?" she said reproachfully. The petite, dark-eyed woman sipped her chamomile tea and glanced over the rim of her cup at Hannah. "This isn't Europe. I don't think American adolescents need to be introduced to alcohol any earlier than when they find it on their own."

She shrugged. "But then again, Gordon thinks I'm a square for drinking herbal tea."

"It's not the tea," Gordon defended. "It's all the chemicals you dump into it." He motioned toward the bowl of saccharin packets. "Wine is better for you than that poison any day of the week."

"*Chacun à son goût*—each to his own, Gordon," Hannah interjected, patting his hand kindly. "Mimi never liked alcohol. Even in college. She'd drink half a bottle of beer and we'd have to lock her in her room." A look passed between the two women that Gordon did not recognize, but Iris did. It was the wordless exchange between women who had been close friends for a long time—an unspoken connection that would always be outside the reach of a man's understanding.

A jealousy knotted in Iris's chest, then quickly passed. That they shared secrets she would never know didn't matter. She wanted this worldly woman and her mother to remain friends. In the long run, she sensed, they'd all benefit from it.

"How are the renovations coming along?" Gordon asked. Behind the question was the not-so-hidden anxiety about needing it done soon. Samuel Fromer had arranged for "California Mornings" to interview the Senate hopeful in three weeks' time. The producer of the show, a staunch Republican, decided it would be to Gordon's political advantage to conduct the interview in his home . . . preferably in a room that reflected style and taste without being ostentatious.

"We're right on schedule," Hannah assured him. "The upholsterers received the fabrics today. The rug Mimi . . ." Hannah glanced at Iris and winked. ". . . *and* Iris chose should be delivered tomorrow."

Gordon nodded absently. Instead of listening, he found himself again wondering what it would be like to bed the White Swan. He guessed it would be a singularly gymnastic experience. The woman was a walking sexual innuendo—tall and slender, large breasts (real, not implants), perfect skin, and a slinky walk that screamed "do me" with every step. She would be one of those rare blondes who were extremely responsive to touch—more like brunettes, whose nerve endings were closer to the skin surface.

He imagined her under him, her long legs scissoring his waist, her nipples hard and deep pink. She would talk dirty to him in that provocative, throaty voice to spur him on. When his crotch started to ache, he forced his thoughts elsewhere. He resolved not to be one of those politicians who gave his opponent any opportunity to smear his name or his reputation as a sterling family man.

God knew he'd been good. Considering the number of beautiful women who had invited him to share their beds, and the fact that he'd turned down every one, he believed he deserved a medal. In light of Mimi's frigidity, he felt he had a claim to sainthood.

He watched his wife chatting happily with the blonde and hoped some of the woman's sensuality would rub off on her. There was no mistake that she had been more cheerful in the last few weeks. He also noticed that Mimi had begun styling her hair and wearing makeup again. When she took the time to care about her looks, Mimi was beautiful; when she was happy, her smile could take one's breath away. From the perspective of a plastic surgeon, her features were ideal—large, well-shaped eyes, full mouth, pretty nose, smooth olive skin. Born of a Spanish father and Jewish mother, Mimi had inherited those finely chiseled, classic features that most women paid him a fortune to create for them.

Mimi's green eyes sparkled as she laughed over some joke that Iris made. The exotic beauty that he had found so appealing sixteen years ago still thrilled him.

"Would you like some more wine, Gordon?" the White

Swan asked. Her light blue eyes shone intensely under dark lashes. She had a natural way of speaking, he noticed, that drew people into an invisible but secure inner circle.

"I'd love some. Thank you." He pushed his glass toward her, flashing his You're-the-only-woman-who-can-save-me look and turned his attention to Iris, who had not touched the food on her plate.

"No appetite, honey? Are you feeling all right?"

Iris sniffed through a stuffy nose. "I'm okay. I think I caught a cold on the plane from this geeky guy who was sneezing and coughing all over the place. He was such a slob, he never covered his mouth. Yeuck."

Mimi studied her daughter with a mother's concern. "Have you been taking extra vitamin C like I told you? Maybe we should have Dr. Bollinger or Dr. Ingram take a look at you tomorrow."

"Oh Mom," Iris said, rolling her eyes. "It's no big deal. It's just a cold. Everybody gets colds. I'll be fine."

Gordon laid his hand against the hot, dry skin of his daughter's cheek. The child was the one true joy in his life. Born on his birthday, from the first moment he held her in his arms, he knew they shared more than just that day—they had a common spirit. Other than those huge green eyes, Iris shared nothing with Mimi. Iris was already five foot seven and had an athletically appealing body. In her wide, freckled face, there was not one trace of her Jewish or Spanish ancestry. Iris was so typically Irish-looking that Gordon at first wondered if she were really his. That fear vanished by the time she was three, and he would catch a certain way she held her lips while working, or her laugh . . . unmistakably Hersh. She was fiercely independent, more clever and savvy than God, and more assertive than any businessman or politician he'd ever done business with.

The child was eerily perceptive, to the point where he'd always suspected her of having some extrasensory powers. Even when she was very young, she could size someone up before he'd even formed an opinion. Like the time when

Governor Green asked if she wanted to play him in a game of Hearts. The seven-year-old had declined the offer. "I don't mean to be overtly insolent," she'd said, using adult inflections, "but I don't play cards with professional cheaters."

Iris was definitely Daddy's girl.

Gordon pushed his chair back, dismissing his concern for his daughter's health. He was a physician, albeit a plastic surgeon, but still an M.D. He would know best when and if Iris needed medical intervention.

"How about if you and I put that wonderful brain that God gave you to work tonight—that is, if you don't have other pressing social engagements?"

Brightening considerably, Iris met her father's eyes, a smile beginning at the corners of her mouth.

"Sam's coming over with the final draft of the speech I'm going to give at the fund-raiser. I'd like you to listen to it and tell me what you think.

"Maybe you can convince Sam that we need to address the concerns of the younger people. Sometimes I think he dwells too much on the hard sell." He pulled his daughter's chair away from the table. "Perhaps Miss O'Hersh would let me know when I sound like a Mr. Oldass?"

Both Iris and her father laughed at the names, which were part of a secret joke they'd shared since she was five. Linking arms, they exited the dining room stage right, leaving the two women at the table to their own devices.

Mimi arranged the coffee cups, glass of iced tea, and the desserts on the silver serving tray and let Hannah carry it into the study, where Gordon was fervently pointing out the weaknesses of his opponent. Iris was an enthusiastic audience, nodding in agreement at certain points, frowning at others, then making a quick note or two in the spiral notebook that lay in her lap. Samuel Fromer sat in a corner chair blinking behind his glasses, also taking notes.

When Hannah entered the room, Fromer raised his eyes

to her bustline and remained fixed there as was his habit.
Irritated, she was momentarily tempted to slap his hand or
offer to send him a photograph of her breasts, so he could
study them on his own time.

She set down the tray and poured coffee from two identical Tiffany sterling silver serving pots. She handed Samuel
Fromer his cup. He smiled at her breasts and thanked them.

She set Gordon's coffee on his desk and handed Iris a
frosted tea glass. "Iced tea for you, sweet pea."

Iris combed her hair back with her fingers, flashed a
broad smile at Hannah, then turned back to give her father
her full, loving attention.

Hannah closed the paint color sample book, glanced at
the clock over the mantel and then at Mimi who was asleep
on the couch. She finished her iced tea and quietly tiptoed to
the study, listening at the door a moment before entering.
Gordon Hersh was talking in what she called his Booming
Republican voice about offshore drilling in California.

Inside, Gordon sat leaning back in his swivel chair with
his feet up on his desk, drinking Iris's glass of iced tea.
Samuel Fromer watched him closely, a frown pulling at his
mouth. It was an expression that made him look even more
like Henry Kissinger than he already did.

Her legs slung over the end of the leather couch, Iris lay
propped against a damask pillow, sipping her father's coffee
from the china cup. She put a finger to her lips, a warning
that her father was in the middle of an important point and
was not to be interrupted. Hannah nodded and began load-
ing the tray with the empty dessert plates.

When Gordon and Sam began arguing over Gordon's pre-
sentation, Hannah sat down next to Iris. "Want to go in to
San Francisco tomorrow with me and your mother? We
need to go to my office to choose fabric for the window
treatments and then your mother wants to find a dress for
the dinner.

"I'll pick up both of you in the morning. Maybe we can have lunch at the Palace Hotel?"

Excited over the prospect of shopping with Hannah, Iris swung her legs to the floor, beaming. "That would be great! Can you help me pick out a dress, too?"

"Might as well," Hannah said. "Can you be ready by nine?"

Iris nodded happily and gave her a kiss on the cheek. "Why don't we take the ferry to the Embarcadero and then cab it from there? It'll be more fun than driving."

"Good idea." Hannah gave the girl's braid a playful yank. "I haven't had a girls' shopping spree in a long time."

Iris stood and yawned. Every eye in the room was drawn to her slim figure; even Hannah couldn't help but notice how much the lithe young girl reminded her of a cat.

"I'm going to bed, Dad. I still think you shouldn't bash Senator McGruder so much in your speech—negative campaigning really turns people off. You really need to put in more down-to-earth and sentimental touches." She glanced sideways at Samuel. "Lay off the hard sell, Mr. Oldass. You've got to come from the heart if you want to win the people these days."

Samuel Fromer ran a hand through his thinning reddish brown hair. "Gordon, I think you've got a bleeding-heart liberal here," he said, wearing a lopsided grin. He turned to Iris. "People may say they like a candidate to come from the heart, but when it boils down to it, Iris honey, they're really more concerned with what comes from the pocket."

"And what goes into it," added Hannah, giving the man a look. She adjusted Iris's headband. "Try to fix an idea of what kind of dress you want to wear to the dinner. Color, fabric, and basic style. It will help narrow the search."

"Black, silky, sexy, but . . ." Iris rushed to finish before her father could object. ". . . sensible."

"Speaking of pockets," Gordon joked, "be kind to your father's. Keep in mind I'm the poor sap paying for all this."

"Oh my God," Iris groaned, her wrist pressed to her forehead. "Mr. Oldass is worried about money. Time to get out the keys to the poorhouse."

As soon as the study door closed behind the girl, the three of them laughed.

"Between the redecoration of the study and the girls' wardrobes," Gordon said, "you're going to break my bank, Hannah."

"Yeah," Samuel agreed. "Thank God you made such a generous campaign contribution, or the doc here would be licking envelopes and carrying around his own soapbox. Stick around for a while—at least until we get into office, would you?"

"A soapbox might not be so bad, you know," Hannah said seriously. "Iris has a point about people wanting their candidates to come from the heart. People like a dashing, personable—*touchable*—leader.

"Maybe Samuel should get you more appearances at all the county fairs and town barbecues, or go to local libraries and town meetings . . . meet the people one-on-one, shake their hands—kiss their babies. Climb down out of your ivory tower. Even John and Marcia Republican don't really want another rich businessman in office. They want rich, real people in office . . . someone just like them, but who was smart enough to make the most of it.

"You should get Iris more involved, too. She's really quite an amazing person, Gordon."

Hannah knelt down to retrieve a spoon from under one of Mimi's garish overstuffed chairs, while both men watched her every move, paying special attention to her legs and ass. "She's so bright it's frightening. A couple of days ago we spent a few hours going over the basic principles of interior design. By the end of the day, she was making design suggestions that it took me years to learn.

"Take today for instance. I was giving Mimi a massage, and I showed Iris a few of the massage techniques I learned in Sweden? She executed them perfectly within a few minutes. It was . . ."

Gordon stopped listening as the vision of the blonde giving Mimi a massage played in his mind's eye. He imagined the big Swede straddling him instead of Mimi, digging into his back with those long fingers.

". . . I enjoy giving massages to people who can take deep muscle work," the sloe-eyed woman was saying, studying him.

For a moment he was caught by the intense, light blue gaze, and held captive. Mesmerized.

"I'm quite good at it actually."

Gordon and Samuel stared at her, both unsure as to whether the woman was aware of the double meaning of what she was saying.

Only a little ashamed of himself, Gordon forced his mind away from the motel bed vision in which he and a faceless man were making a Hannah sandwich, and returned his attention to the present. She was still going on about the health benefits of high colonics and deep Swedish massage. Seeing nothing of the sensual in her look, he decided she was simply enthusiastic about her subject.

"I should fire Sam and have you as my campaign manager," he joked, though the thought had seriously crossed his mind after he'd seen the way she'd handled herself at a recent social event at the governor's home. In a polite conversational political debate with a couple of professional politicians, she'd made mincemeat out of them.

"Is there anything you don't do extremely well?"

She sighed and picked up the filled tray. "Yes, there is," she said with a certain sly smile. "I don't lose well."

After Hannah left them to themselves, Samuel shook his head, turning to make certain the door was closed. "Forgive me, Gordon, and no offense to Mimi, but if the White Swan were in Mimi's place, you'd be a shoo-in. The woman has chutzpah *and* class, *and* brains, not to mention . . ." He made the international doublehanded sign for a curvaceous woman, then kissed his fingers. ". . . she's built."

A pang of deep regret zigzagged around Gordon's gut as he thought about his sham of a marriage. Still, he was insulted by Fromer comparing the two women so tactlessly. Mimi may not have been as socially sophisticated as Hannah, but she'd been a good mother to Iris, and she was a kind and charitable person. It occurred to him that more than once in the not-so-distant past, she had gone out of her way for Samuel Fromer—and then some.

Suddenly enraged, he glared at the man. "You want I should divorce my wife, Fromer? You're an ingrate. Mimi is my wife, and that's what we have to work with, so shut up about her."

Fromer held up a hand and shrugged. "Wait. You misunderstood." He began pacing again, rubbing his chin. "All I'm saying is that you've got a valuable asset in the White Swan, Gordon. She's smart. Very smart. Who said you can't have a woman as a best friend? Look at Clinton. The putz surrounds himself with smart and savvy women who advise him." Samuel shook his head. "Two terms, Gordie. That ain't bad . . . for a schmuck."

"Psssh. Hannah is Mimi's friend. I barely know the woman."

"So? Get to know her. I could think of worse things to do."

Samuel paced some more. "A close woman friend. Think about it, Gordon—it's a show of strength and character for a straight man to have a platonic relationship with a beautiful single woman. Iris and Mimi love her. There'll be no jealousy, no hanky-panky." Samuel Fromer sweated with excitement. "Fuck, the women libbers will love it."

Gordon shook his head and held up a hand. "She's got a history, Sam. That abortion business with Barbara Bush? For God's sake, it made *Newsweek*."

"Hello, Gordon. This is twenty-first century California, my friend, the land of progressive thinkers."

Gordon started to protest, but Samuel held up a hand. "Okay, we'll have her checked out to make sure, but you've got to see this for the gift it is. She's not far enough away from the right that the Republicans will get too bothered by her, and yet she's close enough to the left to make the liberals look twice." He broke off and snorted, "Did I say she'll make the liberals look twice? Shit, every man is going to look twice—first at her and then you. The media love women like her.

"This woman could be very useful to you, Gordon." Samuel bit his thumbnail, his eyes shifting as he thought. "There are some very important men who would do a lot to get next to a woman like that."

Gordon stared at his manager, shaking his head. "You make it sound like she's a high-priced call girl, and I'm her pimp!"

"Not a call girl." Samuel smiled. "Think of her more like the honey that draws the flies."

There is no nightmare that has ever been or ever will be that can compare in horror or bizarreness to the nightmares had by those who become ill while sleeping. Iris Hersh was caught in the vortex of just such a nightmare.

By the time she'd crawled into the antique canopy bed, she'd felt what the little sister at St. Theresa's infirmary would have described as "a bit rummy."

It had been the coffee. It was so dumb to drink it at all, let alone on an empty stomach. She'd only tried coffee once before and had actually vibrated until she'd thrown up. But she'd wanted to show off for her father, proving to him that she was *adult*. On a deeper level, she wanted him to know that if and when her mother failed him, she would be there, ready to fill her mother's shoes. She giggled over the image of her size 9 feet trying to wriggle into her mother's size 5 shoes, thinking that she *must* be rummy to think such a thing was funny.

As soon as her head hit the pillow, she'd fallen into a

strange dream about the upcoming fund-raiser. Standing behind her father at the podium, she was listening attentively to his speech when the audience began to whisper and point.

On the other side of her father, Mimi stood naked except for shoes (tiny) and purse (gargantuan). Worse yet, kneeling in front of her mother, suckling her *there*, was Mick Jagger.

That was when things began to deteriorate. She tried to pull a tablecloth off the nearest table so as to cover her mother's shame, but found she could only move in slow motion. The tablecloth was laden with concrete fruit. No one was listening to her pleas for help. Even worse was that Mick Jagger had sucked the life out of her mother and left her dead on the stage. But no one seemed to notice Mimi's lifeless body, so intent were they in the adoration of her father.

She screamed to Samuel Fromer for help, but realized immediately that he was in league with the Jagger monster. He had a gun and was extending his arm, pointing it at her father's heart. She tried to scream, but the piece of concrete fruit stuck in her throat wouldn't let her.

The Mick Jagger thing came for her. Powerless to move, Iris felt its razor-edged talons slicing through the center of her forehead. Finding the most vulnerable spots, the talons sawed back and forth, ripping at delicate brain tissue, causing excruciating pain and nausea.

Before she sank into the darkest part of a coma, the last bit of her consciousness threw up a flag of panic—not at the thought that she and her father were going to die, but that her father's campaign would be ruined.

At 2:13 A.M., Gordon Hersh's sleep was disturbed by a faint sound coming from the room next door. In the hazy world between sleep and wakefulness, the noise brought up unpleasant memories of his rotation in emergency room when he was an intern. Blood bubbling out of slit throats. Sucking, gaping stab wounds to the chest. Gunshot wounds to the gut. It was enough to wrench him to full consciousness and send him running into Iris's room.

Seventeen minutes after she had slipped into unconsciousness, he found his daughter on the lace-fringed canopy bed choking to death on her own vomit.

TWO

"I WAS TOLD THIS ISN'T THE USUAL RUN-OF-the-mill no-info VIP patient," said Adele. "That's half of why I'm assigning her to you, Cynthia. The other half is that you're the best R.N. we've got available."

Cynthia O'Neil huffed and rolled her eyes. As far as she was concerned, having a ninth patient added to her already heavy patient load was some kind of bullshit—and it wasn't even 8:00 A.M.

"VIP my butt," she snapped irritably. "What did the patient do, get the Hope Diamond stuck up her ass or something?"

Adele Monsarrat, senior R.N. of Ellis Hospital's infamous Ward 8, shook her head and smiled. At times like these it was Cynthia's mortician-turned-nurse sarcasm she depended on to keep her going. In light of being assigned as charge nurse of the ward, dealing with budget cuts due to managed care (she thought of it more as "mangled care"), plus having six patients of her own, today she definitely needed a laugh.

Tina, Ward 8's notoriously cantankerous clerk, answered the nursing station phone with a growl. Without so much as a grunt, she held the receiver out to Adele. "It's some uptight asshole faggot nurse in ER. He wants to give report on the new admit."

Adele put the waiting party on hold long enough to throw Tina a withering glance and place patient report forms in front of herself and Cynthia. Both R.N.'s picked up an extension at the same time.

"Hello? This is Adele Monsarrat, charge nurse. The patient's bedside nurse, Cynthia O'Neil, is on the other line. We're ready for report on VIP Jane Doe."

"And this is uptight asshole faggot Randolph Ingram ready to give report," came the masculine voice.

Adele and Cynthia exchanged glances. Dr. Randolph Ingram was Chief of Medicine for Ellis Hospital and one of the best internists in Marin and San Francisco Counties.

"Tell your clerk," he began with a hint of mirth, "to at least hit the hold button before she maligns the poor caller."

"Sorry, Doctor." Narrowing her eyes, Adele shot daggers at Tina, who used her impenetrable, miserable attitude like a shield. "I'll personally retrain the whelp as to how to use the hold button, and I promise I won't be gentle. If she balks, I'll cut off her ears with a dull butter knife."

There was a pause while Dr. Ingram thought about the woman's response. He remembered the reputation Ward 8 nurses had of being renegades—slightly over the edge and left of centerline. The nurses who were still left after the hospital's budget-cutting rampage were reported to be the cream of the crop in nursing skill and knowledge.

"Okay, good deal. I'm sending you a real mystery this time."

"So, this is new?" Adele asked in her best Barbra Streisandese.

Research of obscure diseases was Dr. Ingram's passion and what made him a hero in the medical community. His subspecialty being infectious diseases, for anyone having a "mystery case" that refused diagnosis—Randy Ingram was the man to call.

Dr. Ingram smiled. "Yes. This one is new and wild. Usually, I've got some clue as to which way is up, but we're operating completely in the dark here. The patient is a fifteen-year-old female—Gordon Hersh's daughter. She's been in boarding school in London, and came home five days ago for summer holiday. No medical history to speak of. She's had all her vaccinations and what's left of the usual childhood diseases.

"Mrs. Hersh said the girl has been suffering from a slight cold. She went to bed about ten P.M. without any specific complaints, then around two this morning, Dr. Hersh heard her choking and found her in a delirious state.

"Rescue Forty got her in here about two-thirty. Her BP was down to sixty palpable, she was febrile at one-oh-two and extremely dehydrated. Gordon said her mattress was soaked through with emeses and urine. I had to do a cut-down to get an IV in.

"She's been coming in and out of consciousness, although she doesn't make much sense when she's in. The nurses say she's more out of it now than earlier and appears to be having a tremendous amount of headache pain—asked her father to pull the knives out of her brain a few times.

"Her pupils and reflexes are sluggish, which made me think maybe we might have had a bleed into the ventricle, but we did a CAT scan and found nothing. We did a spinal tap—again, nothing."

The doctor sighed. "She's presenting like a viral infection. We've done every test we can think of and so far nothing has turned up. Sed rate's normal."

"What about a drug screen?" Adele asked. When it came to other physicians' family members, the docs were sometimes reluctant to order discriminating tests like blood alcohol levels or drug screens.

"Don't I wish it were that easy. She's clean as a whistle—not even aspirin. Her BP is still down around eighty. She aspirated, so she's got a lot of diffuse pulmonary edema on the chest film and her PO2 has started to drop. For now she's on a non-rebreather mask, but I want Briscoe to intubate her when we get there, so make sure there's an intubation set and a ventilator ready to go.

"Hersh insists she be a Jane Doe ID. He also wants one-on-one nursing care, so make sure it's an R.N. with lots of years on her and not some flunky med tech." Under his breath Ingram added, "Hersh hasn't had time to consult with his campaign manager yet about whether they want the news people in on this or not, so keep it a secret up there. I don't want the nurses blabbing this to everybody in the lunch line."

Cynthia put a hand over the mouthpiece and yelled to the imaginary clerk. "Hey, Mac, hold the call to Associated Press on that new admit, will ya?"

Amused, the physician sighed, but was too tired to laugh. "She's got a couple of lines. I've got her on a dobutamine drip and some . . . ahh . . ."

Adele could hear him stretching his neck to read the IV bag.

". . . D five and a quarter. There's—"

"Wait," Cynthia interrupted, trying to stem the rising tide of frustration. "I'm not entirely getting this. What exactly is the diagnosis? I mean, you've got to have some general idea what's going on . . . don't you?"

"Wish to hell I did," the older man grumbled. "This is a previously healthy kid. Last night she was as healthy as you or I with the exception of a head cold. Five hours later she's in a coma. I don't know . . . it could be some exotic virus, maybe sepsis. It might be something she picked up in England or on the plane. Hersh has calls into the airlines and the boarding school, checking to see if anyone else has come down with it. We've got pathology working on it."

"What about isolation precautions?" Cynthia asked. "Shouldn't we do a total isolation until we know what this is?"

"Mmm, I don't think that's necessary. She'll already be in a private room. Just make sure the nurses glove up and do good handwashing."

Cynthia nudged Adele. "He means no French-kissing the patient."

At that Ingram laughed and shook his head. A different breed up there on Ward 8, no doubt about it. Thank God they were as good as they were, or they would have all been fired for originality and insubordination long ago.

"How're mom and dad taking this?" Adele asked.

"Not well. They've got a supportive family friend who's helping out, but I think they're silently coming apart at the seams. I don't need to tell you to use kid gloves in this situation. Treat the patient and her parents like they're the Holy Family."

There was silence from the other end of the phone for a second. Wearily Dr. Ingram added, "I can't tell you what the kid has for sure, but one thing I do know—whatever it is, it's deadly as sin."

"But damn it, Adele, I *hate* kids!" Cynthia pushed the suction canister into the wall outlet with a vengeance and ripped off its thin, cellophane wrapping. "Especially some wiseassed, spoiled rotten, mouthy, teenaged brat of a physician's kid."

Adele had to bite her tongue to keep from laughing at the nurse's dramatic histrionics. "She's going to be intubated, Cyn. And she's unconscious, so you won't have to deal with anything but her body."

"Bullshit!" Cynthia attached the suction tubing to the canister nipple and placed a Yankauer suction catheter nearby. "I have to deal with Dr. Hersh and his wife. What joy. Can't you please give this one to Skip? I'll take the next two admits, I promise. Pretty please?"

Adele shook her head, and continued to set up an intubation tray. The best respirator in the house stood by, ready to be put into action.

"Then what good is it being best friends with the charge nurse?" Cynthia demanded, hands on hips. "I'm asking this as a favor, Del."

The two women had been friends since the day twenty-year-old mortuary student O'Neil was sent to pick up a fresh corpse who had been one of Adele's patients. While Adele helped her do last-minute diapering and zippering up of the body bag—sacrilegiously dubbed the "final vinyl"—they made the curious discovery that neither of them had ever been able to pick out the image of a batperson with wings spread in the Batman symbol—instead, they both saw a screaming baby's wide-open mouth.

It was the start of a solid friendship that, to date, had not let either of them down.

Now, regarding Cynthia with something akin to an older sister's loving tenderness, Adele asked, "How long has it been since you arose from the dead to become a nurse?"

"Five years." Cynthia sniffed indignantly. "You know that."

"Well babe, nursing is a baptism by fire deal. You know as well as any of us that you've got to take the shit with the chocolate. Besides, you're the one who's acting like a spoiled brat—you'll only have one patient. Most nurses I know would kill for that kind of cushy assignment. Kids aren't so bad—you were probably one yourself. Remember? It would have been the period of time right after you were hatched in that very shallow gene pool."

Adele waited for the laughter, but the scowl on Cynthia's face didn't move. "Listen Cyn, don't get unreasonable on me. Skip is the only crybaby wimp I can handle today."

Almost out of last appeals, Cynthia remained silent for a minute longer, then: "I hate dealing with healthcare professionals. Dr. Hersh may be a plastic surgeon but he's still a Medical Deity. Now that he's in politics, he'll be even worse. Besides, what kind of surgeon uses a shar-pei to demonstrate face-lifts to his clientele?"

"That's just a stupid rumor, Cyn. You be nice to him," Adele warned. "Someday he may run for governor and win. And with your disposition, you never know when you might need a stay of execution one day."

Cynthia moved the tip of the suction catheter toward Adele's nose. "Monsarrat, I think I've just come up with a new use for this catheter. Why don't you . . ."

Rhythmic squeaking announced the gurney as it was wheeled into the room. Surrounding the bed were two of the senior ER staff nurses; Dr. Ingram; Dr. Briscoe, the director of the Emergency Department; Henry Williams, the orderly; and at the foot, a distraught Gordon Hersh and a small dark-haired woman. Trailing behind was a tall, blond woman and a nervous, thickset man who closely resembled Henry Kissinger. The only person speaking was Gordon Hersh, who was busy giving orders that everyone else seemed to be ignoring. In general, everyone looked solemn down to their toes.

On the carrier lay a young girl who bore a remarkable resemblance to Cynthia. Right down to the gold and copper highlights in their braids, they could have been identical twins. Even in their state of anxiety, Adele noticed each of the people around the gurney do a double take of Cynthia, then immediately check the girl on the gurney to make sure she was still there and not standing before them dressed in scrubs.

Adele and Cynthia gloved and took their places on the other side of the bed, waiting to transfer the patient. Both of them scrutinized the unconscious girl, gathering general visual data as they went. The teenager's condition was clearly more critical than the picture Dr. Ingram had painted for them earlier.

"She crumped in the elevator," Dr. Ingram said in a low, funereal voice. "We need to get her intubated stat."

Dr. Briscoe gave Dr. Ingram a look that was unmistakable in its message: "Get the parents out of the room." Doctor or no doctor, the last thing any parent needed to see was his own child having a hard plastic tube shoved down her throat.

Adele and Cynthia busied themselves with putting the girl on cardiac monitor and taking admission vital signs while Dr. Ingram expertly corralled the Hershes and company out of the room.

While Dr. Briscoe scrubbed his hands and gloved, Adele did a quick study of the group gathered in front of the room's viewing glass. She guessed the woman wringing her hands was Mrs. Hersh; her staring, on-the-verge-of-hysteria expression was one she commonly saw on mothers' faces. Standing next to her was the striking blond woman, an arm placed protectively around mom's shoulders. She had to be, Adele guessed, at least six foot. After a moment, she reached over and took Dr. Hersh's hand, too.

Henry Kissinger with the wire-rimmed glasses divided his attention between the tall blonde's buttocks and bustline, and Dr. Hersh. Every few minutes he patted Dr. Hersh's shoulder and whispered in his ear wearing a grave expression—as if he were giving away top military secrets.

All four stared at the linoleum floor looking haggard, while Dr. Ingram spoke to them. The blond woman nodded from time to time. She seemed to be the only one who fully comprehended what was being said.

Cynthia stood over her young patient, watching her struggle to wake up. After a few seconds, Iris opened her eyes, mumbling between flagging gasps for air. Her hands flopped around at her sides like newly caught fish on the deck of a boat.

"Where's my dad?" The words were slurred, but comprehensible.

"Relax, Iris. It's okay," Cynthia whispered, caressing the girl's forehead tenderly with her fingers. "Your dad's outside with your mom and the doctors. You're in Ellis Hospital. I'm Cynthia, your nurse. Do you know what made you sick?"

Iris seemed to focus briefly on Cynthia, then closed her eyes, dramatically going from pale to dusky. "Mick Jagger. He tried . . . kill me. He wants . . ."

Adele and Cynthia exchanged glances. The girl was delirious.

Within a second or two, Iris stopped breathing. Cynthia alerted Dr. Briscoe, who was checking the laryngoscope, while Adele felt for the girl's carotid pulse. Pulling the teen's head back so the neck was flexed, she inserted a plastic airway between Iris's teeth. Adele said a silent prayer, pressed the soft mask of the ambu bag tightly over the girl's nose and mouth, and pushed air into the young, compliant lungs.

Ward 8 nurses' station was in the shape of a large oval situated in the center of the unit. Each of the four curves of the oval faced a long hallway—rather like the boulevards of Paris shooting out from the Arc de Triomphe—or, as Adele preferred to think of it, the legs of a large, carnivorous spider. Surrounding the nurses' station were four two-bed acute care rooms, each outfitted with cardiac monitors, wall suction, oxygen outlets, and a stash of advanced life-support medications. Eight of the remaining twelve rooms of the ward also had two beds each. At the far end of each hall were the four "mini-wards" made up of four beds each.

Adele sat alone at the desk, charting on her own patients, plus the eight patients who had been originally assigned to Cynthia. Skip Muldinardo, the only male R.N. on Ward 8, had reluctantly agreed, after much begging and pleading on her part, to take over the basic care of four of Cynthia's patients as long as someone else did the charting. She made the same deal with Linda Rainer, the other regular staff R.N. on duty, for the four remaining nurseless patients.

Grace Thompson, the ward's most recent head nurse, did not want to be approached about such trivial matters as the safety and well-being of the patients. The events of the day had already disrupted her normal nurse-manager's routine of staying cloistered in her office, going over staffing sheets and budget reports, and trying to find ways to cause havoc among the staff.

But today, Grace Thompson found the strength to emerge from her office in order to appear to the VIP brass as though she were indispensable to the efficient running of Ward 8. Adele shook her head as the fiftyish Brit, dressed in outdated, starched white uniform, cap, and white stockings, flitted nervously around the Hersh girl's bedside, trying desperately to appear as though she knew what she was doing.

It was *in spite of* the woman that Cynthia managed to

perform her duties in keeping her patient alive. Twice she had had to fly to the rescue when Grace flipped the wrong switch on the respirator, thus turning off the oxygen, and again when she tripped and pulled out one of Iris's IVs.

It was Adele's theory that so-called professional nurses—those nurses who had a spill of alphabet soup after their names—had had so much theory and so little clinical experience, they were more a hazard to the safety and well-being of the patient than a help. Whenever she had her choice between having a professional nurse or a licensed vocational nurse work on the ward, Adele always chose the L.V.N.

"Get that useless, walking biohazard out of my room!" Cynthia said through clenched teeth. "Invent a crisis, have a code, set fire to her office, just get her out of my hair before I kill her!"

Adele flinched and looked to see if the statement had been overheard; the murder of the former head nurse of Ward 8 less than one year before was still a sensitive issue with the staff.

"Okay, okay. I'll say the director of nurses wants to see her right away; she'll be on a wild-goose chase for hours until someone informs her that old Bess can usually be found down at the Silver Peso, third stool from the end."

Adele glanced over the monitor banks into Iris's room. In the chair placed next to the ventilator, Mrs. Hersh sat holding her daughter's hand. The blond woman held the teen's other hand. Both women wore the same expression of disbelief and shock.

Dr. Hersh had vacated the premises hours before with the excuse that he still had a practice to run. Adele guessed his departure had more to do with not being able to handle his emotions . . . or, more accurately, not letting anyone see him in a moment of weakness. Twice he'd excused himself to go to the men's room, choked up and teary.

Before he left, Dr. Hersh's campaign manager introduced himself to her as Samuel Fromer, then promptly asked if she was registered Republican.

Truly offended by the question, Adele made a face and told him she took it as an insult that she might even resemble a Republican.

Fromer shook his head, looking even more grave than before. "Such a good-looking, smart girl like you?" He'd sighed. "What a shame."

"How's the kid doing?" Adele asked Cynthia when she came out of the critical care room.

The nurse shrugged. "Okay, except I have to suction her every fifteen minutes—she's drowning in her own fluids. Her fever is still up, but she hasn't had any more seizures." Cynthia stared at Iris thoughtfully. "It's almost like having a brainstem injury patient, except she seems to wake up for a few seconds every so often."

"Who's the blond basketball player?"

"If you read the society page of the *Chronicle*, you'd know," said Cynthia. "That's Hannah Sandell. Sandell Design?"

Adele shook her head. The name rang only a very distant bell.

"How can you not know Hannah Sandell?" Cynthia asked in disbelief. "She's famous all over the United States for her interior designs. She renovated the inside of San Francisco Palace Place."

Adele looked blank. The last and only time she'd been in Palace Place had been with her father when she was four years old. A distant memory of crystal chandeliers floating on ornate ceilings of gold and pastel blue came to mind. Now she doubted she could afford to purchase a cup of tea in the wonderful old hotel, let alone go there for dinner or lunch.

"Come on, Del. She's part of your generation—made national news when she turned down Barbara Bush's invitation to redecorate the living quarters in the White House."

"Ding dong. Now I remember. She was the one who said she'd do the White House for free if the administration would stop opposing women's right to abortion? Made the headlines?"

"That's the one. Hangs out with the San Francisco 'In' crowd. She was Mrs. Hersh's best friend in college."

Adele tuned Cynthia out to listen to the bleeping of the girl's monitor. The heart rate had doubled. Through the window, she saw Mrs. Hersh and Hannah Sandell bent over Iris. They looked terrified. Hannah motioned frantically for Cynthia to come back. Something was going wrong.

The patient was clearly agitated; she strained at her wrist restraints and her eyes darted around the room. Iris's respiratory rate went to forty-four, which bucked the respirator and caused the alarms to scream.

Cynthia ran into the room to suction the endotracheal tube and calm the patient. She ordered the two women to wait outside, or better yet, go home. Over Mrs. Hersh's protests, she explained in a clipped, authoritative healthcare professional's tone, that even though her daughter seemed to be semiconscious, she was still very much aware of the high anxiety vibes of those in the room.

That was when Adele stepped in and repeated the same information in a gentler voice while herding them out of the room. She patiently listened to their complaints and answered all the questions Cynthia did not have time to explain. It was a mild version of good nurse/bad nurse.

Mrs. Hersh's questions concerned the care of her daughter, while Hannah Sandell's questions encompassed not only Iris's condition but how best to manage Dr. and Mrs. Hersh's needs. By the time they finally left, Mrs. Hersh ("call me Mimi, dear") hugged her tearfully and made her promise she would call the very second anything changed. Hannah shook her hand firmly and looked her straight in the eyes. There was a momentary gleam and a tiny smile that Adele had seen before—it was a kind of sizing-up—tall girl to tall girl. It seemed silly, but Adele got the feeling that because her own height was only a few inches less than Hannah's, she was being given special consideration she wouldn't otherwise have had, as in: Amazons need to stick together.

It wasn't fifteen minutes after the two women left that Iris's heart rate returned to normal and she seemed to relax for the first time since she was admitted.

Iris thought at first she was in an iron lung. She'd seen pictures of them in her Health History class. What always struck her odd about the machines was the mirror placed above the patient's face. And now she seemed to be staring into a mirror, at a face that was hers, yet not hers. It couldn't have been hers because the face above was speaking, making sense.

She felt every muscle and inch of skin, but couldn't move anything except her eyes. Air pushed into her lungs, and there was a hard pressure in her throat almost as painful as the torment going on inside her head. She shifted her gaze downward and saw the gentle rise and fall of her chest, yet she knew she wasn't breathing. She was too tired to breathe. She drew her gaze away from her body and looked into the mirror face.

Cynthia. That's what the mirror image said her name was. If she was in the hospital, then Cynthia had to be the nurse. But why was she here? An accident? Had there been an earthquake and the roof caved in on her? Had she gone to the mall and been the survivor of a terrorist attack?

She closed her eyes. It was a struggle to keep her thoughts going in one direction, let alone at all. The effort reminded her of when she was three years old and been allowed to play with the record player—it was difficult placing the needle in exactly the same groove every time.

She shivered and turned her head, or maybe she just thought she did. The blond woman was there, and the man who worked for her father. Her mother was holding her hand, looking worn-out. Another woman in a green scrub dress was talking to her father's friend, Dr. Ingram. Dr. Ingram seemed troubled and distracted, like the time Mrs. In-

gram died of breast cancer and they had gone to his house
for the memorial. Except Dr. Ingram wasn't looking into
any coffin—he was staring right at her and shaking his head.

The woman talking to Dr. Ingram had shiny black hair
pulled back into a French braid that hung below her shoulder blades—or wing stumps as her father called them. The
French braid lady had to be a nurse because she wasn't uptight enough to be a doctor.

All her father's doctor friends were uptight and liked to
make believe they were more important than everyone else.
Most of the politicians she'd met were even worse, because
in a way, they *were* more important than everyone else.
They made the rules.

The idea of a room full of her father's friends all trying to
outdo each other made her want to laugh. She started to
smile, but couldn't complete the effort. There seemed to be
tape holding her lips shut around a hard plastic pipe. Tentatively she tried to make her tongue explore, but it was
trapped under the thing that filled her mouth, keeping her
teeth apart. A horse's bit.

The nurse with the black hair came toward her. She
pulled the sheet up to her chin, brought her face close, and
said something Iris couldn't hear. Her eyes were golden
brown.

The mirror-image nurse also approached the bed and gently laid a cool hand on her forehead. Iris noticed that the
nurse was looking at her as if . . . well, yes . . . as if she
loved her.

Sudden realization caused a wave of fear that made her
body tense as if preparing for the worst. How could she
have missed it? Dr. Ingram, the nurses, her mother. Of
course. She was dying. Why else would there be so many
people wearing tragic, tender expressions?

Oh God. Now she'd never get to see her father win a seat
in the Senate, or take a bike trip through France, or feel
what it was like to make love.

Painfully, she moved her eyes, seeking out her mother

and then her father. Her attention was drawn to a flesh-colored object hiding behind the curtains. Slowly it swayed in a spooky, unreal rhythm. Following the movement, she tried to bring it into focus. It took the shape of a hand with talons instead of fingers.

She let her eyes travel up an arm to the head where Mick Jagger grinned back at her with lips that went all the way to his bloodred eyes.

She tried to scream—to warn everybody about him, but the hard pressure in her throat wouldn't give for an instant. Instead she began to choke, unable to breathe. With all her strength, she pushed against the air being forced into her until a high screeching whistle pierced her ears.

People swarmed around her in confusion, saying things she couldn't hear. Her vision blurred.

Before she was sucked back down into the black vortex, she'd started to cry.

Adele was tired. The last thing she wanted to do was listen to dull, incomplete reports from the nurses and med techs. Remaining civil at the end of the shift was a skill she'd had to develop over a long period of time—like for the last twenty years. For the better part of five minutes, she'd been listening incredulously to Skip describe the minute details of Mrs. Bern's morning bowel movement. The nurse was going on with such zeal, that at one point she squinted and pulled back, trying to see behind the glare of his black-rimmed glasses. She thought perhaps he was kidding—but no, it was just weird old Skip being weird old Skip.

She guessed that working with nothing but women all day long would make any normal man a little weird, although one of the Great Mysteries of Ellis Hospital centered around Skip's sexual orientation. She knew for a fact that he'd once been obsessed with one of the younger nurses. True, the girl had resembled an innocent choirboy, but still. . . .

Most people at Ellis were of the opinion that he was gay,

reporting various sightings of him wandering around the Castro wearing heels and white lace. Adele guessed it was more likely that they'd seen Skip's physical double, Marcus—the unmistakably gay nurse who worked on Ward 6's oncology unit. In the end, Adele remained undecided, preferring to think of Skip as a neutered male without any leanings at all.

Skip was now drawing the shape of the woman's bowel movement on the report sheet, giving dimensions in inches and approximating weight in ounces.

"Enough already! I mean, Christ on a bike, Skip—what's the deal? You constipated or something? You sound like you've got a bowel fixation."

The male nurse at first appeared offended, then chuckled. "I guess I was going on there. Sorry."

Adele yawned and let her head fall into her hands. She was very tempted to stay that way and fall asleep. Getting up at four in the morning to run eight miles before coming to work didn't seem like a good idea anymore. As always, she made the vow she wouldn't run on the days she worked. And as always, she knew in the back of her mind that the next day she would wake up promptly at 3:45 A.M. feeling good and ready to run. She was addicted to the exercise, but after eighteen years of running each and every day, there wasn't much she could do about it, except maybe go to bed earlier.

Which is exactly what she tried to do. But, every time, no matter how hard she fought the temptation, she'd inevitably succumb to her other addiction—crime.

Piles of books and magazines about crime investigations, true crimes, make-believe crimes, and forensic studies perpetually surrounded her bed like a fortress. Nor was she above devouring paperback mysteries. Once she was settled in under the covers, she'd pick up a book with the intention of skimming a few pages and end up reading for hours.

Crime had become an obsession at the tender age of eight, when she'd proven herself to be one of those children who ran on a mixture of instinct, lack of fear, and over-whelming curiosity.

Following a hunch that had kept her hyped for days, Adele waited for Mr. DeBergua, their schizoid next-door neighbor, to leave his house. Armed with her Mr. Green-jeans shovel, she diligently dug up the part of his garden where he'd recently been planting fruit trees late at night. It didn't take long before she uncovered a human toe, com-plete with a coat of chipped pink polish on its tiny half moon nail. She recognized it instantly as belonging to Mr. DeBergua's five-year-old daughter—the same little girl who was supposedly visiting relatives with her mother. She thought about trying to find pieces of Mrs. DeBergua, too, but she was shaking too hard to continue digging.

After a short lapse into silent hysteria, Adele wrapped the toe in a hanky, hopped on her bike—a 26-inch Speed-star named Prince—pedaled down to the local police station, and turned the small body part over to the officers at the front desk, and given a full account of what she'd witnessed in the preceding weeks—all without so much as a peep to her mother, who was still planting gardenia bushes in the front yard.

For the months following the investigation and eventual conviction of her next-door neighbor on two counts of first-degree murder, she'd haunted the police detectives until De-tective Sergeant Kitch Heslin dubbed her the official junior trainee of the department. Over the years, the investigators welcomed the gawky tomboy to sit in on their brainstorm-ing sessions. More often than not, she could be counted on to come up with alternative viewpoints on motives, leads to follow, or even suspects. She wasn't always on the money, but the number of times she was, was enough to warrant the detectives' attention.

It had only been a year since she'd been thrown on the garbage heap of semicelebrity for her involvement in solv-ing the Marin County serial murder case—an involvement that had not only left her almost famous, but almost dead.

When the details hit the *Pacific Intelligencer*, people immediately took to sending her crime books, confessions of murder, case histories of unsolved crimes, and pleas for help in finding missing persons. Tim Ritmann, Detective Sergeant for the Marin County sheriff's office, often teased her that if she ever wanted to get rich quick, she could hang out a shingle as a private investigator.

Adele lifted her head and stared into Iris Hersh's room. Obviously dismayed, Cynthia continued to suction her patient every few minutes. That was not a good sign. The overhead lights had been turned off in order to facilitate a more restful atmosphere, and despite the tremendous amount of work and chaos that was frequently involved in caring for a critical patient, the nurse had somehow managed to keep the room clean and orderly.

Cynthia cradled the girl in her arms as she readjusted a pillow. Adele watched the nurse's face, making note that she was looking into the face of human compassion.

Her stomach growled, and it suddenly struck her that Cynthia had not stopped even long enough to sit down since the girl came in. She decided to forgo a set of vitals on her own patients, choosing instead to relieve Cynthia for at least a bathroom break.

As soon as she walked into the room, it didn't surprise her that Cynthia requested to work a double and be assigned to Iris Hersh until midnight. Her decision to say no had been made hours before.

"Why not?" Cynthia asked. Her voice all but broke over the last word.

"I told you—if you work a double, then you can't work day shift tomorrow, and I don't have enough staff for days tomorrow."

"I'm willing to do a turn around," Cynthia pleaded, her Irish stubbornness coming to the surface. "I'm not so fragile that I can't work a few extra hours. I'll sign an overtime waiver. I want to make sure this kid gets the best care."

"But you *hate* kids, remember?"

"This kid is different."

Adele gave her a look.

"I don't know! I don't know. She's scared and helpless and innocent. I mean, there's something to do every second. Who else is going to give a shit enough to suction her every fifteen minutes *and* use strict sterile technique, and make sure she's sedated to the proper degree, and keep her sheets dry, and . . ." The nurse hesitated. "She's right on the edge, Adele. Somebody has to stay on top of every detail every second or we're going to lose her."

"All the more reason to give her up to somebody who's fresh and hasn't been at it for ten hours," Adele said, her expression somber. "Think ahead to ten o'clock tonight when you're bone tired and you can barely think straight. That's when mistakes get made, Cyn.

"Go home and sleep. I'll make sure somebody really good takes her tonight and I promise I'll assign you to her tomorrow."

Cynthia started another protest, but Adele held up a finger and crossed her arms over her chest. "This is a doctor's child. No nurse in her right mind would dare do anything but give her the best care."

Finally the nurse nodded. "Okay. But damn it, Del, there's something about her that really bothers me. . . ." Cynthia's face was drawn and her eyes shadowed. "I just don't know what it is yet."

Adele slipped an arm around her shoulders, and guided the younger nurse to the door. "Come on. You're exhausted. You haven't eaten or sat down all day. Taking care of kids is hard, even when they don't look exactly like you."

At the mention of the resemblance, Cynthia's tension eased. "That's bizarre isn't it? How the hell did an Irish girl and a Jewish girl end up with the same face?"

"The same mailman?" Adele shoved Cynthia in the direction of the nurses' lounge. "Go pee and have a cup of coffee. Tonight I want you to come over and have dinner with me and Nelson and spend the night. As a matter of fact, don't even bother going home. Leave your car here; you can ride with me."

A look of supreme doubt crossed Cynthia's face. "You *know* the Beast wants to kill any human who dares to ride in it, Adele. If I ride with you, it'll try extra hard to kill us—it'll be like a two-for-one deal."

The Beast was Adele's 1978 Pontiac station wagon. It was true the automobile had certain mysterious mechanical idiosyncrasies that might be interpreted as diabolical, but she had learned to live with them or, more appropriately, in spite of them.

"Naw," Adele said. "I'll threaten it with putting a neon orange ball on its CB antenna and withholding its ration of antifreeze if it acts up."

Cynthia considered the proposal for a second, then blew the bangs away from her forehead. After the way the day had gone, she found the prospect of being cosseted by her best friend appealing. "Why not? I don't have any food in the house anyway. I was planning on McDonald's."

A confirmed vegetarian since early childhood, Adele curled her lip. "Forget the Golden Starches; Nelson and I will torture you with vegetarian specialties."

"No wonder Nelson is as screwed up as he is." Cynthia snorted, checking Iris's monitor from over Adele's shoulder. "He's the only dog I know who gets hyped over garbanzo beans and rice."

"Actually, tofu humus with lemon is his latest passion," Adele said. "A neighbor brought him a beef bone the other day. Know what he did?"

Cynthia raised her eyebrows. "Swallowed it whole?"

"He dropped it into the toilet and went back to his humus."

Even though she had devoured an entire bowl of tofu humus and loved it, Cynthia eyed the new dish placed in front of her with suspicion.

"It won't attack, Cyn. Eat it—it's good for you."

"What is it? Looks like maggot eggs laced with mold."

"It's couscous, textured vegetable protein, and fresh spinach mixed with a little tahini and lemon. Eat it."

"Other than spinach and lemon I don't have a clue what you just said." Cynthia tentatively tasted the smallest bite.

Fifteen minutes later, when she reached for thirds, Adele smiled at the nonverbal compliment to her cooking.

"Okay, I'll admit it," Cynthia suddenly blurted, still chewing. "The kid got to me, but there's something else."

Adele stroked Nelson's head while he wolfed down his soybeans and bulgur at their feet. "Let me guess. Taking care of a kid who is the daughter of a famous plastic surgeon, one of the richest men in San Francisco Bay Area, *and* who is a candidate for senator? I'd say that might make anybody nervous."

"No, that's not it." Cynthia pushed her bowl away and took in a deep breath, slowly letting it out. "I can't tell you exactly. It's a feeling I got from the way she reacted a couple of times today.

"It's like she's terrified, but not of being sick. It's the kind of scared kids get when they've been . . ." Cynthia faltered and lowered her eyes.

"What?"

"You know, abused. Or when they're afraid."

There was silence until the black Labrador whined and gave a consoling lick to Cynthia's arm.

"I know that fear, Adele. I know that look; I used to see it in the mirror every day when I was a kid."

Adele nodded and, following Nelson's example, reached over to place a hand of comfort on her best friend's arm. She admired Cynthia because she was a survivor of the hardiest kind. Somehow the former military brat had endured years of abuse from a sadistic, alcoholic father and a strict, cold mother, and still turned out a fairly happy, functional, and compassionate human being.

True, she had a problem with Cynthia's sexual promiscuity

and her chronic inability to commit to one relationship, but she dealt with it, figuring things could have been worse, considering Cynthia's upbringing. The attractive young woman had left more broken hearts in her wake than Adele cared to think about. More than a few of the nurse's discarded lovers had come to her, begging for advice and solace. It was, she often thought, as though they were under some kind of spell.

"The girl is sick, Cyn," Adele said gently. "She's running a high fever and she's delirious. I think you're reading too much into this. Maybe the physical resemblance makes it easier to project your own psychological garbage onto her."

Cynthia went silent, locked in her private thoughts. She rubbed Nelson's neck until he passed gas. Vigorously, she pushed him away, and, holding their noses closed, both women speedily abandoned the kitchen for the bathroom, where they began their individual bedtime rituals.

After her usual five-minute floss with chemically free dental tape, Adele spread her naturally sweetened toothpaste on her natural-fiber brush. Cynthia picked her teeth with a toothpick and brushed with her finger.

"So, have you seen Tim?" Adele asked, trying to sound casual.

Cynthia stopped polishing. Her green eyes narrowed in a stony stare. "Don't start, Adele. I'm not in the mood."

Detective Sergeant Tim Ritmann, Cynthia's last romantic casualty, was a sore subject between the two women. Lasting for just eleven months, it was the longest, as well as the most meaningful relationship Cynthia had ever had with a man.

Immediately following the rather unceremonious abandonment, Cynthia broke down under Adele's intense interrogations, admitting that her decision to dump the good-looking redhead and go on the prowl was made in the split second she discovered that she could no longer tolerate waking up each morning to the sight of patches of auburn hair that peppered his back. It was, she said, like catching him in midtransformation from werewolf to human.

Adele countered that the real reason was because she had chickened out when she realized not that Tim had back hair, but that she was falling in love with him. After all, she hadn't slept with anyone else for almost a year, and for Cynthia that was a major record. Cynthia's complaints of feeling tied down and smothered were met with Adele's accusations that she was a commitment-phobe. Both notions were close to the bone of truth.

Adele shrugged. "Gee, don't get so touchy. It's just that I saw him biking around Phoenix Lake last week, and he looked so unhappy, Cyn. He's such a sweet guy, I hate to see him looking so lonely."

Cynthia was not to be moved. "Then why don't *you* hook up with him?"

"Psssh! Right. I'm old enough to be his mother, for Christ's sake."

Cynthia rolled her eyes. "He's only two years younger than you are, Adele. Don't exaggerate—that's my job."

"Actually"—Cynthia tore off a length of the natural floss and sniffed it—"the thought has crossed my mind a few times that you two would be perfect for each other."

Adele blushed and shook her head vehemently. "Forget it."

"Why? You're both into crime and investigations like it's food for your souls."

"Besides the fact it would practically be incestuous, he happens to be in love with *you,* my dear." Adele snapped her fleshcolored tooth guard into place. "You broke his heart when you left him. He's lost without you."

"Stop." Cynthia held up a hand. "It's over between me and Tim. He's too intense for me. I just wanted a fun thing. At first so did he. Then he turned around and decided one day that he had to have all the things that he knows scare me—a house with a lawn and a lawnmower, a new Volvo and a driveway with the basketball hoop, and kids with the braces and the shots and the diapers. . . ." She shuddered. "No way.

"I don't want to be hooked up with a guy who's a walking target for every psycho with a gun. I never want to be the recipient of a call from the coroner telling me my husband's brains are being scraped off the walls of some alley.

"Besides, I don't look good in black."

Adele heard the conviction in her friend's voice. Tim Ritmann was a good man who would make an even better husband. He was also the best detective in Marin County.

"Okay." Adele begged off. "I won't bring him up again for a while. Maybe you'll miss him when you realize there's nothing but jerks out there."

"I like jerks," Cynthia said and gargled with plain water. "It's not easy being a nurse and dating—I'm never a hundred percent sure if the guy is really attracted to me, or if he just wants a free prostate checkup."

When they were snuggled under the goose-down quilt, Adele ventured to ask: "Okay, so who's the latest victim?"

"Huh?"

"You know—the latest squeeze. You haven't mentioned anybody since your fling with Dr. Wong Dong."

"Damn it, Del. That wasn't a fling."

"Okay, so since your last deeply meaningful three-day relationship with a man who doesn't speak any English except 'thank you, I no understand, Buddha loves you, and fuck me now.'"

"Wing Fat was an extremely spiritual man. We had a lovely sharing experience."

Adele bit her pillow, choking back a scream of exasperation. She had to learn to live and let live . . . not judge anyone, least of all her wanton and lascivious slut of a best friend. "Yeah," she said finally, feeling annoyed, "and welcome to San Francisco Bay, the land of sun, HIV, channeling, crystals, leather, and nipple tethers.

"I'm telling you Cyn, you're walking away from the best thing you've ever had or will have. You should at least talk to Tim."

She could feel Cynthia smiling in the dark and waited for the retort.

After a few seconds the horrid voice from *The Shining* came from the other side of the bed: "I'm sorry Mrs. Torrence, Cynthia isn't here anymore. . . ."

THREE

STEAM FROM THE JACUZZI ROSE INTO THE clear night sky. Hannah sat close to the grieving woman, speaking softly. "You've got to pull yourself together, Mimi. If not for yourself, then for Iris. She needs you to be strong."

Mimi's eyes blurred as she looked imploringly at Hannah, then let herself slump into her friend's arms. "I—I know, and I will. I promise. I need sleep, Hannah. I'll be better in the morning. It's only that I wasn't prepared for anything like this. If I lose Iris, I lose everything. She can't die, Hannah. She can't. . . ."

Mimi pressed her face against Hannah's shoulder and wept bitterly. The woman's sorrow caused a lump to form in Hannah's throat. Swallowing it down, she squared her shoulders. She couldn't allow herself to be weak now; she was needed. She had to think clearly and not get sucked into the emotion.

While Mimi cried, Hannah tuned in to Gordon and Samuel talking in the study. Both men kept their voices low, but it wasn't hard to make out most of what was being said.

Fromer was attempting to talk Gordon into setting up a press conference for the following day on the steps of Ellis Hospital. He had made the suggestion that at least one reporter should be allowed to photograph Gordon at his daughter's bedside.

Gordon's voice was raised in barely controlled protest.

Appalled, Hannah looked back at Mimi for a reaction and

realized she hadn't been listening. Lost in her grief, Miriam sat with tear-stained face, biting her fingers as if she were going to tear them off.

Gently pulling Mimi's fingers away from her mouth, Hannah turned her around and began to knead the tight muscles in her neck and back. She would try to ease some of the grief.

Gordon Hersh stared at Samuel A. Fromer accusingly, wondering for the hundredth time how he could have let anyone talk him into choosing this annoying, corrupt bastard to be his campaign manager. It was true he was a brilliant political strategist and he had a lot of pull in high places, but there were times when Gordon believed the man was not so much clever as a vulgar opportunist.

"I don't want Iris used in a cheap publicity stunt!" Gordon blurted. "I'll make a statement to the press tomorrow—*outside* the hospital—about her condition. That's all."

"Gordon, what is the harm in this?" Samuel removed the unlit cigar from his mouth. "Let people see the human, loving father side of Gordon Hersh. Let them be able to be a part of your grief. You'll have everybody pulling for you." He stuck the cigar back in the corner of his mouth and made a gesture like a man haggling in a marketplace.

"Gordon, Gordon. What could it possibly hurt?"

"Not what," Gordon said, his voice turned solemn. "Who. And the who is my daughter." Gordon uncoiled from his chair, stood to his full height, and fixed the man with a look of distaste. "You can fuck with me on a lot of things, Sam, but not with my family. I don't want any reporters near Iris. She's off-limits, understand?"

Samuel leaned up into his face, his mouth twisted. "Why don't you let me do my job, Hersh? It's what you're paying me for."

"Your job doesn't include Iris . . . or Mimi for that matter." In Gordon's voice was the grim note of warning.

Samuel got up even closer, the veins in his forehead pulsing with his anger. "Everything connected with you . . . right down to the time you take a piss and the arrangement of your hair . . . is my job, Hersh. You want to fire me? Go ahead, but don't tell me how to do my job."

The two men glared at each other. It was Gordon who looked away first.

Gordon Hersh put down the receiver and lay back in the dark, Ingram's voice still echoing through his head. Iris was the same . . . *"Maybe a bit improved."* "Improved," he said after a moment and then allowed himself to smile for the first time all day.

Staring at the bedroom ceiling, he listened to the occasional murmurs of the women's voices drifting up from the Jacuzzi. Hoping for some cool air, and perhaps a glimpse of the Swan unclothed, he got out of bed and pulled back the curtains from the deck door. He searched his robe pockets for his glasses, then cursed himself for leaving them in the study. Still, he looked—even a fuzzy outline of what that body was all about would be better than wondering for the rest of his life. He squinted, craned his neck, blinked, wiped his eyes and looked again.

Through the blurred haze of his myopia, he could make out his wife and Hannah sitting in the Jacuzzi. They were engaged in a serious discussion. A Bach concerto covered their voices.

Pulling at the corners of his eyes—it sometimes helped to reshape his lens enough to see clearly—he thought he saw a breast and some other piece of anatomy but he couldn't quite make out what it was.

A moment passed; then the blonde sensed him and turned toward the window. He let the curtain fall and lay back down on the bed feeling like a teenager who'd been caught peeping in the girls' dorm windows.

He thought of Iris and said a prayer. A deep sadness closed in on him, making his eyes fill and his throat work

convulsively. He found it inconceivable that he had so casually let her go away to boarding school. Now, he was
painfully aware of the time he'd missed with her.

Recalling the day Mimi's mother, Esther, had come to
tell him Mimi was pregnant, he heard himself pleading
with Mimi to have an abortion. He physically cringed with
shame and broke out in a sweat when he considered that had
Miriam listened to him, he might never have known the incredible miracle that was his daughter.

The hulking image of Esther as she was in life—
threatening, loud, opinionated, and devious—lingered in his
mind. Gordon groaned and rolled over onto his stomach. It
was the same double-edged sword that had been hanging
over the heads of husbands since the beginning of divorce
courts—a boring marriage to a frigid wife, but a child he
worshiped beyond all.

Three minutes later, he twitched and fell into a troubled
and restless sleep.

Prompted into finding a husband for her daughter, Esther
Levy-Sandoval, wife of Gustavo Sandoval, set out to make
Rachel Hersh her best friend.

No previous best friend of Esther's had ever been so
pampered. Should Rachel so much as mention a desire to
see a new stage play or hear a particular symphony orches-
tra, Esther broke her neck (and her bank account) getting
tickets. If Rachel admired a piece of her jewelry (Esther
quickly learned never to wear her good pieces when with
the woman), off it came and into the hand of her new friend.
If Rachel wanted Chinese, they ate Chinese. If Rachel had a
headache, Esther tended her with the concern one might
give to the dying. If Rachel had wanted the moon, Esther
would have found a way to deed it over.

Rachel Hersh had never been popular with other women
due to the fact that she had a personality similar to a hedge-
hog's, so she was more than flattered, if somewhat confused, by the sudden attention. Not one to look a gift horse

in the mouth, however, Rachel allowed herself to be captivated
by Esther Levy-Sandoval's attentions.

With Esther's ability to pull the most personal of disclo-
sures from her, Rachel discovered she had been a dam holding back years of repressed parental and spousal injustices
committed against her. What a relief it was to unburden herself to her beneficent new friend.

Although the two husbands grumbled over the amount of
time their wives devoted to spending money during their
frequent shopping excursions, they encouraged the alliance,
since it kept the two women occupied, and conveniently
made for less whining. Frequent invitations to dinners and
plays were soon followed by vacations together, until the
Hershes were as much a part of the Levy-Sandoval circle as
family.

Esther encouraged Rachel to brag about her son, Gordon.
In turn, she boasted about her own jewel of jewels, Mimi.
Sometimes, with real tears in her eyes, she would confide in
Rachel that Mimi—with her looks, brains, and talents—was
a jewel fit only for an emperor among men.

A week before Mimi came home for spring break, Esther
cast her line into the water, watching with a mother's glee as
Rachel took the bait—hook, line, and sinker. It was agreed
that the two golden children would be introduced—casually,
of course—and God willing, they would soon be celebrating
a wedding feast. It would be only a matter of time before
they were surrounded by many healthy and beautiful grandchildren. They went as far as to make up a schedule dividing
the kids and grandkids over the first three years of weekends
and holidays. ("We'll split every other weekend. You get the
first Christmas; I get the first Thanksgiving. You get the babies for one week in spring; I get them for two in the fall.")

As their mothers predicted, the two children took to each
other immediately, and for the ten days of Mimi's spring
break, the handsomest plastic surgery fellow at University
of California, San Francisco, rarely left the Levy-Sandoval

home. More than willing to indulge in the lavish hospitality and attention, Gordon Hersh became, in Esther's words, "a regular part of the family."

Indeed, Gordon Hersh was well versed in endearing himself to young girls' parents. He knew how to play the Eligible Young Doctor About Town game to a tee.

Gordon found Mimi naive and fresh, if somewhat vacant—unlike the hardened sophisticated piranha of the San Francisco Jewish mating scene. Like most of the college girls he'd had (and there had been hundreds he guessed), she was eager to "fall in love." With Mimi there would be no challenge, no fear of being drawn into an emotionally complicated relationship. The delectable beauty was a nice change—a sweet and loving tumble in the sack, someone with whom he could recharge his ego.

He planned to let her go back to school with the appropriate amount of sadness and misgivings. They'd exchange a few sincere and bittersweet letters, then slowly but surely forget about each other. Eventually she'd find a nice, dull college grad who worked with computers, get married, and have babies. Or maybe she'd take a job with a big company in a city Somewhere Else.

It was an old plan, but a good plan, tried and true. But then, even the best-laid plans . . .

Seven days before graduation, Mimi discovered she was pregnant. Disbelieving that the birth control pills she took so diligently had failed her, she considered, among other dramatic choices, suing the pharmaceutical company, joining a convent, going insane, and committing suicide.

Not caring whether it was the failure of her daughter's birth control pills, which she had taken special pains to microwave several times a day for prolonged amounts of time, or the hand of God, Esther wasn't about to let her daughter's hysterics stand in the way of success.

Putting on her most severe Shamed in the Eyes of the World at Large attitude, Esther cornered the prospective father of her first of many grandchildren in the cafeteria of UC

Hospital one busy Monday lunch hour. After an extravaganza of threats, tears, the raising of voices and fists to God, Gordon was finally bribed into holy union.

Years later, on those rare occasions when he was caught with more than one cocktail under his belt, Gordon Hersh had been known to break down and cry over the fact that he'd been "sold into marital slavery" with a measly down payment on a three-room office in prestigious Mill Valley.

The chair squeaked under his shifting weight as Samuel Fromer put down the phone. Thoughtfully, he tapped his pen against the side of his head. Most would have found the news he'd just received disturbing; but for the Jew from New York's east side, bad news was simply a challenging opportunity.

He thought of himself as a survivor with a capital *S*. Starting with nothing except brains and a lack of conscience, he'd ruthlessly hacked out a path for himself and followed it, not much concerning himself with the bodies he'd stepped on and over to get what he wanted. It was, he told himself, all in the name of the big business game—everybody did it—what was the harm in showing his talent for creative (if somewhat driven) manipulation?

Getting the goods on people was his specialty. Most everyone had a dark closet. He had a knack for finding the keys to those closets, then holding the contents over the owner's head. It was, he thought, like investing in insurance. With just a little pinch of dirt, he'd always gotten what he needed—sex, money, position. He did have scruples, however. He used outright blackmail only as a measure of last resort or in desperate circumstances.

Unfortunately there were those few who either did not have a dark closet, or had been successful at keeping it locked. Five years after he'd rammed his way up through the ranks to the top public relations position for the wealthiest corporation in America, a younger—closet-free—and more power-hungry corporate suck stepped on his head and let him take the big fall.

On the way down, he'd grabbed at what seemed like the golden key—Gordon Hersh, Republican, running unchallenged in the California senatorial primaries against incumbent Harold McGruder, Democrat.

With his connections and brand of know-how, there wasn't much doubt he could get the putz through the primaries and elected to office. It would establish him in the political star circle. Senatorial campaign to presidential campaign. The name Samuel Fromer would be familiar to everyone with access to the media. Politicians would clamor for him, the CEOs of rich and powerful companies would want him to consult on big projects.

All he had to do was make sure Hersh didn't fuck it up. It was one thing to project the Dr. Clean image, it was a bitch to run a campaign for someone who really *was* Dr. Clean.

The first time he met Gordon Hersh, he saw the raw ingredients right off—power, prestige, sex appeal, the right amount of arrogance, and connections to the higher circles of San Francisco and L.A. politicians. The downside was that the guy was bright and motivated—sometimes more bright and motivated than what was good for the campaign. The tough part being that when Hersh came up with his own ideas about how he wanted to run things, he got righteous ... wanting to play the game by his rules. He hadn't learned yet that once he signed on, it wasn't his game anymore. The other thing that kept getting in the way was that Hersh had a conscience. It hadn't been easy convincing him that he couldn't run for office and still have one.

Hersh's being a doc was a curse and a blessing at the same time. The man wasn't exactly into extending him-self to the people. Going out and shaking hands and kissing drooly, snot-nosed babies and drooly, rheumy-eyed old ladies wasn't comfortable for him, and it showed. He also wasn't good at speaking the language of the minorities, the poor, and the homeless. He'd been too rich and too arrogant for too long. Minorities found it hard to relate to him; gays hated him for his stand on insurance companies and AIDS; the religious right hated him as only anti-Semites could hate a Jew; and his equivocation on abortion issues had both left and right up in arms.

But—women and Republicans with lots of money loved Hersh. And as far as Samuel Fromer was concerned, that was all that mattered. The best of it was that soon, women and Republicans with lots of money were going to love him, too.

Samuel reached into his top drawer and pulled out a single cigarette from a half-full pack. He smoked one a month; it was all his cardiologist would allow. He walked over to the window, held the flame of his lighter to the end of the cigarette, and inhaled deeply.

Outside the campaign office windows, Miller Avenue was bustling with late night traffic. Down the street, a group of teenagers headed toward the 7-Eleven. On a peal of laughter, one of the girls jumped into the street and did a sort of dance. Another girl joined in, while the boys clapped and made howling noises.

"East side, west side . . ." Samuel sang softly, as he filled a Dixie cup with water from the cooler. ". . . all around the town . . ."

From his pocket he took a packet of Alka-Seltzer, poured it in, then drank the fizzy water.

He wiped his runny nose on the outside of the paper cup and threw it in the wastebasket. A plan of action was forming in his brain—it wasn't exactly a nice plan, but he believed life was dull without some treachery once in a while. ". . . London Bridge is falling down. . . ."

He closed his eyes, and cursed the headache that was threatening to make him barf. He wasn't going to let any rain fall on his parade. ". . . tripped the light fantastic on . . ."

Executing a little shimmy, he threw out his arms and belted out the finale at the top of his lungs: ". . . the sidewalks of New York."

*   *   *

Hannah felt sick. Using the hem of the jacket to cover her nose and mouth, she sneezed, then waited for the throbbing pain in her head to pass. The last thing she needed now was to get sick; she couldn't afford the time. Making a split-second decision, she pulled the Mercedes into the last exit lane before the Golden Gate Bridge, and headed in the opposite direction, away from San Francisco.

Less than six miles from her house, she suddenly leaned over and vomited between her legs onto the floormat. Some of Mimi's vichyssoise slid down the side of her boot.

She pulled over, glad for the lateness of the hour and the absence of streetlights. Light-headed, Hannah lay across the seats and closed her eyes. The trenchant odor of vomit jolted her back through the years to the second-story landing of the tenement house where she grew up.

No longer able to distinguish the pattern in the filth-slick carpet that covered the stairs, nine-year-old Hannah sat and waited, trying not to breathe. The stairway smelled bad. One of her mother's earlier visitors had thrown up in the corner. Someone else, another visitor, had blessed the rug with urine while he waited his turn.

When he finished, he'd sat too close, staring at her. She caressed the fine gold medallion her father had crafted in Sweden especially for her. After a long time, he asked what grade she was in.

"You're too big for fourth grade," he'd said, then pulled her clumsily onto his lap and kissed her. His breath stank of liquor and cigarettes. His fly was unzipped. She felt the wet tip of his penis against the back of her leg, and then his hands groping under her skirt.

Sensing danger, she'd tried to run, but a hand was already on her face being forced inside her mouth while the other pulled at her panties. She held tight onto the medallion. With her free hand, she'd gone for his eyes, clawing like a cat. Not that it had done any good. He beat her senseless as he raped her, screaming the entire time that she was crazy.

But the worst came when it was over, and she lay stunned and bleeding. The man ripped the medallion from her neck, grunted at its weight and slipped it into his pocket.

Half-blind with rage, she ignored the pain between her legs and ran after him. She'd almost caught up with him, but as she made a lunge for the back of his grimy shirt, she tripped on the stairway carpet and fell two flights. When she came to, the man was gone. No one knew who he was, nor did they care to find out. It was best, her mother told her, to keep her mouth shut about the whole business; she had enough trouble without asking for trouble from the police.

Hannah shivered and pulled herself up holding onto the dash of the car. When she was able, she took off the boots, laid them carefully on the soiled mat, and tossed the lot out the Mercedes' window.

It wouldn't harm much if she didn't show up, she decided. She would say she was ill. Hannah smiled to herself as she eased the sedan onto Highway 101 north; for once, she wouldn't have to lie.

FOUR

HOSPITAL STAIRWELLS WERE A PLACE WHERE information could be easily had. Adele and Cynthia referred to the stairwells of Ellis by a variety of names: Eavesdroppers Paradise, Chat Landings, the Reference Library, Stair Wide Web. Anything one would ever want to know about the secrets of a hospital, could be learned by climbing or descending slowly between floors.

Noiselessly the two nurses tiptoed up the back stairs, where it appeared two men were involved in a verbal war on the landing above them.

"Come on, Doc," said a nasal mewl of a voice. "I just want a statement about whether or not the Hersh girl is going to pull through. You've got to—"

"I don't have to do anything!"

Both women recognized the deep, sonorous voice of Randolph Ingram. "This whole thing ... you people taking photographs on the ward, interrogating the medical staff? It's unethical. I don't want anything to do with this."

"Good morning, Dr. Ingram." Adele smiled at the doctor, then gave the stranger with the buzz cut a once-over. She guessed from the notebook and pen held ready in his hand that he was a reporter. All he needed was a checkered jacket to pass for Jimmy Olsen.

The physician snorted, turned, and fled down the stairs. Cynthia fled in the opposite direction toward the eighth floor.

"Hi. I'm Joe Rickie, reporter for the *Pacific Intelligencer*. You a nurse on Ward Eight?"

Adele watched with concealed amusement as the reporter readied his pen. Surprised when she didn't immediately begin spilling her guts, he looked up expectantly.

"What's your name?"

Before she could answer, he narrowed his eyes and pointed his pen at her face. "Hey wait a minute, I know you. You're the nurse who was involved in that murder case, right?"

Adele remained silent, expressionless.

"Oh wow. This'll make a great side story." The reporter lowered his voice, as if to convey an air of confidentiality. "Listen. Off the record, I gotta know. Were you doing that surgeon who bought it over at Bellevue? Me and the newsroom guys got a tip there was some kinda romance connection between you and the doc. True or false?"

"Doing?" Adele cocked her head. "What do you mean, 'doing'? I hope you don't mean what I think you mean." She was advancing on him, backing him closer to the wall. "Because if that's the case, you'd be out of line, not to mention downright rude."

Joe Rickie had opened his mouth to answer, when Henry Williams stepped onto the landing below them. At the sight of Adele, a genuine smile spread wide across the orderly's face. The exposed set of flawless white teeth was impressive.

In spite of the smile, Adele could see Henry was sizing up the situation by the way his eyes flickered and went a little cold.

"Hooooooweee! You sure are one glorious sight. What you say, girl?"

Adele stepped away from the reporter, and slapped Henry's hands in a high five. The handsome African-American frequently tyrannized the nursing staff, insuring his reputation as a man with an "attitude"—an attitude that clung to him like a note pinned to his forehead. During the time she'd cared for his mother, Alva, Adele had come to know the man under the tough crust, and found him a gentle, caring, and intuitive soul.

She smiled at the touch of color he had put to an otherwise dull uniform—the vibrantly purple bandanna tied around his neck went beautifully with the aquamarine blue of his scrub top. Squeezing his arm, she drew him over to the reporter.

"Now *here's* the man—and I do mean *the* man—who really broke that case. Henry Williams, meet Jimmy Olsen of the *Daily Planet*. Why, without Henry's invaluable input, Jimmy, there wouldn't be a nurse or a surgeon alive today in all of Marin County.

"Jimmy was just asking some pretty interesting personal questions about me and our other staff members here at Ellis, Henry. Why don't you give him a verbal dirt tour? I gotta go to work now."

Catching Adele's drift, Henry's eyes swept over the reporter. He stepped close to the smaller man and flared his nostrils, looking down on the top of his buzz cut.

"Say, white boy," Henry said grimly. "You know you got yourself a nasty old sunburn on the top a your head? Maybe you need to get yourself a hat—cover up that ugliness."

The reporter looked up at the powerfully built orderly, and shrank. For an instant, Adele wished she had time to listen to Henry make short work of the reporter; it would be like watching a boa constrictor devour an immobilized mouse.

"Christ on a bike!" Adele whispered and slipped her purse off her shoulder. Alongside Cynthia, she gawked at the group of people gathered outside Iris's room, some with microphones, one with a camcorder marked CHANNEL 4 NEWS. It was no small relief to both nurses that the room curtains were drawn, blocking Iris from public view.

Cynthia marched to Grace Thompson, clamped a hand on her shoulder, and swung her around. The head nurse's smile had always been a little scary—Englishmen with their bad teeth and all that—but, as the prissy, supercilious expression faded into a sneer, the middle-aged nurse's face was positively chilling.

"What the hell is going on here?" Cynthia hunched up her shoulders, making a sweeping gesture toward the reporters. In the silence which settled slowly over the crowd, most of the reporters turned toward the two nurses.

"How dare you manhandle me!" Grace Thompson's jowls jiggled with her fury. "This is none of your business, Miss O'Neil. You are dismissed from—"

"That's my patient." Cynthia pointed in the direction of Iris's room. "You'd better believe she's every bit my business. This is a hospital; the patient has a right to privacy. Why have you allowed these people in here? This is outrageous."

"You will *not* be caring for this patient any longer, Miss O'Neil." Splotches of red covered Grace Thompson's flabby neck. "That's all you need to know. I would appreciate it if you would leave the ward altogether before report begins. You are dismissed."

Dr. Hersh stepped out of Iris's room. At the sight of the reporters, his eyes went wild. The newspeople spoke all at once, firing questions. Several flashbulbs went off and the red light on the camcorder blinked.

Dr. Hersh put up a hand to shield his eyes from the glare of the flash. "What are you people doing up here?" he demanded, a deep color flooding his face. "I specifically said I'd make a statement to the press outside on the west lawn at two this afternoon."

Another chorus of questions was his answer. Gordon Hersh held up his hand to silence the group. "You'll have my statement at two on the west lawn. Please respect my family's privacy and leave now."

Grace Thompson's mouth flapped. "But—but I don't understand. Mr. Fromer said the reporters were to meet you up here. Dr. Zanders himself gave special permission."

His anger under control, Gordon cupped the English-woman's elbow, turning her gently toward him. "I'm terri-bly sorry . . ." He glanced at her name tag. ". . . Mrs. Thompson. Mr. Fromer made a mistake. No one is to be al-lowed near Iris's room except her family and her nurses." He glanced at Cynthia and smiled. "You're Cynthia?"

Hesitantly, slightly distrustful, Cynthia nodded.

"Miss O'Neil has been relieved of caring for your daugh-ter, Dr. Hersh," inserted Mrs. Thompson hastily. "I'm re-placing her with a more qualified R.N." She motioned to Adele.

Adele didn't move.

Gordon sized up the situation between the nurses and turned his back on Mrs. Thompson, gripping Cynthia's el-bow in a personal, confident way. The elbow cupping was, Adele mused, the adult personal touch version of kissing babies.

"Nonsense. Cynthia took care of Iris yesterday, Ms. Thompson," Gordon said in a forceful but patronizing tone. "She proved herself quite capable during the heat of the cri-sis. She's exactly the kind of nurse I want taking care of Iris throughout the course of her illness."

Cynthia pulled back and looked at the politician uncertainly.

"Do you mind taking care of Iris today?" he asked.

"I thought that's what I was doing," Cynthia said, a righ-teous edge to her voice.

Dr. Hersh glanced back at Grace. "Cynthia *will* be in charge of Iris's care today, won't she, Ms. Thompson?"

The gray-haired woman pursed her lips and arched an eyebrow. Exuding reluctant humility, she gave a curt nod of her head. "If you wish, Dr. Hersh."

"Good," he said and began leading Cynthia—still in her coat—toward Iris's room. Head inclined toward the nurse's ear, he began a rambling, disjointed sort of report that was often a physician's style of giving information about a patient.

A flashbulb went off, and Dr. Hersh pointed at the offending reporter. "Get out!" he growled, his voice like ice. "Or I'll have security remove you."

Cynthia, momentarily blinded by the flash, rushed the man. "Damn it! This isn't a photo opportunity, scumbag; this is a hospital!"

One of the reporters snickered. "Look out men, we're under nurses' verbal fire—keep your backs to the wall and watch for sniper enemas."

Everyone laughed—that is, everyone except Dr. Hersh and the nurses.

Dr. Zanders, the five-star general of Ellis Hospital's administration, personally addressed the two shifts of Ward 8 nurses in a bizarre speech of sorts. His thanks to them for their care of the VIP Miss Hersh was laced with thinly disguised contempt for the profession itself as he praised their skills, then in the same breath called them the invaluable servants of the physician.

After he'd lapsed into referring to the staff as "you gals," he went on to say he expected the best care for Dr. Hersh's little girl, hinting in so much administrative double-talk that if other patients had to go without for the child's sake, it would be okay.

Taking his cue from the yawns of the night shift, he ended by saying he hoped that when the time came they would vote for Dr. Hersh because of what he could do for the image of Ellis Hospital.

Several of "the gals" coughed. Cynthia moaned and added under her breath: ". . . and for Dr. Zanders."

The administrator stood smiling at the audience, waiting expectantly—for what, none of "the gals" were really sure. A thin, edgy laughter rippled through the audience and stopped as quickly as it had begun. One night shift nurse who was too tired to know any better attempted applause, but stopped as soon as she realized she was the only one clapping.

Then, as if to blunt the resentment over the publicity circus, Samuel Fromer showed up (*after* Gordon had left, Adele noted) bearing gifts of cheap, greasy doughnuts, a box of campaign buttons, balloons, engraved pencils, bumper stickers, banners, and four large cups of not-so-cheap Starbucks coffee that he hoarded, then distributed to Hannah, himself, Mimi, and Cynthia.

For almost an hour, Samuel danced around Cynthia while she worked, trying to pick her up. It was not uncommon for pretty nurses to be hit on by family members and sometimes the patients themselves. Some unwritten professional code—or perhaps it was because they were always so busy—prohibited most nurses from responding.

Accordingly, Cynthia accepted and drank his coffee because caffeine was her life's blood, but ignored his attentions. Her choices in bed partners were not always sterling, as Adele consistently pointed out, but—she eyed Samuel Fromer—she *was* above scraping the bottom of the sewer lines.

Her assignment was enough to make a good nurse cry or send her gunning for the nurse-manager. But, after seventeen years, Adele knew tears and temper tantrums were pointless, so instead, she spread herself thin by caring for seven seriously ill patients and being charge of the ward. She figured her assignment was part of Grace Thompson's retaliation against her for being Cynthia's best friend.

Mrs. Squires in room 800B was her only documented Class IV acute patient. The sixty-three-year-old's ailments included—but were not limited to—congestive heart failure, angina, end-stage renal disease, and liver failure. Ventilator dependent, with arterial and pulmonary artery lines, and a slew of medications, the woman required enough care to keep two R.N.'s busy every minute. Her other six patients were technically sick enough to be documented as Class III and IV. They had instead been documented as stable, or Class I and II acuities.

It was a prime example of the hospital management's money-saving game: justify high patient acuity to low nurse count. On paper it looked perfectly safe—in practice, it was deadly not only for the patients who did not get the quality care they deserved, but for the nurse whose license was on the line.

Adele stood in the center of mini-ward 816 and ground her teeth into her acrylic tooth guard as she glanced around at what she called her "rainbow room." Bed A was a thirty-five-year-old Caucasian recovering from septic shock secondary to the gunshot wounds in his belly, B bed was a non-English-speaking Latino who had had five days of high fevers, vomiting and diarrhea, but no diagnosis. C bed was a seventy-six-year-old Asian man dying from a gastrointestinal bleed, D was the fifty-two-year-old black man two days out from a posterior myocardial infarction.

"Time to increase my malpractice insurance," she said to the ceiling.

The Czech med tech, Miroslav Dvorak, cocked his head in silent question.

"Never mind," Adele said. "What do you need, Mirek?"

"I do not understand what this means," he said in a thick Czech accent, pointing to the diagnosis box on one of the patient information cards he held.

" 'Peritonitis,' " Adele read aloud. She looked back at the boy in wonder. "You don't know what peritonitis is?"

He indicated he did not. "She has many pains in stomach."

Adele sighed. She had not gotten used to the idea of replacing qualified R.N.'s or L.V.N.'s with lay people who had little or no training. She took the patient info cards from his hand—eight in all—and rapidly perused them. All but two of the patients were moderate to high acuity and deserving of a qualified R.N. Holding up another card, Adele pointed to the name of a common medication. "Do you know what this drug is for?"

Mirek squinted at the name and shook his head.

"Did you take the patient's pulse before you gave this drug?"

Mirek frowned.

"This is digoxin. You don't give this drug without making sure the pulse is above sixty. Didn't they teach you that in med tech school?"

The boy shook his head sadly. "School is for two days. It is too much to learn and I do not speak English good."

"Get outta here," she said in disbelief. "The whole training is only two days?"

Thinking she had dismissed him, Mirek backed toward the door thanking her. She half expected him to bow.

Adele reached out and pulled him back. "No, no. I don't mean get out literally. That's only a saying. It means that I think you're kidding me."

She sighed, regarding him for a moment, then lowered herself onto a nearby chair. "How much do they pay you to work here? How many dollars?"

Proudly he puffed his chest out. "Five dollars eight cents for one hour of work."

Of course. Adele pressed her back into the chair and let out a breath. Why pay a skilled R.N. twenty-five to thirty dollars an hour when a poor sap off the street who can't even speak the language can be put in her place and paid minimum wage? They were all required to wear the same uniform, and were expressly forbidden to tell the patients whether they were R.N.'s or orderlies. How was the patient to know they were being given potentially lethal drugs by someone who, just two days ago, was dipping their cone at Dairy Queen?

She'd seen the increase in mortality rates, but as always, the hospital and medical community joined in the cover-ups whenever the survivors began to ask questions. She swallowed down the lump of frustration and closed her mind to the visions of the disasters possibly taking place in Ward 8 right at that very moment.

"Is it worth it, Mirek? Seems like hard earned money to me."

"Worth it?" he echoed.

"The money," she said. "Is it worth having to work here in the Ward from Hell?"

"I am paid much money to do work I love." He looked at her, then sighed, grinning madly. "In my country this make me a rich person. To live and work in America is a gift."

"Sure, you bet," Cynthia answered with a Minnesota accent over the noise of the wall suction. "Iris is a real trooper; hanging on like a pit bull with lockjaw."

Her jivey tone was meant for the benefit of both parents and Hannah Sandell, who were gathered around the foot of the bed, listening to every word the two nurses exchanged. Cynthia was also taking Iris into consideration—coma or not, patients could often hear and make sense of everything said within earshot.

Adele tried to tell if Cynthia was telling the truth, but was unable to get past the phony grin. "Are you in a position to be able to go to lunch?"

Cynthia scowled, reluctant to leave Iris's bedside.

"It wasn't a question, Cyn," Adele said before she could answer. "It's a command. Linda and Skip have agreed to fill in while you and I take a meal break. Say in about . . ." She glanced at her watch. ". . . one and a half minutes?"

Cynthia vehemently shook her head and pulled off her mask, which was soaked with moisture. "No way. I've got to turn her, empty the suction canister, record a set of vitals and neuro checks, calibrate the machines, do a cardiac output, change her tubing, hang her ceftriaxone and erythromycin, auscultate her lungs, do a—"

Adele held up her hand. "Stop. We'll turn her together. You can empty the canister while I do a set of vitals. The rest, Skip or Linda will take care of. You have to take a break, Cynthia. It's one-thirty. You haven't stopped long enough to go to the bathroom. We're going to the cafeteria and you're going to get off your feet, have some coffee, and eat something. Case closed."

"Yes, Miss Mother." Cynthia curtsied. Behind them, Mimi and Hannah chuckled.

Without further discussion, they fell to work. Adele pulled Iris toward her while Cynthia tucked pillows behind her back and between her knees. In just twenty-eight hours, the girl had lost three kilos. It didn't leave her much to fight with. Her blood pressure, maintained with dopamine to keep it at a normal level, was holding stable, but her temperature remained at 102 despite the antibiotics and the analgesics. Adele could feel the heat from the girl's body while she took a manual pulse.

Cynthia removed the suction canister from the wall bracket, unscrewed the top, and wrinkled her nose. Carefully she made her way toward the utility sink, thinking what a disaster it would be if she were to slip.

It was, as she would say later, a self-fulfilling prophecy thing. With the next step, her legs flew out from under her and she landed on her callipygous rump.

Thick, mucoid secretions suctioned from Iris Hersh's lungs and mouth splashed into her face, dribbled down the front of her uniform and into her lap in great white globs.

"You aren't looking so green anymore," Adele said, trying to sound encouraging. Freshly showered and in a clean set of scrubs pilfered from the OR, Cynthia stared forlornly into her coffee cup.

"Could you eat a little something? Some broth maybe?"

"God, Adele, you're starting to sound like the mother I always wished I had. Believe me, after what I've just had a mouthful of, I'm not going to be able to look at food for a month. I'll stick to black coffee, thanks."

"You have to report to employee health before you go home today," Adele said firmly. "I'll write out the accident form for you. Take it down to Dolores and have one of the

ER docs check you out, okay? If you get sick, I want this all documented."

Cynthia stared at her. She had hoped Adele wouldn't bring the subject up. "Now Adele, you know damned well I'm not going to do that, don't you?"

Adele laughed. Cynthia's reverence for protocol and regulation was lacking to the subminus degree. The woman also believed she was invincible, which might not have been too far from the truth—as far as Adele knew, Cynthia had never been sick a day in her life. Even with injuries, she seemed to heal much quicker than what might be considered normal. Cynthia chalked it all up to being mean and politically inappropriate—Adele thought it had more to do with being from another planet.

"I'll tell you what *does* make me want to blow chunk," Cynthia said, "is that with all Hersh's money and power, they aren't hauling experts in from all over the world to help find out what his kid has. He seems so ineffectual. . . ."

"Oh come on, Cyn, give the guy a break. He's freaked-out. This is his only child, you know. Everybody is doing everything that can be done. Pathology ran tests sixty ways to Sunday, and Ingram has already called in an agent from the San Francisco Center for Disease Control. Most of those agencies have tests for things nobody's ever heard of. If nobody here comes up with the answer, they'll run it by the CDC in Atlanta."

They were quiet for a minute, sipping their coffees, lost in thoughts of another, undiscovered route to take. Finally, Adele yawned and cracked her neck and shoulders. "So, what do you think?" She gave Cynthia a sideways glance. "Is the kid going to make it?"

"Dunno," Cynthia said with a slight shrug. "She's not doing so well on the coma scale, but she's medically stable and her kidneys are working better today than yesterday.

"What drives me really crazy?" Cynthia ran her hands through her hair. "The whole crew is weird. I mean, the mother is Jewish guilt personified. She sits there guilt-tripping herself and staring at the kid like she's already dead. The slime of a campaign manager slash family friend gives me the creeps. He leers at every ass and every pair of tits that walk by. And he's got a cold edge to him, you know, like how a sociopath is slightly aloof? I swear he has all the makings of one of those people who wakes up one day and kills his wife and kids and then blows up the day care center around the corner just because he feels like it.

"Then there's the White Swan. She's . . ." Cynthia waved a hand in the air. "Oh, I don't know, I can't even tell you."

"Tell me anyway."

"I don't know how to describe it. She like *hangs* over Dr. and Mrs. Hersh like she's the attendant in a mental institution or something. Makes me nervous the way she watches everything everybody does, just waiting for the first mistake before she starts screaming 'malpractice.' Oooh, and her eyes are so creepy. They're like . . . like . . ."

"Vampire eyes?"

"Exactly. You know, like Tom Cruise in that Anne Rice movie?"

"Uh huh. Well, get out the garlic and the wooden stake, dear," Adele said, a smile lurking at the corners of her mouth, "because Lestat Sandell is headed this way."

Hannah looked like an ad out of a nursing magazine. All she needed was a stethoscope slung around her neck. Conspicuously overdressed in an elegant white linen suit with a peach silk camisole, she stood holding an orange plastic cafeteria tray on which was a single cup of coffee.

"Mind if I sit with you two?" she asked, pulling out a chair—also orange plastic. If anything, Ellis Hospital cafeteria was color coordinated.

Adele grabbed the chair out of her hand and pushed it back to the table. "You can sit with us only on the condition that you agree to give me all your cast-off clothing."

Cynthia snickered. When Adele was in the right mood, her impertinence could be outrageous.

"It's a deal," Hannah said and chuckled. "I'd love to see them go to someone who can actually wear them. You might have to do some hemming, but otherwise I think they'd suit you well."

Grinning, Adele pulled out the chair again and gestured for her to sit down. "I'm only kidding. Have a seat."

Hannah blew her nose and smiled. She had taken a liking to the dark-haired nurse immediately. Her easy, straightforward manner was a refreshing change from most of the women in her own social circle, most of whom were phony, too wealthy, repressed, depressed, and Prozac-ed into monotoned snobs. It intrigued her that there was clearly more behind those extraordinary eyes than the woman let on.

The other nurse—the one who resembled Iris—was less approachable and more guarded. She had a hard edge that Hannah recognized at once as the self-protectiveness one learns early on when life isn't easy or nice.

"You must be a runner," Hannah said to Adele over the rim of her cup. "You're built like one."

Adele nodded, trying not to stare at the woman's heavy gold necklace and the matching earrings and bracelet—not to mention the solid gold Rolex. They were the best gold . . . nothing hollowed out or fake on this woman. "I've been known to jog around the block once in a while."

Cynthia snorted and rolled her eyes.

"Do you run?" Adele asked.

"Not now. I work out and swim." She lowered the light blue eyes to her cup, spots of color flushing her neck. "But I used to run a lot before my hips gave out. I ran Boston a few times." She shrugged and looked across the cafeteria. "Didn't do so bad."

"Yeah?" Adele smiled. "Like what? Did you come in first or second in your class?"

Hannah shook her head. She felt the flush spreading up

into her cheeks. "Don't I wish." She laughed. "I was the one running with the stroller-pushers and the wheelchairs."

Her smiled faded and she turned her gaze on Cynthia, who was silently studying her. "You got cleaned up in a hurry. Did you hurt yourself?"

"Not really. A bruised pride is all."

"What pride?" Adele asked, sarcastically. "You know your last name is Klutz."

Hannah laughed, then blew her nose again. Her head throbbed with a sinus headache, and the nausea was kicking her stomach around. Reaching across the table, she rested a hand on Cynthia's arm. "How *is* Iris—I mean, how is she *really*?"

Cynthia looked away in order to avoid the piercing eyes. "Stable."

Hannah took a deep breath. "Forgive me for being blunt, but is she going to survive?"

Cynthia stared. Adele blinked. Both nurses were taken aback by the question. Adele wondered if Hannah was afraid she was coming down with the same thing Iris suffered from. The Hershes had told them Iris had been fighting a cold for five days before she crashed.

Hannah sensed their surprise and softened. "Please understand, I'm not the hard-hearted Hannah you've heard about."

She waited for them to smile. Neither of them did. She had to remember nurses were a different breed—strong, independent women. She brought up her bottom-line, businesswoman voice.

"I want to know so that I can somehow prepare Gordon and Mimi. If the child dies, both of them will be devastated, which means the practical tasks of keeping things together will fall to me. That's going to be a major job and I want to be able to prepare for that if it's an eventuality."

"Well"—Cynthia was having a hard time deciding whether the woman's bluntness was offensive or practical—"I suppose the simple answer is that nobody knows. We don't even know what it is exactly that's making her sick. We're just treating her symptoms and making some stabs in the dark at treating an underlying cause."

"But you've taken care of thousands of patients," Hannah pleaded. "You must have some intuition about these things."

Not one who took to being pushed, Cynthia clenched her jaw. "You're asking me to tell you whether or not the kid is going to die, and I'm telling you I can't do that. All my gut tells me is that she's scared shitless, and she's fighting like hell to stay alive."

"She's stubborn like Mimi's mother." Hannah smiled sadly, then: "Thank you, Cynthia. I appreciate your honesty."

Hannah peered into their cups and brightened. "Hey! Let me at least buy you two some coffee." As she knew they would, both women modestly declined her offer. Nurse types—givers, not takers.

"I insist." She stood and briefly glanced at her watch, as did the two nurses. Instantly she felt bad, knowing neither of the women would ever be able to afford anything like it. Covering it with her sleeve, she made a mental note of the time.

"You guys work your buns off. You need a boost. Tomorrow I'll bring in some Peet's Special Mexican Roast for all the nurses."

She pointed at Adele. "You take decaf with nonfat milk, no sugar. And you . . ." She turned her smile on Cynthia. ". . . take the real stuff straight."

"Hit her with more epi!"

The pharmacist looked at her watch and shook her head. "Not time yet, Doc. Another two minutes."

Dr. Briscoe stood with the rest of the code team and stared helplessly at the cardiac monitor. They watched the rhythmic blips march across the screen—translations of Adele's chest compressions.

"Stop CPR and turn off the pacer generator, please, Adele. Let's see what we've got here."

Adele stopped and held her breath along with the rest of

them, watching the screen, hoping for some sign of pump activity.

Someone moaned. Flatline. Asystole. Still dead.

Adele removed her hands from the naked chest and straightened with a wince. She massaged the muscles in her lower back. "We've been working on her for forty-five minutes. She hasn't responded to anything we've done. Her pupils are still blown and fixed."

An interminable ten seconds passed while the code team waited for orders. The quiet in the room was astonishingly loud.

"Okay," Dr. Briscoe said, and with his stethoscope listened to the silence of the still heart. After a moment he stood. "School's out."

There was the instant release of tension as the members of code team each began to gather their various assortments of equipment and drugs.

"How long between the time she extubated herself and the cardiac arrest?" Dr. Briscoe asked the room in general. All eyes went to Adele.

"I don't know," Adele answered, her face burning. "I checked her before I sat down to give report to evening shift at three-fifteen. Her wrist restraints were firmly tied and the endotracheal tube was taped and patent. I finished giving report at four-fifteen, which was when the monitor alarmed."

Dr. Briscoe remained expressionless, though his voice had taken an edge as he shot questions at her one after the other. "Then how did this happen? How did she extubate herself if her hands were restrained? How long did she go without oxygen before she coded?" He glared at Adele accusingly. "I need some answers, Ms. Monsarrat."

Adele shook her head. "I . . . don't know," she stuttered. "Dr. Briscoe, I swear she was . . ."

"I murder her," said a small voice over the confusion of the room. "I make her hands free."

Miroslav, looking small and frightened, took a step forward from the corner of the room.

"You untied Mrs. Squires's hands?" Adele asked in disbelief. "You know that vent patients have to be restrained. That's basic, common sense. You don't have to be a medical genius to . . ."

She stopped. The boy—she guessed him to be all of twenty-two or -three—wore a horrified expression. He was so pale she thought he was going to faint.

"I didn't know," Mirek said, wringing his hands. "She want her hands free. She keep fighting the—the—strings on her hands. Her eyes, they beg me. I don't know she will pull out the air tube."

The few people who had stopped to listen, looked away embarrassed and went on about their business. Adele knew there would be no incident report written—no details about untrained medical personnel making mistakes would be given to family members. The death certificate would read simply "Respiratory failure." Her husband would be told she'd stopped breathing, her heart had stopped beating, and they had tried to save her. No one but the people inside the room would know the truth of the matter.

She wiped blood off the gray face and covered the naked, withered body with a clean sheet. Morgue detail would be left to the evening nurse.

The whole time Adele worked, Mirek stood staring, frozen with remorse. When she was done, she placed an arm around his shoulders and guided him out of the room, away from the wreckage.

"They will come to arrest me, now?" he asked, quiet terror in his face.

Adele shook her head. "No, Mirek. There is no Veřejná Bezpečnost here. No one will arrest you. This was a mistake, but you must not talk about this to people outside the hospital."

Wide-eyed, he held out his hands in supplication. "I did terrible thing. I let her hands free."

"But how could you have known when no one took the time to tell you? You thought you were doing the woman a kindness. No one can blame you for that. It was a mistake. It's done and over."

"A mistake?" the boy repeated. "No one will punish me?"

Adele felt like she was a hundred years old. "No one," she said with a sigh. "No one will punish you but yourself."

Mirek understood her meaning. He resumed wringing his hands.

"And my guess is, Mirek, that you'll be unmerciful."

She found Cynthia lying on the couch in the nurses' lounge, frowning over the afternoon edition of the *Pacific Intelligencer*. The old cowboy's description of a horse who'd been "rode hard and put away wet" adequately depicted her friend.

"What a crock of horseshit!" Cynthia said, flinging the paper into Adele's hands as soon as she entered the room. "Look at this crap!"

On the top page of the second section was the headline: CANDIDATE'S DAUGHTER IN COMA. Scattered around the page were several photos. There was a studio photo of a smiling, radiant Iris Hersh. Another was of a stone cathedral—obviously her school in England. Next to that was a photo of Gordon Hersh striding out of Iris's room, hand over his eyes and looking extremely miserable. In the center of the page was the photo of Dr. Hersh, looking appropriately grave yet in control, speaking in confidence to Cynthia.

The caption under the picture read "Dr. Gordon Hersh consults with unidentified nurse outside his daughter's room."

"An unidentified nurse?" Adele chuckled. "Is that like an unidentified flying object?" She looked closer. Her chuckle turned into outright, wheezy laughter. Behind the pair, the camera had caught Grace Thompson's face, sticking out like a growth from Cynthia's left arm. The hideously twisted expression seemed to emphasize the worst of the painted-on eyebrows and the over-lipsticked mouth. Halfway between a smile and a grimace, it was not the face of a human, but that of a white-haired gargoyle with indigestion.

"I don't know, O'Neil, but I think you should have that unidentified growth excised from your arm—it looks like our head nurse."

She put down the paper and turned around only to find that she was alone.

Adele finished reading the paper, had a cup of decaf for the road, and was hoisting her oversize purse onto her shoulder when there was a knock at the door to the nurses' lounge. She smiled at the rare show of courtesy and opened the door. Miriam Hersh and Hannah Sandell stood in the hall. Hannah waved.

"Hi!" they said in unison.

Adele raised her eyebrows and waved back. "Hello."

The women exchanged a glance in which a whole conversation took place. She and Cynthia had similar glances.

"We were just going to grab a bite to eat at the Good Earth over in Larkspur Landing," Hannah said. "Want to join us?"

Adele smiled, relieved it wasn't something more complicated, like news of a level four virus invading Marin County. "Thank you, but I'm whacked. My dog would kill me if I didn't come home tonight." She shrugged. "Actually, he wouldn't kill me, he'd chew through the front door." She didn't know them well enough to mention what else he'd do.

"Go home and get him and bring him with," Hannah coaxed. "We can eat out on the patio; we'll hide him under the table."

"You obviously don't know my dog." Adele smiled sweetly. "He's a four time flunk-out of Chuckie's Doggie Obedience University. He's the only dog in the university's history to earn an Untrainable Award."

"Oh come on anyway," Mimi said, smiling for the first time since she'd met her. It was a sad smile, but a smile still the same. "You're too skinny, and we're too depressed for our own company."

Adele shook her head. "I really can't. I'll take a rain check, though. Some evening later this week when Cynthia can join us?"

"Okay, you win." Mimi sighed. "If we tried to kidnap and carry you, you'd probably put up a struggle. I guess we'll have to wait."

Mimi took her hand and gave it a squeeze. Adele found the gesture oddly endearing—the wounded giving comfort. "It will be good to have Cynthia come, too. I think all the nurses are wonderful."

Unlike most doctor's wives who hate us with a vengeance, thought Adele.

"Come on, Mimi." Hannah tugged at her friend's sleeve. "Before you start reciting the Hallmark card litany of simpering sayings."

Adele watched them go down the hall—a Mutt and Jeff of a couple—and wondered what the hell *that* was all about.

FIVE

"I DON'T GIVE A GOOD GODDAMN WHAT THE hell it did to my points. I told you I don't want Iris used as publicity!"

"Get over it, Gordon," Samuel said with restraint. "Because people loved it. We got over three hundred calls from well-wishers all over this state within the first four hours after the piece about Iris hit the stands. Our computers are still downloading all the e-mail, and the mail room is jammed with sympathy letters and get well cards."

His head pounding, Fromer rapidly began writing in his notebook as Gordon stared grimly without reply. Without any warning, the campaign manager pitched his pen across the room at the wall and came out of his chair as if there were a fire under him.

"You dumb son of a bitch!" he screamed. He took two quick steps to the wall and smashed his fist into the chart that read MCGRUDER: 49% HERSH: 41% UNDECIDED: 10%

Gordon jerked back reflexively and stared at him in astonishment.

"I am *not*—let me say it again, Hersh—I goddamn *refuse* to allow you to fuck yourself out of this election. You signed on for the ride, and you're going to goddamn stay on the ride even if I have to drag you through it."

He loosened his collar in one fierce tug. "Nine points! You know what that means, Gordon?"

Gordon looked away, rubbing his forehead hard with his fingers.

"Do you?" Samuel took a breath and calmed himself. He was hot and nauseated and fed up with baby-sitting Gordon Hersh. "It means people are starting to notice. It means Mc-Gruder is going to have a run for his money. It means you're on your way for the first time, man. You've got a legitimate shot, now, Gordon. Don't fuck it up."

Unconvinced, Gordon shook his head. "But at what price? I don't want my family paraded around like—"

Samuel exploded. "The fuck you want! Let's get this straight one more time, Hersh—this isn't about what *you* want! It's about what the voters want, and what the voters want right now is to see a human candidate—just like Iris said—they want to see somebody with problems just like theirs."

With a sigh, Samuel picked up his pen from the floor and sat down. He took out his handkerchief and blew his nose. "From here on out you belong to them. . . ." Samuel pointed out the window of the campaign office. "They run your life . . . and your family's lives . . . until you're voted out.

"You do as I say and you'll be the next senator. Think of it like going to the dentist—painful but necessary." Samuel turned his attention back to his notebook. "Now let me hear what I outlined for you about your new welfare program."

Slowly, Gordon picked up a notebook off his desk and began to read.

Nelson finished his portion of ratatouille over rice. Picking up the ragged remains of his beloved Mickey Mouse rug, he ambled lazily to the sink where She was finishing the dishes and laid it at her feet. He burped and nudged Her leg.

Adele wiped Nelson's nose slime off her bare leg and checked the time. She'd do a power poop walk with the dog and still have time for a slow, hot shower before her own treat—bedding down with the new security-systems-update magazine.

She addressed a small group of her closest invisible friends who had gathered around the sink to watch in fascination as she expertly manipulated the soapy dishes. (She'd been assigning personalities to invisible people and inanimate objects since the day she discovered she was an only child.) "I'm the only woman I know who goes to bed with self-defense equipment catalogs instead of a man."

There was a chorus of imaginary but appreciative laughter. A couple of those present made some comments about what a waste it was that she was unmarried—some poor guy was really losing out on a wonderful woman.

Feigning modesty, Adele shrugged and joined in with the conversation. Living alone gave her license to talk to herself. It was mind theater at its best.

Nelson, thinking She was talking to him about the upcoming prowl, waited patiently for his word cue—"Go Out?"

"Nelsie want to go . . . out?"

The black Lab barked once and wagged his tail. He pawed at the door. Adele excused herself from her imaginary crowd with a clever quip about taking Nelson's nose out for a smell. Even though she'd used the same line a hundred times before, they all laughed as though hearing it fresh and new for the first time—just another of the many advantages of having close, invisible friends.

Nelson stopped at the Silver Peso Bar for his fix of a Big Dog All Cereal Doggie Biscuit, and she stopped at Larkspur Books and Office Supply where Jack, the store's proprietor, filled her in on all the local happenings. Somewhere in between the two establishments, an uneasy feeling crept into her psyche and began gnawing.

Normally their prowl took them past the Lark Creek Inn, and down Baltimore Canyon, but this evening she'd avoided the groves of redwoods, preferring to stick to the well-lighted main street. Doggie biscuits and friendly conversations notwithstanding, the bothersome feeling centered in the lower part of her throat, above her sternal notch. Her gut and scalp were tight, warning her to be aware—put up the antennae.

By the time they got back to the house, Adele was spooked enough to double check the side and front door locks. She ran a hand over the .32-caliber Colt she kept in her nightstand, leaving the drawer open an inch . . . just in case.

Halfway through the first article about distinctive monitoring devices for the amateur bugger, the phone rang. "This is it," she said to the lampshade. "This is what I've been dreading all night."

Not wanting to make real the disaster waiting at the other end of the line, Adele paused a minute before answering. As a spiritually confused agnotheist, she would have said a prayer had she remembered any. Instead, she sent a plea to the powers of the earth that whatever it was, it wouldn't be insurmountable.

It was late, and the sounds of the hospital had changed. Gone was the constant babel of the overhead paging system and the noises of busy nurses, ailing patients, and anxious families. In their place was an eerie hollow sound that was broken only by an occasional cry of pain, or the whimperings made by the sick.

Alone with her daughter, Mimi could feel Iris's struggle to survive. It was a vibration, an energy that shot through her every time she took the delicate white hand in hers. She kissed her daughter's fingertips, one after the other, the way she'd done when Iris was a baby. Her fingers were really the only part of her child they allowed her to touch now. From the first day, she'd been warned against disturbing any of the plastic tubes that invaded her daughter's body.

"You have to fight, baby," she whispered. "You've got to beat this thing."

She examined Iris's pale face, no longer delicate and beautiful, but made hideous by the bloodstained adhesive tape wound tightly around the tube protruding from her mouth.

Guilt stuck in her throat and made her temples burn. She gasped for air as a primal doubt clawed at her; perhaps Esther had been right—maybe God had finally found a way to punish her for what she was.

The alarm on the breathing machine stabbed the silence, causing her to jump. The evening nurse came in immediately, looking for the problem. Despite the man's efficiency and sensitivity in caring for Iris, Mimi still wished it were Cynthia. Cynthia never left Iris's bedside. The other nurses didn't stay in the room, much less advise her of what they were doing when they did come in. She might as well have been a stick of furniture.

If Iris made it—Mimi shook her head—no, *when* Iris made it out of the hospital, she'd hire Cynthia on a private-duty basis and pay her fabulously well to take care of her daughter until she was strong.

Iris's eyes opened, blinked, and made an attempt at focusing.

"Hello angel." Mimi willed herself to look confident. "Mommy's right here. You're doing fine. I love you, Iris. Daddy loves you. Please get well. Please . . ."

Iris closed the two green windows and disappeared.

Miriam slumped back into the hard plastic chair, feeling the desperate anguish of a mother losing her child to death. Surely there was *some*thing she could do, some bargain she could strike with God in exchange for allowing her daughter to live. She would give generously to children's charities, or volunteer her time at social service centers. She'd promise never to have another judgmental, unkind thought about anyone, not even Gordon's mother—God rest her soul.

She'd be a good wife, and . . . this one she had to think about carefully . . . she would promise to give up her wicked ways.

* * *

Rosie Martinelli lay with her head on Brian's lap. Her feet, still in brown work boots, were tucked under the tattered orange and brown afghan his mother had knitted. She snapped her gum and giggled.

"Married . . . with Children" was their favorite show. They always watched it together on Sunday nights. Peg said something outrageously stupid and they both roared, Brian's belly jiggling at the back of her head. Rosie sat up and ran a hand through her tangled and dirty hair. Brian took a long hit off his beer, belched, then handed it to her.

"Have we got any more of that wine left?" she asked, rubbing her hand slowly over the front of his pants. Her slow, southern drawl excited him almost as much as her hand.

"In the fridge." He cupped her breasts with his giant hands and tried to kiss her.

Rosie chewed faster. "You aren't supposed to put rosé in the fridge, numb nuts."

He licked her lips, pushing her hand down. "These nuts aren't numb, Rosie. Check it out." He opened his fly. She worked her hand inside. He was right.

Rosie had cheeked her gum and was working him with her mouth when the commercial break came. At the beginning of the fourth ad, his erection suddenly deflated like a balloon stuck with a pin.

"God, how I hate that son of a bitch!" he yelled, giving the television screen the finger. Blinking, Rosie sat up and looked at the TV where endearing clips from Gordon Hersh's life were flashing in a continuous montage across the screen—a baby picture, his Eagle Scout photo, his college graduation, him in a white lab coat working with an elderly woman who was smiling up at him like he was God.

The voice-over was one of those sentimental male voices. It kept saying, ". . . .Gordon Hersh for senator. For the people, with the people, by the people."

"And, given half a chance, he *will* fuck the people." Rosie giggled, pulling her work shirt down and smoothing it over her breasts. "The fucker needs to be assassinated, not elected."

Brian snorted in disgust. "More than that, he needs to be cut down to size. People need to know what a scumbag he really is.

"Why won't you bring sexual harassment charges against him, Rosie? The bastard raped you while you were under anesthesia."

Rose hung her head, her face reddening. Thinking he had caused her to feel bad, he automatically reached out to put his arm around her. But when she raised her face to him, he could see she was angry.

"Why don't *you* bring charges against him, Brian? He disfigured your mom with some oversize implants, then let her suffer for a year with infections? Sounds like a malpractice suit to me."

They both looked back at the screen. A very handsome Gordon Hersh was shaking hands with former President George Bush, smiling and kowtowing like a lackey kissing boots.

"That bastard had Mom coming and going," Brian murmured. "I still can't believe he told her it was her fault she kept getting infected. He kept her on antibiotics for a whole freakin' year before I finally talked her into going to somebody else who took care of the problem in three weeks.

"Then the son of a bitch has the balls to send my mother's account to a collections agency when she refused to pay him."

Rosie turned her gaze back to the tiny, wilted penis and shrugged. She'd heard the story and the curses a hundred times before. She got up to get the wine. "Shit man, ripping off a little piece of ass is nothing compared to letting an old woman suffer for a year, Bri. I told you before—you got a real case for shaking the bastard up. He hurt your mama and messed with your lady." Coyly now, she circled around the couch. "There's ways to make the cocksucker's life a hell on wheels, you know."

Brian flicked off the TV and pulled her back, placing her

in the same position she'd just left. He pulled off her work shirt and began massaging her breasts until she took the cue. Laying a hand on the top of her bobbing head, he leaned back. "Make his life hell? Shit, I'd rather kill the bastard."

For ten years Cynthia lived in the same middle flat of a three-story Victorian situated in downtown Mill Valley, the land of the Terminally Yuppified.

Barely hanging onto consciousness, she lay in the window seat gazing across Sunnyside Avenue at the blinking, pink neon ice-cream cone in the window of Baskin—!31 Flavors!—Robbins.

On. *Pain invaded her head, roaring and tearing in and out of her ears and eyes and throat.*

Off. *Breathe.*

On. *Pain. Nausea coming up like a giant seiche.*

Something wet and warm spread out beneath her cheek, the sour-sweet smell of vomit filling her nostrils. She hadn't puked since the age of fourteen when Zachary Voast got her drunk on alternate shots of cheap Spanish wine and crème de menthe, then took turns screwing her with members of his frat house while she slept and puked simultaneously.

Off. *But she wasn't drunk now. Or, maybe she just couldn't remember drinking. She couldn't remember a lot of things, like how she got where she was, and well, okay—her last name. It was something Irish.*

On. *The pink ice-cream cone. Was it real? Had she ever seen it before? Once in a dirty hotel room in Barcelona there was this other blinking sign and she dimly remembered some guy—a matador?—trying to keep up with the rapidly pulsing beat. . . .*

Focus. Beyond the pain was an agony she'd never known and didn't want to know.

Off. *All kinds of crazy thoughts had been coming . . .*

On. *. . . and off for a couple of hours. The problem had been making her mind stay in one place long enough to concentrate on moving. Her muscles had simply turned . . .*

Off. . . . *and her mind kept shutting down on her. Except if she didn't do something . . .*

On. . . . *right away she was going to die. It was her last chance because she was going out for the count.*

The phone was in her hand. She tried to remember—had she taken it with her when she fell? Lay down? Was dragged? onto the window seat?

Off. *Getting her fingers and mind coordinating was such a difficult task. Almost impossible.*

On. *The nurse part of her that was still awake nagged at her: you're slipping into unconsciousness, your blood pressure is too low, you aren't breathing right. . . .*

Off. *Okay. She forced herself to open her eyes and look at the keypad of the phone. At the top was a programmed number. Help. Who was it? Doesn't matter. When the cone goes . . .*

On. . . . *press down. Press hard. Listen for ringing and . . .*

Off. . . . *a voice. Familiar. But who?*

On.

"Hello? Hello? Cyn?"

Off. *Can't talk! Hear me? Sick . . . need help. Can't move . . . sick. Need . . .*

With a last, tremendous effort, she uttered a thick, agonized groan.

On.

"Cynthia? Is that you?"

Off. *Yes! Oh please God, the pain, the pain, the pain, the . . .*

SIX

TWO NEW COFFEEMAKERS WITH RED BOWS STUCK
to them sat side by side on the nurses' lounge counter. The
machine on the left was perking up Peet's Regular Mexican
Roast, while the one on the right spewed out Peet's Decaf
Mexican Roast. On the counter, next to four extra pounds of
premium coffee beans and a brand-new bean grinder, was a
gift box filled with three dozen still-warm-from-the-oven
muffins. Taped to the top of the box was a note:

> Doc Bryson's Magic Muffins: 0 fat. 0 sugar. All natu-
> ral, "from scratch" ingredients. For the Nurses of Ward
> 8—Thank you for your proficiency at caring
> —The Hersh Family

It was done with taste and style—no half dozen greasy,
sugary doughnuts from Safeway, no two-pound box of See's
creme chocolates carelessly left at the nurses' station to be
picked over, bitten into, and then put back into their sticky
brown paper nests.

It was really Hannah Sandell's doing, Adele thought, as
she relieved her bladder. The Hershes weren't in any frame
of mind to be thinking of gifts and healthy muffins, and the
campaign manager was, as Cynthia so eloquently pointed
out, a slime.

She poured herself a mug of leaded Mexican Roast and
sat down heavily on the couch, a muffin clenched in her
jaws. It was only 8:30 A.M., though it felt much later . . .

days later. She hadn't stopped racing around since she'd driven the Beast at breakneck speed to Cynthia's flat.

Sleep deprivation was the pits, although it gave her a certain choleric edge which she worked to her advantage: Over the course of the night, she'd left a trail of enemies, but that was to be expected in a hospital as incestuous as Ellis. The first half of the night she'd spent in ER, making sure Cynthia received the medical personnel's best efforts.

Cynthia's parents were deceased, which left Adele as the legal guardian and patient's only advocate. Taking full advantage of her role, she demanded and bullied, refused and threatened on Cynthia's behalf. She wheedled Dr. Ingram's home phone number out of the night clerk, called him (he was not on call), woke him up, then spent twenty minutes convincing him he not only had to take Cynthia as his patient, but that he had to get out of bed and come in and see her within thirty minutes.

Further flying in the face of hospital policies and the supervisors to boot, by 6:00 A.M. she'd made it clear that:

One. She was to be Cynthia's and Iris Hersh's nurse. (No one had the slightest objection to that.)

Two. Under no uncertain circumstances would she be charge of the unit. (There were a few grumbles about this, but nobody really wanted to deal with her either—especially after she'd been in contact with the Unknown Contagion.)

Three. She would *not* be taking care of any other patients. (There was an outcry of "unfair!" but her glare was enough to silence the protestors.)

Four. Both patients would be placed in critical care room 802, in strict isolation. That was fine, especially with housekeeping, since it meant they had to do special cleaning of only one room instead of two when the patients were either discharged or died.

By change of shift, a sense of contagion-panic raged throughout the hospital. Word of Nurse O'Neil's admission (Adele thought of it more as an incarceration) spread up and down the hospital grapevine with all the speed and terrifying force of a BB headed for an unprotected eyeball.

Morning rounds stopped before they even began, as physicians hastily rearranged their schedules to bypass their patients on Ward 8. Most of the auxiliary services such as pharmacy, management, and housekeeping, avoided the ward like the plague—literally. Two Ward 8 day shift nurses feigned illness within seconds of hearing about their colleague and were immediately sent home.

Grace Thompson hadn't had the grace to come up with an excuse before she jumped ship—she'd simply gone yellowbelly, leaving the unit before she'd even put her lunch in the refrigerator. It was Adele's guess she'd run home to gargle and do a high colonic with straight bleach.

All that remained of the staff was Tina, Skip, Linda, and four unlicensed assistive personnel—Mirek included. Tina played her usual role as ward clerk, but with enough modifications to put her in a quasi-charge position. Skip and Linda ran the rest of the show, taking the sickest patients themselves and jockeying the four UAPs around. It was, Adele mused, going to be interesting storytelling for those who survived.

Survive. The word had been used carefully when they spoke to her about Cynthia's prognosis. Like Iris Hersh, her decline was rapid, going from serious to critical. Adele recalled how Cynthia looked, curled into a ball on the window seat of her flat, her face oddly lifeless and slack. Unconscious, her head was lying in a puddle of her own vomit. Adele panicked when she'd tried to find a carotid pulse and found instead a barely palpable and erratic vibration. The extreme trembling of her hands had necessitated placing the phone on the floor in order to press 911. As in Iris Hersh's case, the cushions on the window seat were soaked through with what she guessed was the majority of the nurse's bodily fluids.

Adele walked stiffly to the mirror, and without looking at herself, set about reweaving her hair into a smooth French braid. Halfway down the braid, she glanced into the mirror. Tired, sad eyes the color of gold stared back. A choking pressure rose in her throat.

"Don't you dare die on me, Cyn," she said in a stern prayer. "You're all I've got besides Nelson and sometimes my mother. You can't do this to me. You need to finish serving the rest of your sentence in this hellhole. I couldn't work here anymore if you . . ."

Her voice was strangled off by the throat lump. Tears rolled down her cheeks. "Don't. Just don't, okay?"

The lounge door opened and Skip appeared, his face flushed with anger. "Hey Del. We're out here busting our humps and you're in here fussing with your hair? What the hell are you . . . ?"

He gaped at Adele Monsarrat crying, not wanting to believe his eyes. The sight triggered all his abandonment fears and brought up a devastating memory of finding his mother in tears when he was five. Who would take care of him (and the ward) if Mom (Adele) broke down?

Tentatively, then deliberately, the nurse wrapped his arms around his colleague. "I'm sorry," he said, fighting to keep himself from choking up. "She's your buddy. You've been here all night. I wasn't thinking."

Adele wiped her tears and nodded. "It's gonna be okay. Cyn's strong. She'll come out of it."

"She should," Skip said, separating himself from her; being physical with a woman made him ill at ease. "She's got the best nurse in the county taking care of her."

She blew her nose into a paper towel and smiled crookedly. "Now I know for sure you're a lying sack of shit, Skip."

"You need more time?" he asked.

"Naw. I've got to get back; they're both due for the works."

"Need any help?"

Adele raised an eyebrow and stared at the man who consistently refused to take care of all patients suffering from anything even remotely transmittable. "Do you still remember how to do isolation technique?"

Behind the Coke-bottle-thick glasses, the male nurse rolled his eyes. "Psssh! Like, does a bear shit on the pope?"

"I can use your help before lunch. I'll be doing linen changes about then."

"I'll be there," he said, making his way to the muffins and coffee. "Who're these from?"

"The Hershes. Well, actually they're from Hannah Sandell."

"That the bombshell who's taller than a basketball hoop?"

"Uhn huh."

Skip fit an entire muffin in his mouth and still managed to talk without sounding garbled. He raised his eyebrows a few times. "Very wow."

"You think she's attractive?"

He chewed, pouring himself a cup of the decaf. "Yeah . . . well, I mean, she's not *my* type, but going by your typical American male hormonal standards, she'd be considered hot goods in most locker rooms."

Secretly amused, Adele wondered just what or who Skip's type was—considering that no one had been able to verify for certain which way he swung. To settle the matter once and for all, Cynthia had volunteered to seduce him, but hadn't quite been able to bring herself to actually do it. That, in and of itself, was saying something.

"I've got to get back," Adele said, a sudden urgency overcoming her; she'd been away from room 802 for more than fifteen minutes.

"Me, too. I only came in to tell you that the Hershes, the bomb, and the pushy guy with the wire rims all want in to see the kid. I put them in the Queen Mother's office and told them they couldn't go in until you talked to them. The doc and the old lady are bickering with their jaws clenched. I heard shouts when my ear got accidentally pressed against the door."

Adele bit her lip. She wondered if the Hershes were upset over Iris having a roommate. Whatever the problem was, she figured she'd have to deal with it sooner than later.

* * *

Mimi could see the panic in Gordon's eyes. In a rare show of temper, he grabbed her by both arms, pressing his fingers into her flesh.

"Damn it, Miriam," he said, his voice rising, "you've *got* to show some strength. The voters don't want to put some putz into office who falls apart at the first sign of hardship."

"Is that what your dying daughter is to you, Gordon?" Mimi returned bitterly. "A hardship?"

Gordon stared at her in disbelief. In fifteen years of marriage, he'd never known his wife to put up a fight over anything he wanted; she'd always given in without a whimper. "Of course not! But people will feel we've let them down if we cancel this dinner."

"*We've* let them down? This isn't *my* campaign, Gordon." Her voice began to rise. "I'm only the adoring wife who follows three steps behind. I dress well, but not too flashy, put on the dinners but never eat lest I should gain an ounce, and make damned sure I never give an opinion that doesn't in some way glorify you."

Gordon let go of her arms. He was afraid of her like this. He could see the unraveling of his political career before it even had a start. When he spoke again, it was in a defeated voice. "The wife of a senator is as important as the man himself. You *know* that, Miriam. You said you wanted this. You said you'd be behind me every step of the way." He jammed his hands into his pockets and paced as much as he could in a ten by twelve room crowded with office furniture.

"McGruder will have a field day. I can hear him now— 'Conflicts in his personal life prevented Gordon Hersh from appearing at a fund-raiser dinner—think what he'll do when he's called upon to handle the demands of the voters.' Christ!"

Mimi stubbornly stood her ground, her chin jutting in resolve. Hannah and Samuel exchanged glances, their expressions those of unwilling, innocent bystanders who had been caught in the cross fire of a marital war.

A moment later, Gordon turned to his wife and took her by the shoulder. "Say something! What is it? Do you want to bury me, is that what you want?"

"I can't leave Iris," she said softly. "I . . . don't want to go to the dinner and have to put on a phony act. How would it look if both of us are kibitzing and having a grand old time while our daughter lies dying?"

She pulled out of his grasp. "People—decent people—will think we're monsters. I . . ." Mimi looked to Hannah for support. The blue eyes told her she was doing the right thing. She straightened her back. "I won't leave my daughter. It isn't right and that's the end of it, Gordon."

Gordon grabbed a handful of his hair and pulled. "But I need you there, Miriam. For God's sake, the Belvedere Hotel is only five minutes from Ellis. Please, I'll hire a . . ."

He stopped at the sound of himself pleading, suddenly mindful of the two other people in the room. At play inside him were conflicting feelings of a newfound respect for the mouse he'd married, and the desire to kill her for standing up for herself. How dare she develop a backbone now!

After a deafening silence, Samuel rose from his chair holding up a finger. "Okay Gordon, hold on a minute. I think Mimi's right about this."

Mimi sighed and sent Samuel a grateful look. Gordon closed his eyes and took a deep breath. When he opened them again he stared hard at his campaign manager in challenge.

"A concerned mother who forgoes an important social event to be at the bedside of her gravely ill child will go over far better with the contributors and the voters, than whether you have an attractive wife and cohost at your side.

"People—especially the voters—are human, Gordon. And everyone—well, *almost* everyone—who attends will have had a mother."

Despite his frustration, Gordon smiled.

"How about if someone else stands in for Mimi?" Samuel said in a calculated way. "We'll find someone to oversee the pomp and circumstance, and stand in as hostess at the same time. Before you give your speech, you can explain why your cherished wife and the devoted mother of your only child can't be there. Turn the situation to your advantage. Make them blubber like babies."

Samuel rubbed his hands together and laughed. "My God, they'll love you for it."

Gordon stared at the floor of the cramped office, feeling better than he had all week. Samuel Fromer might be an obnoxious ass, but he was sometimes absolutely brilliant in his assumptions. He could play Mimi's dedication as a mother to the winning hilt—the dedicated family woman. Automatically, Gordon's mind began to tick through the lists of women he knew who held political offices. It was an unattractive lot.

"Okay, I admit it's a good idea, but who the hell is going to agree to do this with twenty-four-hour notice? It's crazy."

Samuel stroked his chin. "A close friend to both Dr. and Mrs. Hersh, perhaps? A self-made woman who is not only successful, intelligent, *and* beautiful, but also a great humanitarian." He nodded at Hannah, his eyes shining.

Hannah wasn't having any of it. She shook her head. "No way. I'm an interior designer who contributes regularly to charities. You can find someone else who would be much better for the job. What about Judge Hill? She'd be a perfect cohost for you. I'm not qualified. I don't know anything about political campaigns. Hill would . . ."

Gordon screwed his mouth sideways in regret. "Jane Hill's rulings on the homeless and illegal alien cases are in direct opposition to my views."

"What about Congresswoman Dorman? She's . . ."

"Dorman doesn't know her ass from a hole in the ground," Samuel countered, losing patience with her reluctance. "She's a housewife from Lake County. Come on, Hannah! You're perfect for the job. At least consider it."

"Do it, Hannah," Mimi said in a low voice. She gently squeezed Hannah's arm. "Please. Do this for me."

Hannah stood regarding the three of them for a long time before she finally sighed and threw up her hands with a smile. "All right, I'll do it."

A sly smile escaped Samuel, who leaned back, unconsciously smoothing his wavy auburn hair—or the lack of it.

Mimi kissed Hannah on the cheek.

"Are you sure this is okay?" Gordon asked her, taking her hand. "You don't have to, you know. Playing hostess at a political event as big as this one can be tedious. Ask Mimi, she hates these things."

"I'll be delighted." Hannah smiled. "And ..." She weighed whether it might be a bit much, considering her reluctance of three minutes before. ". . . honored."

At once all business, she turned to Fromer. "If it's possible, I'd like to have the list of guests and the participants—everyone from hotel managers to the caterers, and I'd like to go over the menus and the schedule of events."

"See?" Sam said to Gordon, rubbing his hands together. "She's already taking charge." He turned back to Hannah and put a hand on her arm. "Miss Sandell, you can have anything you want. I'll have a messenger deliver all the information to you here within the hour. Most everything is done. It's only a matter of making sure you're there and looking beautiful as always."

"What say, Mimi?" Hannah said, turning to Mimi. "Do you trust me to escort your husband?"

But Mimi was barely listening. Her mind had wandered to Iris and worrying over why they'd been shuffled off to someone's office instead of being taken directly to her daughter's room.

"Sure," she said dully. "Whatever works."

The room was more crowded, but other than that, everything was status quo. Iris was in and out of consciousness. Cynthia was consistently out. The three people who'd most often sat at Iris's bedside before, sat there again except in complete isolation gear—paper shoe covers, masks, head covers, gowns and gloves. The individuals were identifiable only by size: the Swedish bear, the papa bear, and the mama bear.

Under her mask Adele laughed the laugh of someone who was past exhaustion and on the verge of insanity. She'd surprised herself at how calmly she'd broken the news to the Hershes that Cynthia was in critical condition, apparently suffering from the same thing as Iris.

As she expected, Dr. Hersh questioned the wisdom of having both patients in the same room, but eventually agreed with her rationale that it was a matter of efficiency.

Mimi and Hannah initially seemed uncomfortable with her taking over Iris's care. She could feel the two women watching her every move, judging, comparing, to see if she was as good a nurse as Cynthia had been. Adele was glad she was giddy or she might have been irritated by the constant scrutiny.

When he left, Dr. Hersh made a point of giving her his condolences over the illness of her friend and colleague. She initially dismissed the remark as a politician's effort to secure a vote for himself, but then she caught the glint of real empathy, as in: You have a friend—I have a daughter.

Skip, gowned to the gills, came in at noon as he had promised. Under the pressures of an understaffed ward, however, his earlier charitable mood had changed to something less than civil. He helped with the countless chores required by the critically ill: taking vital signs, auscultating lungs, calibrating monitoring devices, bathing away diarrhea and perspiration, measuring urine, answering Mimi's and Hannah's questions, giving IV meds, switching cooling blankets on or off, and checking placement of various invasive tubes and wires.

Twenty minutes later, only a dozen words had passed between the two nurses, but their dispositions were considerably altered: She felt less tired; Skip stopped grumbling under his breath.

The male nurse was finishing a cardiac output on Cynthia

when Adele noticed for the first time that he was gloveless.
A ripple of alarm went through her brain and out her mouth.
"Christ on a bike. Have you been ungloved this whole
time?"

Skip looked down at his bare hands and then back at her.
His expression was one of extreme dismay, like a sky diver
at the end of a free fall who has just realized he's forgotten
to pack his parachute.

"Oh shit. I—I'm—I took them off to change the arterial
line tubing and forgot to glove up again."

"Do a five-minute scrub down right now," she said with
authority. "And use the nail scraper."

Mimi and Hannah exchanged alarmed glances over the
rim of their masks, then looked to her for explanation of
Skip's panic.

"Don't worry. Iris and Cynthia aren't in danger from
Skip—it's more the other way around. He left himself
unprotected."

"Sounds like you're talking about condoms." Hannah's
mask breathed.

"I am. Hand condoms; the nurse's best friend. It gets to
be second nature after a while. Even at home, whenever I
wash my hands, I find myself looking for the glove box."

"Oh how sterile for you," Hannah remarked dryly.

Adele laughed. In spite of Cynthia's cool attitude toward
the woman, she hadn't been able to dislike Hannah. To the
contrary, she was drawn in by her dry humor and common
sense. And really, was the woman's protectiveness of the
Hershes so different from what Cynthia had shown toward
Iris, or what she herself had recently demonstrated toward
Cynthia? Hadn't one of the ER nurses found it necessary to
take her aside and warn her to chill out or everyone would
begin to think she and Cyn had some sort of "unnatural" relationship going?

Nor was Cynthia above jealousy; the nurse liked to say
she admired strong, independent women who made it to

success on their own without a man to pay their way, but perhaps Hannah Sandell had made it *too* well.

Skip finished his scrub looking suicidal. On his way out of the room's degowning area, he brushed past Dr. Ingram, who wore a similar expression. Adele cringed at the sight of the physician. She checked his hands for weapons.

"Do you need anything in here, Adele?" Dr. Ingram asked from the door.

Mimi was on him before he could take another breath. It was the type of assault the physician endured daily—a family member demanding answers he did not always have. She grabbed the physician's hands and wrung them. "Is there anything new, Randolph? Have the laboratory reports come back?"

"Sorry, Miriam. I spoke with the head of the lab this morning, but nothing definite has been pinpointed. Yesterday I was leaning toward the possibility of some sort of poisoning, but now with the nurse coming down with the same thing, it's thrown a wrench in the works."

He shook his head. "We've sent off Nurse O'Neil's specimens for comparison tests, but so far the preliminaries are all coming back clean."

"Did anyone mention to you that Cynthia was splashed in the face with Iris's . . ." Hannah searched for the proper term.

". . . secretions." Adele finished for her.

"Yes, Ms. Monsarrat told me when she dragged me out of bed in the middle of the night." The older man sighed and looked at the nurse with one eyebrow arched. "Anything new you have to tell me?"

Adele picked up the two critical-care flow sheets and the most recent lab work. Ingram would rely on her report instead of examining the patients himself—it was a compliment of sorts she supposed, although he would be the one collecting the two-hundred-dollar hospital visit fee.

She spread out the large, awkward sheets over the degowning area counter and commenced to give a full report of both patients' various systems and vital signs. Overall, Iris was beginning to lighten neurologically, and her liver functions were improving, while Cynthia remained considerably less stable and still comatose.

She asked him to write orders for different IV solutions and a sliding scale guideline for adjusting the rates of infusion, then requested that several of the respiratory and medication orders be made "At nurse's discretion." He did so willingly.

Unlike most physicians, Randolph Ingram encouraged the nurses to take the role of collaborative practitioners. Instead of playing the supercilious dictator-physician who often ridiculed or even dismissed the nurse for providing detailed information about a patient's needs, he actively sought out their input and opinions.

Ingram listened to Adele's suggestions, nodding his head in agreement of some, and questioning her rationale on others. Both Hannah and Mimi listened in with keen interest. Hannah asked intelligent, appropriate questions about the physical data, while Mrs. Hersh asked the harder questions about future neurological function and residual disabilities.

As was the custom, Dr. Ingram made no predictions and no promises, and left patients and visitors to the nurse's care.

Adele did hourly vitals. Cynthia's respiratory rate was beginning to climb, and she was bucking the ventilator. Adjusting the amount of delivered oxygen, Adele applied ointment to Cynthia's lips, which were swollen and beginning to crack around the endotracheal tube.

"It's okay, Cyn. I'm right here. You're going to be okay. Iris is better today. You'll follow her course, but you've got to do the fighting Irish number, okay?" Her voice broke.

She was swallowing down the lump in her throat when a long, strong arm went around her waist. Hannah. Immediately, a small hand took hers and squeezed. Mimi.

"You're very close to her, aren't you?" Hannah asked, tenderly smoothing a stray lock of hair back under the blue paper hair cover.

watched the entrance to the cafeteria while she waited for her party to come to the phone.

"This is Maurice. How may I help you, Ms. Sandell?" Maurice spoke with a heavy accent—Belgian probably.

Automatically, Hannah's hackles went up. She had never relished dealing with the egos of European males who were in service-oriented positions; those who weren't gay usually treated American women with disdain, regarding them as crude whores. If a woman showed spirit or a sense of independence, she was immediately labeled as a lesbian.

"I'll be standing in for Mrs. Hersh at the Hersh fundraiser at the Belvedere tomorrow night. I've gone over the lists of the food to be served and I'm faxing over a list of dishes I'd like added to the hors d'oeuvres menu. I also want two choices of meatless soup, and another choice of green salad added to the menu. This being the Bay Area, I'm sure there will be more than a few vegetarians in attendance."

She heard his silent disapproval in the hesitation before he said, "Very good, madam." His voice was clipped and chilly.

"Also, Mr. Fromer and I will be there early to personally survey the food before it leaves the kitchen. I'd like—"

"That is really quite unnecessary, madam," the man interrupted with a modicum of indignation. "Chez Bleu has the highest reputation in all of San Francisco Bay Area. We are rated in—"

"We will check the food before it leaves the kitchen," Hannah repeated, carefully enunciating each word.

There was a pause. "No. *N'est pas possible*. I'm afraid that will be out of the question, madam. I don't think . . ."

"Yes, I can see that you aren't thinking, Maurice. And you should be afraid not of what is out of the question, but rather, of losing this job."

The silence on the other end of the phone deepened. When the man finally spoke, the strain of contained anger made his voice rise an octave. "It is illegal for nonfood workers to enter the food preparation area . . . madam."

Irate at the man's impertinence, Hannah forced a laugh. "Oh Maurice, you are such an *enfant gâté*. And so witty." Her voice dropped. "Mr. Fromer and I will arrive at the Hotel Belvedere kitchen at approximately five-thirty. I'd like the first round of hors d'oeuvres to be served no later than six. I want . . ."

"I am so sorry, madam, but you cannot survey the food before it is served." He sent the words out like guttural daggers. "The reputation of my business is flawless, Madam Sandell. I will not allow it."

"No?" Hannah swallowed, as the veins in her neck distended with rage. She hated to lose her temper—a reminder that she was, after all, her mother's daughter. Her mother's blind rages and the savage beatings which followed were things she still had nightmares about.

There was stubborn silence from the other end of the phone. Hannah could feel herself losing control despite her resolve. "Maurice, may I ask . . . are you a philosophical type of arrogant bastard, or are you the pragmatic kind?"

She waited a beat, to compose herself. She blew her nose and blindly searched the bottom of her purse for her pill bottle. Finally, she took a breath and spoke in a reasonable voice.

"Okay, Maurice. I will give you the benefit of the doubt and believe you are a businessman with some sense. As such, think on this for a moment if you please: Don't cross the White Swan. With one call, I assure you, you will never rip off another ignorant rich American with your substandard food and that fake Parisian accent again. I will personally make sure that happens. At the end of two months you'll wish to God you never left whatever nasty little European hole it was that you came from."

The silence on the other end of the phone lasted a few moments.

"Maurice? Are you there?"

Was it just her imagination, or did she hear the grinding of teeth?

"Now, once again: Mr. Fromer and I will be there at approximately five-thirty to go over the food. Is that understood?"

"Yes." The word was spit out with disgust.

"Good. Have your best people ready to begin serving the hors d'oeuvres at six sharp. When I say your best people, I'm talking about hygienically sound humans with IQs above seventy and whose first language is English. Am I understood?"

"Perfectly . . . Madam."

"Thank you, Maurice. We'll expect to see you tomorrow in the main kitchen."

Opening a small bag of M&M's, Hannah emptied them into her mouth, chewing rapidly. She blew her nose, and swallowed her antihistamines and Advil dry. At the count of ten, perfectly poised, she opened the telephone booth door and stepped onto Skip's white NurseMates shoes.

SEVEN

THE WIZENED OLD LADY BEHIND THE GLASS counter barely cleared the top of the tray rail. Only her eyes, long nose, and the top of her poofy blue hair cap showed— like a "Kilroy Was Here" cartoon.

"Nope," she said in a rusty crank of a voice. "The garden chow mein gots no meat. Not even no meat juice."

"Are the vegetables fresh?"

"Picked 'em myself this morning, dearie."

The server next to her, an obese, rosy-cheeked woman with a beehive hairdo, snickered.

"How about MSG?" Adele asked suspiciously.

"MG? Ain't that one of them sporty cars?"

"MSG is a food additive. It's very bad for your body."

The crone's eyes didn't flicker. "Nope. Ain't got no MG neither. You new here, honey?"

"Nope." Adele shook her head. "I'm old here by about seventeen years."

Violet (that was her name—after her Aunt Milly's second cousin's wife) was shocked. In her twenty-six years of slinging vittles, she thought she'd met everybody who ever worked at Ellis, except maybe for the physicians who put on airs and thought they were too good to eat her food. (After twenty-six years, she thought of it as *her* food.) Now she wondered who else she'd never seen.

"Well, you want the chow mein or not?"

"Sure, why not? If I'm not dead by now, nothing's going to kill me."

102

"You want the rice under the hill or on the bank?"

Adele blinked. "Under the hill?"

"Rice, deary. Under or on the side?"

"Better put it on the side . . . just in case."

The rheumy gray eyes disappeared, leaving only the poofy part of her hair cap bobbing and weaving like a blob of blue cotton candy. Adele leaned down and peered through the space above the aluminum bins of food. Through the lights of the food warmers she saw the old lady elbow the server next to her.

"Just in case," Violet snorted, ladling out a scoop of the Chinese stew onto Adele's plate.

Both women wheezed out a couple of cackles.

Most of the tables were occupied, but she'd found a table in the far corner of the cafeteria. Hidden from general view, Adele warily studied the multi-colored gelatinous mush on her plate and sniffed. She did not recognize any of the forms on her plate as vegetables she was familiar with on earth.

It smelled good, but then again, she was so hungry, she'd find the smell of a dead coyote appealing. In seventeen years, it was only the second time she'd purchased Ellis cafeteria food. Overpriced, overcooked, and small portions had kept her safely at bay.

She went for the rice first—just in case. It was white and gummy, exactly the way she liked it. Two chews into it, she detected a funny iodine aftertaste that she obliterated by sucking down a packet of soy sauce. That would play havoc with her sodium-potassium levels, but it was better than the funny aftertaste.

The chow mein tasted like the insides of a twice-smoked, nonfiltered cigarette. She ate as much as she could. When she couldn't take it anymore, she relied on her coffee to take that taste away.

She checked her watch. Exactly nine minutes had passed since she left the ward. Thanks to Miriam Hersh, she could relax for five more before having to head back. Mimi had proved herself to be more proficient at nursing than most of the med techs. An astute observer, the woman was not hampered by squeamishness or her emotions once she began technical hands-on care of her daughter.

She had actually learned how to suction using sterile technique in one session. Though tentative at first, by the time Mimi pulled the catheter out of her daughter's endotracheal tube a last time, she was even sounding like a nurse, saying things like: "Oooh, look at all the great stuff I got!"

Adele couldn't wait to run the idea of a millionairess becoming an R.N. past Cynthia so she could write one of her funny short stories about a rich nurse ordering hand-tailored latex gloves by Dior.

She watched the people in the cafeteria. The normal people—nonmedical personnel—were always interesting to observe, but she found healthcare personnel downright riveting.

The ER nurse who went by the name of Xena stood in the opposite corner of the room talking nonstop to a bored-looking echo tech from cardiology. The echo tech kept backing up, and the nurse followed. In the span of a few short minutes, they'd made it clear across the room and out the door.

An entire table of African-Americans wearing various uniforms all got up, as if on cue, and vacated the table in front of her. Within a few seconds, a table of Hispanics did the same. Then the Asian table. It seemed the cafeteria was clearing out by race.

As soon as the Asians left, Adele saw the wide back of Hannah Sandell. Sitting opposite her, listening impassively, was Skip. She squinted. No, not Skip. She'd left him upstairs manning the ward and her two patients. It had to be Marcus.

Everyone has a double wandering around the earth. Marcus Weider was Skip Muldinardo's twin. Same face, same pattern of baldness, same build, same black-rimmed thick glasses, same whiny voice, same spare tire around the middle, even the same uniform.

The only things different were that Marcus was an artist, quite bright, and militantly gay, and worked in oncology; Skip had no creative talents, kept his intelligence *and* his sexuality a secret, and worked the Ward from Hell.

Hannah grabbed Marcus's arm. The male nurse looked down at her hand as though something peculiar—like kangaroo droppings—had pooled there. He removed his arm from the table. The two talked for a while longer, sipping at their tea. Hannah was gesturing in a way that suggested she was talking about curtains and windows, or perhaps the colors of the sky.

That would fit, thought Adele, since Marcus was an artist of some merit. Several of his canvases—a colorful series originally entitled *HIV Suns*—graced the walls of the hospital lobby under the administration's revised title, *Dorchester Gardens*.

In the side entrance to the cafeteria, Gordon Hersh's campaign manager came into view, sucking on a toothpick and scanning the tables. When he spotted Hannah and the male nurse, he watched them for several minutes, never taking his eyes off Marcus. He stopped a passing employee, pointed out the table, and said something. The woman—a Ward 6 clerk—looked where he pointed and said something back. Adele couldn't be sure, but his expression seemed to be one of irritation.

By the time Adele left the cafeteria, slinking along the far wall so as not to be seen, Hannah and Marcus appeared to be blushing and having a grand old time.

"Oh God, I am so sorry," Hannah said, grabbing the nurse's arm. Her cold had settled in her nose and throat, making her voice low and whispery. "I wasn't looking where I was going. These damned antihistamines make me spacy."

Marcus bent to rub his foot where the woman had accidentally stepped. She had to weigh more than Baby. When he straightened he looked over the tops of his glasses. What he saw almost took his breath away—a real, honest to God Marc Jacobs with matching pumps and purse. And oh that royal blue! It would look absolutely divine on him. The outfit was probably worth at least six months of his salary.

The woman pointed to the cafeteria. "I'm taking a coffee break, want to sit together?"

"Sure," he said. Who was this woman and what did she want? She was nice-looking in a big Norwegian way—kind of like Roxie in Baby Sex's Castro Street Cavalcade of Vestites show. It was simply too perfect. He decided to call Baby the second he got home.

He paid for his lunch and found the woman sipping an iced tea at a corner table. He sat down and began to eat like a hungry ranch hand.

"May I ask you a question?" she asked, touching his arm again.

Marcus stopped dead in the mastication of his fruit salad concoction. "Ah, I guess. Depends. You can ask."

"Do you like being a nurse? What I mean is, you work with all women. Doesn't that make you . . . uncomfortable, or resentful?"

Marcus shifted his eyes suspiciously, wondering if sticking this woman on him was another one of his lover's practical jokes. He decided right away that it wasn't any joke. Stevie didn't know anybody north of Mission Street, and nobody south of Mission could afford The Gap let alone a real Marc Jacobs.

"Nursing is okay," he said hesitantly. "Most of the girls are fun, though some of them do get bitchy. But really, doesn't *everybody*?"

Hannah coughed. "Doesn't your wife or girlfriend get jealous?"

Marcus looked at her uncertainly. Was this girl for real, or just dumb? "Ah, no, I'm not . . ."

"It must get hard for you working so closely with so many attractive females." She gave him a playful glance from under thick lashes as she blew her nose. Reaching across the table for his hand, she pulled it toward her. She had a grip like one of the leather boys. She was coming on to him! Oh God, Baby would die laughing. Really! "... *get hard for you?*"

He stared at her hand, not quite sure of what to do with it.

"You have the hands of an artist." Her voice was husky but he couldn't tell if it was because she was trying to be sexy or if it was just a cold.

"I am," he said. "I mean, I'm a painter. They call me the Mapplethorpe of Marin; most of my work centers around gay issues and community; AIDS ... that sort of thing." He was eager to get the message across.

The woman seemed slightly put off for a second. She drew back her hand. "I suppose you could say I was an artist of sorts, too. Did you know that I'm an interior designer?"

"Oh, how exciting!" Marcus whispered in his faggiest of voices—the one he used at the baths. He threw in a limp wrist salute for good measure. "I just knew you were a designer of some sort the second I saw that divine dress. I said to myself, 'Now there's a woman with impeccable taste.' " He fingered the material of her sleeve. "It's a Marc Jacobs, isn't it?"

"Ah, yes. Yes it is."

He nodded approvingly. He was busy constructing the story for Baby and Stevie. They'd love it even though Stevie would pretend to be jealous. It'd be a fun story for the baths on Friday night.

"Interior design is like working with large canvases in a way," Hannah said, waving an arm at the far wall. "I start with the natural light in a room and blend everything outward from there. The walls, the floor, the furniture ... everything must reflect the natural light and color."

She turned her gaze on him. For the first time he noticed that her eyes were such a light blue they looked almost white . . . like the eyes of a malamute. *A few tattoos, a radical haircut, a spiked dog collar, black lipstick and nails,* he thought, *and she'd be perfect for the Castro. Femmes and dykes would be killing themselves over her left and left.*

"Do you know what I mean by natural color?" she asked.

Marcus stopped sucking on his straw just on the edge of making those impolite suctioning noises that made his mother slap him upside the head. "The color of the atmosphere," he answered without hesitation. "Not exactly plain air, but the essence of color collected and reflected in one specific space."

Hannah was impressed and looked at him with new respect. "Yes, that's exactly what I mean. Do you ever show your work? I'd love to see it sometime."

"I have a series in the lobby titled *HIV Suns.*"

She recalled the three canvases. They were well done, with clever blending of color. For a moment, she felt dizzy and slightly out of balance with reality. The feeling threatened to send her into a hypoglycemic-induced anxiety attack. She sucked at the sugar at the bottom of her glass and studied her Rolex for a moment. She drew instant reassurance from the thought that someone had taken great pains and expense to make the timepiece the perfect instrument that it was.

She looked up in time to see the nurse gathering his lunch dishes. "I've got to get back now," he said.

"You nurses work so hard," she said, rising. "I truly admire all of you." They turned in opposite directions. "See you on the ward."

Marcus waved, wondering which of his patients she was related to. He couldn't remember seeing her on Ward 6 before.

A sudden dark fear about premature AIDS dementia and losing his mind threw a shadow across his path. He squelched the terror with the thought that it was too early for that. But maybe forgetfulness was a side effect of the AZT. Sure, that was it. Said so right in the PDR—or was that another one of his drugs?

He'd *definitely* call Baby when he got home. Baby would know all the answers.

Tim Ritmann, Detective Sergeant for the Marin County sheriff's office, tapped on the window. The only part of him that was exposed was his eyes and forehead—everything else was blue isolation wrap. The blue of the wrap matched the redhead's eyes.

Adele looked up from the Foley drainage bag which held a measly 300 ccs of Cynthia's urine and her heart muscle threw a premature ventricular contraction at the sight of him.

Nip it in the bud, Monsarrat! she mentally reprimanded. *He's just a man—Cynthia's man. Put the hormones on ice and think of him as a brother.*

Oh yeah, but he's such a lovely, warm, intelligent, gorgeous brother.

Forget it! How can you think of him like that with Cynthia dying?

She is not dying!

Okay, then nip it in the bud.

The muscular man gave her a hug. "How is she?" he asked. Then he took in the sight of his ex-lover lying still in the bed. "Jesus," he whispered, astonished at what he was seeing, "What the hell happened? Why didn't anybody call me?" She was so pale, sunken and invaded by hideous medical equipment, Tim was having a hard time recognizing the wasting body in the bed as the vivacious and voluptuous woman he'd made love to a few hundred times.

"I was going to call you when I got home," she lied. "I haven't left her side since nine last night.

"Nobody knows what it is, Tim. This girl," Adele nodded toward Iris, "came in three days ago. Cynthia took care of her and then yesterday she got splashed with some of her secretions. By last night she was out of it. Somehow she managed to call me before she lost consciousness."

"But what is it? A virus or . . . ?"

She shrugged. "Nobody's seen anything like it before. Blood samples have been sent to San Francisco CDC and just about everywhere else."

His voice and eyes were so full of fearful concern that for a second, she felt scared, too.

"What's going to happen?" he asked in a somber voice.

She opened her mouth to say no one knew, and that it was up to the fates, and that they had to think positively, and all the other happy horseshit medical people traditionally shoveled out, when, instead, she slowly sank into the chair next to the bed, covered her face, and sobbed.

His knees cracked as he knelt beside her. His arms went around her, and she felt the warmth of his face against her neck. She wound her fingers in the blue paper of his gown. They stayed like that until her sobs melted down to sporadic gasps for air. When she opened her eyes, he handed her a tissue and told her to blow her nose. Her mask was soaked through.

Mimi came in at the end of her outburst and stood at bay, wringing her hands. Her latex gloves were squeaking. "Are you okay, Adele?" she asked, her eyes wide.

Adele nodded and removed her mask. "It had to come out sooner or later. I'm glad I wasn't on the freeway—the Beast would've killed me for sure."

Over Tim's shoulder and through the crook of Mimi's elbow, she saw the swing shift nurse who was going to take over from her walk into the unit and check the assignment board. The nurse's hand flew to her mouth in a gesture of shock as soon as she saw Cynthia's name.

Adele rose from her chair feeling tired and heart weary. Still, she didn't want to give up her two patients to someone else. She now understood Cynthia's concern about turning over a patient to a nurse who wasn't so emotionally attached.

"I've got to get ready to give report," she said. "I'll call you tomorrow and let you know what's happening."

"Why don't I buy you dinner?" he said consolingly. "I'll wait for you downstairs."

She shook her head. "I don't think I can stand upright that long. I expect by the time I get home I'll be crawling on all fours."

"Nelson will love that."

At the mention of her roommate, she groaned. Nelson had been left alone for over twenty hours. He'd be furious with her for bringing up all his abandonment fears again. She hoped he hadn't resorted to his usual retaliation of chewing holes through the front door or peeing on her pillow, because then she'd have to threaten him with sending him to doggie day care, and then it would escalate into the never-ending cycle of punish and strike back. And God, she hated getting into that with a dog—it could really turn vicious.

Instead of the elevator, Hannah took the stairs to give herself time to think. There was so much to do. She would have to find a dress, go over the menus again, make sure Mimi was okay, stop by the Hersh house to make sure the underlings were following her orders, check in at her office and then Gordon's office.

Hannah heard someone coming up the stairs behind her and moved to one side. Rubbing the back of her slender neck, she was aware of the ache cutting through the Advil. She would have to resort to taking some of the Demerol left over from her last visit to the dentist.

She heard her name and then felt someone's hand slide under her dress and pinch her inner thigh. She whirled around, her leg kicking out at the same instant. Her foot grazed the side of Samuel Fromer's head. In a flash, he had grabbed her ankle and held it in one powerful hand, forcing it outward.

"What the hell do you think you're doing?" she demanded, kicking at him again. This time, her foot made a solid connection.

Fromer staggered against the railing, rubbing his ear. He was out of breath and perspiring heavily, as though he'd been running. "You've got a hell of a kick." He stepped up closer. "Not to mention a hell of an ass."

Hannah glared at him, clenching her jaw. "You're disgusting," she snapped. "Why would you do such a thing?"

His smirk turned into a leer. "I noticed you chatting up the faggot nurse in the cafeteria. You that hard up, Ulla?"

"You . . ." Whatever she meant to say died in her throat. She stood motionless.

Samuel moved to the stair below hers. "What's the matter, Ms. Nyquist? Did I scare you?"

He studied her face as she transformed before his eyes. The ball-busting untouchable was gone abruptly, leaving a scared girl in her place.

"How about going someplace for lunch? We can talk about the fund-raiser and . . . other things."

"No thanks," she said, pretending to recover. She turned and continued climbing the stairs. A fine line of perspiration formed on her upper lip. "I don't bring animals to restaurants."

He grabbed her arm and pulled her back. "Let's get some exercise then."

Hannah twisted away from him. "What *is* your problem, Fromer?" she asked in a voice laced with frost.

He chuckled. "Well, you are right about there being a problem, Ulla, but it sure as fuck ain't mine."

"Stop with the cat and mouse routine," she snapped. "I don't feel well, and I've got a lot to do before tomorrow night. I'm not up for games."

He leaned against the rail and ran his fingers across his lips. He liked the fact that she was nervous, yet not willing to crump. She was feisty. That was good. He liked women who had an edge.

"Tony Saludo," he said finally.

Hannah blanched. "What?" she whispered. Her hand tightened around the large Styrofoam cup of iced tea.

"I said, Tony Saludo."

"Who's that?"

Fromer laughed derisively. "Shit, I don't know, Ulla, but it would seem to me most women would remember the name of their mother's pimp, especially when he's her pimp, too."

Hannah wiped the moisture off her upper lip and said nothing.

"It would make a hell of a story for the *Intelligencer*, don't you think? 'The White Swan, queen of San Francisco's social circle; daughter of a Swedish whore success story.' Or, how's this?" He held up his hands as if framing a marquee. " 'My mother's pimp put me through college on the money he made from my mother's porno flicks.' Or, 'How I got my start in business with the help of a mobster.' "

Her heart raced. She started to say that that part of her life was ancient history, that she'd erased the humiliation and the abuse, but stopped herself. She refused to show weakness in front of the man . . . especially this man.

"What do you want?" she asked.

"All I want . . ." He let his hand slide up the outside of her dress to her breast. ". . . is a little piece of the White Swan."

"What's the matter," she sneered, "you can't get a woman to screw you without blackmailing her?" She gave him a look. "No, I guess you couldn't. Not many women would allow an ugly pig like you near them."

Momentarily stung, he narrowed his eyes and then threw back his head and laughed. "I got this reporter friend named Joey? Well, Ulla, Joey owes me a few favors. I wouldn't get too cocky if I were you. Those headlines won't be too good for business."

"You wouldn't dare," she said in a monotone. She did not move.

Fromer smiled. "Try me," he said. There was an underlying tone of malice to his voice. He slid his hands around to her buttocks and pushed her into him. "If you don't play nice you've got a lot to lose. If you play nice with Sammy, I'll make sure you get more than you ever dreamed was possible."

He was breathing heavily, his face an inch from hers. "I'll bring you to the top. San Francisco is gonna be small-time compared to where we're going. You want to get into the White House? You want the palaces of Europe? They're yours if you behave."

He pushed her away. "You get uncooperative, and you're a dead duck, Miss Swan.

"Come on." He pulled her down two or three stairs. "Let's go for a drive to my place and have a little fun. You'll like it, Ulla."

"I can't . . . Mimi expects me back." Hannah backed up the stairs, holding up the cup of iced tea, as if it were a shield.

He took the Styrofoam cup out of her hands and dropped it over the railing. A sound like shattering glass came back immediately, as the cup exploded several floors below.

"I've already told her that you were involved in a heavy conversation with that dorky nurse in the cafeteria. She doesn't expect you right away.

"Let's go." He pulled at her wrist.

She allowed herself to be pulled down the stairs, staring expressionlessly over his shoulder. She had ceased to feel anything. It was a trick she learned early in life.

Iris swam under warm, thick water. They must be visiting Aunt Andra at Lake Sunipee. She frowned. She couldn't remember how she got there, or why she was so tired. Maybe it was because she was breathing water. It was easy, and she wasn't drowning.

She struggled to open her eyes even though Grandmama Esther warned her not to ever open her eyes underwater. Grandmama Esther said bacteria would get inside and she'd get pinkeye and go blind. But she didn't care; she had to see what was going on around her.

Slowly she forced her lids to part. Through the murky brown she saw blue walls, glass windows, and bright lights. Figures were moving around, but she wasn't sure if they were human or not. They had large, odd-shaped white or blue heads and no mouth or chin. The rest of them were shapeless inside long blue robes which went all the way to the floor.

She closed her eyes. Aliens. She'd read about the abductions in a book she took out of the library last summer. She must have been taken aboard one of their ships.

Her eyes opened again, easier this time. The brown had cleared to an overcast of tan. One of the aliens came closer to the bed. She was startled to see it had eyes like her father.

"Iris?" it said in the voice of her father. "Are you waking up? Please, sweetheart. Wake up for your Mr. Oldass papa."

She forced herself to blink. Tan lightened to a soft yellow. The figure pulled down his mask to reveal the face of her father. Something warm was put into one of her hands.

"Squeeze my fingers, Iris," her father commanded.

Working very hard, she tightened her grip on his fingers.

Her father laughed loudly, and shouted, "Thank God! She's lightening up." She couldn't understand what had made him so happy. Her mother appeared next to him. She looked frantic—like always.

"Dreidela?" It was the pet name her mother had used for her when she was a baby. "Dreidela, are you awake now?"

She squeezed more fingers which created more excitement. Her mother disappeared out of her range of view.

There was a rapid clearing of her consciousness. As she grew more aware, her surroundings became clearer. A hospital room. Another bed next to hers. Or was it?

No. It was a mirror. She could see herself lying in bed, her head surrounded by blue and white tubes and IV bags on poles and . . .

It all came back. London, drinking coffee, listening to her father's speech, going to her room, hearing noises and getting out of bed to see what it was. She remembered seeing something through the crack of a door and then getting sick. Iris closed her eyes again, too tired to keep them open any longer. Too tired to think.

Her father said something unintelligible.

She wanted so badly to tell him what she'd seen before she forgot. For a moment she thought she would go insane with the clear image of the horror. Instead, merciful unconsciousness erased everything and let her drift back to peace.

Adele was brain-dead and her body was numb. It made the eight-mile run more bearable than had she been mentally present to hate it. She'd missed her 4:00 A.M. run, but rather than give herself a day off, she decided to run after she got home from work. Most people would have ragged on her for pushing herself, or called her addicted, but running was the only thing that would bring her back to some kind of mental and emotional balance.

Nelson ran at her side, alternately ecstatic, confused, and frustrated. He loved being with Her in the Out, but he didn't like it when She left him for so long. Today, the water bowl had gone dry and he'd had to resort to drinking out of Her toilet. Then it had gotten cold and She wasn't there to make the wall blow warm air at him. The worst, though, was having to wait until he was forced to wet the rug by the door. It was enough to make him take a few nibbles at the front door.

By the time the clock on the mantel chimed seven, she had showered, jammied-up, and, bouncing off the hallway wall only once, listened to her phone messages.

Her mother had called wanting to know if she'd read Daniel Weiss's book about cockroaches, and in the same breath asked if she'd like to come over for some meatless lasagna. Mrs. Coolidge, the neighborhood gossip, was next, asking if she would look after her cat—the fiendish, twenty-four-pound Queen Shredder—for two days while she visited her brother in Healdsburg. Then Miriam Hersh called to ask her to please call; she wanted to know if she'd consider working private duty for them once Iris was discharged.

Adele paused the tape. By the time Iris was well enough to be discharged, she would be the one needing a nurse. Mimi was such a worrywart. Earlier in the day, she'd worried because Iris put out ten ccs less urine than the day before, then she had been anxious over Cynthia's fever, not to mention the woman's reaction to her emotional outburst over Cynthia. Even when the campaign manager told her Hannah would be delayed because she was talking to a male nurse in the cafeteria, she'd gone slightly frantic.

When Hannah failed to show up at all, she'd pressed Adele for details about who the nurse was, and did she think Hannah would be safe? Inside, Adele had howled, and told her Marcus was as safe as they got.

Denise, the swing shift nurse, left a message saying to get some sleep and that Cynthia was stable and that Iris was waking up and beginning to respond and she would call her if there was any significant change in Cynthia's condition.

Nelson crawled into her lap and licked her face. "No, no." She pushed him off. "No body fluids, Nels. You might get sick, and then you'd have to go to the doggie doctor and be put on a respirator."

Nelson whined and barked as if to say *Not me!* and trotted off to the kitchen to beg a second dinner.

With the news that Cynthia was stable, a weight lifted from her shoulders and her appetite returned with force. She paused the machine again and headed to the kitchen, where she burned rye toast and spread it thick with cottage cheese and catsup. Then she prepared an escarole salad with six cloves of raw garlic cut into it, and shared it with the dog.

Dessert was half a bowl of puffed wheat with a banana, honey, and rice milk. A banana hater, the dog turned his nose up at that concoction, but eagerly accepted his vitamins, which had been specially formulated for vegetarian dogs.

Nelson licked her hand begging for more. She knelt down

next to the dog, wondering if it were possible to spread the virus to an animal. For that matter, she wondered what it would take for her to get it. She had taken extra precautions to protect herself from the moment Iris was brought into Ward 8. Still believing that handwashing was the single most effective way to prevent illness, she silently thanked Mrs. Mau, her first-year nursing instructor, for drumming the basics of disease control into her head until it became second nature.

She returned to her answering machine and picked up from where she'd left off. At the sound of Tim's voice, her stomach went into hyperspin-digest. How are you? How's Cyn? How about dinner tomorrow night?

She rewound the message six times, dissecting every minute change in his intonation, and weighing how he said her name as opposed to how he said Cynthia's name, and was the feeling behind the invitation simply friendly, or was it a *date* kind of invitation? She was listening to it for a seventh time when she realized she was obsessing and reset the tape to the beginning.

No matter what happened, she would *not* let herself get involved with Tim Ritmann. He younger than she, he had red hair, he was in love with her best friend. End of story. Amen.

Her head hit the pillow in the middle of a thought about how it had felt inside his arms, and his soft breath on her neck. There was a fleet of random thoughts about having forgotten to floss, her ex-husband, naked men, and exploding Winnebagos. And then she was out for the count.

Gordon looked at himself in the mirror and stuck out his tongue. It was coated.

"What's the matter?" Mimi asked, standing at the next sink over.

"Nothing." He flicked on the battery-powered toothbrush.

Mimi continued to rub a thin film of cold cream and lanolin over her face and neck. "You don't look well, Gordon.

Take some vitamin B and C." A thought stopped her hand. "You don't think you, Samuel, and Hannah have what Iris started out with, do you?"

Gordon shrugged. "I don't think so. We've been careful."

She did not miss the look of concern behind her husband's eyes. "What about starting some antibiotics?"

He finished polishing his back molars, then shook his head. "Antibiotics aren't going to help. I'll give Sam and myself a B-twelve injection tomorrow. You and Hannah, too.

"Samuel missed an important meeting with our attorneys this afternoon." He looked at her out of the corner of his eye. "You wouldn't know where he was, would you?"

"No." She screwed the lid back on the jar of cold cream and frowned at the wrinkles around her mouth that only she could see. "Why would I know where Sam was? He's *your* campaign manager."

Mimi began brushing her hair. Gordon caught the warm smell of her perfume coming off her like a faint cloud. She threw back her head and closed her eyes, swaying slightly.

The unprocessed, natural sensuality that came from her mesmerized him. It was an erotic, animal sensuality that he could not remember in her. Without thinking, he touched her neck and then her hair.

Mimi froze under his touch. Opening her eyes, she looked at him with such repugnance, he pulled his hand back as though he'd been burned.

Brian removed his face guard and rubbed his temples where the headache throbbed. Carefully putting the test tube down on his work table, he went to the sink and lowered his head under the tap. Through the noise of the running water, his stopwatch beeped, reminding him it was time to have something to eat. Rosie had convinced him he needed to have frequent snacks—especially on the days she or his mom didn't come to cook and he worked late at the laboratory.

She told him that as his blood sugar fell, he was fifty

times more likely to make a mistake, and with his kind of job, mistakes could prove deadly to a lot of innocent people. Brian snorted and opened the laboratory refrigerator. In the back, behind the racks of test tubes and the heat-sensitive bottles of chemicals, he saw the paper bag Rosie had filled with "health food" snacks.

He closed the refrigerator. Behind him, in its cage on his workstation, the mouse squeaked once and went stiff as it went into a seizure.

Dropping his lunch in the sink, he picked up the violently twitching rodent with tongs and put it under the exam light. By the time he'd prepared the instruments he'd needed, it was dead.

He whistled under his breath, and noted the time of death to the second. He turned the critter over. Dark red fluid ran from its nose and mouth. "Hey there, Gordon." He smiled down at the mouse. "That was pretty damned fast."

EIGHT

ADELE BLESSED THE GOODWILL UMBRELLA AS she fished it out from under the front seat. The mold-tinged, red and white nylon panels sporting Sapporo beer advertisements made the ancient bumbershoot one of the few material possessions she would be hard-pressed to part with.

The unpredictability and sometimes rapid change of Bay Area weather necessitated that one carry various changes of clothes, shoes, and various instruments of weather protection. A former Girl Scout, Adele believed in being prepared. In its spare tire well, the Beast carried a duffle bag filled with blankets, warm hats, sun visors, shorts and down-filled ski pants, a long wool coat, tank tops, heavy snow boots, and flip-flops.

Alighting from the Beast, she struggled with the rusted clasp of the umbrella until it sprang up like a rocket, giving her wrist bones a good rattle. She searched for her favorite denim jacket, couldn't find it, and settled on her 1946 navy blue (with red lining no less) nurse's cape instead.

Her apprehensions grew with each step that brought her closer to the ER entrance. She could almost swear the phone had rung a couple of times during the wee small hours of the morning. Then she had a vivid dream of Cynthia lying at the bottom of the morgue wagon. When she woke promptly at 3:45 A.M., her unconscious vomited the fuzzy memory onto the floor of her conscious mind. Bolting out of bed, she tripped and bounced her way to the answering machine, which remained in its cruel, You-have-no-messages mode.

That cinched it—the phone *had* rung, and it was most certainly the night nurse calling with such devastating news that she couldn't bring herself to leave it on the answering machine. Not entirely a disbeliever of oneiromancy, she'd pushed the Beast upwards of seventy miles per hour to get to the hospital.

The ER doors swung open automatically. Inside, Adele took a breath and held it. It was okay—if there was going to be bad news about Cynthia, she would rather get it in person with other people around than at home with Nelson—the dog took her bad news worse than she did.

She was over two hours early, but who cared? The night shift nurse would be happy to see her—especially since something had most certainly gone sour during the night. Entering the warm, dry hallway, she saw several groups of night nurses, supervisors, and housekeeping people clustered together in the ER lobby, talking in low voices. She wondered if this was a regular thing night shift people did at 4:45 A.M. ("Hey, Jack! Big doin's down at the ER lobby around 5:00 A.M. Everybody's gonna be there!") Night shifters were strange people—a culture unto themselves— like the undead who were in need of immediate blood transfusions.

The second they saw her they went silent and stared in a shifty-eyed way that reminded her of the final scenes in *Invasion of the Body Snatchers*. Their gazes fairly screamed: "Outsider! Day shifter! Outsider!" Or, then again, maybe they were plotting to blow up the building, or perhaps they were simply waiting around to get their packaged transfusions from the blood bank.

Or, it might have been the sight of her umbrella and cape, but she really didn't think so. She tried not to stare back.

"Good morning, everybody," she said cheerfully, as she snapped the bumbershoot closed.

They glanced at each other with wide, "oh-oh" eyes.

At once, her blood turned to ice and her mind went twisty

at a hundred miles an hour as all her suspicions were confirmed.

Cynthia! There'd been a code and Cynthia didn't make it. The night shifter cult had brought the body down to ER for some sort of weird ritual, and were about to be caught red-handed by the deceased's best friend. No wonder they were all so pale.

She was raising her right foot to fly through the ER doors, when one of the supervisors (supervisors could be identi-fied by the clipboards they regularly kept clasped to their bosoms—like breast plates) took a step nearer—though not too near—and said: "You're Ardel from Ward Eight, right?"

Her heart was going too fast. She was getting dizzy. Her head nodded.

"How did you hear about this? Were you a friend?"

Adele opened her mouth, closed it. *This is only a dream,* the Emotional Emergency Broadcasting System radio voice chanted in her head. *This is only a dream. In case of a reality emergency, you will be instructed to tune to your lo-cal adrenaline pump for emergency infusions. This is only a dream.*

She could feel that her pupils were wide open. A strangled croak came from her throat. "Aggh?"

The supervisor pulled her clipboard tighter so that it crushed her nipples. She took a step back in alarm, afraid the woman, whose face had drained of color in four sec-onds, was going to fall on her. "Excuse me, aren't you Ardel who works on . . . ?"

The ER side door opened and a slender, long-haired man burst out of the ER doors, wailing at the top of his lungs. As he ran past, she thought she recognized him as one of Cyn-thia's past lovers.

Next emerged an orderly pushing the morgue cart in front of him. From the solid, *full* sound it made as it moved, she knew it was occupied.

Tearing past the groups of hospital employees, she grabbed the orderly by his shirt and pushed him aside as easily as though he were a cardboard cutout. She clawed at the lid. Several of the nurses made futile attempts to restrain her. The supervisor (still clutching her clipboard armor) shouted to the switchboard operator to call Crisis Unit Intervention Team stat.

Adele heard and felt nothing except her own panic. When the latch on the false-bottomed cart snapped open, she was suddenly faced with the problem of what she would do when she saw Cynthia's mottled face, gray with death.

That was easy, her brain said, steal Cynthia's body, run away to someplace safe (for some reason, she pictured her kitchen) and fix her ... make her live ... spoon-feed her blue-green algae, royal bee jelly, shark cartilage and rice milk.

She threw back the lid and with eyes that were no longer able to focus, looked into the well of the cart. Falling against the orderly, she clamped a hand over her mouth so as to muffle the scream. The resulting noise sounded like a Bronx cheer.

She blinked and focused on the corpse. There was a religious medal hanging from a chain nestled in a clump of dark chest hair. There were no soft, melonlike breasts, although the nipples on the breasts before her had been lipsticked red and pierced.

It wasn't Cynthia unless her friend had been keeping some pretty major secrets.

"Oh thank you thank you thank you," she whispered, clutching the startled orderly.

But then, another, more subtle type of panic started at the base of her liver and worked its way up into her temples. She let go of the orderly and again brought her face close to the corpse in the cart. "Skip?" she whispered. "Skip, is that you?"

Wait. Skip was an atheist and wouldn't wear religious medals ... let alone have the nerve to pierce his nipples. She looked closer and jumped back.

"Jesus Christ on a bike in hell," she said to an elderly, silver-haired woman who suddenly appeared at her side.

"I'm *so* sorry," said the Crisis Unit worker. She had the face of someone who'd spent many years in the desert without sunblock. "You must have loved Marcus very much."

Adele gave the silver-haired lady a blank stare, trying to control her urge to break into the crazy woman laughter that was right *there* waiting, at the back of her throat. She bowed her head, pinching the corners of her lips toward each other in order to stop the grin. She nodded. "Uhn huh."

They were locked in the Quiet Room, that place reserved expressly for the purpose of delivering Bad News to the survivors of departed or badly maimed loved ones. All the physicians and many of the nurses, including her own, wonderfully alive Cynthia, had used the room for quickies.

She glanced once more into the sympathetic (emphasis on the pathetic) face of the woman. Suddenly, a deep, long snort escaped from her throat and out the unguarded tunnels of her nasal passages. Adele covered her face and tried to make her howls of hysterical laughter sound like weeping. Her cousin Jimmy made a convincing sobbing noise when he laughed— she hoped the skill ran in the family. Maybe this woman had heard all kinds of crying; she certainly *looked* like she'd been hearing people cry her whole, sorry life.

The crisis worker scribbled something in her notebook and tried to force a Kleenex (Medical World Rule #405: All psych workers carry inexhaustible supplies of Kleenex) in between her fingers. She inadvertently poked Adele's eye, which made Adele laugh harder.

When she came up for air, the clock read five-fifteen. Immediately she sobered and stood, wiping away the crazy woman laughter tears. The nagging worry about Cynthia, which had been biting at her temples, was now gnawing in earnest.

"Thank you for your support," she said, reaching to unlock the door, "but I must go to work now."

As if stricken with palsy, the older woman awkwardly jerked at the wattles of her neck. "But—but you *can't* go back to work! You've had a terrible shock; someone close to you has died. You need time to repair and heal your psyche.

"You don't have to be to work for two more hours. Let's walk down to the Crisis Unit and have some coffee, why don't we? Perhaps one of the medical people can prescribe a sedative or some sort of prophylactic antidepressant to help you through this difficult time."

It was just the thing to piss Adele off. The woman was doing what all medical and shrink people were automatically trained to do in any emotional crisis—medicate and suppress the mind and body's natural response. As far as she could tell, over half the population of the United States was on Prozac and were all the weirder for it. As far as she was concerned, Prozac was the actualization of the drug Soma from Huxley's *Brave New World*.

"I don't need anything, thanks. I can weather this from here on out by myself."

"But ... you can't. . . ." The woman was practically gasping.

Adele smiled kindly and opened the door. "Oh yes I can. I've worked without a safety net for years."

Adele pulled down the dress box with her name printed on the outside from the top of her locker. Pushing back the first layer of tissue paper, she gasped at the blue Isaac Mizrahi dress. Under that was an autumn brown cashmere Gucci sweater and a pair of black Prada slacks. Inside the pocket of the slacks were a pair of solid gold hoop earrings from Tiffany's.

The note was written in ink on handmade paper. The handwriting was precise, yet at the same time, artistic.

Adele,
Just a few things I pulled out of the closet earlier this

evening. I thought these colors and textures might set off those beautiful eyes of yours! Hope you like them.

If you do, we can raid the rest of my closets and drawers together. I desperately need to weed the wardrobe!

The note was signed with a bold, artistic *H*.

Reluctantly, Adele repacked the clothes with the note and put them into her locker. She never dreamed Hannah would take her seriously. Unwritten code #790 stated that individual nurses were not allowed to accept personal gifts of more value than a cup of coffee or a box of candy. Immediately, Adele replaced visions of how the Mizrahi dress would look on her with thoughts of how to return the clothes without seeming rude or ungrateful.

Her preliminary check-in in room 802 both reassured and worried her: Cynthia had not improved, but Iris was conscious and her lungs were less crappy.

According to her watch, she had a small window of time to play with. It took her two seconds to decide where she would most likely find the clipboard-chested supervisor.

Caught in the angled corridor between Wards 4 and 6, Mattie Noel realized there was no place to hide from the nurse barreling down on her with all the speed of an express train.

She was fully aware of course that most of the Ward 8 regulars were not like her other nurses; there was always something *wrong* with them that made them less respectable than the rest. The one who was about to accost her, Ardel something or other, had made herself a public figure the year before—getting right in the middle of that disgraceful murder business. Rumor had it, she'd been fornicating with the murderer and several of the murderees.

Mattie's thin lips tightened to a disapproving line, giving rise to the tic in her right eyelid. She held her clipboard closer and gave the annoying tic a wipe with her Kleenex.

"Mrs. Noel?"

Mattie forced herself to smile, but her bloodshot eyes remained locked in her most deadly look. "Yes, Arlene, I mean Ardel?"

"It's Adele. Could you help me?"

"Perhaps." She felt instantly relieved that the woman was calmer and that she'd shed that absurd nurse's cape. "Are you feeling better?"

"A little. I'd like to know what happened in ER with . . ." She looked down and let her chin quiver. ". . . dear Marcus."

"Were you very close?" Mattie asked sympathetically, at the same time hedging on an answer.

Adele knew the tactic well. The woman wouldn't give out the particulars unless she told her copious and major lies.

"He was my half brother. We have the same mother. Our fathers were brothers, though."

Clearly startled by the news, Mattie unclamped her lips *and* her clipboard. "Well, my *goodness*, Ardel, why didn't you tell me or the crisis person that earlier? Your mother was right in my office. She didn't say anything about Marcus having a sister. . . ."

"My mother and I haven't spoken in twenty years. Marcus was always trying to patch things over, you know. He loved us both so much, and it always tore him apart that Mom and I . . ." Adele let herself cave in at the middle, upping the intensity of the quiver.

"I need to know, Mrs. Noel, or I won't be able to get through this." She looked at her pleadingly. "Was it his . . . AIDS? I don't know how it could've happened so fast. I mean, when we left the hospital yesterday, he was the picture of health. We hugged and kissed like we always do, and he said, 'Hey big sister, I'll see ya tomorrow.' Just like that. He was so happy and . . ." She covered her face, waiting for Mrs. Noel to talk.

Silence. She peeked through her fingers and saw Mrs. Noel scowling, as she flipped through the top layers of papers stacked on her clipboard. Her lips made a thin, white slit in the lower half of her face.

"According to yesterday's staffing sheet, Ardel, Marcus went home earlier than usual. When he left, he was complaining of feeling sick. The day supervisor gave him a ride home because he was too sick to drive himself."

"Oh. Well, it must have been the day before. Forgive me, Mrs. Noel. I'm confused and upset, I can't believe this is happening."

Mattie looked at her watch. She was going to be late reporting off if she didn't make it to Ward 5 pronto. No way did she want to deal with that bitch of a day supervisor. She pinched her ass cheeks together and decided it would be much easier to tell the woman what she wanted to know. "Dr. Briscoe said your brother may have died of the same influenza that Nurse O'Neil and Ms. Hersh have. Marcus was compromised by his AIDS, so he didn't really have a fighting chance. He went into a coma early this morning. His . . ." Mattie hesitated, restraining herself from using the popular San Francisco terminology—"lover." ". . . friend, Stephen, called nine-one-one.

"They weren't able to determine exactly how he would have come into contact with the infected patients, although Mrs. Hersh did spend some time with him early yesterday afternoon."

"Miriam Hersh?" Adele stared at her. "You mean Hannah Sandell. He had lunch with Hannah San . . ."

"I don't know about any Hannah. The charge nurse on Ward Six said Mrs. Hersh came to their ward yesterday and spoke to Marcus for quite some time in the nurses' lounge.

"I must caution you, Ardel, that if you were hugging and kissing your brother, I strongly suggest that you report to ER and be seen by the ER physician right awa—"

Adele cursed herself for lying without forethought. Unless she squashed this right in the bud, all sorts of administrative red tape shit was going to hit the fan.

"It's okay, Mrs. Noel." Her face was burning, and she

smiled sheepishly. The woman already thought she was a freak, now she'd probably wonder about her mental stability. "I lied. Marcus wasn't my brother. I said that because I had to know how Marcus died. I haven't had direct contact with Marcus since the opening of the new ICU ten years ago. Sorry, but I knew you wouldn't tell me unless I said I was a relative."

Mattie Noel might have been stiff, but she wasn't stupid. She'd put the whole story together instantly: the nurse lied because she'd slept with that Stephen pervert who'd also been sleeping with Marcus. Ardel was probably terrified of coming down with AIDS—this was a Ward 8 nurse after all. Fornicating deviants, every last one of them.

From deep within the dark cellars of her heart a muffled murmur of pity was heard. "You're right," she said sternly, moving away, her clipboard tucked reassuringly against her breasts. "I wouldn't have told you. But, seeing as how your ward has both of the two affected patients, you should look on the bright side."

Adele waited.

"The young man's postmortem may shed some light on what's causing this plague."

"I hope so," Adele muttered. "We're all dying to know."

Mimi didn't know what to think. Everything had started out fine. Samuel came by early to go over last-minute details for the fund-raiser with Gordon. Then she'd driven to Hannah's, where she was given a private showing of the Versace gown she was wearing to the dinner. On the way to the hospital, they'd stopped for a pastry and coffee.

They hadn't even gotten to the lobby elevators before Hannah suddenly snapped at her over nothing, and then rushed her upstairs as if there were a fire in her pants. At first she thought it was Hannah's hypoglycemia, the way she'd gone all pale and mean. But they'd each had a maple bar (dripping with maple sugar) at Lady Baltimore's only minutes before, so it couldn't have been that.

Once gowned and gloved, Mimi eagerly launched into the routine tasks of caring for her daughter. She kept up a steady stream of questions, which Iris answered by raising her eyebrows or squeezing her fingers—two for no, one for yes.

Adele's sixth sense kept kicking her, which made her on edge. She wasn't sure, but she thought she might be waiting for something really bad to happen.

Adele didn't have to wait long. Around midmorning Cynthia's kidneys failed, and her liver enzymes shot off the chart along with her temperature. Her lungs turned into a chest X ray whiteout, which seemed to be the main indicator that the Mystery Plague was at its fastigium.

Dr. Ingram was a tortured man. He ordered more tests, and then tests on test results. He changed medications, and initiated new treatments and procedures. He even went the final mile and canceled his morning appointments. When he left the young nurse's bedside, he did not believe she would survive the day. Wisely he did not tell anyone his prediction; if the girl died, well then, that was the end of it. There was no cause to put everyone through the dread before they had to. Too, he did not believe in diminishing the loved ones' hope—only God was allowed to do that.

Adele worked as one does when driven by fear. She said almost nothing except to answer direct questions from Dr. Ingram or the lab people, and to direct Mimi in Iris's care.

By three, Cynthia stabilized enough to allow Adele a three-minute bathroom break. Using the wall phone over the toilet paper holder, she called Tim Ritmann's voice mail to let him know Cynthia was not doing well.

Brian raised the binoculars to the trees beyond his intended mark. The approaching steps stopped. An elderly couple shaded their eyes and looked to where his binoculars were pointed.

"What you got there?" asked the man quietly.

Brian did not turn nor did he lower his binoculars. "A double-billed pom pom," he whispered like a bird watcher who meant business.

The man and the woman nodded, shaded their eyes some more, strained their necks, squinted, then, bored with the whole thing, wished him good luck and continued their walk down Monte Vista Avenue. As soon as their footsteps could no longer be heard, Brian lowered the binoculars back to their original position and refocused on the brown shingled office building across Miller Avenue—campaign headquarters of Dr. Gordon Hersh.

At 5:30 P.M., Hannah entered the hotel kitchen and felt better at once. Gleaming on hooks and stovetops, stainless steel and copper pots of all sizes and shapes gave a sense of order and cleanliness. The rich colors of the foods arranged on humongous round platters made her salivate.

A drop-dead gorgeous man in his midtwenties approached, moving with all the self-possession of a man who had the world swinging between his legs. She guessed he'd been in lackey training for a long time. The minute he opened his mouth, she knew he'd started out as a waiter/surfer-dude in L.A., went through the Motion Picture Industry Mill of Extras Hell, and then the male modeling agency/escort service merry-go-round. When he'd grown tired of Tinsel Town's bullshit, he'd migrated to San Francisco to start over. He was good at taking orders, and nothing ever ruffled him—mainly because he just wasn't all that bright.

"Ms. Sandell?"

She smiled and held out her hand. "Yes, but you are *not* Maurice."

"I am Kevin [he pronounced it Kee-von], Monsieur Lepre's assistant? Monsieur regrets he cannot be here personally, but he has been called away to an important . . . ."

Hannah laughed out loud and patted the young man's arm. "Don't bother making excuses for him, Kevin, just go over the hors d'oeuvres with me."

Kevin smiled and relaxed. The broad wasn't so bad; Moe the Toe had told him she was a major cunt from hell.

"I'm really not the nasty old bitch he told you I was, Kev."

Kevin's eyes—sparkling from the joint he'd smoked twenty minutes before—widened appreciably. "Ah, Monsieur Lepre didn't say . . ."

"Yes he did. And that's okay. I didn't really want to meet the bastard. I'd rather deal with a young, good-looking guy like you. Has Mr. Fromer arrived?"

"He was here already, ma'am. He inspected the hors d'oeuvres and said they looked fine to him, but that you were a better judge of the food."

Hannah snorted. "Horsemeat would look fine to him."

Kevin didn't know what to say to that, so he relied on the curt head bow—a move he'd learned from watching old black-and-white movies. He used the gesture in all sorts of situations and no matter what, people always thought he was cool.

"Mrs. Hersh said she was really glad you ordered the additional dishes."

Hannah's eyes stopped roving over the food and returned to the young man's face. "Mrs. Hersh came here?"

"She and Mr. Fromer came in about five o'clock." Kevin's right index finger twitched slightly. He suddenly had the feeling he'd said something he shouldn't have. The White Swan got a strange, twisted look in her eyes, and for a brief instant, he knew what Moe the Toe must have run into over the phone.

Together, they passed by the hors d'oeuvres trays. One by one, Kevin pointed and recited the name of each in French. *Oeufs de Pluvier, Poitrines d'Oie Fumées, Anchois Roulés, Petits Coeurs d'Artichauts, Gougères, Anguille Fumée, Paupiettes de Choux.*

At the last tray—*Cervelle de Mouton Poché*—she let go of his arm and smiled warmly. "Perfect. At six P.M. I want half these trays circulated by hand. At six-thirty I want the other half brought out and placed two trays per buffet table. Tell the bar people to go easy. I don't want a bunch of drunks puking up eel and cheese before we even sit down."

"Cool." Kevin giggled, then corrected himself. "Very good, madam."

"Kevin?"

"Yes, Ms. Sandell?" God, he wanted to call her Ms. Swan in the *worst* way.

"I want you here in the kitchen making sure everything goes smoothly. Keep a close eye on everyone who comes in and out of this kitchen. I want everything to be perfect."

She smiled a sensual, coy smile and leaned against his muscular body so he could feel the warmth from hers. "And Kevin? Save me a hit for when this is all over, would you? I think I'm going to need it."

He did the curt head nod thing, grinning like a wild man. "Of course, Madam Swan."

Despite the headache and the runny nose, Gordon Hersh was handling his glory like a seasoned politician—with the boyish charm of JFK, and the sagacity of Gandhi. It was easy for him. He'd discovered early on that being a politician was very similar to being a plastic surgeon: all you had to do was chat people up and boost their egos with promises of wealth, power, and beauty. As Fromer put it, "Once you sell them, most people will turn over their souls without a second thought."

It was a funny business. Rich Republicans lined up to shake his hand after paying a thousand dollars a plate just to hear what line of goods he had to sell. Each of them was going to pay a lot more for a promise—You take care of my interests, I'll take care of yours.

Then there were the do-gooders. The do-gooders were those civic-minded, special-interest groups who represented the voice of the common man. They got some decent press, and once in a while could create a real stir, but in general, they didn't have a pot to piss in. The heavy guys had all the gold pots.

It was the golden-potted who would put him into office in exchange for favors and deals. In the end, if he did everything right and didn't screw up, he'd end up with a gold pot of his own with which he could help out the do-gooders. It would be, he liked to think, like playing Robin Hood of California Forest.

At his side, the White Swan glowed like a ray of blond sunlight in a formfitting gold-toned gown that made it difficult for him to keep his eyes off her breasts and his hands to himself.

"I don't know, Senator, but I'd have to say you have a lot of support here tonight," Hannah said, touching his arm. "Harold McGruder hasn't been able to pull this kind of weight in his entire political career."

"I think you're right about that, Hannah." Giddy with the success of the turnout, he leaned forward. "Have I told you yet that you are the most beautiful woman here this evening?"

Hannah smiled warmly and opened her mouth to answer, when a series of flashbulbs went off, blinding her. Almost immediately, a voice came through the circles of purple blocking out her vision.

"Excuse me." The voice was aggressively insistent. "May I get your name please?"

Reporters. Hannah disliked them immensely, blaming them for a large percentage of the world's troubles. Rarely did she ever talk to them, preferring to keep her private life private, but, she decided, for tonight she would drop her Greta Garbo routine and dazzle them.

"Hannah Sandell, president of Sandell Designs, San Francisco," she said.

"Ms. Sandell is a very close friend of mine and Mrs. Hersh's," Gordon cut in, speaking over the noise of the crowd. "She's been instrumental in making this dinner a success tonight, and in aiding my wife and me during our daughter's illness."

The reporter pressed her with a question about the work she was reportedly doing on the Hersh residence. She winked at Gordon and began explaining the project, when Samuel Fromer advanced on them. Hannah stiffened perceivably, the smile fading. She turned sharply away.

Gordon couldn't help but notice that Samuel seemed to gloat when he smiled at her. He had a fleeting worry that something had happened between the two.

Samuel grabbed his arm, leading him to an uncrowded spot. "We've got to talk," he said hurriedly. The collar of his dress shirt was soaked with perspiration. He pushed the plate of hors d'oeuvres he was carrying into Gordon's hand. "You should eat something, you look pale."

"What is it?" Gordon asked, eyeing the food distastefully, a habit he'd acquired at three as a result of his mother's extraordinarily bad cooking. The thought of her leaden, pasty latkes still made him want to hurl.

"Smoked eel, anchovies, liver paté, and cheese puff pastries. Eat. Listen, we've got a little problem . . ."

Gordon pointed to the *Cervelle de Mouton Poché*. "And that?"

"*Cervelle de Mouton Poché*. It's delicious. Hannah ordered it special. She said Bush and Reagan had it served at all the major White House functions."

Gordon picked up the scallop-shaped appetizer, sniffed it, and rapidly put it back on the plate. "What's in it?"

Samuel sighed. "Sheep brains. Gordon, listen to me, this is important."

Gordon looked at Samuel and noticed for the first time that there were dark rings around his eyes, and his breathing was labored. "What? What's wrong?"

"You had a death threat. Some guy called headquarters this afternoon and said he was going to kill you."

"A death threat? On me?" Gordon was mildly amused.

The thought that someone found him significant enough to want to kill him almost bordered on flattery. It put him in the same category as JFK and Lincoln. "Who was it? What'd they say?"

Samuel slumped at the shoulders, rolling his eyes. "Jesus, Gordon. You think they're gonna announce themselves and give me their address and phone number? The guy said he was going to kill you, your family and every 'fucking Republican pig' connected with you."

At the mention of his family, Gordon's breath caught in his throat. "Did you call the police? Have you . . ."

"No police. Get that look off your face and keep smiling. You start with the police and you're going to end up with negative publicity. I tripled security here, and sent someone to watch your house and outside the hospital ward. The—"

"The police need to know this." Gordon began to pull away; he wanted to get to a phone. "I want Iris and Mimi covered. I won't have my family . . ."

"You'll do as I say, goddamn it," Samuel said through a clenched-teeth smile. "You will not call the police. You will stay calm and close to me. Iris and Mimi are fine. I just talked to Mimi at the hospital."

Gordon saw Martin Gerber, president of Southern Pacific, and his wife Sophie, coming across the room to meet him.

"Eat some of the hors d'oeuvres, for Christ's sake," Samuel said. "You don't look so hot. I don't want you passing out halfway through your speech."

"I'm too nervous to eat," Gordon replied. "Besides, I don't do sheep." Under his breath he added quickly, "and I hate fish."

Samuel winced and swiftly looked around. "Jesus! Don't say that so loud! We need the endorsement of the commercial fishing companies and the meat packers."

Samuel stared at the hors d'oeuvres for a moment, shrugged, then stuffed one into his own mouth. "What are you drinking, then? You're too stiff."

Gordon grasped the hand of Mr. Gerber and dutifully bent

to kiss Mrs. Gerber's sagging neck, wondering if he should tactfully offer her a gratis, full lift. Still wearing his show smile, he turned back to Samuel. Out of the corner of his mouth he said, "Gin and tonic. Not so easy on the lightening."

NINE

ADELE LEFT WARD 8 AFTER SHE WAS SURE Cynthia was stable. When she got to her car, Detective Ritmann was waiting for her, leaning against the Beast's driver's side door (or arm, as she preferred to think of it) listening to a ball game on his radio headset. Over her protests, he insisted he take her to dinner. He warned that if she wasn't ready in the time it took him to visit Cynthia and then drive to her house, he'd put her under arrest and drag her by the handcuffs.

In the past, the three of them had had dinner together probably twenty or thirty times. The only difference this time was that Cynthia wasn't present . . . not in body anyway.

Rushing home, she'd fed Nelson, rinsed off in the shower, and brushed her hair so it hung softly around her face and shoulders. She tried on a drapey blouse and skirt—both slightly new from the Goodwill—but decided the outfit was too sexy, and traded it for a pair of jeans and a white cotton shirt. As reflected in the mirror, the outfit seemed more sensuous than the skirt and blouse.

Adele was unzipping the jeans, ready to slip into a pair of overalls, when the doorbell rang. Her shirt got caught in the zipper, and no matter how hard or gently she pulled, she couldn't get it up or down. As she yanked at the shirt, her bra strap pulled loose of its moorings.

"Christ on a bike!" she said to the group of invisible friends who'd come to watch her dress. "I need this now?"

The doorbell rang a second time.

139

Just go answer the door, Adele, said the smoke detector. *It's only Tim; he's seen you looking worse than this!*

It was only too true. Instant recall delivered an image of herself in a ragged Goodwill bathrobe, her hair done up in a hundred tiny pink curling rags, eyebrows unplucked and leg hair long enough to put it in curls, too, no makeup or deodorant—sitting with Tim and Cynthia in her living room one cold November night playing Scrabble and comparing Most Embarrassing Moment stories.

Had she *really* allowed another human being—let alone someone of the opposite sex—to see her like that? "Christ on a bike," she whispered in disgust. "Where was my mind?"

The bell rang a third time. She peeked at herself in the mirror. Not displeased with her reflection, she shook her head in amazement. The miracle had happened again—she'd never figure out how it worked, especially since on some days she could look so very, very bad.

Still struggling with the stuck zipper, she headed for the door. Oh well. She wasn't trying to impress him, anyway.

Oh. Uhn huh.

Tim had to wait a beat before he could greet the striking woman standing in the doorway with her jeans unzipped. He was afraid something else would come out of his mouth like, "How can you not know that I'm madly in love with you?"

He could never ever say that to *this* woman. To her he was only a friend and nothing more. Sometimes when he and Cynthia would get together with her, he'd had a hard time not staring at her or pulling her into his arms for a deep, passionate kiss.

Using that special perception possessed only by women, Cynthia guessed early on in their relationship how he felt about her best friend. She'd even teased him about it. He'd denied it, even though Cynthia insisted it didn't bother her. More than once she'd said he and Adele were better suited to each other, and that they had a lot in common. Cynthia was always commenting on how much his and Adele's minds worked alike. Frequently one or the other would verbalize exactly what the other was thinking or say the same things at the same time.

How he ended up with Cynthia instead of Adele wasn't a complicated thing to figure out. Big One Eye and the Boys (the name he'd given to those bodily appendages, that, up until his last birthday, had made ninety-eight percent of his life's decisions) were behind that mistake just as they had been the cause of the majority of his relationship mistakes. It was how most men made their way in the world, but he, for one, was tired of it. Cynthia's and his relationship had been based on having a good time. Cyn didn't want more than that, nor did he—until he got to know Adele.

Adele refrained from sucking in her breath at the sight of him. "Hi." She indicated her open fly. "I'm caught."

He handed her a small cardboard box. Inside were six red, perfect tomatoes, each nestled in its own piece of tissue paper.

"They're Organic. From Healdsburg," he said. "Got a pair of pliers?"

Deeply touched, she accepted the gift and inhaled the delicate fragrance of the fruit, before stepping aside to let him in. "Thank you. Follow me to the tools."

On the way to the kitchen he stopped to speak to Nelson as though the dog were a human being. Unlike some men who made jokes at the dog's expense, Tim treated Nelson with the respect due the leader of the pack, or, in human terms, the male head of household.

Nelson, on the other paw, could smell the mating urge on the man, and did not stray more than a few inches from Her side . . . just in case.

From the cabinet under the kitchen sink, she pulled out two of three tool boxes and opened them. The smell of linseed oil wafted up from the neatly organized cases. Everything in the boxes was beautifully crafted. There was none of the cheap, mass-produced garbage they sold in the stores now.

He made a low whistle, admiring a wooden-handled drawknife. "Where did you get these? They're beautiful."

"Most of them were my father's," she answered matter-of-factly. "He died when I was pretty young. When I missed him, I'd go into his workshop and take the tools down one at a time; I loved the way they felt and smelled. I think I got to know a part of my dad that even my mother didn't know through handling these tools.

"Because I spent so much time with the tools, my mother thought I was interested in building things." Adele laughed. "Being the librarian she is, she started bringing home books about woodworking and how to make things with tools." She made a one-shouldered shrug. "So—I learned how to use them."

She picked up a ball peen hammer. "As soon as I got over the rumor that because I had ovaries, I was missing the part of my brain that handles things mechanical, I did okay. I like being able to make and fix things around the house."

A comfortable silence took place while he examined the contents of the boxes, running his fingers over the richly grained handles of chisels, screwdrivers, and an ancient block plane. The smell of linseed oil now seemed more erotically stimulating than any perfume he'd ever smelled.

He picked out a pair of sturdy needle-nose pliers and went after her zipper.

Quietly, she went out of her mind. He was so close, she could feel the heat from his hands. With the slightest movement, she could have touched the careless hair and kissed the back of his neck. She closed her eyes, but instead of seeing his hands roving over her body, she replayed the vision of how he had caressed the tools and called them beautiful.

His heart racing, he worked at freeing her shirt from the zipper, listening to her stomach complain of hunger. No matter how hard he tried not to, his fingers kept brushing against the smooth skin stretched taut over her flat abdomen. Knowing that she didn't wear underwear wasn't helping any; each time he felt the warm skin of her belly, his hands shook harder.

He bit his lip and corralled his mind away from the prurient, and toward what he sensed was going on with her. She had something on her mind other than Cynthia; he could tell by the way she kept going inside her head and working her thoughts around. When he finally freed the cloth from the zipper, he asked where she wanted to eat. He wasn't the least bit surprised when she asked if they could go to his office first.

The soft glow from the screen of the computer bounced off their faces—hers an inch behind his.

"Start with the local field investigation cards," Adele directed eagerly.

Tim's fingers flew over the keys until a screen with the name FROMER, SAMUEL AUGUST came up. Listed after the vital statistics were several codes that Tim interpreted. "Well, the most current citizen contact for Mr. Fromer was a couple of weeks ago. He reported that someone had broken into his apartment in Mill Valley and stolen a pair of gold cufflinks and about two hundred dollars' worth of CDs. Probably local kids."

Adele thought about Sam Fromer for a minute and decided differently. "I don't know about that. What kids nowadays would want to listen to Mantovani or Nancy Sinatra classics?"

Tim scoffed at her. "They didn't want the CDs, Adele. They wanted some quick money. You've got to think in terms of resale.

"The only other contact was one month ago when he reported another break-in at the Hersh headquarters on Miller Avenue. Nothing was reported missing, but someone had written their opinion of Gordon Hersh all over the walls using dog shit."

After a moment of flickerings and computer scufflings,

the State of California file came up next. Blank. Typing in a
request for an FBI number, they waited again through another series of computer noises—like the sounds made by
an unhappy pig.

Samuel Fromer's federal record burst forth on the screen
in brilliant blues.

"Well, well, well. Looky here."

Adele's eyes flew over the FBI rap sheet. The Stock and
Securities Exchange Commission had brought charges of
fraud against him ten years before.

"There's a contact reference number for the U.S. Attorney in the Dallas office," Tim said. "Want me to call and
check on the disposition of the case?"

Before she could answer, he picked up the phone and
dialed.

"Well?" Adele asked, when he hung up twenty minutes
later.

"Fromer did fourteen months hard time for money laun-
dering. He was partners with an investment shark by the
name of Andrew Baldwin. The two of them headed up a
Dallas-based investment firm whose profits were being
routed to the Mob.

"Fromer pleaded innocence based on his claim that Baldwin duped him into selling investments that he swears he
didn't know were phony. Six hours before the Feds were to
move in on Baldwin, the Dallas police found him locked in
his car in a deserted parking lot, decomposing nicely. He'd
been dead for three days. The coroner eventually ruled cause
of death as a coronary infarction and severe pulmonary
edema."

"What do you mean, eventually?"

"Initially there was some question of foul play. They
were sure someone was with Baldwin when he died."

"They think Fromer iced him?"

Tim shrugged. "They didn't charge him. The coroner's
reports cinched that."

"How old was this Baldwin guy?"

Tim studied his notes. "Sixty-five and not in the best of health."

Adele bit her lip. "Can you check out two more names?"

"Sure. Lay it on me." Tim cleared the screen.

"Last name Sandell, first name Hannah, and then Miriam Hersh . . . not sure what her maiden name was."

The computer clicked and whirred, producing another screen, the top of which read SANDELL, HANNAH, SEX: F, RAC: W, POB: NY, DOB: 080258, HGT: 600, WGT: 147, HAI: BLD, EYE: BLU, SKN: FAIR, AKA: NYQUIST, ULLA, AKA: SANDELL, HANNAH ULLA NYQUIST.

"Nothing," Tim said after going through the files in the same order as he had Samuel Fromer's. "Not even a parking ticket."

"What are those?" Adele pointed to the list of codes on the federal screen.

"Pffft. Minor offenses from fifteen years ago. College kid stuff—freedom of choice political rallies, women's rights, sit-ins in the administrators' offices—that sort of thing."

Tim typed and the screen flickered again. HERSH, MIRIAM ESTHER, AKA: HERSH, MIRIAM LEVYSANDOVAL.

"Zilch," they said in unison.

Disappointed, she rolled her chair away and sat biting her lip as she stared into space.

"You going to tell me what this is about?" he asked.

Adele shrugged and shook her head. She glanced over at the phone on his desk. She wanted to call the hospital and check on Cynthia again, but she didn't want to make an enemy of the nurse on duty. It had only been an hour and fifteen minutes since the last time she called.

"Adele?" He waved his hands in front of her eyes. "Anybody home?"

She smiled into the beautiful blue eyes that made her self-conscious when staring directly into hers.

"Bring me up to speed here, Del. Who are these people and why are you so interested in them?"

"Sandell is a friend of the Hershes. A rags to riches, self-made woman. To hear Cynthia tell it, she's the founding mother of San Francisco's social set. Fromer is Gordon Hersh's campaign manager. Miriam Hersh, obviously, is Hersh's wife, and the mother of Iris Hersh."

"So, why are we checking them?"

Another shrug and avoidance of his scrutinizing gaze.

"Do you think they have something to do with Cynthia and the Hersh girl getting sick?"

She thought for a minute and stirred uneasily in her chair. "No. I mean, I don't really know for sure. It's intuition. There's something hinky going on, and I just want to check all bases." Smiling apologetically, she picked their jackets off the desk and went to the door.

"It's been a long day. Let's go to dinner."

"Rabbit food, or a good, old-fashioned Canadian restaurant?" he asked.

"Don't care. I'm codependent tonight. You decide."

"Don't care either. A mason jar of one, half dozen of the others."

His habit of bastardizing adages could always make her laugh no matter what. "Okay then," she said decisively. "Let's do the mason jar and then have one of those tomatoes and a game of Scrabble for dessert."

Bill and Ivy Lundgrin, seventy-eight and eighty-two respectively, huddled together in their foyer. They knew each other better than they knew themselves, which was part of why they hadn't talked much in the car on the way home from the dinner.

"Not feeling well, either, huh?" Bill tapped an ice-cold, bony finger on the back of his wife's pale hand. After sixty years of marriage, he really didn't need to ask—it was more a conciliation.

"You don't think it could have been the food, do you, Bill?" She read the lines around his eyes.

Shuffling stiffly, he made his way to the heater. "Don't

know. Going to build a fire. It's cold in here." He turned the thermostat to 78 and put some wood in the fireplace. "You wouldn't think they'd serve bad food at those prices," he grumbled. "A thousand dollars a plate for God's sake."

"Can you imagine that?" Ivy whispered in awe, dimly remembering what a thousand dollars would have bought in 1915.

"Republicans get greedier and richer every damned . . ." Bill doubled over as the first searing pain ripped through the right side of his brain. It took his breath away.

When he stood, Ivy was staring at him, her heart jack-hammering in her chest. "Bill?" Hurrying as best she could, she prayed the dizziness and nausea she felt would not over-take her before she could tend to him.

He'd eased himself onto the couch, where she loosened his tie and unbuttoned his shirt. Both of them were perspir-ing, although they felt colder than if they were in a meat locker.

Bill felt the vomit coming up his gullet and reached for the first thing his hand could find—a doily she'd cro-cheted before their first was born. He hated to do it, but he had to . . .

"I'm sorry, Ive," he said afterward, ashamed of himself. "What a god-awful mess I've made." His eyes filled with tears as she wiped his mouth with the matching doily.

"Shhhh. Don't you worry. I've cleaned lots of messes be-fore. Yours isn't special."

He vomited again, this time not even bothering to try and stop it. When he finished, she looked at the rug.

"Oh dear God . . ." Ivy covered her mouth at the sight of her husband's dentures lying in a puddle of blood.

Bill did not see the blood for the black cloud that was crowding out the light. He touched her leg, said her name once, and slumped back against her.

For some fool reason (one she would not have time to fully understand) she leaned over and kissed her uncon-scious husband. The kiss grazed the corner of his right eye

and ended up in the white fringe of his hair. She eased herself out from under his weight and got unsteadily to her feet.
Instantly, the ground came up to meet her knees and chin. A
snarl of pain ripped up her left arm into her throat. That and
the pain of having bitten through her tongue, competed for
attention. Bleeding and nauseated, she crawled to the phone
thinking of how she had kissed him. An odd thing for her to
do now that she thought about it.

When the seizure hit her, she was hoping that when they
both felt better, he wouldn't chide her for being a silly old
woman.

Adele was dreaming that Hannah Sandell was the stew-
ardess and Samuel Fromer was the pilot of the plane she
was taking to Disneyland. She'd only just realized they'd
been in the air for seven hours and was beginning to
panic—John Wayne Airport was only an hour's flight from
San Francisco.

She'd asked Hannah if they were in trouble. Instead of
answering, Hannah forced a royal blue mummy bag—the
outside of which had HALSTON printed down one side—
over her head.

It was during the drawn-out molasses dream sequence of
unhooking her seat belt and repeated slow-motion attempts
to run to the speakerphone to warn the rest of the passengers, that the red alert alarms went off inside the aircraft.

The plane turned upside down and she bounced off the
other passengers' inflated Halston bags. A bag holding an
unconscious Cynthia slid by, then Marcus, dressed in scrubs
and a hat the shape and color of a banana, landed on top of
her, shouting, "Adele! Wake up."

She pushed him away. "We're goin' down!" she yelled
above the roar of the alarms. "Put your head between your
knees."

Tim laughed briefly, then swore as he fumbled with his
pager, searching for the "off" switch.

As soon as the noise stopped, Adele awoke with a start

and looked around. Right. They'd fallen asleep on her living room floor playing Scrabble.

Tim was on his knees leaning over her. Nelson was stretched out beside her, his head resting on her shoulder. She sat up too quickly, accidentally banging her forehead into Tim's chin. They both fell back from the impact.

"Oops sorry," she said, rubbing her forehead, then immediately wiped at the mascara she knew was smudged under her eyes, making her look like a raccoon.

In his sleep stupor, Tim tried to focus on his pager. An *H* (four points) Scrabble square was stuck to his temple. They both yawned and looked at the mantel clock. They were simultaneously shocked at the time.

"Someone's paging you at one-thirty in the morning?" she asked. The thought that he might be currently involved with someone who had expected him in her bed hours ago gave rise to a short-lived jolt of hollow despair.

He raised his eyebrows and shrugged. The *H* scrabble square fell off his face and landed on his sleeve. "Nine-two-five-seven-two hundred? Doesn't ring any bells. Can I use your phone?"

She waved him toward the end of the couch, the number running through her mind. It was familiar, but she needed to visualize the numerals. She wrote them down on the score pad (he'd won three games to her one) and yelped.

"Hey! That's Ellis's ER—one of the back line numbers. What are they doing calling you?"

"Probably a shooting." He picked up her phone and punched in the number.

Five minutes later, he replaced the handset and put an arm around her shoulders. The feel of his muscular body against hers set free a barrage of hormones she normally kept under lock and key. Never, she thought, had she wanted to kiss anyone—not even Ricky Linscott at their sixth-grade spring dance—as much as she wanted to kiss him right at that moment.

"Are you scheduled to work tomorrow ... I mean, today?"

"No. Why?"

"Well, babe, put on some coffee and grits, because you are now." He hitched up his pants and shuffled toward the bathroom. "Not only that, but you're going in early again."

Hannah sat perfectly still under a hot shower, holding the nausea at bay by concentrating on a minute by minute replay of how things had gone wrong.

Gordon's speech met with a standing ovation, but even then she sensed an underlying tension in the audience. Two of the campaign aides left early, complaining that they didn't feel well, and soon after, she'd noticed a stray guest here and there making his way to his car looking like death warmed over. She watched as one older man made it as far as a potted plant in the lobby before he was sick. That was when her own splitting headache and nausea had begun.

The private party, consisting of her and Gordon's entourage, had retired to the penthouse suite in the hotel around ten-thirty to do a "strategy regrouping." In a scene worthy of a Peter Sellers movie, Samuel made his announcement about the death threat and then vomited and passed out. Against his will, he was loaded into a taxi and sent to Ellis ER.

Hannah closed her eyes and willed the pain slicing through her head to stop. Falling forward onto her knees, she heaved, bringing up a minute amount of blood. Her face turned toward the spray of water, she filled her mouth and let the water run out the side until the sour taste was gone. The pain in her head subsided, and her thoughts returned to the sequence of events.

After Samuel left, she saw her reflection in the bathroom mirror. She was gray and sweaty. It seemed strange to her now, but at the time, the alarm she felt was not because she feared death, but because the thought of having one of those plastic tubes shoved down her throat and attached to a machine which breathed for her was unbearable.

The campaign headquarters secretary went down next, and then Gordon. Following them was the campaign consultant and the last of the inner circle aides. While they waited for the limos to transport them to the hospital, the phones began ringing off the hook with news of the others.

By eleven-fifteen, she and Gordon had left the hotel and were headed toward Ellis Hospital in the back of the limo, both vomiting into separate champagne buckets. It was the Ellis ER clerk who told them Samuel never made it to their ER, and did they want her to call around to see if she could find him?

Hannah bent over the shower drain, and gagged once again. She'd been lucky, though not as lucky as Gordon, who seemed to sail through the best of all.

TEN

GEORGE CALDWELL, M.D., WAS MOONLIGHTING at Ellis ER because he desperately needed the money. The job he was so sure he'd landed (the senior partners had flown him and the current squeeze to Vail, all expenses paid for three days) had gone straight to hell in a handbasket. In anticipation of a junior partnership in a thriving private practice (starting salary: $243,500 plus malpractice, health benefits, retirement, and a share of the firm's stock in Marin Labs, Inc., and Bliss Pharmaceutical), he'd purchased two items that were considered basic necessities to an unmarried Marin physician—the two-bedroom, waterfront Tiburon starter condo ($580,000), and the Mercedes ($75,000) convertible.

Now he was having to work days at an HMO known as FHP (he referred to it as "Fatal Health Plan"), and Ellis emergency department at night. That made him tired, horny, and ornery. He'd averaged four hours' sleep a night, the week's current squeeze was cutting him off, and to top it all off, he hated sick people.

Settling old scores, hatred, and the desire to make others as miserable as himself, were the motivating factors behind his decision to tip off the *Pacific Intelligencer*.

After the first Mystery Plague victims started rolling through the pneumatic doors around ten, it hadn't taken long to figure out that all twenty-two patients had several things in common—most important of which was that they had all attended the same political brouhaha and had direct physical contact with Gordon Hersh. "Handshaking, kissing, and dick sucking" he would tell the *Intelligencer* reporter.

Lack of time made reading the newspapers impossible, but he had not missed the recent *Intelligencer* photo of Dr. Hersh outside his kid's room. It didn't take a degree in neurosurgery to know that the general public, as stupid as they were, could put two and two together.

As a representative of God, his statements about the situation would be quoted in all the Bay Area papers. He'd pepper each sentence with key words guaranteed to start a mass panic. Highly contagious . . . Mystery Plague (*M* Plague for short) . . . No treatment . . . Epidemic . . . Ebola . . . CDC . . . Excruciating pain . . . Primary carrier . . . Gordon Hersh . . . Criminal disregard for the health and safety . . . Hersh. Tragic price paid . . . Five innocent people dead . . . Hersh.

The twenty-two patients exhibited varying degrees (mild to fatal) of the same symptoms as the first three—Hersh's brat, the Ward 8 nurse, and the faggot nurse. Whatever the bug, it wasn't exactly picky about who it hit—age, race, or social standing meant nothing. Of the victims, those who were aged or seriously compromised had died rapidly—that included an eighty-two- and seventy-eight-year-old, two AIDS-infected men fifty-four and sixty-one, and a twenty-two-year-old anorexic with an existing cardiac condition.

Of the seventeen survivors, only six (one of whom—surprise surprise—was Gordon Hersh, Mr. Plague Carrier himself) were mild enough to be discharged to home. The rest were divided up and spread out over the critical care units at Ellis and Bellevue hospitals. At least three of those eleven patients did not have a promising prognosis.

Lacing his fingers together at the back of his head, George leaned back in his chair and smiled at the ceiling. The night had turned out better than anything he could have imagined. It had even had its share of pussy promise. The moment he'd laid eyes on the tall blonde with the more than fuckable body, he knew getting her into bed would be a cinch. Her type was easy to spot—she had the look of a rich slut; one of the ones who got off on being humiliated. He'd attended to her as soon as she'd rolled through the door. There wasn't any doubt in his mind she'd call before the week was out. He discharged her first, not missing the fact that even puking and a steel-clad headache hadn't stopped her from taking his pager number.

He closed his eyes. The memory of Gordon Hersh puking on his sneakers caused a swell of deep satisfaction. Not to mention that he'd made the bastard wait until last to be seen. The damage he caused Hersh would about even the score. "What goes around, comes around, motherfucker," George whispered to the ceiling.

To make the revenge sweeter, he pulled a file out of his locker and reread for the hundredth time the letter Hersh sent out to the Medical Ethics Board of the hospital less than a year before. In it Hersh complained about a suturing job he had done on some overindulged Marin brat's forehead.

George recalled that the miserable two-year-old had bitten him and drawn blood. He remembered it well because it was also the night the security guard walked in on him sticking it to the Ward 3 clerk in the physical therapy whirlpool. It had cost him a bundle to keep the son of a bitch quiet.

. . . *criminally sloppy job worthy of a drunken butcher,* and . . . *innocent young child scarred for life due to Dr. Caldwell's gross incompetence,* were the two sentences that still stuck with him.

Unfortunately, they'd stuck in the minds of the senior medical partners, too. Which was the reason he did not get the junior partnership, which was why he was having to work his balls off in the shitholes of the earth taking care of mindless cretins.

Lowering the front chair legs to the floor, he picked up the phone, dialed the number of the *Intelligencer*, and asked for Joe. The brother of Last Month's Main Squeeze, Joe was a reporter who hung from the lowest branches . . . a dirt dig-ger . . . an ambulance-chasing blood and gore man.

Joe was gonna eat this story up.

Besides being a dirt digger, Joe Rickie liked being in bed with cops and politicians. One thing he knew for sure: To survive as a reporter, you had to be in bed with the fuzz, or you didn't go anywhere. If the cops liked you, they wouldn't break your nuts every time you showed up at a scene. You scratch my back, I'll scratch yours—that's how it was with cops and reporters. Playing kiss the brown hole with politicians was trickier. It was suicide to get on one horse—one had to know how to ride the fence.

Twenty-five minutes after arriving at Ellis emergency and getting the full lowdown from the doc, he called Detective Hurley at Larkspur PD and Tim Ritmann over at the Sher-iff's. Tipping off the McGruder people had been a judgment call. If Fromer had tipped him off sooner about Hersh's kid getting sick, he might have not made the call.

Joe chided himself. Who was he trying to kid? He would have made the call even if Fromer were his mother.

He dictated the exclusive to the flunky at the newsroom with the air of a man holding a winning lottery ticket. This one, he thought, was gonna put him at the top of the cops' and McGruder's excellent credit list.

Mattie Noel was debating possible desperate options when her jaw flapped open. There, standing in the door of her stuffy cubicle at 2:45 A.M., was Ardeen from Ward 8 saying she'd work extra—starting immediately.

Just for a second, Mattie thought she knew what Bernadette Soubirous must have felt like when the Virgin Mary materialized before her at Lourdes. And it *had* been a miracle—looking up from the list of "no responses" and seeing the nurse standing there *offering* to work?

On red alert from ER, she'd begun calling every nurse in

the county to beg and offer extra cash bonuses for coming in
to take care of the Mystery Plague patients. By 2:00 A.M.,
there were at least thirty-five answering-machine recordings
on which she could be heard pleading on the verge of tears.

She lost it on the thirty-sixth answering machine, fairly
screaming into the receiver, "I know you're listening! Pick
it up, goddamn it. We're desperate! This is an emergency!"

Her next step was to call the head nurses of every unit
and tell them they had to come in for a county emergency.
Two of them didn't answer their phones, one said she was
too drunk, one said the "C" word and hung up, and one said
she'd think about it, promptly fell asleep, and snored in her
ear. Finally, in a daring, uncharacteristic move, she'd contacted the police and asked them to go to the nurses' homes
and haul their asses in under threat of arrest. The desk
sergeant laughed and thanked her for the best crank call of
the evening, then hung up on her, too.

She was seriously contemplating going out and hiring a
few of the prostitutes who hung out at the Bermuda Palms,
dressing them in scrubs, and putting them on the units, when
suddenly there was this Ardeen . . . Ardel? Whatever. She
was a capable nurse despite her personal problems. Mattie
Noel restrained herself from kissing the woman—God only
knew what diseases she was carrying.

The nurse was willing to work only on certain conditions.
"Anything," Mattie had told her, and considering what she
could have had, her requests were nothing.

Mattie sighed. Shifting a few nurses around so this Arden
woman could have her pick of patients was preferable to
paying golden time or promising favors.

Heart pounding out of his chest, Brian steadied his feet
on the rim of the toilet seat and braced himself against the
sides of the stall. The door to the women's room squeaked
open and the lights flickered on. Brian held his breath,
praying the security guard wasn't any overzealous Rambo
type. From the ease with which he'd sneaked into the build-

ing, he was of the mind that the old man was more a Helen Keller sort.

A second later, the lights went off and the door closed. Brian strained to hear the footsteps fade. When they were completely gone, he eased out of the rest room and noiselessly made it across the hall to the campaign headquarters. He felt in his pocket for the key that Rosie had left for him and put it to the lock. It snapped back the lock with ease. He smiled, and made the thumbs-up sign to the door. Rosie refused to tell him how she'd come by the key in the first place, and warned him not to ask. He knew her temper well enough to sidestep it—he had enough gouges and bruises to last him a lifetime. Why she'd made him go to the trouble of picking it up in such a wild place was beyond him, but again, he knew better than to ask. With Rosie he did as he was told.

Brian entered the dark reception area and walked into the main office. He waited until his eyes adjusted to the dark before untying the canvas drawstring bag from his waist. Idly, he scattered papers from the desktops and shelves onto the floor. He opened a bottle of copier toner and smeared it over the desks and chairs.

He pulled down the poll chart, then sliced through Hersh's name with his Swiss Army knife. Across the top he wrote DEATH TO THE FASCIST BASTARD HERSH in black permanent marker. He could barely contain himself; these were things he'd always wanted to do in college, but never had the balls to actually go through with them. "Harvard scientist nerd makes up for lost time," he whispered to himself and chuckled.

On the wall was a poster-size picture of Gordon Hersh with the motto FOR THE PEOPLE printed underneath. Standing on the desk, he wrote NOT before the word FOR. Then, drawing a statement bubble coming out of Gordon's smiling mouth, he extended it to the wall and wrote in a bold print TRUTH: I AM A GREEDY SCUMBAG. VOTE FOR ME THEN BEND OVER AND GREASE UP!!!

He was admiring his handiwork when a door slammed somewhere on one of the floors below him. He waited until he was sure no one was coming, then rapidly searched the walls and ceiling for the central air vent. He found it dead center in the ceiling of the main room.

Standing on a chair, Brian removed the vent cover with a battery-operated screwdriver, detached the air filter, and lifted the rest of what he needed from the canvas bag. The small wooden box and the travel clock he placed inside the lip of the vent. He checked the clock against his watch; both read twelve-fifteen. As he tightened the last wire around a terminal, he heard the unmistakable sound of someone climbing the stairs. Promptly setting the grate back into place, Brian shoved in the screws and haphazardly tightened them. The footsteps were slow and erratic coming down the hall toward the office.

Frantically, Brian looked for a place to hide. Someone stopped in front of the frosted glass door, fumbled with their key, and pushed it open. Propelled by fear, Brian blindly leapt. When the lights were switched on, he found himself squeezed into a corner of a combination broom and office supply closet behind some file boxes.

Sweat ran in rivers down his shirt as he pressed his bulk farther into the corner. He knocked over a sponge mop, but caught it before it hit the floor. Just in front of him was a box of plastic garbage bags. Brian pulled one out, peering through the crack of the door.

A man dressed in a tuxedo reeled slightly as he studied Brian's graffiti. He stretched out a hand as if to pull down the defiled poster, but instead leaned forward to steady himself, then vomited violently against the wall. After a few minutes, he straightened with a groan and headed straight for the supply closet.

Heart racing, Brian ripped two eye holes in the plastic bag with his teeth and slipped it over his head.

"Fucking cops," the man mumbled as he entered the small space. "Fucking flu. Sons a bitches going to be sticking their fucking noses up our asses." He threw up again, but didn't bother to bend over. The mess cascaded over the front of his ruffled shirt and down his pants.

Brian silently cursed his fat belly, stopped breathing, and squeezed himself even farther against the wall. He was less than three feet from the man's back.

The man split open one of the cardboard file boxes and began pulling out files and throwing them haphazardly over his shoulder. One hit Brian in the head. When the box was empty, the man ripped through the middle of all four sides, then threw it to the floor.

"What the fuck did I do with those goddamned envelopes?" The man hoisted another box—one box away from where Brian stood. Up close, Brian could see the guy looked really bad. His breath was wheezy and bubbly, as though he were breathing through water. Sweat dripped off his face, and his pants were soaked with acrid-smelling piss.

A coronary, thought Brian. His father had the same look the night he dropped dead at the dinner table—facedown in the roast beef and mashed potatoes.

Dumping the files out onto the floor, the man again ripped the box apart and flung it away from him. He had started to grab for the one next to Brian when he stopped, reached inside his breast pocket, and pulled out a tiny, dark brown bottle. Brian recognized it at once as one containing nitroglycerine tablets.

The man put two of the tiny pills under his tongue and rested his head against the wall.

Samuel closed his eyes against the pressure in his chest and tried to calm himself by deep breathing the way they'd taught him to do in the biofeedback training. He couldn't. All he could think of was how incidental shit always managed to get in his way and keep him from what he wanted. First there had been that miserable nothing of a fuck who'd stepped on his head in Texas, and then Baldwin and the Feds and now this fucking flu bullshit.

Just when he was so close to having it all. Christ! He'd even had the White Swan on her knees gobbling him. It had been sweet while it lasted—which wasn't more than a few seconds. "Fucking medication," he said aloud. The god-damned know-it-all doctors hadn't told him the heart pills would keep him from getting it up. Chest pain or no chest pain, he'd thrown the lot down the toilet.

He clutched his chest and gulped air. He reconsidered about the pills—maybe that hadn't been such a good idea. Maybe he should have kept some of the other pills besides the nitro. He sure as shit didn't want to end up like Baldwin.

The thought of his ex-partner made the pain in the front of his head worse. At least Baldwin hadn't died alone. So what that he'd just finished blackmailing the old guy, at least he'd been there to hold his hand as he went out.

It wasn't like he'd been blackmailing him for something really big—like some of the guy's millions. His demands had been insignificant—complete exoneration from the SEC charges. Compared to leaking info to the Feds about Baldwin's "acquaintance" with Raul Sanchez, Mr. Colombian Drug Lord himself, that was small potatoes.

How was he supposed to know Baldwin had a heart like soggy oatmeal? Had he not insisted they meet in that parking lot in the middle of the night, the Feds would have tried to pin Baldwin's death on him, too. Those bastards were almost as rabid as the Big Boys . . . almost.

"So fuckin' close," he said, his eyes squeezing shut again with pain and disappointment. As soon as the speech was over, there wasn't any question in his or anyone else's mind that Hersh would be a shoo-in—a landslide victory. The Republicans loved him. The contributions were pouring in. Promises—big promises—were made.

It was all going to be so perfect. Gordon Hersh would be the solid, upstanding family man, run like a puppet by Samuel A. Fromer, aka "The Handler"—tag compliments of the Organization boys.

By the time Hersh was running for governor, he'd be one

of the Organization's most valuable players. That is, if he could pull Hersh out of this bullshit mess. It was going to take a lot of ass kissing and promises, but if he had the right information on the right people, he just might be able to pull it off.

He retched and spit out a mouthful of blood. "Son of a bitch!" he gasped at the sight of it dripping through his fingers. Ignoring the competition of pain between his head and his chest, he snorted at the sudden thought that he could die from something so pointless as a goddamned flu bug. But then again, he supposed it didn't matter whether or not he survived the clogged arteries and the flu—he was going to be a dead man if the police discovered the lists.

He shouldn't have made the lists at all, let alone kept them around. The Organization's Number One Rule: Forget names and places, or get your memory erased for you with a bullet or an underwater tour of the bay. Keeping lists had been such a dumbshit thing to do, no matter how much of a temptation it had been. These boys weren't exactly the types you wanted to piss off. Even the FBI couldn't save his ass if the boys got the idea he was saving shit he shouldn't be saving. Hell, he could have plastic surgery, dye his hair, cut off his legs, and then ship himself to a shack in the far reaches of Antarctica, and the Organization would still find him.

"Nope," Samuel wheezed, reaching for the next box. "Don't want to fuck with the big *O*. Not this boy."

As his hands gripped the edge of the storage box, his fingers grazed something warm and hairy. Startled, he looked first at the large hand and then upward at the hideous, white, shapeless head towering over him. The eyes of the Devil stared at him through two ragged holes.

Samuel Fromer's scream was lost inside the roar of the number 13 Muni bus headed toward Marin City.

She waited for the Marin City bus to pass before turning the lock in the outside metal door. From experience she knew the door that led to the basement of the Miller Avenue building squeaked on its hinges loud enough to wake the dead—or the retarded night watchman Gordon Hersh had hired to watch the place after the last break-in.

Inside the building, she put the stolen key in the pocket of her pelisse and noiselessly made her way to the campaign office.

Pulling out the gun, she stepped inside the lighted office.

Samuel Fromer wasn't going to get away from her this time.

Hannah swept the Versace gown and her cape off the bed to the floor. With a pair of nail scissors, she cut the yellow plastic hospital ID band from her wrist. It fell onto her foot. Kicking it off, she sneered at the memory of Dr. Caldwell, the cockalorum with the overload of testosterone. From the moment she walked into the ER, he was too involved with working his way into her pants to even ask her name. It was exactly as her mother told her: scratch any man—doctor, lawyer, Indian chief—and find a good-for-nothing animal.

Still damp from the shower, Hannah lay naked on her bed staring up at the ceiling fan. She didn't know why so much had gone wrong—but she was determined to find out.

Suddenly chilled, she threw on a robe and tried to walk. She made it as far as her desk and sat down, shivering. She was going to have to start thinking straight, sick or not. She couldn't let them down—especially Mimi.

Opening the top desk drawer, she pulled out a sheet of handmade paper with the intention of writing down everything that had happened, when her eyes fell on a creased and soiled business card that lay forgotten underneath the rubber bands. She picked it up and read it word by word, number by number. Then, using the gold-plated letter opener, angrily stabbed the card through the middle, pinning it to the desk.

Adele took her third M. Plague patient, admitting the seventeen-year-old male to the acute room next to Iris and Cynthia's. Derek had brown hair, dark bedroom eyes

with lashes out to there, and dimples. A ham radio operator someone said—he'd built his own set. He'd won first
prize in the Tam High Future Journalists' contest—a guest
pass to the Hersh fund-raiser and a byline in the *Intelligencer*'s "Youth Perspective" section for a series of three
paid articles.

He'd rolled in the door breathing like a hurt animal. With
each ragged breath, he made an eerie, high-pitched noise.
The ER reported he was one of the lucky ones—he was
stable. At the first sight and touch of the boy's dusky, cool
skin, Adele knew differently—the kid was circling the drain,
ready to go down.

"This kid is gonna crash pretty soon," she announced to
the room in general.

Dr. Caldwell looked her over like a piece of merchandise
and decided she was too skinny for his taste. "Oh really?"
he said sarcastically. "Since when did they start handing out
medical degrees in nursing schools?"

While she hooked the patient to the cardiac and oxygen
monitors, Adele gave the arrogant man a thin-lipped smile.
"Probably about the same time you were getting yours
through that home study program out of Mexico."

The respiratory tech and the ER nurse laughed. George
Caldwell silenced them both with a look and made note of
the nurse's name tag—Adele Monsarrat. He'd remember it
long enough to report her insolence to the director of nurses.

Adele watched the boy's chest carefully while they trans-
ferred him from the ER gurney to the bed. Before the
stretcher was out of the room, he'd vomited, and stopped
breathing.

The intubation was difficult with the stomach contents re-
fluxed into the airway. Adele had to suction him three times
before Dr. Caldwell was able to guide the endotracheal tube
down the boy's trachea. It was while the resp tech was se-
curing the tube with adhesive tape that the cardiac monitor
alarmed.

Adele and the other staff stared, not quite believing the

profound bradycardia that turned at once into an unbroken flatline flowing across the screen. "Has to be a loose electrode or a lead," she said, not wanting to believe in her own prediction ten minutes earlier.

But there were no loose leads; his seizure confirmed that.

"Start chest compressions and somebody get the crash cart and a transcutaneous pacer set up," she yelled, then hastily changed the leads in order to look at the still heart from another angle—it didn't much matter; a dead heart looked the same from all directions.

As soon as the red metal cart was inside the door, she pushed a milligram of epinephrine into his IV, followed by an equal amount of atropine. The pacer arrived, and they continued their efforts until it was clear that the heart was not going to respond to any amount of drugs or electrical stimulus.

When it was over, Adele stared at the floor strewn with post code debris—equipment wrappers, empty IV bags, gauze pads, blood, needle caps—and wondered what he would have written for his first article.

She washed his face, cleaning the crusts of vomit and grunge from the stubble of his chin, put a clean gown over the pale muscular body, then led his brother and mother in to say goodbye.

After all the times she'd heard it before, the sound of raw grief in the form of female shrieks and a young boy's broken sobs still chilled her to the bone.

ELEVEN

GORDON HERSH SLAPPED THE FRONT-PAGE HEAD-line with the back of his hand and threw the *Pacific Intelligencer* down on the breakfast table in front of his wife.

MYSTERY PLAGUE KILLS SIX AT HERSH FUND-RAISER

Mimi scanned the first few paragraphs, a look of dismay clouding her face. "My God, they're blaming you for the deaths of these people. How can they do that?"

Gordon coughed into his handkerchief and stood too quickly, having to wait a minute until he got his vertical legs. "They can't. That's why I'm calling the attorneys. You call Sam at home. Tell him I don't care how sick he is, he needs to get on this now! I want a full rebuttal and a printed apology by the time the evening edition of this rag hits the streets."

He stalked away. Before he reached the door, his anger welled up again and he wheeled around. His face was red and the vein in his forehead was visibly pulsing. He jabbed the air with his finger.

"Ingram had better start coming up with some answers, goddamn it, because if he doesn't . . ." Nausea choked him. He pressed his thumbs against his temples, trying to rub out the pain behind his eyes. ". . . I'm dead in the water."

Mimi stared at him, a subtle fear biting at her throat. He was pasty white with the exception of a ring of darkish flesh around his eyes. "Please, Gordon, calm down. You're supposed to be in bed. The doctor said . . ."

"Oh for Christ's sake, Mimi, *I'm* a doctor!" he shouted. "Caldwell is a walking medical malpractice file. He hates my guts. Who the hell do you think called the paper and told them this goddamned crap in the first place?" Shoulders and neck held rigid, Gordon marched off in the direction of his study. "Don't you worry about me, I'm fine. After I talk to Sam, I'm going to Ellis to see Iris. You can reach me at campaign headquarters after nine. I'm not going to let this—"

Mimi jumped to her feet, sending her coffee cup clattering across the table. "Don't you dare go near Iris!"

His eyes widened at the hysterical quality of her voice.

"I mean . . . we don't want to reinfect her. She's so weak, she couldn't survive another bout with this—this mystery virus . . . or whatever it is."

"My God, don't tell me you believe this contagion crap too?" He hit the paper again. "No one is going to reinfect her. She's been in the same room with another infected patient for over twenty-four hours and has improved. This isolation business is prehistoric medical nonsense."

On a sudden impulse, Gordon went to his wife and put an arm around her. "I love Iris. Do you really think I'd ever put her in danger?"

Mimi moved away from him, pretending to busy herself with mopping up the spilled coffee. "No. I—I don't know, but let's not take chances."

Gordon started to argue and cut himself short. Studying his wife's back, he realized she wouldn't listen no matter what he said. He picked up the paper again. McGruder would hurt him with this. Cream him. He and Fromer couldn't let that happen.

Mimi was at first appalled by Hannah's appearance, then secretly resentful. It was almost as if by her pale, hollow-eyed appearance, Hannah had proven herself a stronger, more worthy woman than she.

"How's Gordon?" Hannah asked, gingerly toweling herself off. It was her fourth shower of the morning.

She shrugged, trying to ignore the definition of muscles in Hannah's arms and thighs. Next to her, Mimi believed she looked like the Pillsbury Doughboy. "He says he's fine, but he looks terrible. He threw up all night."

Mimi fell silent for a moment, watching Hannah get dressed. "He thinks he has to go out and meet the challenge instead of hanging back. He's going to the campaign office to work on a rebuttal to the *Intelligencer* article.

"Did you read it yet?"

"Only the front page," Hannah answered calmly. "I rarely ever read the paper. It takes too much time and it's all hype anyway."

"You should read the piece, Han. Really, it's libelous. They've all but come right out and said Gordon was responsible for those people dying."

"The *Intelligencer* is a small-town rag, owned by Democrats, Mimi. Don't worry, by the time the story comes out in the *Chronicle*, it'll have a different slant. Gordon will make sure his sterling reputation is restored to its original flawlessness. He's the great white hope, remember?"

Hannah pulled a salmon cashmere sweater over her head and faced her. "Why didn't you come to the hospital last night, Mimi? It didn't look good."

"I—I didn't hear the phone." Mimi turned her gaze away. "I decided to take Gordon's advice and have a glass of wine before I went to bed. You know what wine does to me."

"Yeah," Hannah said, arching an eyebrow. "I know."

Gordon stood outside the window, declining to go inside the room. They spoke from opposite sides of the doorway.

"How is she?" he asked, craning his neck to see Iris.

"Getting better," Adele answered. "Ingram wants to start weaning her off the ventilator soon."

"And Cynthia?"

"Stable. Her lungs are a bit clearer, and neurologically

she's lighter. It's a recovery course similar to the one Iris
went through, only not quite as speedy."

They nodded, staring at the two patients. The soft click
and whoosh of the respirators filled the silence.

"How're you?" she asked. "I understand you got sick last
night?"

He blew his nose. "I'm still queasy but a lot better off
than everybody else." Depressed, his gaze wandered back to
Iris. "I'm lucky, I guess."

"Is Mrs. Hersh okay? She's usually here by now."

"Miriam's fine. Ingram can't figure out why, but she is.
The officials here have contacted the Center for Disease
Control in Atlanta this morning. They're going to need more
help with this thing."

Gordon checked his watch. "Mimi will be in later; she
went by Hannah's house to check on her."

"Ms. Sandell is sick, too?"

"Yeah. She got hit along with everybody else."

Gordon interpreted Adele's change of expression as disbelief. "Yeah, I know what you're thinking," he said with a
wry smile. "She looks healthier than a moose—like nothing
could get her down short of a wrecking ball."

They laughed, Gordon keeping his eye on Iris. As soon as
she was looking at him, he blew her a kiss. In return, Iris
managed to raise her eyebrows and wiggle her fingers.

"Do me a favor and tell her I've got a touch of a cold and
I don't want to take a chance at giving it to her while her immune system is still fragile. Tell her Mr. Oldass loves her."

"Mr. Oldass?" Adele smiled. "Sure, no problem."

She watched the man blow another kiss to his daughter,
and for one moment she saw him in a new light; he was no
longer the wealthy, arrogant physician or the blowhard Republican running for office—he was just a regular dad who
loved his kid.

The fury Gordon Hersh felt at finding the door to his office
unlocked melted into a stunned awe when he was faced with

the graffiti and the mess inside. By the time he stumbled to the phone to call the police, he was in a rage. That was when he tripped over the arm, stiff with rigor mortis, and fell next to the corpse.

He'd gone through medical school and seen some pretty horrible disfigurements and plenty of corpses. But at close range, the mask of terror frozen on Samuel's dead face had been enough to make him gasp.

He couldn't remember for certain what happened next, but it seemed to him he'd made it to his knees when he heard a loud blast and then smelled the gut-wrenching odor delivered on clouds of thick, brown smoke. He was vomiting uncontrollably when the phone rang.

Gordon groped for the receiver, believing in his confusion that it would be the police on the other end of the line.

"You're gonna die, Gordo," said a muffled voice. "You and your whole fucking family of rich, Republican pigs have got tickets to hell."

His rage resurfaced and he began to bellow into the mouthpiece, demanding the coward come and take him on one-to-one like a man. He was still yelling when the day security guard came in and took the phone away from him.

Tim's eyes still watered from the smell. He'd smelled plenty of stink bombs and seen lots of military smoke grenades—but nothing like the one that had gone off in Gordon Hersh's office. It was, the detective guessed, a most unusual blend of chemicals to have made it smoke, stink, and linger the way it did. No amateur chemist had made that bomb—unless he'd recently visited the bowels of hell for the ingredients.

"You sure you're going to be okay?" he asked the man sitting on the couch in the reception area. "Do you want me to call an ambulance?"

Still in shock, Gordon Hersh feebly shook his head, trying to make sense of the events that had taken place that morning.

"Jesus," he murmured again. "This is like a nightmare from Alfred Hitchcock."

Tim nodded. "I need you to come with me to the office, Dr. Hersh. Do you think you can do that?"

Gordon nodded and attempted to stand. "I'm okay. It's just that I've got so much work to do. I've got to . . ." He stopped himself before he could finish his sentence with ". . . find a new campaign staff and manager." It sounded cold and inhuman. He looked at the detective and smiled. ". . . work. My best aides and my advisors are in critical condition. Somebody has to keep the shop open."

Tim shook his head. "I'm going to have to close this building as a crime scene; I'm sorry. It's probably not a good idea for you to be here, anyway, Dr. Hersh. Lots of people carry guns, but from experience I also know that your regular garden-variety vandal doesn't usually carry a gun, and they certainly don't shoot people."

Tim heard the words as he said them and again felt the glitch of a misconnect. People who set off stink bombs and wrote nasties on the walls *didn't* carry guns. The bullet hole through Samuel Fromer's neck didn't make any sense. Even if the campaign manager had surprised the vandal, vandals rarely resorted to physical violence—they ran. Vandals were shit disturbers, not murderers.

That all ten file boxes and most of the desks had been rifled was another misconnect. It wasn't a robbery—the petty cash and the computers were still lying around. Somebody was looking for something, and his guess was that Samuel Fromer knew what the something was.

"You might want to think about hiring some protection for yourself and your family, sir. It doesn't look like these people are fooling around."

Gordon shook his head. "Not for me. I'll have someone look after my wife and daughter. I don't want to have to walk around under guard. Negative publicity. This—this is bad enough."

"Are you ready, sir?" Tim extended a hand to help the

man up from the couch. "If you'd feel more comfortable, I can ask you these questions at your home."

Gordon took a deep breath before pushing himself up from the couch. "Could you meet me at my surgical suite in San Rafael in about an hour? If you don't mind, I'd like to stop by my house first to shower and change. I have some surgical patients coming in this morning, and I don't want to be late."

"I don't mind at all." Tim looked at the man with concern. He was shaking, and he'd grown more pale from the exertion of standing. "Are you sure you don't want me to call your wife, Dr. Hersh?"

Gordon's jaw tightened as a fear wrapped itself around his guts. "No. I'll tell her myself. She'll be upset. Mimi liked Sam a great deal."

Rosie pressed her fingers against the cool sheets of the bed, watching Brian undress. The sheer size of his mammoth body rendered him slow and clumsy. He put her in mind of a manatee.

She closed her eyes and willed her headache back into hiding, while trying to think about something else. The quote from Lady Alice Hillingdon, "I lie down on my bed, close my eyes, open my legs and think of England," came to mind. Except England was such a damp and dreary place—rather like Dr. Brian Macy himself—the brilliant scientist without a left side brain cell to his head. It made her wonder that someone so intelligent could be so stupid to risk so much for revenge.

Rosie closed her eyes and rubbed her temples, remembering the day they'd met four months before. It was while she waited to be seated at Mama's Cafe in Northbeach. For the sake of saving time, they'd agreed to share a table. Considering his social ineptitude, it was amazing to her now that he'd actually initiated a conversation. But then again, his bravery was sparked when he saw the front page of the paper she was reading—the one that featured the quarter-page photo of Gordon Hersh announcing that he was entering the primaries.

Their mutual hatred of the physician-politician drew them instantly to each other. Before they'd even finished their cappuccinos, he told her he was a research chemist for a pharmaceutical company. On his own time, he said, lowering his voice, some government people had hired him to develop nondetectable toxic agents.

He'd gone on for a full hour about D-7, his quarter-million-dollar baby, and how it could kill a man, be mistaken for a virus, and never be detected. Jokingly he'd asked if she had anyone she wanted to "do in" and not get caught.

She'd taken his phone number.

It didn't take long before Rose Martinelli, the lowly upholsterer for a famous antique furniture restoring firm, worked her magic, telling him her hard luck stories about growing up an orphan in Arkansas. She played him until he was completely in love with the sweetest, most erroneously persecuted girl in the world. She'd even cried after the first time she'd seduced him, letting him believe he was her first and only lover—outside of the rape, of course. Anyone, she'd decided, who was stupid enough to believe that yarn, deserved to be lied to.

On their first date she discovered that alcohol acted as a sort of WD-40 for his mouth. He'd have an occasional beer, but most alcohol didn't appeal to him. On their second date, she discovered that sweets were his weakness. After that, she never showed up without bringing a bottle of some sweet, Kool-Aid type wine like Ripple or liebfraumilch. She thought of it as supplying the water to prime the pump.

And talk he did. About everything—his mother's "smother love," his social isolation, his work, various scientific discoveries, his love of his mother's cooking. She mentally dozed through most of it, but when he talked about his private research, she woke up, transformed into the wide-eyed student; fascinated by, but not really understanding, what he did for a living. With her steering the course of his monologues, he'd told her everything about D-7, short of giving her the formula and the name of the group putting out the quarter of a million dollars for its development.

A small amount of the white powder could kill a man— or a whole roomful of people—and not be detected. It mimicked all the symptoms of a flu, acting not immediately, but four to eight hours after it was introduced into the body. He was, he bragged, about to become a very rich man.

Two weeks before—after his second glass of Strawberry Wine Cooler—he told her the D-7 first round trials were suspended for three weeks while he worked on a special rush project for the laboratory.

She felt the other side of the bed sag as he slid in beside her. Turning to face him, her body tensed under his touch. She breathed away the instinct to recoil and in direct opposition to her body's natural desire, put her arms around him, pulling him close, allowing him to kiss her.

Stroking him into hardness, she pushed him inside her, then began to move mechanically under him, concentrating on waves of the ocean. Yes, that would do. She pictured herself floating in the Caribbean.

He tried to slow down—begged her to stop, telling her that he wanted to make it last. Rosie sped up, wanting to get out from under his incredible weight as quickly as possible. She felt like she was going to suffocate.

"Faster, faster. Don't stop!" she commanded, pretending to orgasm. Roused further by her excitement, he couldn't hold back.

When he rolled onto his side still breathing in gasps, she pressed her face into the pillow and sighed at the relief of having him gone from her body. He wound his fingers through her damp hair, then let them stray to her face. Pulling her close, he forced her head to rest against his shoulder. The smell of his perspiration made her sick to her stomach. She moved to get out of bed, but the dull ache behind her eyes forced her to lie still.

"Don't go back to work, Rosie," he pleaded. "Let's do something crazy like go to Fisherman's Wharf and act like tourists. We'll have lunch at that restaurant you like so much down on Union Street? Or . . ." He sat up, his excitement growing. ". . . tonight I promise to make a dinner that'll make you want to marry me. It's Mom's lasagna recipe. I'll substitute nonfat cheese and cut down on the olive oil just for you. I . . ."

Rosie glanced at the clock radio on his nightstand. It was late. "I can't. I've got a meeting at the shop. The boss wants me to go over the new shipment of fabrics. Next time I promise I'll stay longer."

He looked miserable, like the family dog about to be left behind. "Damn it, Rose. You say that every time and you never do. You know Tuesday is the one full day I have off from work. Can't you ever plan ahead?"

"Knock it off, damn it!" she snapped. "We've only been seeing each other for a few months. We're taking it slow is all."

He suddenly looked lost and sad. He took her hands in his and stroked them tenderly. "Don't you *want* to be with me, Rosie?" he pleaded. "Don't I make you happy?"

"I swear you're more like a whiny girl than a dude," she said in a softer tone. "Come on into the kitchen, honey. I brought fixings for lunch."

He hesitated, then looked at her.

Rosie stiffened. She knew the expression. It meant he'd done something he hadn't told her.

"What?" she asked. "What did you do?"

"I didn't do anything, Rosie. I swear I didn't."

The woman drew up, nostrils flaring. "Goddamn it! What didn't you tell me, Brian? What did you do?"

Brian looked away and got out of bed. "I didn't—"

She was on him in an instant, grabbing a fistful of his balls before he could finish the denial. He sucked in a breath at the pain, clawing at her wrist.

"Tell me now, you son of a bitch, or you will *never* see me again!"

"Last night . . . I . . . there was this guy." Brian tried to pry her fingers off. The pain was excruciating. "He came in while I was setting the bomb. Please, Rosie, let go. You're hurting . . . please."

Still holding onto him, she pulled him across the room and then yanked him down into a chair. She knelt in front of him, keeping her grip on his testicles. He was crying, gasping in torment.

"What guy, Brian? What did you do?"

"Nothing. I . . ."

"What did he look like?"

Brian screamed as she twisted his balls and punched them up into his body.

"A Jew!" he screamed. "Wavy red hair. Big nose. Glasses."

"What did you do, Brian?" Patiently she waited until he was able to talk in short gasps.

"I hid in the storage room. He came in there. He was wearing a tuxedo. He was sick. Puking. He took nitroglycerine and his breathing was bad. He was looking for something in the boxes. Envelopes or something. Said the big *O* was going to kill him. I had a plastic bag over my head, and when he saw me, he freaked. Passed out and had a seizure. A heart attack. I think—I think he was dead. I couldn't find a pulse."

She jerked him up off the chair and pulled him back to the bed and straddled his legs. He groaned. She studied his face for a moment, began to let up, then punched his balls again. This time, he saw stars as the burning in his groin transcended pain.

"What else, Bri?"

"A woman." He gasped as soon as he could breathe again. His body was shaking out of control, and his eyes were rolling back in his head.

Rose let go of him and sat back. She cocked her head. "A woman? What woman?"

He cried out with relief and lay back panting. "I couldn't see her. She had a long cape thing on. The hood was over her face. She had a gun."

Rose squinted. "You sure you didn't recognize her?"

He shook his head. "She came in while I was checking to see if the guy was dead. I ran. She got in my way and I knocked her over." He shuddered. "It—it was okay, Rosie. She didn't see me. I still had on the bag."

Slowly, Rosie smiled and leaned over him. For a long time she caressed the tender, reddened sac. His pain excited her.

Then, when he was ready, she mounted—touching him as little as possible—and rode.

The fear hit as she was driving to the hospital. She swerved into oncoming traffic, then yanked the wheel back just before a pickup rounded the curve at a tremendous speed.

How could she have been so stupid, she wondered, slapping the steering wheel. She'd had all that time before Samuel's body was discovered to go back to his apartment for another search. Now it was too late. Every place Fromer had a connection would be crawling with policemen.

But then again, maybe it was just as well. The man with the bag over his head might have had the same idea. He might try to kill her if he ran into her again.

Taking a deep breath, she shook off her fear. She hoped Samuel was as smart as he said he was. She hoped he hadn't lied when he said he'd hidden the envelopes where no one would ever find them.

David "Boxer" Takamoto, Marin County coroner, looked at his new arrival and shook his head. The place was getting crowded with M. Plague victims.

Picking up the stack of files—one for each corpse—he leafed through them carefully. Medical histories, social habits, environmental histories. The only commonalities were that they'd all attended the same social function at the same time, and the stomach contents all had traces of one particular type of food.

When the first bodies came in—even before he'd autopsied them—he'd had the foresight to ask for local police cooperation in making an immediate search for all leftovers of food and beverage served at the dinner. He'd explained how important the leftovers could be, stressing that even if they had to go through bags of garbage, they had to find them, freeze them, and bring them to the lab, where they'd be analyzed and then sent to the CDC in Atlanta.

Dr. Takamoto felt something akin to excitement. Even though it was a terrible thing, the M. Plague was a relief from the banality of suicides, stranglings, and gunshot wounds.

He was elated. This, he thought, was going to be a real adventure in forensics.

TWELVE

ADELE SET HER STOPWATCH FOR FOUR MIN-
utes and thirty seconds from the second Tim answered.
"Tina said you called and left a message to call ASAP.
What's up?"

"Trickles of shit are hitting the fan. Dr. Hersh walked into
his campaign office this morning and tripped over his rather
stiff campaign manager."

Adele sat at attention. "Christ on a bike! Fromer's dead?"

"Most definitely."

"M. Plague?"

"One might think so from the ankle-high sea of puke, but
I don't think the bullet through his neck was the treatment
of choice."

"Somebody *shot* him?" Adele was incredulous.

"Yeah, but it gets better."

She waited, devouring the news.

"The office was vandalized; papers thrown around, hate
slogans written on the walls. A stink bomb planted in the air
vent exploded a minute after Hersh found Fromer. The
bomb wasn't any toy that could be bought at the corner radical upstart store, either. It was a homemade job, but very
professional, very sophisticated.

"There was nothing missing from the office that Hersh
can tell. Petty cash was untouched, all the computers still
there. I checked the report from the last vandalism, and it
was the same sort of deal only without the stink bomb . . . or
the dead body.

"The other thing that was different was that the place was torn apart, like somebody was looking for something specific. It wasn't just vandalism; it was a search."

"Maybe it's the same people who broke into Fromer's apartment?"

"I've got Cini over at his place now checking to see if he can find anything. My guess is that Fromer caught somebody in the act and swallowed a bullet for it. He took a death threat call yesterday from a man who said he was going to kill Hersh and everybody connected with him.

"Immediately after the bomb went off, Hersh got a call from the same guy who repeated his threat."

"What about a security system? Anything on tape? Wasn't there a burglar alarm?"

"No forced entry, no alarm, no tape. Everybody and his pet baboon had a key to the office. There was an older than dirt security guard. Useless as snail slime. Slept through the whole damned thing until he was relieved this morning at seven. He said he made his last rounds around eleven forty-five last night, and that he specifically went inside Hersh's office to check the place. Didn't see a thing, which is neither here nor there. The guy could have been hiding."

"And, exactly how do you know it was a guy, Detective Ritmann?" Adele asked with a sarcastic edge.

"Sorry." Tim sighed. "I keep forgetting about political correctness and the abolition of genitals. Hersh told me this morning that Fromer was the first of the campaign group to get sick and the first to leave for the hospital.

"But he never showed up at Ellis. The cabbie took him from the Belvedere to his apartment, waited outside for over an hour, then dropped him at the campaign office around twelve-fifteen. He remembers Fromer vividly because he puked all over the back of his cab.

"I've talked to a few of the people who work at the campaign office—those who aren't on respirators—and haven't turned up anything. Everybody seems on the up-and-up."

"What about Mrs. Hersh and Ms. Sandell?"

He snorted in disgust. "Been trying to get a hold of Sandell all day. Her office said she was sick, but she isn't at home. When I called earlier, your clerk said neither she nor Mrs. Hersh had been in.

"I followed Dr. Hersh home from the campaign head-quarters this morning. Mrs. Hersh had already gone, and I didn't see either her or Sandell's car there."

"Mrs. Hersh still hasn't shown up yet," Adele said in a hushed voice, as if she could be heard through the walls. "Usually both women are here first thing in the morning—before night shift even reports off."

"I suppose they could be off making funeral arrangements or something."

"Don't think so, Adele. No information has been released, and we've asked Hersh to keep it to himself and his wife. He's been sworn not to tell her about the bullet to the neck. We're going to try and keep this thing quiet for now."

"What does the coroner's office say?"

"I expect to hear from Takamoto any time. He's got us collecting leftover food for the CDC in Atlanta." He let out a breath and continued. "Our lab is going over the bomb. Ballistics is checking out the bullet. Pete Chernin's checking out some local sources who might know about any radical Hersh haters."

He paused, staring once again at Samuel Fromer's FBI file on the computer screen. He tapped his finger on the desk and bit his lip. "Do me a favor, would you?"

"Shoot."

"Check what time Mrs. Hersh left the hospital last night."

"No problem. Why do you want to know?"

"Hersh got real nervous whenever the old lady's name came up. He was overeager to keep her out of it. I think there's something going on there."

Adele's watch went off in short, shrill blasts.

"What the hell was that?"

"My egg timer." She stood up and opened the stall door. "I've got to get back to the trenches before the next attack."

* * *

"Okay, well, how would a CIA agent go about murdering Saddam Hussein at a cocktail party?" Rosie asked, tossing the salad. "I mean, couldn't he dump some D-seven into his martini and be done with him?"

Brian put down the paper. "If you left out the booze it would. It's complicated, but in simple terms, alcohol reacts with the chemical structure of the D-seven and denatures it—makes it unstable. Of course there are other chemicals besides alcohol that would denature it as well, but they wouldn't be consumed—at least not voluntarily—by humans."

"Oh. Well, what would be the best thing to put it in?"

"Since it's tasteless and odorless, water is the best medium, but almost anything will work."

"Are there any foods that might inactivate it?"

He came into the kitchen and kissed her on the neck. "Food is fine."

Taking the baking dish out of the oven, Rosie tasted the steaming garlic, cheese, and rosemary polenta. "Oh mama," she said in the Arkansas accent that drove him wild. "This here fancy cornmeal mush is gonna set you free, baby."

He took a heaping forkful of polenta, making the whole thing disappear in a single bite. Mushroom gravy dribbled down his chin and onto the fat of his second chin.

They both shuddered. She, because the sight of him eating made her sick; he, because his taste buds were having orgasms all over his tongue.

He closed his eyes and moaned. "God that's good, Rosie. Don't tell anybody I said this . . ." He giggled. ". . . but it's even better than Mom's."

"I'm glad," Rosie purred. She moved the serving dish closer and spooned another steaming portion onto his full plate. "Have more. Have as much as you like."

Later, Rosie insisted on washing the dishes while he relaxed on the couch. She was thinking about the woman with the gun when Brian's voice broke through her thoughts.

"Hey, Rosie, come here. Take a look at this!"

He was hunched over the society page of the *Chronicle*, his finger resting on a photo of Gordon Hersh and a blond woman in the ballroom of the Plaza. He squinted, patting his shirt pocket. "Where's my glasses?"

Rosie shrugged, closed the paper, and knelt down in front of him. "Enough, Brian. Give this shit a rest."

He reached around her and tried to open the paper again. "Come on, Rose, I want to see this picture. I want to see the smug asshole hobnobbing with the richy riches. And look at this woman here. Shit. Where's my glasses? Did I leave them next to the bed?"

He started to get up, but she pushed him roughly against the back of the couch, grabbed his shirt by the neck, and brought his face close to hers. It was his natural reflex to cringe.

"You hard of hearing, Bri?" She dug her nails sharply into the flesh of his neck. The skin broke and began to bleed a little.

"I—I—Don't hurt me, Rosie. I prom—"

His words choked off as she pressed against his throat with her clenched fist. "Let me repeat myself, Brian. I said enough is enough. You scared the shit out of the asshole, you fucked with his head and his political career, you messed up his office, now forget about Gordon Hersh and everybody connected with him. I mean it."

He was panicking, unable to breathe. The ache in his throat had turned into a burning pain, and he could feel his eyes bugging out of his head. He wanted to beg. Rosie liked it when he begged, but he couldn't talk because his throat was frozen. Instead, he nodded as best he could, hoping it would make her ease off.

"I don't want you calling me from jail, wanting me to come and hold your hand while you sweat out a murder charge. Count your blessings that you didn't get caught last night and forget it."

She abruptly let go of his throat. He grabbed at the flesh where her fist had been, massaging the area to ease the pain.

"Besides . . ." She unbuttoned her blouse and rubbed her nipples against his thighs. "I've got something better for you to do."

He looked down at her, puzzled and confused. "What . . . ?" he croaked, coughed, and tried to speak again. "What's gotten into you today, Rosie? You're never like this."

She smiled mysteriously and unzipped him. "You're wrong. I'm always like this."

"But that woman . . . She's . . . Oh." Brian let his head fall back. "Oh Rosie, what you doin' to me?"

Rose used the newspaper to wrap the wet garbage.

Brian came out of the bathroom, frowning. "You sure my glasses aren't in the bedroom? Maybe on the floor next to the bed? I remember taking them off before we . . ."

"Hey!" she said, irritated. "Who do I look like, your goddamned mother? Go look for yourself."

"Maybe I left them in the car. I'll walk up to the garage and get them later." He pulled her into his lap and nuzzled her neck. "You are a dish, Rosie. Why don't you stay for fourths?"

She checked her watch. "Sorry. Mr. Nokomi wouldn't like it if he found out I was screwing on his time."

"Screw Mr. Nokomi."

She made a face and pushed off his lap, slapping his hands away as they tried to pull her back. "Always leave 'em wanting more," she said, pulling on the cheap denim jacket covered with rhinestones.

Brian's heavy-lipped mouth settled into an unhappy pout. She slipped her bare feet into a pair of scuffed cowgirl boots, feeling like Cinderella on the flip side of a glass slipper.

Rose gave him a light kiss on the cheek. "See ya around."

"When?" It was undisguised begging.

Rosie shrugged and was gone.

* * *

In the parking garage ladies' room around the corner from Brian's apartment, Rose Martinelli tore off the cheap denim jacket and the cowgirl boots and stuffed them into the trash container. From her bag, she pulled a pair of pumps and a neatly folded sweater and put them on. She ran a comb through her hair, applied a fresh coat of lipstick, and looked at herself in the mirror.

"Well," she said with a bright smile. "That's more like it."

In the name of privacy, Adele led the newly arrived Mimi to Grace Thompson's empty office and pushed the blinking hold button on the line where Dr. Hersh waited to speak to his wife.

Hurrying back to room 802, Adele used the phone next to Cynthia's bed to dial an in-house extension number. She waited to be connected to David Takamoto, silently thanking Cynthia not for the first time for having chosen him as one of her paramours.

After Cynthia broke off the relationship, Adele remained the man's friend—just as she had with most of Cynthia's romantic casualties. Adele liked to think of herself as the Good Samaritan—picking up the mangled and bloody pieces of her best friend's heartkill.

"What took you so long to call?" David asked dryly when he finally answered. "I've had this bullet hole down here for almost four hours, and I've already had an outside call on him."

Adele lost her smile. "You're kidding. Who?"

"Don't know for sure. A woman called first thing—we hadn't even gotten him out of the bag and onto the slab yet. She said she was his sister. Outside of his mother, I knew the guy didn't have any family, so my natural curiosity kinda got the better of me. I strung her along by asking about the family health history, and when she last saw her brother, and how he was feeling at the time, that sort of thing.

"She wasn't interested in giving any answers, but boy, was she hot to find out what the specific cause of death was. I gave her the old 'confidential information' rap. I said I hadn't completed the investigation and she'd have to call back in a week.

"When she figured out that I wasn't going to give her any information unless she gave up a few goodies, she vaguely remembered that he had a cold, and asked if the M. Plague had killed him or if it was something else. I asked what she meant.

"We went around the bush a few times, and she finally called me a rather quaint name she probably picked up in a men's room somewhere, and hung up.

"I didn't say a word about the strange, circular hole through his neck, of course, but I got the feeling that's what she was after."

"Do you remember anything unusual about her voice?"

"No, it was a normal voice."

"But what *kind* of voice?" Adele pressed.

"What do you mean what kind of voice?" the coroner said, getting cranky. "How the hell am I supposed to . . . ?"

"Okay, okay. What I mean is, was there anything distinguishing about the voice? High? Raspy? Maybe an accent?"

"She had a slight southern drawl and she sounded like she was under sixty years of age."

Adele glanced out the room window. The door to Grace Thompson's office remained closed.

"Okay, so what *is* the deal with Fromer?"

"It's pretty strange."

"The stranger the better."

"The guy had some crummy-looking coronary artery disease to begin with, so he actually died from a myocardial infarction which was secondary to the stress of this M. Plague. The clincher is that he'd been dead for at least an hour or more before he was shot. The bullet entered the anterior neck and passed through to the floor, which would indicate that he was shot at fairly close range by someone standing directly over his body."

Adele pursed her lips slightly. "Who the hell would stand over a dead man and shoot him?"

"Beats me. I said it was strange. It might have been somebody who wanted to make sure he stayed dead, although you'd have to be blind not to have known he was deader than a doornail already. The guy looked like shit."

Adele snorted. "How can you tell he looked like shit? He was dead."

"Some dead people look shittier than other dead people, Adele. This was a very dead-looking corpse."

"Maybe it was an accident," Adele mused. "Or maybe someone was trying to warn Hersh . . . as in, the next bullet could be yours."

"Pretty weak conjecture, Monsarrat, but since we're speaking of accidents," David's tone turned serious, "how is Cynthia doing?"

"Did you hear me, Mimi?" Gordon strained his ear, as if he would somehow be able to see her reaction if he listened hard enough.

"My God, who would do such a thing?" She traced a pearly white fingernail around her lower lip.

"I don't know, but this is confidential, so you can't tell anyone, not even Hannah. The police are working on it. They dusted for fingerprints, took photos and pieces of the bomb for analysis. The detective doesn't really think it was vandals, he thinks it was someone searching for something."

"Searching for what?"

"I don't know. There's nothing here that would be important to anyone and I don't think even McGruder would go this far to dig up dirt." He considered something for a moment. "After last night, I'm sure McGruder thinks I'm out of the race, anyway."

"Where are you?"

"Back at headquarters. The main office is sealed off,

but the police said they'd take the scene tape down tomorrow. I'll need you to help the girls sort through the personal files if—"

"No!" Mimi practically shouted. She composed herself immediately and lowered her voice "I don't want to see that office."

There was silence. Then, "Mimi?"

"Uhn?"

"I don't want to argue about this again, but where were you last night?"

"I told you this morning—I left the hospital late and took a drive up in the Headlands before going home. I needed to think."

"Were you alone?"

"Of course I was alone," Mimi said, keeping her voice even.

Gordon put his head in his hands. "I don't believe you, Mimi."

"I don't care, Gordon."

"I do," he said with soft deliberation. "Do you think I don't know what was going on between you and Sam?"

Her guts cramped. In a hollow, dry whisper she asked, "What are you talking about?"

"That night last month that you and Hannah were supposed to go to the opera? I followed you, Mimi." Gordon stopped to control the emotion in his voice. He didn't want to show weakness now.

"I'll admit, I was surprised when you went to Sam's. I thought you were seeing someone else. I watched you come out with him two hours later. I saw the looks on your faces."

Mimi let out the breath she'd been holding, and her body relaxed. Instantly she started to laugh a deep, hearty belly laugh complete with wheezes. "Oh God," she said, trying to get her breath. "You thought I was romantically involved with *Samuel*?" She bent over, again helpless with laughter.

Confused, but still angry, Gordon raised his voice. "What were you doing with him, Mimi? What were all the hushed phone calls? Did you think I didn't notice the way you were always whispering to each other, making excuses to be alone together?

"You were with him yesterday afternoon. The clerk at the hospital told me you left together and didn't come back for two hours. Where did you go?"

Mimi wiped away laugh tears and coughed. "You're an idiot, Gordon. We were planning a surprise double birthday party for you and Iris. I wanted it to be a quiet family affair, but Sam insisted it be a major publicity event.

"He wanted to take me by the Belvedere yesterday so I could see the food for the fund-raiser. He was going to hire the same caterer for the birthday party, but I thought it was too expensive.

"The opera with Hannah was a ploy; you're right." She started to laugh again. "I went to Sam's apartment so we could put together a guest list. We couldn't agree on one person other than Hannah and your campaign aides. What you saw on our faces was frustration and anger, not lust. He wanted to have an open invitation to the public—I didn't. I was ready to kill the stupid—" She stopped abruptly.

Gordon wasn't going to let go of his anger and suspicion so easily. He'd spent months stewing over it. "Then where were you last night?"

"Driving," Mimi said. "Just driving around."

"Don't lie to me, Mimi."

She didn't say anything, but watched the tiny, blinking light on Grace Thompson's answering machine.

"Miriam?" Gordon's voice was hard.

"Uhn?"

"My keys are missing from my key ring. One to the back door of the office building, and the one to the office. You wouldn't know where they might be, would you?"

"Of course not," she said, a little too quickly.

So much for confidentiality, Gordon thought when Hannah entered the Miller Avenue office. He'd been sitting at the reception desk brooding over the morning edition of the *Pacific Intelligencer*, a deep frown etched into his face.

Placing a large espresso in front of him, Hannah took the lid off her own cup and peered past him into the darkened main office. She could see papers and file boxes thrown everywhere. The stink of the bomb lingered in the air even though every window in the place was open. A single strip of yellow police tape was across the doorway swaying with the breezes coming off Miller Avenue.

"When did you find out about Sam?" he asked. He wondered what the real reason was that she'd come; somehow he couldn't imagine it was to give condolences. He hoped to God she wouldn't try to seduce him—he didn't have the strength to deal with anything that physically challenging. However, a sudden fantasy about her raping him under his desk made him check to make sure the reception window blinds were down and closed.

She turned away from the inner office and pulled a small bag of pretzels from her purse. "Here. I thought you could use a cup of coffee and a snack," she said. "They're the only things that have relieved my headache and nausea so far."

He pried off the white plastic lid and took a sip of the bitter coffee. "Thanks. I'll try anything. I've gone through a bottle of asprin. I'm about ready to write myself a prescription for morphine." He glanced at the pretzels and looked away; just the sight of them made him want to hurl.

"Mimi said you had to vacate this morning?"

"Yeah." He nodded. "They sealed off the whole building initially, so I went up to my surgical suite thinking I was going to be stuck up there for three days. The detective called a little while ago to say they were taking down the scene tape except for the room where Sam was found." He shrugged. "They're going to release that tomorrow. They think they might need to get a few more photos."

There was an awkward pause, and when she raised her head to look at him, tears stood in her eyes. "I can't believe this," she said in a shaky voice. "When Mimi told me what had happened, I thought it was a bad joke. I mean, I wasn't Sam's best friend, but . . ." She looked at him helplessly. "What the hell is going on, Gordon? Why is this happening? Aren't you scared? I'm scared. I'm scared for everybody." She put her hand over her mouth as the tears spilled down her cheeks.

He started to go to her, to put a comforting arm around her shoulders, and thought better of it. Keeping the desk between them was the best way to go . . . much safer.

"I think Sam had connections with some bad people, Hannah. Who knows, maybe he pissed them off. Maybe he had something they wanted." He waved a hand in the direction of the destruction. "The detective said it looked like somebody was seriously searching for something."

"What?" she asked, still crying a little. "What would Sam have that was so important?"

"I don't know." Gordon shook his head. "Sam always had dirt on people. Maybe he had dirt on the wrong person."

"Do you think McGruder's people did this?" Her gaze slipped back to the main office.

"Don't I wish it was something that benign." Gordon sighed. "All I know is that I've got to keep going. I've been on the phone all day. Rob Byrd has agreed to come out from D.C. to run my campaign. He said he could bring some of his best people with him. Rob's a good man . . . I think he can help pull me out of this."

"The *PI* article was a low shot," Hannah said, blowing her nose. "I can't imagine what they'll do with Sam's death. How much is this going to hurt us in the polls?"

He raised his hand and let it fall. A gesture of futility. Still, he was secretly pleased she'd used the word "us." "It sure as hell isn't going to help. I had two patients to see today at the surgical office. Both of them canceled. Then I met with the San Francisco Presidio Planning Commission, and not one person would shake my hand." He raised his shoulders in a shrug. "I mean, what kind of a politician can't shake hands or kiss babies?"

She shook her head.

"A dead politician," he said glumly. "In the public's eye, I'm no longer a senatorial candidate, I'm a leper. God only knows what will happen when Fromer's death hits the papers." He eyed her. "Mimi wasn't supposed to tell you anything about Fromer. The police are keeping Fromer's death quiet until they know the exact cause. I'm sure—"

"I wouldn't tell anyone, Gordon," she interrupted, sounding slightly offended.

Watching her for a moment, he entertained the idea of asking about Mimi and Sam. Surely women told one another those kinds of secrets. But, the Swan would be loyal. She wouldn't tell him anything Mimi didn't want him to know, just as he believed she would not spread the word about Fromer's death.

"You've got pull with the *Chronicle*," she said suddenly. "Surely they can help."

"They're running a piece tonight downplaying the virus and building up the main platforms of my campaign." He sneezed and did a one-handed fumble through his suit pockets for the handkerchief he'd forgotten.

"They're good platforms, Gordon," she said, producing a clean linen handkerchief from her purse. "You had them on their feet cheering through their tears. They ate up every word—they're hungry for someone they can trust."

"Yeah," he said, wiping his nose. "That was before I became the official carrier of the black plague. Mr. Level Four himself.

"McGruder was on KPFA first thing this morning, giving out details of the people who died—he actually started bawling on the air. Then he went right into pontificating about my irresponsibility and disregard for the common man. I never realized how much he sounds like Ross Perot. All he needs are a few charts and a pointer."

Momentarily amused, they both laughed. The tension eased.

"Has Dr. Ingram come up with anything yet on the virus?" Hannah asked.

He snorted in disgust. "Each of the preliminary autopsy reports are showing similar inflammation and degeneration of the major organs, but no definitive cause . . . no virus—nothing.

"No one can come up with a plausible explanation as to why some people who have been exposed are immune, and others aren't. There isn't any real concrete common thread among the people who were affected or, for that matter, there isn't any between the ones who weren't. The local agencies have finally contacted the CDC in Atlanta." He put an emphasis on the word "finally." "Now we're going to get somewhere. Atlanta doesn't fool around."

She pushed her chair back and got to her feet. "Well, I've got to get back to my office. I just thought I'd play Jewish mother and make sure you were drinking your fluids."

"Thanks, Esther," he said wryly and took another swallow of coffee. He saw the Swan's momentary quizzical expression and explained.

"Esther—Mimi's mother. Ever meet her?"

Involuntarily she made a face. "Briefly. She hated me. Interesting woman, though."

Gordon laughed. "How charitable of you. She was a bitch with a capital *B*. She hated everybody. I never saw anyone who got as much pleasure out of manipulating people and making them miserable as she did." He fixed her with an amused gaze. "And what, pray tell, was her reason for hating you?"

"She thought I was going to drag Mimi down into the sewers of pot-smoking, bra-burning, political radicals."

He rubbed his chin. "I didn't think Esther was too concerned with politics. As far as I knew, Esther thought Stalin was a German poet who was burned at the stake for defending the Bible." He paused for a beat. "She probably didn't like you because she thought you and Mimi were sexual together."

Hannah gaped, then laughed. "Do you really think so? I wouldn't think she knew about things like that. Esther was so . . . prehistorically straight."

"Were you?" His gaze did not waver.

"What? Sexual? With Mimi?" She made a face at him. "Oh don't be ridiculous, Gordon."

He waved his hand nonchalantly. "But didn't you know? Esther was convinced Mimi was sexual with every woman friend she had. At some time in her narrow-minded life, she'd seen Lillian Hellman's *The Children's Hour* and it freaked her. She interfered with all of Mimi's female friendships— even after Iris was born. Every woman was a threat."

She picked up her purse. "Sounds like Esther was the one with the problem. Projection perhaps?"

"I thought so," he said decisively. "She always reminded me of a constipated Gertrude Stein."

"I don't think you ever need to worry about Mimi," she said dryly. "I don't think she'll be leaving you any time soon for another woman."

"That really would cinch the election, wouldn't it?" He smiled. "I can see it in *People* magazine now: 'Plague, perversion, and politics . . . the demolition of senator-hopeful Gordon Hersh.' "

Brian Macy was prying off the childproof cap to a bottle of oral Demerol when he remembered the plastic reading magnifier his mother gave him for his birthday. It was still inside the jumbo card with the airplanes on the front. "For a Loving Son on His Birthday . . ."

Magnifier in hand, he opened the copy of the *Pacific Intelligencer* that he borrowed from Mrs. Duggan next door. It took him ten minutes to read the entire article twice through, starting with the headline and finishing on the last page of section two. He studied the photographs of Gordon Hersh and his wife, Miriam, and his daughter Iris. Then he studied the faces of the dead and the survivors.

Growing increasingly anxious, he read the interviews with the medical examiner and physicians several more times, going down the list of symptoms. Then he went back to the photos of the fund-raiser dinner.

He let the paper drop to the floor and willed himself not to throw up. It was the migraine that was making him sick—nothing more than that.

Thoughts slipped in and out of the pain, mostly about Rosie and how much he loved her. She had a violent temper, that was sure, but she was the only woman who'd ever taken the time to get to know him.

"But . . ." His mother's warning echoed through his brain. ". . . what do you *really* know about *her*?" Not much, he had to admit. He had her pager number. That was it. No address, no work number. She'd always been careful about what she said about herself. Never once had she invited him to her apartment, and she always refused to let him give her a ride home. She said she loved riding the bus.

How the hell could anyone love riding buses?

His shirt was soaked through. He got up to change and saw that the couch was wet.

In the shower, he strained for some piece of information. Her parents were dead. Originally raised in Arkansas? Texas? No. Someplace in the South.

The smell of the shampoo sent him to his knees, and he vomited over the drain, watching chunks of undigested yellow polenta circle and disappear.

A sister. Engraved on the gold compact she used were initials—not hers. When he'd mentioned it, she said the compact had belonged to a married sister who had been killed in an auto accident. He tried to envision the compact.

On hands and knees he crawled out of the stall, pulled down a towel, and wiped his face. His breathing was becoming labored. Using the door as a support, he pulled himself up on rubbery legs. Several times he fell against the walls, making his way back to the living room. The newspaper photos were still there on the floor, looking up at him.

He focused on one, and then he remembered the initials on the compact.

At 4:00 P.M., Marcia, the day supervisor, tapped on the window of what was now referred to as "Ebola Room One." Adele, in the middle of suctioning Cynthia, raised her eyebrows. Marcia went away and returned with a sign written in red Magic Marker on the back of a progress sheet: RELIEF NURSE CALLED IN DYSFUNCTIONAL. CAN YOU STAY OVERTIME 4 HOURS? MAYBE 5??

Adele nodded. Marcia smiled and made the thumbs-up sign. Adele looked at Cynthia. "You've got me until seven or eight tonight, girlfriend. Prepare for an ugly evening."

Gordon found the vein on the back of his right hand and inserted the needle. He injected 25 milligrams of benzquinamide and let his head fall back against the Jag's head rest. Despite the pain and nausea, he chuckled—it would be just his luck for someone to come along and see him injecting the antiemetic. SENATORIAL CANDIDATE SHOOTS UP ANTIEMETIC FOR KICKS. He could see it all now.

Thirty minutes later, a round of vomiting shook him down to his toes. "I'm a physician," he addressed the floor of the Jaguar out loud. "I never get sick." Sitting up slowly, he felt the world roll upside down as the pain seared through his head. A phrase in LED lights began running across the back of his eyelids. It said TIME TO GO TO THE HOSPITAL, GRACIE. He put the car into gear and touched the gas. It was only five miles to Ellis by the Mill Valley–Corte Madera hill.

The same testosterone imbalance that made it impossible for men to ask directions would not allow him to call someone for a ride to the hospital.

He rolled out the driveway and into the busy fray of Miller Avenue. The sounds of angry horns and maledictions

aimed at the asshole driving the Jaguar never took his notice. Ed, the motorcycle cop who routinely patrolled Miller
Avenue for odd driving behaviors, did not see the weaving
Jag. Less than twenty yards away, the policeman was busy
pulling over a precocious nine-year-old who was driving his
mother's BMW down to Peet's Coffee on Throckmorton,
for a quick cappuccino.

Halfway over the curvy, narrow hill, Gordon saw Hannah
and Mimi walking hand in hand on the verge of the road,
kissing and fondling one another. Mimi's breasts were exposed. Moving logical thoughts through the sludge of the
drug and pain was difficult, but he knew he had to stop them
before someone else saw them.

His right foot did not obey the "Brake Now!" command.
His head dropped to the side until he could feel his ear
pressing into his shoulder. His neck was too weak to lift his
head up again.

In the last few seconds before the front end of the Jaguar
met the trunk of the eighty-year-old redwood, he became in-
credibly lucid, rather like having one's life flash before
one's eyes before death. Except this wasn't his life that
flashed before his eyes—it was the events of the last three
months.

Suddenly everything was very clear. In his lucidity, he
realized exactly what had happened and why. He made a
valiant effort to veer . . . a common man would not have
tried.

But then, a common man didn't have a daughter to save
from a murderer.

THIRTEEN

ADELE LEANED OVER HER SLEEPING FRIEND AND kissed her forehead. From her pocket she took a small spray bottle of Paloma Picasso—Cynthia's trademark perfume— and sprayed it liberally over the light brown hair. It seemed to her that Cynthia's nostrils flared . . . just the minutest bit.

"Wake up creep," she said tenderly. "I'm tired of confiding in Nelson." She thought for a minute and added, "Plus you owe me money." She pulled back in time to catch a tiny twitch at the corners of Cynthia's mouth.

"Listen," she continued. "You and I both know that you set your watch a half hour ahead because you're one of those persistently tardy people. But honey, you're running really late on the waking up phase of this escapade. I also want my favorite rhinestone denim jacket back, missy. You know, the one you stole from the Beast's duffle bag? I've willed it to you, so I *have* to die first."

The woman lay still with the exception of the rise and fall of her chest under the covers. "Okay." Adele sighed, her good humor fading fast. "I didn't want to have to play hardball with you, but you aren't cooperating, so here's the deal: You've got until three P.M. tomorrow afternoon—three-thirty your time. I mean it, O'Neil. If you don't wake up by then, I'm going to tell everybody about what you did behind Christian Brothers' winery last October."

The slightest bit of a frown crept between Cynthia's eyes.

"Go ahead, mull it over. Sleep on it, even. Just be awake by tomorrow evening, or you'll never be able to walk down

a street anywhere in Marin without people pointing at you
and laughing."

It took some doing, but Brian managed to find the number
he was looking for. Dialing it was another matter. He could
barely see the numbers through the searing pain in his head,
and his hands were so clammy, they kept slipping off the
buttons. After six attempts, he got through to a recorded
voice offering him a menu.

Forcing himself to concentrate, he punched in the appropriate numbers and listened to another, more familiar voice.

A few minutes later, he hung up, his heart thudding in his
temples. Somehow he made it all the way to the locked refrigerator he kept in the back hall next to the washer and
dryer. His fingers slid off the lock several times before he
managed to get the key in and turn it.

Behind bottles of chemicals was a rack of four polyethyl-
ene test tubes, each one three quarters filled with fine white
powder. Resting his head against the top shelf, he cried out
with relief until a paralyzing thought caused him to pull a
tube from the rack.

He trapped it between his arm and the front of the crisper,
and unscrewed the cap. After six tries, he managed to slip
his little finger far enough into one to coat it with powder.

He smelled it, then touched it to the tip of his tongue. As
though jolted with a current of electricity, he dropped the
tube and scrambled on all fours out of the kitchen toward
the phone.

Halfway across the living room, he vomited, reached
out for the coffee table, and grabbed hold of the edge of
darkness.

Seven o'clock came and went. At seven-fifteen, Marcia
called from the nursing office to ask if she could hold on for
another hour or so; her relief nurse had overslept and was
driving in from Berkeley.

It was fine with Adele; she hadn't really expected to be

relieved before the end of swing shift, anyway. She hadn't even begun to clean up the room. Twenty minutes later, she looked out the glass windows toward the nursing station and saw that there was a sudden storm of activity. She motioned to Malloy, Ward 8's evening clerk and resident Buddhist, to come to the outside door.

Malloy's head bobbed inside the gowning area. The man had his head shaved to the scalp in what she called a Zen Center cut. Two small gold hoops pierced the cartilage of his left ear.

She raised her eyebrows. "What's up out there?"

"Gordon Hersh is coming up on a respirator from ER," he whispered rapidly in a thick Bostonian accent. "He demolished his Jaguar. Got bilateral wrist and rib fractures, a deeply lacerated thigh, a serious relapse of the plague, and . . ." He looked at the admit sheets in his hand. ". . . a pneumothorax."

"Where's he going?"

Malloy jerked a thumb to 801. "Next door."

Adele thanked him and swiftly drew the curtains across the viewing windows between the rooms so Iris would not see anything of the mass chaos that was about to go on.

Three minutes later, she peeked out of the front window to see the nursing staff running wild. Dr. Hersh's bed was surrounded; Drs. Ingram and Briscoe, and Mimi and Hannah were anxiously huddled around him as if in conspiracy. Mimi was weeping, Dr. Ingram looked grim. Dr. Briscoe was rubbing the back of his neck, an expression of grave concern bothering his face. Hannah looked sicker and more gray than the patient.

Adele pulled back and went to Iris. She would get the details later from Tim as to what had happened. Clearing away IV tubing, she rubbed Iris's cool hand and sat on the edge of the bed.

"Hi, sweetheart. How do you feel?"

Iris's hand went to her throat. She grimaced. "Throat hurts," she said in a hoarse whisper.

Adele nodded. "Your throat is still irritated from the tube that helped you breathe."

Iris pointed at Cynthia. "She looks like me." She smiled. "I thought I was looking in a mirror. In my dreams, she kept saving me from . . . she saved me."

There was an abrupt change in the girl; a thought that evolved rapidly into panic. "Where're my parents?"

Adele hesitated. "They're next door talking to Dr. Ingram." It was a generic answer . . . not exactly a lie.

Iris closed her eyes in apparent relief. "She hasn't gotten him yet, then." The statement was mouthed with barely enough air behind it to make it audible.

"Who?" A generic question.

The girl's eyes opened and with some effort looked to the windows facing the nurses' station. "My father. She wants him out of the picture."

Adele's heart skipped a beat. "Who wants your dad out of the picture?"

Iris's eyes again scanned the room and finally settled on Cynthia's sleeping form before they closed. "My mother," she said as if it were understood. "Miriam Hersh."

Her report finished at nine-thirty, Adele crouched below the windows between the rooms and took advantage of a passing laundry cart to escape the notice of the Gordon Hersh entourage.

In the locker room, the package from Hannah fell out of her locker when she opened the metal door. Hastily, she scribbled a couple of regretful lines about it being against nursing policy to accept expensive gifts from patients or their families. Like the coward she was at that moment, she called Malloy from the phone in the nurses' lounge and asked him to deliver the package to Ms. Sandell as she was leaving. She didn't dare trust herself to return the package in person, afraid she'd give in at the slightest encouragement and keep it.

In the stairwell between the third and second floors, she

heard someone coming up the stairs singing. The voice sent her into a moment of vanity-alert. She listened to "By the Light of the Silvery Moon" while shaking her hair loose of its braid, and pinking up the skin over her cheekbones. She would have gone all the way and applied a light coat of lip gloss had she had time to rummage through her voluminous purse.

They met in the middle of the second-story flight.

"Don't tell me you're just getting out of here?" Tim asked.

"They asked me to work overtime," she explained hastily. "They were short staffed. Nothing out of the ordinary for us. What brings you here this late?"

As soon as the question left her lips, she realized that he was there to see Cynthia. Of course—he'd come by to see the woman he was still in love with.

"I was called by Corte Madera PD about Hersh's accident. We're going to handle the investigation."

As soon as the words were out of his mouth, it occurred to him that Adele might think he was an uncaring and insensitive male if he didn't mention Cynthia. "I thought I'd check to see how Cyn was doing while I was here."

"How is she?"

"Very late on the waking up part. I'm worried."

"Cynthia O'Neil," Tim said in a consoling tone, "has never been on time for anything in her entire life, including her own birth."

They both laughed; it was known to them both that the habitually late Cynthia O'Neil was a documented ten-and-a-half-month gestation baby.

Adele shuffled her feet. "So, is this an accident?"

He shrugged and shook his head. "The lab is going over the car. So far, all the obvious stuff seems to check out okay . . . no cut brake lines or anything like that. There was a witness in an oncoming vehicle who said Hersh looked like he was already unconscious when he went over the side of the road.

"The janitor saw him go to his car about six. Said he looked pretty unsteady on his feet, like he might have been drunk, but his blood alcohol level checked out at zero. Seems he sat in his car for about fifteen minutes, then took off. He probably thought he could hold out until he got to the hospital.

"Takamoto said he talked to you today, so I don't need to tell you about how Fromer died."

She frowned and shook her head. "Yeah, isn't that weird? Why would somebody shoot a dead person?"

"Could have been a mistake, could have been a warning. The range was so close, the bullet passed through the vertebral bones and lodged in the wood floor. The gun used is a real piece of shit—a three-inch barrel, double-action revolver; probably a Harrington and Richardson. Something you'd find on the street."

He leaned back against the wall and put a hand in his pocket. "Did you check what time Mrs. Hersh left last night?"

"Linda said she left about eleven."

He nodded, then after a silence asked, "What do you think?" There was something like regret in his voice. In the worst way he wanted to pull her into his arms. Instead, he pulled a stray lock of her hair. "Come on. What's cooking in that brain? You didn't have me check out those people last night for nothing—and today one of them is dead.

"Are you going to share, or are you going to save it so you have something to spread on your toast points later on?"

She opened her mouth, unthinking, to tell him what she suspected, then changed her mind. It was too soon. "Well," she hedged, "if you're very, very good, I'll think about sharing the jam when the time is right. You'd just better make sure you have your own toast points in order."

He laughed, knowing that she meant exactly what she said. Getting information out of Adele Monsarrat was tougher than rock rinds.

"But for now," she continued, tugging on his shirtsleeve, "you can tell me all the information you're holding back."

Acutely aware of her fingers wound into his shirt, he was also aware that they were flirting. More than anything he wanted to please her . . . give her presents . . . hell, give her anything she wanted. He was about to tell her things that he knew he probably shouldn't; he also realized he trusted and respected her, much in the same way he trusted his partners.

"I cleared the Miller Avenue office building about noon—all except that main back office. Hersh came down and worked out of the front reception area, and our guys went in and did a few more photos and left. The janitor says he saw a woman go in sometime between one and five, but all he caught was a pair of off-white or beige high heels, and a woman's hands carrying two coffee cups.

"And yes," he said, forecasting her next question, "I've sent a scene guy back over there for another look around.

"I called the Dallas DA again and spoke to one of the guys who actually worked on Fromer's case. He said Fromer's game was blackmail. He had some major connections with the Mob, and I figure he probably had some informa—"

The approach of footsteps and a conversation in hushed, urgent voices, caused him to stop. Both she and Tim stared at the two sets of feet—one in beige heels, the other in gold flats—rushing down the steps.

Mimi and Hannah entered the landing, startled to see them there. While Adele made the introductions, Hannah scrutinized her and Tim, sizing up the situation.

Adele experienced a flash of annoyance as Tim examined Hannah carefully while he shook her hand. He started with Hannah's shoes and worked his way up to her eyes. He seemed to find the woman's eyes particularly interesting.

He looked, thought Adele, like he wanted to lick her clothes off. That he blushed and stammered while saying hello, forced her to look away in disgust; men turned into such fools over a pair of gorgeous breasts, a perfect body, and a pretty face.

"How is Dr. Hersh?" Tim asked.

"He's stable, thank God," Mimi said with obvious relief. "It's a miracle he's alive. The paramedics said there wasn't anything left of the car."

"I saw it briefly on my way over here. It's not as bad as some I've seen go off that hill, but bad enough. I'd have to say your husband is a lucky man."

Tim's eyebrows lifted with another question. "And how's your daughter doing?"

While Mimi waxed euphoric over Iris's progress, Adele grew uncomfortable under Hannah's steady gaze.

"I am so sorry about the clothes," she said finally, pointing to the box Hannah held conspicuously under her arm. "It's hospital policy not to accept personal gifts."

"I'm sorry, too." Hannah smiled. "The earrings match your eyes. Perhaps I can give them to you sometime when you aren't on duty . . . that is, if there ever is such a time."

"Not lately," Adele said, setting her ear to keep track of the conversation between Tim and Mimi. Tim had just said he needed to ask Mimi a few questions and was making a time to meet the next day. "Even my dog is divorcing me. I caught him packing a suitcase last night."

Hannah blew her nose. "How do you manage to have a personal life outside of this place?"

Adele thought she heard a slight reproach in the tone of her question. "I don't sleep," she answered. "Not that I have a personal life anyway."

Tim turned to Hannah and then looked back at Mimi. "By the way," he said, with a businesslike inflection, "did either of you happen to visit Dr. Hersh today at either the head-quarters or his medical office?"

Mimi and Hannah exchanged glances. It was so fast, Adele couldn't tell what meaning was passed.

"No," Mimi answered slowly, concerned. "But he left a message on our voice mail at home before he left the Mill Valley office. He said he was heading for the hospital. He didn't say anything about being sick, but I could tell from his voice that he wasn't feeling well."

"Did he say anything else?" Tim asked. "Give you any details about what kind of a day he'd had, or mention anyone who might have come by to see him?"

"Why do you want to know all this?" Hannah asked, cutting to the chase. "Are you thinking this might not have been an accident?"

"I'm thinking I want to be thorough, Miss Sandell," Tim answered, watching her carefully. "A woman was seen going into the campaign office earlier this afternoon."

"Oh for goodness sakes, that could've been anybody," Mimi said casually.

"Maybe," Tim said. "But whoever it was might be able to give us a clue as to why he went off the road, or if he was ill at that time."

"Oh come now, Mr. Ritmann," Hannah said. "I've had a touch of this virus myself, and I don't think I could have driven out of my driveway let alone over a narrow, winding road."

"Just one more question, Mrs. Hersh," Tim said. "Did you go home last night after you left the hospital?"

For a fleeting moment before she answered, Mimi looked as though she'd been kicked in the throat. "Yes," she said haltingly. "Yes, I did. I had a glass of wine and went right to sleep." She laughed nervously. "I'm afraid I don't usually drink alcohol and when I do, it knocks me for a loop. Gordon called from the emergency room, but I slept right through."

Tim turned to Hannah. "How about you, Ms. Sandell? Did you go straight home after they released you from the ER?"

"Yes," Hannah answered stiffly, as though offended by the question.

The detective gave her a searching glance. "Would you mind stopping by my office tomorrow with Mrs. Hersh? I'd like to ask both of you a few more questions."

"Well, if you'll excuse me," Mimi said, already heading

for the stairs. "I'm exhausted and need to get home and get my feet out of these shoes before they swell up any more than they have."

Automatically, they all looked down at her feet, which seemed impossibly small inside the beige pumps.

"It was nice meeting you, Detective Ritmann," Mimi said, waving. "See you in the morning, Adele."

As soon as the two women disappeared, Tim and Adele raised their eyebrows at each other. "Did you say the janitor saw beige heels?" Adele said.

"Yeah," Tim answered. "Something's floating sideways in the fish tank."

Adele pulled the shreds of the Mickey Mouse rug out of Nelson's mouth and gave him a stalk of peanut butter-stuffed celery.

"Chew!" she commanded, then watched as the dog swallowed the vegetable whole.

"Christ on a bike, are you part pelican or what?"

The black Lab cocked his head, checking out the Food Hand for more treats, or maybe his favorite of all—one of Her dirty running socks. Smelling no evidence of either, he returned to suckling his old pal, Mickey Rug.

Adele took two more bites of burnt toast slathered with nonfat cottage cheese, three more forkfuls of broccoli stems, then clicked the microtape she'd "borrowed" out of Grace Thompson's answering machine into her minicassette recorder.

"Invasion of privacy or sleuthing?" she asked the bowl of broccoli stems.

Don't worry, they said. *You'll never tell a soul you accidentally pushed the two-way record button for the express purpose of recording someone's private conversation.*

Satisfied that broccoli stems did not lie, she hit the play button and listened to Dr. and Mrs. Hersh's phone conversation from earlier in the day.

* * *

The thoughts that would not let her rest finally caused her to bolt out of bed and check the clock. It was early. In terms of San Francisco nightlife, ten-thirty was the time when the night people were just waking up. Most of them were only beginning to think about which stimulant to take first and wondering which nipple and navel rings would best go with their leather outfits and their designer tattoos.

She dressed quickly and pulled out a black canvas duffle bag from the back of her closet. At the smell of it, Nelson whined.

"Oh come on, Nels," she said, checking out the bag's contents. "I'll be back before you know it."

He whined again and pawed at her foot.

"I know, I know. I promise I'll be careful. I can't afford to get hurt now, not with Cynthia still sick."

Nelson barked.

"Don't worry. I'll be home in time to make you some onion pancakes for breakfast."

Sycamore Avenue, Mill Valley. Adele found the narrow dirt path between the two houses that were half Victorian, and half forty-niner rustic style. Noiselessly she ran past fenced backyards and crossed the old wooden bridge over Miller Creek to the dead end of Willow Avenue. Miller Avenue was less than fifty yards in front of her. To her right was an empty parking lot, and to her left, sitting on the creek bank, was the back of Gordon Hersh's office building.

She picked her way through the thick undergrowth of olallieberries and stopped when she reached a flat metal door. There were no lights on inside the building and no cars in the parking lot—nothing to indicate human presence. The metal door had the type of lock that was so easy to open, she wondered if the manufacturers of such doors had a pact with burglars. From her duffle bag she took what she called her lock and key kit, found the perfect lock pick, inserted it, and stepped inside the dark of the building.

* * *

She sat cross-legged on Samuel Fromer's desk, chewing a mocha-flavored PowerBar and studying the mess around her. It was pure, wondrous fortune that the crime scene had not yet been dismantled, and for that she was supremely happy.

As her jaws worked over the candy, her eyes went from the chalked outline of Samuel Fromer's body, to the bullet hole, to the mess of files and file boxes.

There was a subtle regularity to the mess. It was so subtle, she broke out in goose bumps when she finally saw what it was. The thrill and the satisfaction together were exactly why she loved medicine and crime—the highest forms of puzzles and riddles. Having the type of mind that ran on less obvious paths was helpful.

Tim, she guessed, would notice it eventually when he settled down to study the photos of the scene, but then it would be too late. The scene would have long since been disturbed.

"This," she whispered to Sam Fromer's chalked form, "is better than any sex, running high, or bungee jump I've ever had."

She stuck the PowerBar wrapper in her duffle bag and walked over to the empty file boxes. Ten in all, only two of which were ripped apart in a particular pattern—all four sides ripped through the middle. None of the tops or bottoms had been bothered with.

On a hunch, she picked up one of the intact boxes and pulled a number 12 scalpel from her duffle bag. Carefully, she slit through all four sides, and picked up the next box and did the same. The third box proved to be the winner. Halfway down one side, her scalpel dragged as it hit a thicker material than the box itself. Adele pried apart the cardboard.

Stuck between the layers was an envelope. Opening the flap, she found two sheets of paper filled with handwritten names and addresses, none of which she recognized. She checked the handwriting on Samuel Fromer's desk calendar with the sheet of paper. The distinctive, masculine script was indeed Samuel Fromer's.

On boxes seven and ten, she found two more envelopes similarly hidden. One held a sexually explicit love letter signed by Mimi. The other contained six pages of incriminating information about three people. Two of the names she didn't know . . . the third she did.

She put each file box back exactly the way she'd found it and gathered her duffle bag. It was time to start pulling in the loose threads.

"No cups in the office or the car. No clues to indicate foul play anywhere," Detective Peter Chernin said, perching himself on the edge of his boss's desk. "You really think this is homicide?"

Tim shrugged. "You got a better idea?"

Peter didn't, but gave voice to anything that came through his head. He enjoyed brainstorming with the younger detective almost as much as he enjoyed watching movies. "It's a weird virus bug is all. Hell, AIDS started out the same way. Didn't you see that two-hour TV movie with, ah, Lily Tomlin? Nobody had a clue what the hell AIDS was for years. Some people got it and died, some didn't. For all we know this plague thing could be a mutation of the AIDS virus."

"I'd think they'd know that by now if it were a mutation of AIDS." Tim tapped his pen on the blotter. "It's not that simple. It's got lots of people scratching their nuts. The victims are within too small a circle. If it were a bug, it'd be wider spread than it is. Adele's been up to her elbows in the shit, and she hasn't gotten sick. Neither has the kid's mother."

What Tim didn't say was that Adele's intuition was the main motivator for his suspicions. He didn't have to—Chernin had already guessed.

"And what does Detective Nurse Monsarrat think?" Peter said in a taunting way, hoping for some information about the nurse with the reputation for being a poor man's private eye. He'd been thinking about Adele Monsarrat on and off for a long time—actually, since the first moment he'd laid eyes on her a few years back when she filed a missing persons report on her psycho husband. In the middle of an ugly divorce himself, he'd filed the leggy dame away in his daydream file.

He was working on another case when she became part of the doctor-nurse serial murder case. Detective Enrico Cini was assigned to interview and tail. She'd gotten under Cini's skin, too—only in a different way. Almost every day, the vertically challenged detective came back to the office ranting about that "ball-busting, know-it-all bitch." Then at various social events, he'd hear Ritmann and his ex-squeeze talk about Adele in shades of Mother Theresa, Florence Nightingale, Marilyn Vos Savant, Uta Pippig, and Sherlock Holmes. The more he heard, the more it served to pique his interest.

"Her woman's intuition thing is working overtime," Tim admitted. "But she's not talking right now. You know women."

Peter ambled to the bulletin board. He stared unseeing at an FBI's Most Wanted poster. "She still single?"

Tim quickly glanced at the detective, who closely resembled Richard Burton; he could see that the back of the man's neck was flushed red.

"Why?" Tim forced a laugh as his stomach poured acid into his esophagus. "Thinking of trying to hook up with her?"

"Maybe." The older detective shoved his hands in his pockets. "What do you think?"

Tim felt the vein in his forehead get bigger. The rock and the hard place squeezed.

"I don't know, Pete. Don't you think you're a little old for her?"

"Psssh. How much younger can she be? I'm only fifty. She might be the type who likes older, more secure men.

You know what women say these days: Be secure—go mature."

Peter checked his watch. It was only ten forty-five; not too late to give her a call. Everybody knew nurses kept owls' hours.

Tim went over the logistics in his mind. Adele was an eccentric, adventurous wild woman—Peter Chernin's idea of a wild adventure was to shower without his bulletproof vest on and watch *Ocean's 11* in the nude.

Adele had a quick, dry wit—Peter was into Benny Hill.

Peter raised rabbits for his dining pleasure—Adele was a strict vegetarian and abhorred the killing of any animal, and certainly nothing that had a name like "Fuzzy Girl," or "Hoppy Bunster."

Adele's IQ was high. Peter's was . . . well, lower.

Never in a million years would she go out with the guy.

"Go for it," Tim said, finally, enthusiasm born out of his relief. "What have you got to lose?"

Adele sat in the Beast's lap and read Mimi's love letter for a third time. The date on the top was three months old. The salutation read "My dearest love." The body of the letter held passionate sexual passages among which were couched declarations of undying love. The letter ended with the promise that she would soon be freed from her prison.

The Beast was cresting the Gough Street hill at Jackson when it decided to play its going-to-sleep trick. Other than approaching a crosswalk full of children at a high rate of speed, Adele couldn't think of a worse time and place for the 1978 Pontiac station wagon to shut down, leaving her behind the wheel of a couple of tons of steel without steering, brakes, or lights.

Firmly grasping the wheel in both hands, she threw her weight onto the steering wheel as the yellow monstrosity coasted to the middle of the intersection and stopped. She got out and pushed the disabled vehicle forward, then jumped back in and pulled on the wheel until it drifted to the side of the street.

The Beast came to rest in a bus stop. A one hundred and twenty dollar ticket, no excuses. San Francisco parking patrol were not known for their sweet or brilliant natures—they had been known to give tickets to people who'd died while driving and then had the car towed as the body grew stiff behind the wheel.

For a few moments she entertained herself with clips from a movie version of her calling Tim from a San Francisco jail and asking him to come over and bail her out. He'd think she was kidding until she handed the phone over to the desk sergeant who would explain that she'd been arrested for assaulting a traffic cop.

She pounded the Beast's dash chest. "You're going to the junkyard for this one, you goddamned rotten rust bucket piece of shit!" Hoping the threat would sink into the brain (and it most certainly had one somewhere—a diabolical working of wires and spark plugs), she turned the key. Nothing. Not even a fart of a spark.

"I swear I'm going to buy that damned neon orange ball and stick it right on top of your CB antenna, like a clown's hat. You'll be the laughing stock of every car on the road."

She gave the keys a twist.

The automobile's silence fairly screamed, "Fuck you!"

"I give you the best of fuel, get you lubed, and nice fresh oil every two months, and what do you do?"

She tried again. This time the Beast managed a wheeze and a cough—just to let her know he was present and listening to every word she said.

"Whitewalls, for Christ's sake. I give you four beautiful new whitewalls, and for this I get the sleep trick? You *owe* me, babe!"

The motor turned over, purred, then went silent.

"What is it?" she asked finally, in a tone of defeat. "You want a hot wax, now? Is that it? That's it, isn't it? Okay, okay. I'll give you a hot wax next week."

She turned the key chanting "hot wax, hot wax, hot wax . . ."

The Beast woke up and purred.

She patted its dash chest, gave it an encouraging word (*wax*), and sped off toward Polk Street.

FOURTEEN

MIMI TIPTOED DOWN THE STAIRS TO THE KITCHEN.
At another time, she might have turned on the television and
watched an old movie while sipping tea, but her worry was
about to kill her.

She opened a drawer and reached behind a package of
flour. As soon as her fingers touched the cold metal handle
of the revolver, she felt better. That part would be okay. No
one could trace it to her. She'd purchased it years ago from a
man who had approached her on the street begging for
money. She told him she would give him five hundred dollars in cold cash if he brought her a revolver and some bullets to go with it. It didn't seem important anymore to
remember why she'd wanted it badly enough to do such a
thing, but she liked knowing it was nearby. It was an added
bit of security that was her own.

Overcome with sudden despair, she dropped her head in
her hands and wept as bitterly as she had when she'd found
Sam dead. As long as he was alive, she at least knew the letter he'd stolen from her—the letter he could ruin their lives
with—was in his keeping and hidden.

Hidden well, Mimi thought, thoroughly frustrated. All her
searches of the office and Sam Fromer's apartment in the
last few weeks had turned up nothing.

She took out the revolver, rubbed her temples, and paced.
It was really her mistakes that were worrying her. She had to
really concentrate on what she'd done. She'd have to go

over the details. She played back through her conversation with the detective and winced; they were bound to find out she'd lied, and then they'd become suspicious and start prying. Mimi made a fist and pressed it hard into her forehead.

The call from the emergency room clerk, informing her that her husband and Hannah were there being treated, had come shortly after she'd arrived home Monday night. The clerk gave her what details she could about what had happened at the Belvedere Hotel, then inquired as to whether or not she'd seen Mr. Fromer or knew where he was.

She'd answered that she hadn't seen him since earlier in the afternoon, which had been the truth. What she didn't say was that she knew where he could be found. Samuel Fromer wasn't a stupid blackmailer; he would be gathering his golden eggs and moving them to a safer place.

The mistakes she'd made and the chances she'd taken crashed in on her, making her cringe. She'd been so careless, blinded by her desires. The argument with Gordon at his office—people were certain to have overheard them. Forgetting to replace the key on Gordon's key ring—pure stupidity. And the most senseless of all: the mistake she made the night Iris got sick.

Now came the torture, she thought, letting her nails bite into the flesh of her palm. Now she would have to wait to see what her mistakes would cost her.

The Duck and Swallow, a Polk Street bar, more popularly known among the gay population of San Francisco as the Suck and Swallow, had a reputation as an open gay bar, which meant it catered to all members of the alternative lifestyles group. Transvestites, transsexuals, lesbians, gays, cross-dressers and "Other," called the bar on the fringe of the tenderloin section of the city home.

The Duck and Swallow did much more than serve alcohol to the lonely, horny, and chemically dependent. It served as a meeting place for curious midwestern tourists and those weary of judgment. ("Say, are you guys real San Francisco homosexuals? Oh yah? Well, do ya think we could get ya to pose in front of the cable car there?")

Adele found a parking space on Sacramento Street. Covering the six and a half blocks at a jog, she passed window displays of garish, spindly-limbed manikins dressed in the sexual raiment of those belonging to the far, far left. She raised her head long enough for a quick peek at one display. Three white manikin bodies, red lips, black eyes and hair. One was on its hands and knees, a studded black dog collar choking its thin neck. Across the manikin's face was a black patent leather mask with only an *O* cut out for the mouth. There were twenty or so silver rings pierced through the nipples and navel. A clear plastic pair of panties with black trim and a split crotch was worn over the not-so-private private parts. A triangle of wiry black pubic hair was much in evidence.

The male manikin holding the other end of the leash was clad mostly in leather and studs. A strap-on dildo had been applied and the appendage, decorated with sequins and rhinestones, artistically placed. He was walking arm in arm with another male manikin dressed as a construction worker complete with hard hat.

Despite its location next to an adult book and toy store, the Duck and Swallow was a fashionable establishment— one of those seasoned San Francisco bars that sported a wealth of mahogany, brass, and potted palms without coming off too stuffy or yuppie for its own good. A ray of streetlight had managed to squeeze in between the buildings and pierce the stained-glass window taking up most of the south wall. It illuminated the middle section of the bar where the bartender stood drying rocks glasses by hand.

Adele took a seat at the bar so she was at the edge of a red spotlight that shone from the ceiling. For her the place had the feel of old San Francisco—sophisticated, liberated, and a touch of the outlandish, all at the same time.

"Oh my God, will you look what the dog dragged in?" The bartender grinned so wide, the corners of his mouth seemed to slide off toward his earlobes. The muscular, good-looking man leaned over the bar and kissed her.

Adele hugged her ex-husband. After three years of a somewhat unconventional and unsatisfying marriage, Gavin Wozniac goose-stepped out of the house one sunny afternoon and disappeared without a trace. When he reappeared a year after, without explanation as to where or why he'd gone, Adele had already divorced him. There was a brief but bizarre volley of attempts to reunite with her, all of which were firmly rejected. When he knew there would be no going back to the trials of wedded mediocrity, the former combat training officer for the Green Berets astonished her yet again by coming out of the cross-dressers' closet.

After the initial shock, it hadn't actually upset her, but it did explain the sporadic mysterious disappearance of her clothes while they were married.

Gavin had always been off-center. Indeed, his unorthodox behavior was one of the reasons she'd married him . . . who else would wake her up in the middle of the night to howl at the moon or do combat drills?

"Hey Gavin, what's up?"

"Besides the cost of living? Not much." He waved the dish towel toward the tables. Along with a waitress of dubious gender, there were only fifteen or twenty customers inhabiting the place. "It's early. The place doesn't fill up until eleven, but as long as it fills up, I don't care."

He put a wineglass in front of her and opened a bottle of dry sherry. For himself he poured a wineglass of Perrier with a twist of lemon. They clinked rims.

"What brings you to this side of the bridge?" He took a sip of his expensive water. "You working in the city now?"

She shook her head, noticing his polished wedding ring. "No, I'm still at Ellis. I actually came over especially to ask you something."

He eyed her with an impish smile. "I'm sorry, Charlie, but I'm remarried now and Debbie's jealous of you."

Hearing him use his pet name for her brought up memories she thought she'd forgotten. She smiled, not because they were fond memories, but because she was so glad not to be married to him anymore.

"Well, she has no reason to be jealous. She's the one with the perfect shoe and skirt size."

Gavin stepped back so she could admire his black denim miniskirt and three-inch patent leather heels. She sipped her sherry and gave him a thumbs-up, wondering if it was sick that she was bothered by the fact that his legs were better than hers.

"You ever hear of Hannah Sandell?"

"Sure. Who hasn't heard of the White Swan?" He resumed polishing the rocks glasses. "She's the wet dream of every dyke in San Francisco. You know her?"

"I've met her. She's a friend of one of my patients."

"And?" Gavin's impish smile returned. "What's the story, Charlie, you couldn't find anybody to measure up to me, so now you're gonna try the other side of the swing?"

"Not quite," Adele said, lifting one eyebrow, "but I am curious about her personal life. Do you know anyone who might have been involved with her? Someone who might know for sure if she's . . ."

"Gay?"

"Yeah." She took another sip of sherry and let it roll around her tongue. She could already feel her lips getting tingly. "That's what I mean."

He lifted his chin in the direction of the androgynous waiter/waitress dressed in white tie and tails. He/she was a dead ringer for Pat from "Saturday Night Live."

"Pat's the one to ask."

Before she could stop him, he'd hailed the waiter/waitress over. He/she lumbered across the room like a two-hundred-pound salmon loaf.

"Pat, this is Charlie, my ex-wife. She's got a question about Hannah Sandell."

Pat raised his/her eyebrow . . . the one that went straight across the ridge of his/her forehead. Adele interpreted it as eyebrow talk for "Yeah?"

"Hi Pat. Listen, would you know if Hannah Sandell is . . ." Adele forced her eyes away from the scraggly mustache. "I mean have you ever heard whether or not she's gay?"

The eyebrow went down in the middle, making a V of a frown.

"Cripes, I'd have to give a positive on that one," Pat said finally in a voice that gave direct testimony to an overabundance of testosterone—or estrogen, whichever the case was.

"I had a friend—Sandy? She told me the Swan picked her up at a bar down in the Mission once. Gave her a phony name, got her drunk on Sunrises, then took her home, gave her lots of expensive clothes and jewelry, and then screwed her brains out for three days.

"Sandy swears it's true. The Swan never called her or saw her again. Broke Sandy's heart."

"Have you ever seen Ms. Sandell in here?"

While Pat thought, he/she commenced to play with the growth of hair festooning his/her upper lip. Adele wondered if he/she went to a barber or kept it trimmed him/herself.

"I've been here three years, and I think I've seen her in here maybe three times."

"When you saw her in here, was she with anyone?"

Pat nodded. "The Swan usually comes in with a guy. Big. Dark like an Italian. Older. They sit at the corner table, she orders a Stoli—chilled, straight up—drinks it down in one shot. He orders a Roy Rogers which he never drinks. She pays—they leave. Tips fair, not great."

"Do you have any idea who the man is?"

Pat's eyebrow talked. "Yeah. One of the regulars said he was Mafia. Tony something."

"Tony Saludo?"

Pat twirled out her 'stash. "That's it."

Adele nodded. "Well, okay. Jeez. Thanks for the info, Pat." She put out a hand, which was engulfed by Pat's huge and slightly hairy one.

After Pat had plodded back to his/her station, Adele finished her sherry and prepared to leave. Gavin came around the bar to walk her to the door.

"You need a boyfriend, Charlie," Gavin said, giving her a peck on the cheek. "You're looking peaked."

"I need a boyfriend," she said dryly, "like I need a toothache."

Gavin shook his head sadly. "Don't say that, Charlie. Everybody needs somebody. It's what makes the world go 'round."

"I have Nelson. What more could I possibly want?"

"Well," Gavin said, pulling up his fishnet stockings, "it's not too late to start thinking about trying for a normal life."

"Yes it is," she said, falling into the old depression. "Any hope I may have had of being normal was destroyed the day I became a nurse."

It was almost 2:00 A.M. before Adele put away her notebook and lay down to talk to the ceiling light fixture.

"Detective Chernin? He's the one who looks like Richard Burton, right?"

Right, answered the light.

"What do you think prompted him to ask me out?"

Lust?

"Nah. Maybe . . . shit, maybe Tim asked him to."

A mercy date?

"Oh shit." She sat up, felt dizzy for a second, and began yanking off her black leggings. "I thought only Cynthia tried to fob those off on me."

Tim probably feels sorry for you, Adele. After all, you haven't had a date in a long, long time.

"You know what, goddamn it?"

What, dear?

"I'm going to call this guy back and tell him I'll go out with him on Friday night, and I don't care if he is almost as old as my mother. I'm going to enjoy myself. I deserve it. I'm tired of always having Nelson for my date. I'm tired of . . . oh forget it!"

You're tired of Tim not wanting you? Is that it, dear?

"Shut up."

Tim's in love with Cynthia, Adele. You can't blame him for just wanting to be friends.

"Oh yes I can," she said bitterly and turned off the light.

Gordon forced his eyes to move from square to square of ceiling tile with each breath the ventilator delivered to him. And with each breath, each tile, he struggled to remember each hour of his day. Most of it he could not.

He knew Samuel was dead, but couldn't recall how that had happened. He remembered being furious with Mimi about some keys she'd taken off his key ring, but couldn't remember why he was so scared about it. He remembered every detail of the morning's conversation with Adele and blowing kisses to Iris.

He'd been asked questions by the police at his office, but couldn't remember about what. Then he'd called Rob Byrd, and remembered doing a hard sell and offering a lot of money, but couldn't remember the details of that either. Later, Hannah had visited with the intention, he was sure, of seducing him, except he couldn't remember the act itself. He prayed to God he hadn't.

Reluctantly, he did remember Mimi's visit. She'd brought him a too-sweet apple strudel and insisted he eat it despite his nausea. They'd argued violently, but he couldn't remember exactly why, except it had to do with Sam Fromer and something else.

Excruciating pain tore at his head and he closed his eyes against the fluorescent lights. He could never have imagined such pain existed.

The thought that Iris had experienced this, that his innocent girl had gone through this, tortured him with another, almost worse kind of agony. In his mind, he bore down and screamed.

A nurse suddenly appeared, looking concerned as she stared first at him and then at the monitors over his bed. She busied herself with checking his IVs and then adjusting his respirator. He felt the increase in number of delivered breaths, and guessed she had also increased the oxygen concentration from the surge of dizziness. The presence of the nasogastric tube threaded down his nose to his stomach was irritating to his nostrils and the back of his throat. On the wall behind the bed he could hear the constant suction pulling out probably nothing but bile—and what was left of Mimi's strudel and Hannah's coffee.

My daughter! He tried to form the words around the endotracheal tube. *Watch my daughter!*

The nurse drew up something in a syringe, told him to be calm, and plunged the needle into the IV medication port.

He opened his eyes as wide as he could. He fought the wrist restraints that held his hands. *Goddamn you! I have to save my daughter!*

His heart was thudding heavily in his chest, protesting the strain being put on it with a dull ache. The nurse was nervous, motioning for help. He didn't care. He needed to save Iris no matter what. Even if it cost him his life.

He began to kick. If he kicked hard enough, he thought he might be able to loosen the ties on his hands, and then he'd be able to tell them that Iris was in danger.

The medication—he correctly guessed Valium—made his limbs feel like they weighed a hundred pounds each. Blinking, he tried to keep the ceiling in focus, but it kept sliding away, like it was spiraling down a funnel. A man he knew, but couldn't name, stood over him now telling him to relax and asking him stupid questions. "Are you air hungry, Gordon?" "Are you in pain?"

Iris! He tried to scream, except his scream was no more than a whisper of air . . . a puff from his endotracheal tube. *Save Iris!*

FIFTEEN

"WHAT TIME IS IT, HAN?"

Hannah glanced at her watch and internally flinched. It was almost seven. Shifting her gaze from the large round window overlooking Mount Tamalpias, she studied the petite woman resting in her arms. "Enough time to make love again," she teased, caressing the woman's breast.

Miriam Hersh closed her eyes, arching toward the other woman like a cat stroked. "You never quit, do you?"

"When it comes to loving you?" Hannah shook her head resolutely. "Never." She nuzzled Mimi's soft black hair. "This time I'm not letting you go."

The sun reflected off the swimming pool, causing shimmering patterns to dance over the bedroom ceiling. *This time,* she thought, *I mean to have you for good.* She pulled Mimi closer, holding her as tight as she dared without hurting her. She'd let Miriam Sandoval-Hersh go once before, and had spent sixteen years agonizing over it.

Through the wonders of computer science, they'd been matched as ideal roommates in their junior year at Skidmore College in upstate New York. She was an art major; a free-thinking, left-wing radical who had her own pillow at the Saratoga Springs jailhouse. Mimi, a liberal arts student heavy into home economics, was naive enough to be proud of being a registered Republican.

They'd hated each other on sight. It was forced propinquity and time that eventually broke down the false barriers and made them inseparable. Her initial attraction to Mimi was generated by the delicate beauty's immense need of her. Mimi's vulnerability made her feel worthwhile, as though protecting her was the purpose for which she'd been born. Unlike any of her myriad radical causes, Mimi's need for the security of her arms was tangible.

They made an odd couple. As the brooding artist, she rarely said more than a few words to anyone unless it was from a soapbox; Mimi talked incessantly to anyone about anything. At six feet tall, Hannah slouched and hid her striking Scandinavian features under curtains of long blond hair. In contrast, Mimi's one hundred pounds was neatly packed onto a voluptuous five-foot frame. With her shining jet-black hair and green eyes inherited from her mother, and smooth olive skin from her father, Mimi's exotic beauty was a hit with the boys from surrounding colleges.

College boys being college boys, they indulged in the age-old campus sport of finding the prettiest package, going for the challenge, conquering, and moving on to the next target. Each time she was dumped, Mimi ran to Hannah—her Gibraltar, her unconditional comfort, her protector.

While not lacking in her own brand of good looks, Hannah seemed impervious to the charms of the college boys. She had no yearnings to sample anything having to do with her mother's profession; her initiation to the world of sex had been far too traumatic for her to imagine that there could be anything at all pleasurable about the experience.

A few years after her rape, her mother's pimp set out to groom her for the world's oldest profession. Tony Saludo's first meeting with the needy, sensitive thirteen-year-old was not what he had expected. While he didn't find the girl to his own sexual tastes, something about her appealed to his more enlightened core. She had a drive and an intelligence that was more like a man's than any woman he knew.

A wise investor, Tony smelled a return on her potential and invested in her future. He figured he could afford to take the chance—he spent more on racehorses in a week. The bargain was set: in exchange for her education, she would extend to him her services once a month. After college, he would send her to a fancy Swiss finishing school for polishing. Then, he would sit back and watch his finished product make it to the top. He was thinking along the lines of Hollywood. He had connections with the studio bosses who owed him big favors. Making her the next Ingrid Bergman wouldn't be difficult.

In her early college years, Hannah claimed to live for her art alone. Other than the monthly visits to her benefactor (she thought of the brief, overnight affairs the same way she thought about having her period—messy, unpleasant, but necessary), she said no to the two most powerful drugs known to the human race—love and sex. Looking back on her resolve, she found it ironic that from the first time she and Mimi made love, she'd lived for nothing else.

Their love came as a complete surprise to both of them. Although she had already had sex with several women older than she (the mobster's sexual tastes ran more to watching her perform with other women than using her himself), neither she nor Mimi considered herself a lesbian. In the beginning, Mimi had been shy, though not reluctant. Through patience and gentle coaxings, Hannah eased her lover's inhibitions and delivered her to her true inborn passion. During the first year of their intimacy, they lived content and happy under the umbrella of security new love brings. Their select inner circle of friends never guessed their secret, although when they described the two women, they never used the term "best friends," but rather, "soul mates."

Inseparable and passionately in love, the strength of the relationship seemed to defy all the odds against it—except one. Their devotion would not protect them from the intricately engineered schemes of Mimi's mother to drive them apart.

Possessed of a mother's uncanny ability to see all from eyes placed in the back of her head, Esther Levy-Sandoval had not missed her daughter's infatuation with the blond shiksa. She'd heard the whimpering through the walls during that first Christmas break when Miriam surprised them by bringing home her roommate. Esther had suspected the worst from the moment she'd laid eyes on the amazon and the unnatural way she was always touching her daughter. Resolved to save her child from falling into her grasp, Esther devoted herself to finding an appropriate arrangement. It was during the Golden Daze Bridge Tournament that Esther found the ticket to her daughter's salvation in the hand of Rachel Hersh, wife of Dr. Ira Hersh and, more important, mother of Gordon Hersh, M.D.

Valentine's Day decorations weren't even up before Esther's letters were full of the gorgeous Gordon Hersh, prince in waiting. Intuitively Hannah knew what the game was and took the challenge. From that time on, she devoted herself entirely to Mimi, loving her to the point of exhaustion.

None of it had mattered. Hannah blamed herself only in that she'd been stupid to think Esther would not resort to hitting below the belt. She was devastated when she learned of Mimi's pregnancy. In vain she tried talking her beloved into an abortion, pointing out that it couldn't be considered murder since "the thing" wasn't even an inch long and had no consciousness, therefore no soul.

Failing to get through Mimi's pro-life resolve, she proposed that they live together as an alternative lifestyle nuclear family. She would get a job and take care of her and the child, raising it as if it were her own.

Mimi sneered at the idea, and added the touch of killing truth by stating the obvious—that being a new college graduate with a degree in art history, Hannah could not afford to give her and her child the security she so desperately needed to be happy.

Turning a deaf ear to Hannah's diatribes about gilded prisons of security versus true inner happiness, Mimi handed the controls of her life over to Esther, who soon turned them over to Gordon Hersh in the San Francisco society wedding of the year.

Hannah followed her obsession and moved from upstate

New York to San Francisco. At night and on Saturdays, she would sit for hours in the front west window of the Twin Peaks branch of the San Francisco Library, keeping one eye on her design books and the other on the apartment building across the street where Dr. and Mrs. Hersh lived.

Once in a while she was lucky enough to get a glimpse of the young couple leaving the building. Mimi always looked strained and worried, as though she were afraid of the outside world.

After the baby came, there were fewer and fewer sightings, although one night, Mimi did venture out with the stroller by herself. She'd gotten as far as the corner before she hurried back to the building in what appeared to be a terrified panic.

After a year's apprenticeship with an award-winning interior design establishment, Hannah went out on her own. Sandell Designs started in a one room apartment, and over ten years had become the most prestigious of all interior decorating businesses in California. It had taken a lot of hard work, a little luck, and a moderate amount of help from Tony Saludo. Soon connected with the wealthiest and most famous of San Francisco society, it didn't take long before she was a card-carrying member of the limelighted crowd.

Gone was the curtain of straggly hair, the ragbag castoffs and the slouched shoulders. The Swiss finishing schools had successfully mined the diamond out of the rough. Known in the inner circles of San Francisco society as the White Swan, the stylish Hannah Sandell was taken seriously by all those who were considered to be "somebody." Celebrities from George Lucas to Nancy Reagan paid handsomely for the privilege of a consultation with the Swan. Herb Caen frequently mentioned her in his column, always with a hint that he was half in love with her himself.

But still, at each step, Gordon Hersh had beaten her to the next higher rung on the golden ladder. His small Mill Valley office had long since been traded in for lavish surgical suites in both San Francisco and Marin County. Catering to the same wealthy clients for whom she did interior designing, Gordon Hersh, plastic surgeon extraordinaire, did the exterior design.

Over the years, Hannah and Mimi brushed shoulders a few times as guests of the same fund-raisers or charity balls, but Mimi always managed to keep a distance between them, clinging hard to Gordon's arm whenever she was physically near. Their contact had been limited to a nod, or, if it was Christmas and the feeling of goodwill toward men was high—a smile, a hello, but nothing more.

It didn't upset her. On the contrary, the way that Mimi fought contact confirmed for Hannah what she suspected to be true—that no matter what kind of life Dr. Hersh provided for his exotic wife, she was the only one in the world with whom Mimi had shared her true nature.

When she'd read in the *Chronicle* that Gordon Hersh had entered the primaries for a seat in the senate, she'd opened a bottle of her best champagne, sat back, and waited for the deserted, unsettled Mimi to call. She didn't wait long. One month after the celebrity surgeon entered the race, Mimi called the office under the pretense of wanting to redecorate the study of their three-million-dollar Sausalito home.

As the official interior designer of the Hersh showplace, Hannah was there every day lending her own special touch, making sure each detail was perfect. Their reunion was sweet and steamy. At first she'd been startled by Mimi's unbridled passion. Miriam Hersh, for all her money and social standing, returned her love like a woman starved.

Mimi ran the tip of her tongue along the curve of Hannah's palm and swung her shapely legs off the side of the bed. "We'd better shower now. I want to get to the hospital early."

"Let's work ourselves into a sweat first," Hannah said and reached over toward her lover.

Slapping Hannah's hand away from the sensitive inner surface of her thigh, Mimi clucked her tongue in feigned vexation. "Why, Hannah Sandell, you're a shameless pervert!"

"Not so perverted, my love. Here, let me show you." She picked up the smaller woman and carried her into the shower. Locked together, they made love once more as the warm water flowed over their bodies.

As soon as Adele came within view, the med tech pulled away from the wall and stood straight. The woman was strong willed and made him nervous, yet she was the only one who would care enough to be honest with him.

"Good morning, Miss Monsarrat?"

Adele stopped reading the *Intelligencer* and looked up. Mirek stood before her wringing his hands.

"I knew you come here early. Please may I talk to you?"

"Shoot."

The med tech was momentarily silenced. He frowned and looked around.

She remembered hearing that in 1984, during staunch Communist suppression, he had escaped Czechoslovakia in a wardrobe trunk stuffed in the back of his parents' car. The vehicle had been shot at and he'd taken a bullet in the foot.

She corrected herself. "I don't mean shoot as in guns, I mean yes, what do you need?"

He handed her a form. It was an application to Bellevue Nursing School. "I want to do the right thing," he said carefully. He'd practiced his plea a hundred times in front of his American-born cousin, Petula. "I want to help people. I need American nurse to write down that I am worthy to become a nurse."

She looked at him doubtfully, wondering why a young man with his whole life before him would want to join a dying profession of women. "Do you really want to be a nurse? I mean, you see what goes on here every day. Why in God's name would you want to do this?"

His expression remained deadly serious. "I wanted to be nurse for a long time, even when I am in my country."

"Yeah, okay, but why?"

After a second or two, he touched the center of his chest. "Because my heart is smarter than my brain."

It was one of those innocent, spontaneous statements that stopped her cold and gave her goose bumps—miniature life rafts made out of words for when one was drowning in self-pity and frustration.

She would quote him when she wrote his reference. It would be all the explanation anyone would ever need.

Dr. Hersh looked smaller and more frail, and somehow, thought Adele, more Jewish. Like an old rabbi.

"You're definitely one of God's Chosen, Gordon." Dr. Ingram laughed. As his caseload of M. Plague patients grew, he, in turn, grew to look more like Ichabod Crane—gaunt and tired.

Gordon closed his eyes as if to say, *Oy vey, I'm dying, and he vants to do a comedy act?*

"What do you mean, Randolph?" Mimi asked.

"It's good news," Ingram said. "If you'd held a gun to my head last night I would have told you with absolute certainty that Gordon wasn't going to survive through the night. Today I checked his chest X rays and I actually bawled out the X-ray tech because I thought she'd given me the wrong films. His lungs have improved dramatically. I want to wean him and Nurse O'Neil off the respirators over the course of the morning. If they do okay, I'll extubate both of them this afternoon."

Hannah entered the room in time to catch the last of the good news. Beaming, she placed an arm about Mimi's shoulders. Mimi promptly shrugged it off and leaned over her husband. "Gordon?" she whispered, anxiously touching his shoulder. "Did you hear?"

With his eyes closed, Gordon nodded and tried to say something around the tube that put his breathing pattern out of synch with the machine's fixed rate of breath delivery. The respirator alarmed. Mimi moved out of the way, in order that Adele might silence the machine's wail, and as she did so, Hannah once more reached out and slipped an arm around her shoulders. That was when Gordon opened his eyes and saw the pair of them. His heart sped to triple its previous rate. He lifted his head off the pillow, trying to talk.

"Relax, old man," said Dr. Ingram. "We don't want you to relapse. Save your strength. Breathe with the ventilator. Easy."

Gordon shook his head and bit down on the endotracheal tube. His hands strained, trying to get free of his restraints. The ventilator was going into hyperalarm mode. The alarm—someone must have fashioned it after a train whistle—was blowing out their eardrums.

Adele herded all of them toward the door. "Okay, the peanut gallery has to clear out now. I need to do my assessment and clean him up. Let's give the poor man a rest."

When she was alone with him, she drew the curtains and gave him a squirt of Valium . . . not enough to make his jaw go slack, but enough to relax him into a slow drool. She didn't want him too groggy; he needed to be able to breathe on his own so they could extubate him.

She could hardly wait to hear what he had to say.

The gain her father made, Iris lost over the course of the night. She'd required sedation after the night nurse—a cold, sulky woman whom Adele had not entirely trusted—pulled back the curtains from the viewing windows that separated the two rooms and told her that the patient she was watching with great interest was her own father.

It was at this point that Adele wanted to ask if she'd gone to the Adolf Eichmann School of Nursing, or if sadism was a natural part of her personality. She held back the question by biting the inside of her lower lip.

The nurse then reported, with genuine bewilderment, that soon after Iris had been told about her father, the child had grown restless and needed to be sedated. After receiving the medication, the girl had grown confused and needed to be

placed on a non-rebreather mask. Her decision to continue
to administer more and more sedation until the young girl
was unconscious was, in her opinion, "the best thing for
the kid."

When Adele tasted blood, she unclenched her jaw, but sat
on her hands so as not to throttle the woman where she sat.
She knew that the nurse had kept Iris sedated for one reason
only: so that she wouldn't have to deal with her on any level
other than purely physical.

Adele asked why she hadn't called Mrs. Hersh to come in
and calm the patient. Unashamed, the nurse boldly replied
that she didn't see the need since it was so much less trouble
to sedate the girl. Scanning her nursing notes, Adele saw
that the nurse had provided written documentation as required by law of what her justifications were for sedating
Iris Hersh so heavily. She'd written simply "Patient disturbed and exhibiting agitation; ranting and raving, trying to
get out of bed, and not making sense." Nowhere was there
one word written regarding the fact that the patient had just
learned her father was seriously ill, and then was allowed to
view him in that state.

"What . . ." Adele asked, her hands struggling to make
fists under her, ". . . didn't make sense in her rantings and
ravings?"

"I couldn't even tell you, it was so crazy." The woman
waved a hand in dismissal of the question.

Adele pushed again for an answer. One hand was working its way out from under a buttock; it wanted to grasp
firmly the doughy padding of the nurse's throat.

"Honest, I don't remember. You know how crazy patients
get sometimes. It was the same old ranting, crazy talk."

"Actually I don't know how crazy patients get," Adele
said, giving her a look that should have scared her. "I do
know how people act when they've been told bad news, and
then seen a loved one in distress. I also know how patients
'get' when they're overmedicated, so I suggest you try very
hard to remember what Iris was 'ranting and raving' about."

Normally slow on the uptake, the woman was just beginning to realize the level of Adele's irritation. "Something
about murder. Someone trying to kill her and her father."

"Did she mention any names?"

"I don't remember." The nurse crossed her arms over her
chest—a gesture of defiance.

"Try."

"Okay. How about Mick Jagger and Minnie?"

"Mimi," Adele corrected. "What else?"

"That's it."

"Don't make me dig. Give me something else . . ."

"I told you—none of it makes sense."

"Try me."

"Coffee. She kept going on about drinking coffee. I told
you it didn't make sense."

"Hey," Adele said, shaking her head, "makes perfect
sense to me."

Cynthia's body was slowly on the mend; it was her mind
that Adele was worried about. Dr. Ingram finished his neuro
check muttering under his breath. She caught the words
"neurological damage," and folded in at the middle. In her
fear, she wished she could call up Cynthia and tell her about
her best friend who was in the hospital not doing very well.

As with Dr. Hersh, Cynthia's ventilator settings were
changed every hour or so in the attempt to shift more and
more of the responsibility of breathing to the patient. Referred to as "weaning," the process sometimes went rapidly
and well. If it didn't, it left the patient in a private hell of being "ventilator dependent." Adele was thankful that although her mind was still lagging, Cynthia wasn't having
any trouble breathing without assistance.

At noon, Detective Ritmann tapped on the viewing window and asked Adele to take a break. She kissed Cynthia
tenderly and whispered in her ear, "You've got three hours
left, dickhead. At three-oh-one P.M., I'm going to start telling the world about that little comedy of personal errors that

you acted out behind Christian Brothers. I'll start with Tim, and then Skip. Then, I'll tell Nettie 'The Mouth' Wecheski." Adele pinched Cynthia's cheek. "You know Nettie, don't you, Cyn? She's the blabbermouth switchboard operator over at Bellevue? By the end of the day, Nettie will make sure that the rest of Marin County is informed."

In Ward 8's kitchen Adele made them each a cup of instant decaf.

"A big negative for finding anything at the Hersh office," Tim said, taking a sip of the dark brown liquid that tasted like burnt water and tar. "I've requested the clothes Dr. Hersh was wearing when he came into ER from Admissions office; maybe we'll find something there. The ladies are coming in later this afternoon to make statements.

"Seems that Mrs. Hersh and Ms. Sandell have selective memories. The ER clerk who worked the night of the fundraiser said she spoke with Mrs. Hersh at length around quarter to midnight. She told Mrs. Hersh that her husband wanted her to come to the ER, and asked if she knew where Mr. Fromer was.

"Mrs. Hersh said she hadn't seen Fromer since earlier in the afternoon and that she'd leave for Ellis immediately. She never showed up.

"Hannah Sandell went . . ." The detective made the sign for quotes. ". . . 'straight home' from the ER by way of a tour of Mill Valley. She slipped the limo driver a C-note to drive her partway up Summit Avenue—which was where Fromer lived—then down Miller before taking her to her car in the Belvedere parking lot."

"What time did the driver drop her at the hotel?" Adele asked.

"He thinks it was around midnight." He paced in the tiny room, able to take only two strides in each direction. "He thought she was checking for someone's car."

She leaned back against the counter, her eyes sparkling. "Would you check out a couple more names for me?"

He pulled out a pocket-size notebook from his jacket pocket. "If you tell me why."

"I'll tell when you give me the information," she said, handing him a pen. "Tony Saludo and Greta Nyquist. They both lived in or around New York City at one time."

She rinsed out her coffee cup and placed it, still wet, back in the cupboard that held the staff's mugs. "Have you traced any of the evidence found at the Hersh office yet?"

He mimicked an exasperated expression she frequently gave him. "I'm following the Adele Monsarrat school of investigation work—I ask the questions and don't give anything away until the time is right."

Grinning, she understood by his answer that he hadn't.

He shuffled his feet. "How's Cyn doing?"

"I've told her she's got three hours to snap out of it, or I'm going to tell all her dark secrets." She grew serious. "She's okay, I guess. All her systems have kicked back in except her brain."

"How can you tell?" Tim fought back a smile.

It took her a second or two, then she laughed and socked him in the arm. "Oh you're so bad. I'm going to tell her you said that when she wakes up."

"I used to check her for brain death every day," he said lightly. "I never did quite determine whether or not she was all the way with us.

"Want to have dinner tomorrow night?" he asked, hoping it came out sounding casual and *friendly*.

She felt the scarlet blush start at her armpits and spread upward to the roots of her hair. "Can't. I'm . . . um . . ."

She looked to the refrigerator for answers. *Should I tell him? Will it ruin my chances? Will he ever want to eat with me again?*

What chances? answered the refrigerator. *He's only being* friendly—*you can hear it in his voice. Tell him so he doesn't feel like he has to mollycoddle you or set up any more mercy dates.*

". . . catching a movie with Peter Chernin."

Immediately his anal sphincter tightened in response to his guts turning to water. *Never in a million years, huh, smartass? Son of a bitch didn't waste a fucking minute.*

"Oh. Well. Another time." *Smile, you sap. Why shouldn't she go out? She's beautiful and smart. Any man would want to . . .*

She pushed away from the counter and washed her hands.

He watched her, basking in the sight of her hands moving gracefully around and over each other, making love. The smell of her—a flower mixed with citrus—triggered a fantasy of her lean body moving over him in candlelight. He looked down and immediately stuck his hands in the pockets of his sports jacket, using the flaps to cover his erection.

She dried her hands and checked her watch. "Christ on a bike, I've got to get back."

He followed her for a few steps wondering if he looked part basset hound. He felt like one. Then, they waved goodbye, strained smiles on their faces—two emotional train wrecks heading in opposite directions on the same track.

Iris kept getting sucked down and pushed up, in and out of somnolence. Even in her unconsciousness, it infuriated her to know that the stupid nurse had snowed her with drugs. It wasn't like she'd been biting and kicking or anything like that.

As an added torment, she was caught in one of those frustrating molasses type dreams that came in installments, like a miniseries on TV.

The first part of the dream had been about waking up and seeing her mother and Hannah trying to cut through her oxygen tubing with a pair of kindergarten scissors. The second part put her standing among people crowded around a grave, looking in. Looking down into the six-foot hole, she saw her father, floating in the air with tubes attached to him—like in the book, *Coma.* Her mother was kneeling at the edge of the grave with the kindergarten scissors in hand, slashing at his air tube.

The third part of the dream-turned-nightmare was different from the rest—more detailed, and somehow more real. There was a figure sitting at her father's grave, except she couldn't tell who it was—or even *what* it was in terms of gender. At first she thought the figure was knitting, using her father's IV lines as yarn, but as she walked closer to the window, she saw the person wasn't knitting at all—they were using a needle to poke holes through the IV. Iris squinted and tapped on the glass. She hoped whoever it was would stop what they were doing. But they didn't.

She tapped again, louder this time. Her father woke. Returned to life, he tried to get free of the ropes which held him to his coffin. She could read his thoughts. He wanted to get away. He wanted to make the person leave him alone. Frantic in her need to help him, Iris pounded her fists against the window.

That was when the person turned around and snarled at her. Except it wasn't a person at all; it was the Mick Jagger thing. The nightmare.

A rat scurried over her bare foot on its way toward Cynthia's bed, where it joined in with the five or six tarantulas crawling up the sheets toward the nurse's face. When they began scurrying in and out of her mouth and ears, Iris got back into bed, closed her eyes, and waited for the movie to end.

Miriam sat at her husband's bedside thinking about her future. Her mouth was dry and she was trembling. At first, she marveled at the hole she had dug for herself, then despaired over the depth of it and wondered how she would ever climb out. A decision about what she was going to do would have to be made quickly.

Across from her, Hannah sat dozing in her chair, still holding her half-full cup of coffee. She looked worse than death.

Mimi leaned over Gordon, and curled her fingers comfortably around his arm. His IV line, which had tangled around her hand, felt cool. She wondered briefly if the liquid felt cool on the inside of his veins as it dripped into his bloodstream. Idly twining her fingers around the plastic line, she also wondered how much he remembered about what had happened.

She raised her eyes and was startled to see Gordon staring at her, as if he saw her from very far away. His face was full of accusation and anger. A chill went through her body and she swallowed hard.

"What?" she asked in a harsh whisper. "What is it? Why are you looking at me like that?"

He attempted to talk around the tube, grew frustrated, and shook his fists against the bed.

"Stop it!" she murmured in a desperate, hushed voice. "Stop doing this." She brought her fists to the sides of her face and then bit the back of her hand. "I'm through pretending it's all fine. I'm tired. Do you understand what I mean? I feel like I'm losing my mind."

On the other side of Gordon's bed, Hannah stirred and woke with a start. At once she tried to stand, but her knees buckled, and she landed back in the chair with a hard jolt. "Mimi? What's wrong? What happened?"

"Nothing," Mimi said determinedly, her face streaked with tears. "I've . . . I'm tired." She turned her back on the bed and walked to the medical supply cabinet. There she found a clean washcloth and held it under the faucet.

Hannah attempted standing again, only slower. She gained her feet, then walked to where Mimi was wiping her face and neck with the damp cloth. "What do you want me to do for you?"

"Nothing," the dark-haired woman said, ignoring Hannah's outstretched hand. "Go sit down and finish your coffee."

She closed her eyes and tried to shut out the vision of her husband's eyes boring into her. Mimi took a deep breath. "For once," she said bitterly, "I'll take care of it all by myself."

* * *

Entering Dr. Hersh's room, Adele was focused solely on getting to the call light release. The body falling to the floor in front of her didn't register until the ground shook under her feet. She had noticed, however, that Hannah missed cracking her head on the corner of the bed by less than an inch.

Yelling for assistance, Adele did a quick ABC check on the woman—Airway: open. Breathing: irregular, shallow. Cardiac: thready, faint pulse. The peculiar bitter smell that came from the pores of all the M. Plague patients was unmistakable, as well as the dusky pallor and cool, clammy quality of the skin. While Adele waited for the gurney to arrive, Hannah completed the M. Plague profile by urinating and vomiting large amounts of fluid simultaneously.

When she came back from the cafeteria and was told what had happened, Mimi seemed locked in an odd sort of controlled hysteria. Calmly she wrung her hands and pinched her neck, all without a whimper. She clung to Adele as if she were some kind of savior.

Adele practiced the first principle she'd ever learned in nursing school: In order to lessen anxiety in the walking wounded, assign them simple tasks. She ordered Mimi to spend fifteen minutes at a time in her husband's and her daughter's rooms, talking them through their sedation.

Halfway through her first potassium-laced IV, Hannah regained consciousness and looked around the room.

"You're lucky," Adele said, finishing her physical exam. "Your lungs aren't too bad."

Hannah licked her lips. "Where's Mimi?"

"I sent her in with Iris and Gordon." Adele draped the skirt over a hanger and hung it next to the pink silk blouse. The skirt was of a delicate flower pattern with gold threads woven through the material. The outfit seemed grossly out of character—more feminine and relaxed than the elegant, tailored outfits the White Swan usually wore.

Mirek came in and handed her Hannah's shoes and purse.

She started to give the purse back to him to give to Mimi, but changed her mind. After Hannah drifted off again, she took it into the bathroom and dumped the contents out onto a towel.

A key chain with a white plastic swan charm attached played leash to a half dozen keys. She wrapped them in a length of toilet paper to render them jingle-free and placed them in the bottom of her pocket. In her other pocket she put a Tylenol bottle in which was a variety of powder-coated pills. The rest of the contents—a purse-size spray of Chanel No. 5, several samples of perfume, a gold compact, a wallet, a credit card case, a bottle of foundation, blush and lipstick—all went back into the purse.

Returning the purse to the closet, she hoped Mimi would be upset enough to forget about details like Hannah's keys. She closed the closet door and went back to her patient, who was attempting to get out of bed.

"Where do you think you're going?"

"I've got to get to Mimi before she ... I've got to go home."

Adele recognized the look of confusion that was part of the M. Plague patient profile. She drew up two and a half milligrams of droperidol—a tranquilizer she favored using. "You can't go home, Hannah, you're ill. You've got to stay in the hospital for a while. Don't worry about Mimi; she's better off than you are right now."

"I've got to go home." Hannah threw a leg over the side rail. "Get organized."

Adele pushed her leg back and injected the clear medication in the port of the IV, watching it make swirls in the saline. "You don't need to organize anything except your health."

Hannah lay back, her blond hair, dark with sweat, sticking to the sides of her face. The overall effect was to make the ice-blue eyes more piercing, and the hollow cheeks even more sunken.

Conversely to her appearance, a smile slipped over Hannah's lips. "I know you."

"Oh yeah, what do you know?" Adele said casually, giving her patient a sidelong glance.

"You're clever." The woman's hand made its way to the side of Adele's face. The long manicured fingers stroked her cheek.

"What else do you know?" Adele kept her voice low and calm. She placed the woman's hand back under the covers.

"You're in love with the cop."

The droperidol was beginning to hit . . . her enunciation was going soft and her heart rate dropped out of the fast lane. She seemed to have forgotten about needing to go home. The medication wouldn't last long, though. It rarely did with type A's.

"I feel dizzy." Hannah looked at her accusingly. "What have you done?" She made an attempt at sitting up and collapsed back onto the bed. "You don't understand. None of you do. I need to be with Mimi. She's not herself. I'm afraid she's going to do something . . . stupid."

"Like what?" Adele asked.

"She's going to try to hurt . . . herself or . . . She's desper . . ." Hannah closed her eyes and dozed off. Adele found a restraining jacket in the linen cabinet. Getting it on the woman wasn't going to be a one-person job. At the window, she scanned the nursing station and the acute rooms for a nurse or tech to help. The place was devoid of either.

She'd started back toward Hannah's bed, when she caught an odd movement from across the hall that made her stop. She looked closer into Dr. Hersh's room.

Dr. Hersh was arching up off his bed. His arms and legs were rigid, as his entire body rhythmically shook in a seizure.

Not bothering to take off her isolation wrap, Adele sprinted across the station and into his room. On the bedside monitor screen was a fine, ragged pattern of ventricular fibrillation.

She couldn't even guess how long it had been going on, because all the monitor alarms, along with the automatic print-out button, had been turned off.

CPR and a long, drawn-out code made no difference in the outcome—Gordon Hersh's luck had run out. He was no longer one of God's Chosen or a candidate for a seat in the senate; he was a permanent absentee voter.

"Get your nondenominational Bible-thumping butt up to Ward Eight," Adele told Roger Wynn, hospital chaplain.

The momentary silence on the other end of the line was almost enough to make her smile. Roger Wynn was a man caught between two extremes in morality—Victorian and the twenty-first century. An anal-retentive by upbringing, the Satanish-looking man was only just beginning to dig out from under the moral codes that plagued the Victorian age.

"What's going on?"

"Dr. Hersh has expired, and his wife needs someone to take her home. Nobody up here has time—I think you're the man for the job."

Through a crack in the door, Adele could see and hear Mimi wailing and falling on her husband's chest. She had seen grief-stricken widows, and she had seen grief-stricken widows—Miriam Hersh was afflicted with something traumatic, but it wasn't grief. It was, Adele guessed, something closer to fear.

Mirek stood by, gingerly patting Mrs. Hersh on the back, tears flowing down his face. In comparison, the boy's grief was more real than the show going on next to him.

"I liked Gordon Hersh," Roger said finally. "He was a good man and a fine doctor. I'm very sorry to hear this." He added, "Is Ms. O'Neil okay?"

His infatuation with the morally challenged nurse was well known to everyone except Roger Wynn.

"She's okay. We just extubated her, but she's not waking

up. Stop by and see her, too; maybe a little shot of religion would boost her into a verbal tirade."

"Tsk. You talk about the ministries as though they were a drug."

"Now Roger, you know better than to get me going on this."

He sighed, silently saying a prayer for the misled heathen. "Okay. I'll be up in five."

Per instructions, Adele waited for the tone before she began leaving her message on Detective Ritmann's voice mail recording. She played with the keys in her pocket, trying to decide whether or not to complain about how officious and arrogant his message sounded.

The tone came. "Hey, it's me. Get rid of your message; you sound like a neurosurgeon. Good news is that Cynthia's breathing on her own. Bad news is that she's still lollygagging around lala land, refusing to wake up.

"Other bad news is that Gordon Hersh just expired, which is extremely bizarre since his doctor gave him a gold star for recovery this morning. That's a little too weird for me, how about you?

"As far as I know, the only people to enter that room were the nurses and techs, Dr. Ingram, Hannah Sandell, and Miriam Hersh."

Down the hall, Adele could see Roger leading Mimi into a vacant patient room. The tiny woman pressed against him so hard he could hardly walk straight. She looked like she'd been drinking.

"Before he went down the tubes, Sandell was scraped off the floor of his room and admitted with a relapse of the plague—just like Gordon. She's not in the greatest of shapes—well, not health-wise anyway, but she's not intubated yet either.

"Miriam Hersh is . . ." She paused, trying to think of how to phrase it. "I can't tell *what* state she's in . . . maybe shock, but not really. Not really grieving or remorseful either. Sort of hysterical, but without the sound turned up. I don't think she's going to make her afternoon appointment with you."

She lowered her voice. "I think Nancy Drew might have to do some serious surveillance soon. Talk to you later." She started to hang up, when she thought of something else.

"And don't call to tell me not to. I hate that."

The receiver was again almost on the hook. "Oh, and by the way . . . did Cynthia ever mention to you what she did behind the Christian Brothers' winery last year?"

Grace Thompson stood over Adele's shoulder pursing her lips, working them in and out. "You'll have to write an incident report in regard to the monitor and ventilator alarms being left on hold."

Adele didn't look up from her charting. "They weren't left on hold, Grace. They were put on hold on purpose."

The Brit bristled. "By whom and for what purpose?"

Adele shrugged. "Wish to God I knew, because then you'd have to go ask *them* to write the incident report, and I could be left in peace to chart so I can get out of this place at a decent hour and not have to charge overtime."

Laden down with several charts, Skip sat in the chair directly behind the head nurse, so that the woman was wedged between him and Adele. "Excuse me," Skip said impatiently. "Could you please move?"

Grace Thompson made a huff over being crowded out from the desk, continuing to harp on Adele. "That monitor was on hold for at least twenty minutes before you noticed Dr. Hersh's ventricular fibrillation."

Adele stopped in her charting and fixed the woman with a stony look that went on forever. "And how, exactly, do you know that, Grace?"

"Well . . ." The Brit hesitated, realizing her error. "I—I saw it on hold when I went to my office."

"So, if you saw it on hold, why didn't *you* go in and take it off hold?"

Skip snickered. The head nurse's morbid fear of having direct contact with sick people was no secret.

"I—I thought you would take care of it. It was your responsibility. You were his nurse, after all."

"I was busy admitting another patient as you well know since you're the one who insisted I take another patient."

"I refuse to engage with you any longer on this matter." The older nurse sniffed. "Please write the incident report and have it on my desk before you leave."

"Oh I will, Mrs. Thompson, believe you me." Adele left the sentence hanging in the air like a command to aim and fire.

"Oh-oh," said Skip, without bothering to look up from his charts.

Adele put her finger to her lips and sat down on Iris's bed.

"Where's my mother?" the girl asked. She was coming out from under the sedation.

Adele shifted uncomfortably. Mimi insisted Iris was in too delicate a physical and mental state to be told about her father.

While the teenager slept, everything possible had been done to ensure she would not learn anything of his death by mistake. The staff had been warned, a notice put in her chart—even the power controls for the television and radio had been removed from her room so there would be no chance she would catch one of the news bulletins about her father's death.

"She's with Hannah," Adele lied. "Hannah is . . ."

"Why are those curtains closed all of a sudden?" Iris pointed to the window between her room and her father's. "And why did someone take the TV control?"

The questions made Adele flinch. Although she'd spent years either withholding information or outright lying to patients for what had been determined as their own good, she didn't like it. Suddenly a part of her now thanked the night nurse for having overmedicated the girl—had she not been sleeping it off, she would have been at least a partial witness to her father's code. "You need to rest, not worry about what goes on in your father's room. And your control was broken, so I sent it to the engineers to be repaired. Anything else you want to know, missy?"

Iris lay back without taking her eyes off the closed curtains. "Sorry." She took a deep breath and let it out. "I had a bad dream, it wigged me out."

Adele sat closer. "What was it about?"

Iris pushed herself up again and sipped some ice water. "I keep dreaming about this monster?"

Adele nodded. "The one that looks like Mick Jagger?"

"Uhn huh. Well, today I think I had a dream that it was in my father's room and it had this knitting needle and it was sticking it into my dad's IV? Then everyone fell into this grave. . . ." The girl stopped. "You won't think I'm crazy if I tell you this?"

"On the contrary," Adele said. "I think you're doing fine."

Cynthia stared at her without saying a word.

"Talk. Blink. Do something so I know you're in there, Cyn. I'm not kidding. Ingram thinks there's been permanent brain damage. He doesn't know that's your normal personality."

She stuck her fingers inside Cynthia's curled fist. "Squeeze my fingers."

Cynthia blinked.

"Not good enough. Squeeze my fingers and talk."

Cynthia blinked and closed her eyes.

"No cigar, babe. Say hello."

Blink. Blink.

"What's that? Am I supposed to be reading Morse Code by blink? Forget it. I want meaningful conversation, Cyn."

Silence. Blink.

Adele called over her shoulder. "Hey Iris!"

"Yes?" the girl answered.

"Want to hear a really funny story about the time Cynthia and I went to the Christian Brothers' winery?"

Cynthia's eyes snapped open. "Up yours." Classic O'Neil— it was barely audible, it was froglike, but it was there.

Adele's eyes filled with tears. "Welcome home, sweetie," she said, "and up yours, too."

SIXTEEN

A REDWINGED BLACKBIRD SANG OUTSIDE THE bedroom window as Adele laced up her running shoes and studied the early evening sky. She figured by the time she ran to Ross Commons, it would be dark enough to break and enter without being seen.

In such a Waspy, wealthy conservative neighborhood as Ross, the residents were, more often than not, overly protective of their territory. Most of the mansions in Ross had fifteen-foot-high iron gates with electronic eyes, sound systems, and surveillance cameras. Prisoners of their own riches, the inhabitants of these showplaces activated 911 over the slightest thing . . . like if the paperboy stopped to tie his shoelaces, or if the leaves dared to fall on their lawn without permission.

At her feet, Nelson whined.

"What's a matter boy, huh?" Furtively, she looked around, to make sure they were alone. Her manner of speaking to the dog would have been condemned by most Marin County animal psychiatrists as being dysfunctional and harmful to the pooch.

"Is Nelsey Welsey confoozed that mommy's going running again? It's okay Bun-Bun. Mommy's doing some snoopy detective work."

From under the top shelf of her clothes closet she pulled a plastic shopping bag filled with wigs of various colors and lengths. She chose one closest to Hannah's, put it on, and made one last check: she left the room, and several minutes later, walked back in. Nelson cocked his head, then crouched and barked *at* her, not *with* her.

"That's good enough for me," she said, and headed out.

The bells of St. John's chimed seven times. She didn't have to work the next day, and, at the moment, there was nothing more pressing than making some major breaches of security. Keeping her visor pulled low, she entered Ross Commons and turned right onto Shady Lane—a street of mansions.

Adele slowed her pace to a jog in order to check out the addresses that were visible. There weren't many. In their struggle for simultaneous ostentation and obscurity, the wealthy seldom advertised their mansion numbers. She thought of opening one of the numberless mailboxes to check the addresses, but couldn't be sure if they were rigged with some sort of internal alarm system.

Embedded in the stone gate of one gothic style castle, she spied an oxidized copper plate bearing the Roman numerals XXII. Counting by twos, the house that should have been thirty-six was dark. A good sign.

She turned sharply into the driveway, moving onto the grounds through a gap in the tall hedges that surrounded the house. Without leaving the shadows, she sprinted up a set of steps to the wraparound porch. The hand-painted tile above the front door featured a white swan in a pond, erasing any doubt she had about who lived there.

Adele checked the key ring and singled out the front door key and then another, smaller, oddly shaped key. It was, she knew, the key to a relatively rudimentary and archaic alarm system. Whether or not there was a backup system was one of the gambles she was willing to take. Considering the psychological aspects of someone who would depend on such an outdated alarm for security, she seriously doubted there would be.

During her junior year in high school, she worked part-time for a security systems business. By the time she began her senior year, she had learned the working details of every basic security system and a few of the unconventional ones as well. She also came to know that certain types of people consistently ordered certain types of security.

Without hesitation (she believed wholeheartedly in the old adage "she who hesitates is lost"), she inserted the door key, let herself inside, began the countdown on her stopwatch, and searched for a black box with a blinking red light. There was no doubt in her mind that Hannah Sandell would have the alarms set to go off at sixty seconds.

At fifty-one seconds, she found the box inside a counter cupboard at the entrance to the kitchen. She disarmed the alarm and set about turning on all the lights. After conducting a quick search for a second security system, Adele pulled a pair of black kid gloves from the back of her leggings and began the search of the house.

Whether Hannah's neighbors were the types who might stop over to borrow a cup of Beluga caviar or a spare magnum of Dom Pérignon, was another chance she was willing to take.

Adele marveled over the sunken living room, the parquet floors, and four-foot-tall alabaster vases on plinths of black marble. The overall effect of the decorating style was both elegant and relaxed, albeit somewhat sterile.

The library was her favorite room. Unique in its design, the six-tiered, built-in bench and shelf system could be climbed all the way to the high ceiling. At any point, one could sit comfortably to read or browse among the shelves.

The master bedroom and the mirrored workout room were connected by a walk-through closet the size of Rhode Island. Adele gaped. Never in her life had she seen so many clothes and shoes belonging to just one person. Every blouse, every shoe, every dress was perfectly arranged, pressed, and dry-cleaned and held a faint scent of lily of the valley.

She tried to imagine having to choose and coordinate an outfit each day from the magnificent collection, and couldn't. Her sparse, mismatched collection of Goodwill creations was more than she could deal with as it was.

Adele recalled Hannah's invitation to weed through her drawers and closets and snickered. It had been a creative come-on, she had to admit. Certainly much more creative than men's "Come upstairs and see my etchings on CD ROM." This was definitely a gay person's come-on: "Come and let me take you into my drawers and closet so I can free you from yours."

In the spacious bedroom, the contents of the bedside tables were all perfectly organized—a concept she found odd. In reflection on her own bedside table drawers, loaded with every bit of junk and clutter known to woman—fingernail clippings, Nelson's shed whiskers, glass beads, bits of broken jewelry, an unopened melatonin bottle, disfigured globs of melted candles, I Ching coins, matches, a dried sprig of California pitcher sage, loose ibuprofen and Tylenol, several 12L scalpels, a hemostat, a Swiss Army knife, and a dusty condom packet—anyone snooping through them would think she was either a conjuring witch or a Lorena Bobbitt trainee.

The bathroom fixtures gleamed as though they'd never known a water spot in all their existence, and the toilet and shower were squeaky clean. "Why is it rich people's houses are always spotless?" Adele addressed her invisible audience and whatever expensive furniture was interested in listening.

Could it be the illegal alien housekeeper who comes in six days a week for four-fifty an hour? replied one of her wealthy and cultured invisible friends, looking at his Rolex. He curtly reminded her she shouldn't tarry; each minute she fooled around was a minute closer to being caught, which was when the platinum wig and the black gloves became a liability rather than an asset.

The most interesting of her finds was a worn business card that had been stabbed through its paper heart and pinned to the desk by the letter opener. She copied the information on the card in her notebook, then flopped down on the California King. It was so firm, she was sure she'd injured herself.

On one corner of the bed—that seemed like it was a half mile from the opposite corner—lay a pair of sewing scissors, the ones with the bird design on the handles. Bits of pink patterned rayon shot with gold thread and a threaded needle lay nearby. It took her notice immediately, only because it was difficult to imagine Hannah Sandell doing her own mending.

Under the bed in a plain, brown cardboard box, was a collection of sex toys. A few she recognized; most were too complicated and bizarre to fathom *what* they might be used for. She held back from picking them up for closer examination out of fear—not of disease, but electrocution. Next to the toy box, away from the rest of the herd, Adele found a pair of size 10 pumps in beige. Picking them up one at a time, she carefully examined them under the desk lamp and then put them back as she'd found them.

Downstairs, the kitchen invited her in for a look. The bright hand-painted tiles, gleaming copper, and polished steel were right out of *Architectural Digest*. Work islands topped with real Italian marble holding a built-in coffee maker, cappuccino maker, pasta maker, bread maker, dehydrator, and water purifier were almost overshadowed by the three ovens, two stoves, and the refrigerator-freezer that took up half a wall.

She opened the refrigerator and laughed; in the acreage of sparkling glass shelves was a two-pound cello bag of carrots, one withered apple, three bottles of Pellegrino water, a cheap bottle of Gallo White Zinfandel, six European chocolate bars, a jar of capers, one half loaf of rye bread, and a jar of mayonnaise with the purchase receipt still stuck to the side.

Almost on reflex, she reached for a carrot.

The invisible man with the Rolex gasped. *What do you think you're doing, Detective Monsarrat?*

Adele pulled her hand back and closed the door. He was

right—there was an outside chance Hannah might suffer from the same paranoid affliction as other rich folk and count the carrots. Collecting herself, she went into the informal dining room. At the bottom of a small built-in cabinet, she found a manila envelope full of loose photographs concealed between the folds of an Irish linen tablecloth.

It wasn't until she'd started going through the old black-and-white photos and yellowed Polaroids that it dawned on her that the house was devoid of personal artifacts. No framed photographs, or humorous notes and sentimental postcards held to the refrigerator by eccentric food magnets were in evidence. No mementos of achievements, not even a theme among the art which adorned the walls. It was good art, but antiseptic—still lifes of flowers and fruit. Now that she thought about it, even the library seemed fairly generic. There was nothing that might give someone snooping around a deeper insight into the heart and soul of the person who lived there.

Adele spread out the photos on the Persian rug. In one, a younger Miriam Hersh smiled shyly at the camera while a serious Hannah knelt at her feet, untying the pretty woman's hiking boots. Behind them was a long, beautiful valley. On the back was the notation "Me and my baby—1st camping trip—Hudson Valley."

Adele picked up a black-and-white with curled, yellowed edges. A smiling man wearing a sailor's uniform from some foreign country held a towheaded toddler. The somber child frowned at the camera, a bit of the defeated about the slump of her small shoulders. In a careful hand was written "Ulla and Daddy. Easter."

Another, taken a few years later, was of the same towheaded child standing barefoot in a gutter outside a rundown tenement house. The somber expression had been replaced with one of angry defiance.

The last photo she studied was one of a big, bleary-eyed woman sitting on a bar stool holding a cigar in one gaudily bejeweled hand and a bottle of beer in the other. She was leaning toward the camera, her more than ample breasts not well covered by a too small halter top of polka-dot material. Her platinum hair was pulled back into a ponytail. Sparkling earrings dangled past her chin almost touching her collarbone. Her mouth was a full-lipped, sensuous red gash set in a pale white face. The light eyes, which showed up red in the camera's flash, had been heavily outlined in black.

The white short shorts did not look bad on her despite her size. Down at the end of long legs, the feet, which appeared too small for the rest of her, were shod in black espadrilles—the kind where the laces crisscrossed and tied halfway up the calf. The back of the photo read simply "Mama—Brooklyn."

In the library, Adele climbed the tiers, scanning the collection of books. Classics, fairy tales, Russian, Scandinavian, and English histories, contemporary fiction, sci fi, mysteries, a whole tier devoted to architectural design, a wall of biographies of famous—and infamous—women, books written by women for women, and, on the shelf closest to the ceiling, were psychology books about lesbianism and histories of women's struggles for equality.

Thirty minutes later, Adele turned off the lights and reset the alarm. On the run back, the list of events from the previous forty-eight hours used her mind as a playground, jumping from one swing to the next. But, like the ace of spades, the piece of strangeness that kept turning up as the top card was Iris's nightmare Mick Jagger.

Passing Tamalpias Theater on Magnolia Avenue in Larkspur, a flash of a thought caused her to execute a sharp hairpin turn and pick up her pace.

Ahead, the bright lights of Ellis beckoned.

She entered the back stairwell, taking the steps two at a time. On the third-floor landing Skip sat cross-legged in the corner smoking a cigarette. She greeted him with a smile.

Skip frowned and then put his hand to the side of his face.

"Shit, what did you do to your hair?" he whispered, staring at her head. "You look like hell. I didn't even know who you were at first."

Her hand followed his eyes. The wig! She'd forgotten to take off the platinum wig. "Don't you like it?" She patted down the sides. "I thought since you said Hannah was such a knock-out, I'd try something new."

The male nurse covered his mouth. "Oh my God, tell me you didn't really."

"Don't worry, I can dye it black again."

"Jesus!" He got to his feet, still staring at her head, and shuddered.

"Are you working a double?" Adele asked.

He nodded miserably. "My MasterCard is blackmailing me."

"Who have you got on your patient load?"

"Everybody who isn't in isolation. It's my punishment for refusing to take a plague patient."

"Did Mrs. Hersh go home?"

"She spent some time with Iris and then Chaplain Wynn took her home." Skip hesitated. "Ingram talked her into telling the kid about her old man. Poor thing. She's majorly bummed."

Adele's heart sank into her stomach. "Oh man," she said gravely. "Did they sedate her?"

He shook his head. "The kid wouldn't let them. She didn't want any part of her mother either. It about tore *me* up for both of them. The mother was a sorry mess, the kid was a sorrier mess; it was awful.

"You going up?" He paused. ". . . looking like that?"

Adele put her arm through the nurse's and nodded. "Yeah. Maybe it'll cheer somebody up."

Adele went immediately to what, until recently, had been Dr. Hersh's room. She breathed a sigh of relief—it was still vacant, although it had already been cleaned. Her jaw tight-

ened in disappointment when she saw the wastebaskets had
been emptied. She next looked inside the sharps box to see
if it had been replaced. It hadn't.

Internally rejoicing, she took the container to the dirty
utility room and placed it and her wig inside a large red isolation laundry bag. With a Magic Marker, she wrote M.
PLAGUE—SAVE FOR INSPECTION across the side and left it in
a corner. It was a well-known fact that nurses never threw
away anything that had the word SAVE written on it, even if
it sat for six months gathering mold.

The force with which Iris threw herself into her arms almost knocked her over when she entered the room.

"My dad." The girl sobbed piteously. "My dad died,
Adele."

"I know, honey." She rocked the girl in her arms and tried
not to cry at the sound of her anguish. "I am so sorry."

"Why didn't you tell me before?" Iris pulled back, her
face full of betrayal and anger, yet not willing to break
physical contact. "I thought you would tell me the truth."

"I wanted to, but I wasn't allowed." Adele felt Iris's eyes
holding hers. "I'm sorry. Your mom was afraid you'd . . .
she didn't think you were well enough to handle it."

Iris pushed herself into the protection of Adele's arms
again. For a long time while the girl cried, Adele stroked her
head and rocked her. She said nothing to the girl, who was
still too raw with grief to hear anything she might have said.

When the sobs turned to whimpers, there came a rustling
noise from the other side of the room.

Both Adele and Iris directed their attention to Cynthia's bed.

Looking bleary, the nurse propped herself up on one
elbow.

"Poor Mr. Oldass," she said in a hoarse whisper. "I'm
sorry, too." Cynthia fell back, too weak to hold her body up.
"Mr. Oldass was an okay dad."

* * *

Adele agonized for all of two minutes over the problem of walking home with a bright red plastic bag that had DANGEROUS BIOHAZARD printed all over it in stark white letters.

Wrapping the bag holding the sharps box inside a bath blanket, she arranged the wig at the opening and carried the odd-looking infant out of the hospital, smiling at the security guard. She willed herself to glow like a new mother.

At the front lobby doors, an elderly woman—already cooing—craned to have a peek at the baby. Before Adele could stop her, she'd pulled back part of the blanket and gotten a glimpse of red plastic and a black hole rimmed with lots of blond hair. The cooing turned to a loud scream.

The security guard, who'd been watching the scene, came running. "What's the problem here?" he demanded, grabbing for his nightstick. Adele knew the type . . . small dick, big stick.

"My little Joey Bob here is the only hirsute thlipsencephalic alive in the United States today," Adele said in a tone of motherly pride. "The doctors say it's to be expected if you take drugs and practice self-abuse during pregnancy like I did. Why, my boy is going to be in medical journals!"

Embarrassed and horrified, the guard and the old woman silently backed off while she hurried out the door with her tragic bundle of hair.

She could barely wait for Cynthia to recover so they could both get short of breath in hard laughter over the story.

In her driveway under the garage light, she shook the contents of the sharps box onto a plastic tarp and sorted through the contents with a curved long-handled hemostat.

There was a moderately large assortment of blood-encrusted scalpel blades, suture needles, IV catheters, one half-eaten Milky Way bar, a hundred empty glass medicine vials, and at least twenty syringes of the insulin, tuberculin, and intermuscular varieties.

Three quarters of the way through the biohazardous medical debris, she clamped onto a syringe that was different from the rest. She'd never seen one like it used at Ellis by either the lab or the nurses. Placing the bandit syringe inside a clean olive jar, she put the rest of the medical waste back into the box.

She wondered if Tim would mind her calling him at home, thought better of it, and paged him instead. On the border between the boomers and the new generation, she still could not bring herself to call a boy.

SEVENTEEN

RULLI'S WAS A EUROPEAN CAFE THAT SERVED UP lousy coffee, great pastries, and a whole lot of Old World charm. It was one of Adele's self-treats to sit at a window table and watch the goings-on in downtown Larkspur.

Tim slipped the olive jar into one of his jacket pockets, and opened one of the two envelopes she'd handed him—it was the one with the page of rather nefarious information about Ulla Nyquist, aka the White Swan. She could tell from his lack of expression that he wasn't impressed.

Then he opened the second envelope. His eyebrows shot up, and in true surprise, he said: "Holy shit!" as he read down the lists of names. Adele thought there might have been a touch of awe in his expression when he finally folded the papers and put them back into the envelope.

"Do you know who these people are?" he asked in a low voice, scanning the surrounding tables.

Adele pursed her lips. "Well, two of them are household names—that is, if you read the paper or listen to National Public Radio on the weekends. Those are the only ones I recognized."

"These are high organized crime people, Adele, some of the deadliest in the business. There are a few in here who masquerade as Washington power brokers. One of them used to be a top CIA officer, another is connected to a White House chief of staff."

"Why would he have them?"

"Oh, I'd imagine he used them as sort of inducements

from time to time." Tim sighed. "It might explain a few things about why he was at the office the night he died."

"The info on Sandell shouldn't be too hard to verify. You're sure this is Fromer's handwriting?"

"Check it out yourself."

He looked upwards, as if imploring heavenly aid. "Are you going to tell me how you knew where to find these?"

Adele shook her head after the manner of a petulant child.

He adjusted his jacket and regarded her with half a smile. "Okay then, are you going to share your game plan with me?"

She shook her head again.

"Are you in your Nancy Drew mode now?"

She nodded. He laughed. There was silence for a beat or two.

"I'm serious, Adele. Now is the time to lather up your toast points. Why don't you tell me what you've got in mind?"

"Naw," she said, watching Magnolia Avenue. Across the street, a young couple paused for a passionate kiss in the doorway of an insurance office. "The Polaroid is still developing. I'll tell you when I've got something to tell."

He arched an eyebrow. "You mean like when you're face-to-face with some psycho holding a scalpel to your throat?"

"I'm smarter now," she said, a tiny stir of temper rising over his reference to an incident that had taken place a year before. "I'll never get caught like that again." She narrowed her eyes, sending not quite daggers, but needles. "And thank you so much for your lack of confidence; it's so reassuring, Timothy."

He sat forward and their hormones went wild, both extremely aware of how close his face was to hers. Adele covered her nipples with her sweater.

"I know lots of cops who've said the same thing," he said, and touched the back of her hand. It seemed to her to be a token of friendship touch. "They're all dead now."

They fell silent.

"Did I tell you that I spoke briefly to Mrs. Hersh this morning?" he asked.

"No. When?"

"Early. She called to ask if we could meet later than three. I agreed, and figured I could get away with asking a few questions right away." Tim crossed his arms. "She was nervous as a cat, but she kept her stories straight, I have to hand her that much. She seems jumpy around the issue of Fromer's death, so I pushed her a little. She admitted that Dr. Hersh thought they were having an affair. She says she wasn't but Hersh wasn't having any part of it."

"She's telling you the truth about that," Adele interrupted. "I overheard an argument they had." She made a face. "Plus I really don't think Fromer was her type."

"So you don't think she was having an affair?"

Adele held up a finger. "I didn't say that, Detective. I think she was, but not with Fromer."

"Sandell?" he asked, as though it were the next logical choice.

She nodded and gazed out of the window, thinking of the expression on Mimi's face as she cared for her daughter. Then she thought of Mimi's letter to Hannah and her reaction to Gordon's death. "Boy, I don't know. There sure are a lot of pieces missing." She paused and resumed looking out the window.

The kissing couple had moved on and was replaced by a trio of giggling teenaged girls talking loudly. They reminded her of Iris and she wondered how long it would be before the girl would heal from her wounds and resume a normal life.

Her sad expression made him think he'd offended her. In an effort to break the descending mood, he suddenly reached out and put a hand on each side of her face, holding her head so she couldn't move. His voice boomed over the cafe, trembling dramatically.

"Dear God, Doris! You haven't rented the children out

again? You know how those medical experiments upset their little systems."

Several people at nearby tables stopped sipping or nibbling and turned in the direction of the unfolding interpersonal drama.

Adele lowered her eyes. "I couldn't help it, Malcolm. It was the most money yet, and they'll only have to keep them in isolation for two months this time—just to make sure the experimental drugs work."

There was dead silence and then a harried-looking woman with two young, very assertive children called out: "Where do I sign them up?"

The whole cafe broke up in laughter.

Only in Marin, thought Adele, could such irreverent, impromptu comedy routines be so well received.

Hannah lay on her side. As soon as her eyes focused, she was aware of a plastic emesis basin resting against her face. Immediately, she used it, relieving herself of more bile.

A pretty face floated over her for a minute, removed the basin to the sink, and reappeared, observing her with concern. "Are you okay?" said a gentle voice—the bedside nurse voice.

She nodded. "I want my clothes."

Linda slid a cool hand under her back and readjusted her body so it was more comfortable. The motion was effortless and fluid. "Why do you want your clothes?"

"I need to go home," Hannah answered, wishing the trembling in her arms and legs would stop.

"Yeah, me too," Linda said dryly, "but I can't right now, and neither can you. You should try and rest."

After the door closed, Hannah relaxed, pressing her cheek against the cool pillowcase. She had to think of something other than the smell of sickness and death. She had to concentrate on getting home. Mimi. Where was Mimi?

Her fingers went to the pendant hanging from her chain. The Chilean five-peso coin was a recent gift from Mimi. It had been expertly chiseled so that only the symbol and the word *Libertad* remained inside the coin's rim. She brought the pendant closer to her eyes and studied the figure: a winged woman with arms outstretched to the sky. Around her wrists were manacles which had been broken.

According to Mimi, it was a symbol of the freedom of women. For her it meant more—it signified something well crafted and true. It had required a steady hand to chisel out each tiny letter and detail. The feel of it momentarily transported her away from the pain and nausea. She took a deep breath and coughed up blood-tinged phlegm, which she spat into the basin.

The nurse would be back soon. Panic, that anguish she had known only a few times in her life, cut through her brain like an ice pick and forced her over the side rails. On legs she no longer felt, she inched away from the bed, taking extreme care not to stretch the wires or tubing which attached her to the monitor and the IV. She made it as far as the closet. Ignoring the shafts of pain hurtling around her head, she was pulling her skirt over her hips when the nurse rushed in and asked what she thought she was doing.

Before she could manage an answer, the pain, followed by a black nothingness, claimed her once again.

At eleven, Adele settled into bed with both of her substance addictions—a bowl of plain popcorn, and a teaspoonful of peanut butter. She licked up half the peanut butter, savoring every bud of flavor and, thus buoyed, called Ward 8.

Linda Rainer answered in the exhausted voice of one who was carrying a heavy cross and just wanted to be crucified to get it over with.

"How're my girls in eight-oh-two?"

"Iris is still a mess. I had to change her pillow twice. Emotional kid. Chaplain Wynn is up here with her now. Her mother has called twenty times, but Iris refuses to talk to her.

"As far as Cynthia goes, I'm having a hard time getting used to her being so . . . inert. Otherwise she's fine. Just very quiet."

"What about Sandell?"

"Sick, but not over the edge. I had to put the restraining jacket back on her; she got out bed and was already half-dressed by the time I got in the room."

In the background, Adele could hear call lights going off.

"Noticed you're not scheduled for the next two days," Linda continued. "Want to work night shift? We're really short for nights."

"We're always short, Linda." Adele sighed. "I may act like a ergasiomaniac, but that stems from my thassophobia. I need a couple of days off so I can get reacquainted with my dog. I've been working so much lately, that when I do make it home, he thinks I'm a prowler."

"The FBI should posthumously award Fromer the Medal of Honor," said Tim, sounding tired. She'd called him at his office and was speechless when he answered. Talk about your average ergasiomaniac.

"Every name on that list is a major league mob man."

Chin resting on her knee, Adele held the phone to her ear with her shoulder and rubbed sesame oil into the tiny spaces between her toes.

"There are a few people on this list who the FBI had lost through the cracks. The agencies have been looking for them for years."

"But that isn't where the bullet hole came from," she said, and accidentally drooled on her knee. She sat up and wiped it off with her towel.

"Those guys don't shoot dead men. I doubt that they knew anything about this list, because if they had, Fromer wouldn't have been around to get the M. Plague. Fromer was going after it because he knew the cops were going to start looking around. He couldn't afford to have that list found or for anybody to know he was connected with the Organization."

"But that still doesn't tell us who put the bullet hole through Fromer's neck, does it?" she asked tauntingly.

"Gee," he said sarcastically, "I thought you could tell *me* that, Monsarrat."

"I could," she said seriously.

He waited in silence.

"But I think you should find out on your own."

He laughed, wondering what she was wearing to bed. He intuited it was white and cotton and smelled of clean laundry.

"Did you ever look up Saludo and Greta Nyquist?"

"Oh my God, Monsarrat." He shook his head, amazed at her impertinence. "Just what are your balls made out of—granite?"

"Stainless steel," she said and chuckled. "So, what did you get on them?"

"Saludo was a mobster. Not big time, but no small change either. He dabbled in a little of everything except drugs. He retired to Palm Springs about five years ago and died last July of a stroke.

"I did a little checking around and came up with his attorney's name. The old geezer left most of his dough to his sister and her kids. The rest he left to Ulla Nyquist."

"How much did Hannah get?" Adele asked, working the oil into the area she considered the ugliest part of her body—her elbows.

"Half a mil."

Adele whistled, moving the oil around the second ugliest part of her—her knees. For a half second, she thought of asking Tim over for a nightcap, got into wondering exactly what a nightcap was, and then snapped out of the temporary lapse into lust.

"What about Greta?"

"Greta Nyquist is more intriguing. She was a prostitute with a few reels to her credit, mostly loops—the three-minute kind you see in the backroom booths at adult video stores for a quarter. Really down and dirty.

"Disappeared without a trace about five years back. NYPD were glad to see her go, and nobody filed a missing person. She surfaced—literally—in San Francisco Bay two years ago. ID was made, death was ruled a suicide, and her daughter—who claimed she had not seen or heard from her mother for over ten years—was notified. The remains were cremated. End of Greta Nyquist."

There was a long pause. The thought that he'd put her to sleep crossed his mind.

When she finished writing, she asked, "So Tim, tell me, why is it you never have any quarters?"

Exhausted, Adele put the assortment of Hannah's pills back into the Advil bottle. She'd matched them to the photos in her *Police Guide to Common Drugs* book. It was all legal and boring kind of stuff: Motrin, Aleve, Benadryl, Zovirax, Lasix, OTC diet pills, and Xanax.

She dropped her "brilliant ideas" notebook on the floor next to the bed and turned out the light. Nelson backed himself over to the other side of the bed, dragging his Mickey Rug with him. Within minutes he was snoring like a full-grown man.

Sleep did not come so easily for her. In the darkness she lay awake staring at the vague, monsterlike outline of Nelson's huge head. Like a pinball, her thoughts bounced around from subject to subject. After a while they came to rest on Kitch Heslin.

"Where do I go from here, Kitch?"

The white-haired detective leaned back in his swivel chair, making it squeak. The sound was as familiar to her as her own voice. *Do just like I told you,* he said in his round, calm tone. *Start with the basic motivations: love, hate, sex, money, power, sometimes freedom.*

Move to logistics, timing, and check for cracks in the plaster. Put yourself in the other's shoes. Make a plan and start asking questions. Be assertive, but don't get caught.

It had been Lesson One in the long line of endless things he'd taught her.

She turned on the light again and picked up the notebook. At the top she wrote MOTIVATIONS/DETAILS and started making notes of everything she knew so far.

When she was done, she sat on the edge of her bed and studied the page for a long time. The answer was hiding in the clues like a snake hides in the grass.

"It's coming," she whispered to Nelson finally. "It's beginning to take a shape."

An hour later Adele stood on the side of a hill a quarter of a mile away from the Hersh residence, a pair of small but powerful binoculars held to her eyes. She imprinted the layout of the place in her mind and made some quick conclusions. Sliding down through the tall, dry grass and the packed dirt to the street, she became just another runner out for a night jaunt as she ran the streets surrounding the house. No one would have thought anything of it unless they'd watched her carefully—noticing how she searched every detail of the surrounding grounds.

It was her fourth time around the northeast corner of the house when she veered briskly to her left, took a slight hurdle over a low concrete ledge, and scrambled up a short, steep lawn and through a narrow space where the wrought iron fence met a stone pillar. It had been the least daunting entrance she could find.

She circled the house, praying to the trees for anything that might signal Mimi's presence on the ground floor. For a while she moved silently through the still, dark air, examining the house. Her eyes moved slowly over every window, every deck and balcony. No motion sensors. No hidden surveillance cameras.

She crawled toward the back of the house, making her way to the lowest window.

Inside, Mimi sat on the floor of what appeared to be a fancy study or library. There was a brandy snifter half-filled with a dark amber liquid on a low coffee table beside her. The woman was huddled, her head almost touching her knees. In the light coming from the fireplace, she rocked herself gently.

Adele crept to a window that was closer to where Mimi sat, until faint sounds coming from within the house caused her to stop and listen. Only a few inches from the window, she fought the desire to put her ear to the glass.

Mimi bolted upright and the noise stopped. Adele stepped back quickly, away from the light falling from the window. In that split second, she saw the revolver in Mimi's hand, its chrome finish gleaming dully.

The woman lifted the snifter to her mouth and took several large gulps worthy of a longshoreman. She replaced the glass on the table, her eyes going to the window. Adele shrank back farther, burying herself inside a large juniper bush that she knew was full of spiders—junipers always were. She just hoped there wouldn't be any black widows in with the mix.

After a few minutes, the faint sounds began again and Adele looked once more into the window. At first she had to strain, but then Mimi's voice rose, until it was almost a constant scream.

"What have I done? What have I done? What have I done. . . ."

Adele backed up a few feet and listened to the mournful sound until a plump, dark spider crawled off her hair and across her mouth. Instinctively she spit, shook herself like a person gone berserk, and ran.

EIGHTEEN

SHE HADN'T BEEN INSIDE THE MORGUE EX-
cept for the one time when she delivered a body deprived of
its life force by an African art object in the shape of a five-
foot-long spear which that had been shoved through the
skull, temple to temple. She was the one elected to run the
curiously mangled corpse, too conspicuous and horrifying a
sight to be left in the ER, down to the morgue. Making sure
not to scrape the walls with the ends of the spear, she ma-
neuvered the gurney through the halls to the freight elevator
that made an express drop to the basement. She didn't really
get to go all the way inside the morgue and remembered
only that the place seemed spooky and very odoriferous.

The smell was the same. No way anyone could ever forget *that* smell once it had gotten inside the olfactory glands.
The greasy, sweet-rotten smell engulfed her, making her
stomach roll. It was the stench of old blood, decomposed
tissue, and formalin. She was extremely sorry she'd eaten
breakfast.

The long narrow room was lit primarily by hanging surgical lamps; one lamp per steel table. Against one wall was a
seven-foot-high steel cabinet filled with the accoutrements
of a morgue—saws, pruning shears, scalpels, trocars, tubing, plastic specimen bags, and glass slides. The sign taped
to the top of the cabinet read

!DANGER!
PLEASE KEEP MONKEYS OFF THE EQUIPMENT!

She glanced at the steel tables, and got the impression it must have been a very bad night in the ER. Six corpses lay on gleaming tables. All except two were draped with a white sheet.

On one of the corpses left uncovered, the *Y* incisions had been made, ribs cut through and breastplate removed. The scalp had been cut behind one ear, over the top of the head, to behind the other ear, and then pulled away from, and down over the face. The end result was beyond macabre—the inside of the scalp lay folded back, obscuring the face. It looked like the inside of a humongous lower lip fringed with hair.

The dome of the skull had been sawed open, and the brain was displayed. The control center, she thought, the seat of everything that person had been—although she couldn't be sure that the carnage on the table really had been human. It didn't look like anything she recognized as human—except the limbs.

Working over a body at the far end of the room stood a good-looking Japanese-American man dressed only in a face shield, exam gloves, brown Italian loafers with grey socks, and white boxer shorts with bright yellow suns and blue moons printed on them. Over his boxers, he wore a plastic apron that was smeared with blood, Jackson Pollock style.

"Hey, Del!" David Takamoto, the new chief medical examiner of Marin, waved her over with a bloody scalpel.

Adele waved back and gave him a genuine smile. Long ago, David had managed to hang in as one of Cynthia's lovers long enough for Adele to get to know him socially. As it turned out, he proved to be one of the nicest men Cynthia had ever dragged home and violated. Whereas most of Cynthia's men had rough edges on their various personality dysfunctions, "Boxer" Takamoto was almost without snags . . . except perhaps for his odd choice of undress while doing autopsies. Cynthia put it perfectly when she dumped him—"He was too nice."

The smell stopped her about four feet from where he stood working. The body that lay under the glare of the surgical lamps was that of Samuel Fromer. The first thing Adele noticed—other than the smell—was the fact that his mouth was pried open to its maximum. David Takamoto had finished severing the tongue from its base. A dribble of dark—almost black—blood oozed onto the corpse's chin.

"What's up?" David asked, carefully placing the tongue on the scale that hung above the table. She waited until he finished naming the organ and then giving its weight in grams into the microphone that hung from the ceiling.

"I came to pick your brain."

Her statement hung in the air for about three seconds before they both laughed. David pointed his scalpel at the uncovered corpse with the monster hairy lip. "I'd rather you picked that one down there," he said. "Save me some time."

Adele glanced back at the exposed brain and couldn't help but think of a ball of congealed noodles sitting in a white bowl. "Hold on a sec," David said. "Let me finish this and we can talk as long as you want."

Adele watched him work, feeling both repelled and amazed at the science of the postmortem. She knew from watching other autopsies that the heart had been removed first, since it was closest to the top and most likely to give up a cause of death. Then the lungs had been taken and examined, followed by the stomach, intestines, liver, kidneys, adrenals, spleen, lower bowel, internal genitalia, and bladder. Next came the tongue and then the throat structures. The head and brain were usually left for last.

David finished taking out the throat, then took a dozen photos or more of the same. Then he cut through the scalp ear to ear.

Grabbing the hair on the front part of the scalp, he pulled it gently away from the skull and part of the forehead.

Her stomach lurched.

David picked up a saw much like the ones used to cut through plaster or fiberglass casts, turned it on, and sawed a wedge out of the front of the skull.

The smell that filled the air made her hold her breath and take a few steps back. She bumped into the steel table holding the uncovered corpse.

Reaching back to steady herself, her fingers grabbed hold of something cool and slimy. She almost gave herself a whiplash turning around to find the fingers of her right hand holding onto the exposed brain. Wildly she ran to the nearest sink and washed her hands with the bacteriocidal soap provided. Then she washed them again, scraping her fingernails this time.

David lifted out the wedge of skull bone, watching her with amusement. He lowered his face shield again and turned his attention back to the job at hand.

"Okay," he said. "So what do you want to know?" With the proper respect due a human brain, he scooped the organ gently out of the cranial vault and weighed it.

"Did you do the autopsies on all the plague victims?" she asked in a weak voice. She wasn't feeling well.

He set the brain on a small steel side table and waved the scalpel around again. "I did everybody here except the one on the end down there. They're all plague casualties."

"Are you finding anything in common on them?"

"They're all dead." He shrugged. He placed his hand over the dome of the brain and began slicing through it like a meatloaf.

She was surprised to see that the grayish squiggly outside layer, known as the cortex, was only about a half inch thick. Everything else looked like packed lard. She wondered if this was where the expression "fathead" came from. It was one of those moments she was happy to be a vegetarian.

"See this?" He motioned toward a kidney. He pushed a large magnifying glass that was attached to the table by a flexible arm toward her and nodded. "Take a look."

Adele flipped on the halo light and positioned the magnifier directly above the organ. Using the tip of the scalpel, he pointed to a darkened section.

She leaned forward, then moved back in order to focus. The area consisted of blackened, necrotic tissue.

"In each victim," he explained, "the brain, lungs, liver, and kidneys have these diffuse areas of hemorrhage and necrosis."

She studied the damaged tissue closer, a depression settling in over the fact that Cynthia's and Iris's organs had probably undergone similar ravages. "What causes it?"

He went back to his work, took a piece of brain tissue and put it in a bottle of fixative. The rest of the brain he placed in a white plastic container and snapped on the lid. It was another use for Tupperware she doubted was ever mentioned at Tupperware parties.

"Off record?" he said after a moment.

Adele nodded.

"Personally I think it's a hemotoxin. A nonreplicating toxin that only mimics a viral infection. It's more like a cholinesterase inhibitor—like a pesticide. It's harmless in the stomach, but once it's in the system, it causes major damage to the target organs.

"I could be wrong, though. The CDC might find that it's some exotic virus, but it just seems too far off the viral course of communication."

He walked with all the grace of a cat to the table next to the uncovered body, the brain of which bore her fingerprints, and pulled back the sheet. "Take this fellow here for example."

Adele looked into the face of a heavyset middle-aged man who closely resembled Garrison Keillor.

"This man was found approximately eighteen to twenty hours after death on the bathroom floor of his San Francisco apartment. His skull had been cracked open on the rim of the john, and his right wrist was broken from an attempt to break his fall. He sustained a large subdural hematoma.

"To somebody who wasn't looking for it, he would have presented like a straightforward case of a big, clumsy guy who slipped after taking his shower and sustained fatal head injuries."

He held up a finger and cocked his head. "But the San Francisco coroner read the notices sent to every coroner's office in the state describing what we were looking for. Being an exceptionally bright woman, she had a diener put him in the wagon first thing this morning and bring him over for reautopsy. His tissues and blood samples matched the others, with the exception that his hemorrhage is more extensive than the rest."

David held up his scalpel, looking like an Asian version of Sherlock Holmes. "Now as far as we can tell, this guy hadn't had any contact with the original sources."

He shook his head resolutely. "The immunity issue is too selective. If this were an airborne or body fluids transmission, we'd have a major epidemic on our hands."

He pointed at her. "You yourself, Ms. Monsarrat, are a case in point. You've been up to your eyeballs in this shit and you're healthy as an ox. Viruses aren't normally so picky about their host. A host is a host is a host. They'll replicate anywhere they can."

He thought for a minute. "The other sticky wicket is: if this virus was supposed to be initially picked up and carried by the Hersh girl from England, why didn't any of the other people on the aircraft come down with it too? Not one other passenger on that flight suffered from anything more serious than a cold, and everybody knows the air filtration systems on those commercial planes are breeding grounds for viruses."

Absentmindedly, the coroner grabbed the band on his underwear through the plastic apron and snapped it. "Whole planeloads of charter passengers frequently come down with the same nasty virus or bacterial infection. Lawyers love those class action suits."

Respectfully, Takamoto covered the body with the sheet

and moved to the table where the uncovered body lay gray and still in all its Clive Barker-ian, hairy-lipped horror.

"Now here's another interesting case." The medical examiner grasped a handful of hair and pulled the face and scalp back up over the skull—exactly like an elaborate rubber Halloween mask—except it wasn't Richard Nixon or Bill Clinton in rubber, it was Derek—the seventeen-year-old boy they'd tried to save.

"This kid was in perfect health. He didn't have any congenital malformations or . . ."

Adele stopped listening and stood stunned. Uttering a cry, she stepped back from the slab, a cold, prickling sensation settling into her temples. Everything suddenly seemed so *unnatural.* Her composure started to slip, and when she spoke, her voice was far away. "I'm—I'm not going to faint," she said. "I'm a nurse." It seemed like a strange thing to say, and for a minute, she wasn't really sure it was her voice that said it.

David Takamoto's smile turned to an expression of concern. The woman's face had gone from a healthy flush to the color of his tabled subjects.

"Oh yes you are," Dr. Takamoto said in a slightly disgusted yet amused tone as he got ready to catch her.

"No I'm not," she heard herself insist from the other end of a long tunnel. "I'm a nur—"

And then the nurse fainted.

Think about something else, she said to herself. Think about Nelson chewing his rug. Think about Tim's hands. Think about swimming on the backs of dolphins in the Gulf of Mexico.

Adele avoided looking in the mirror as she splashed cool water over her face and ran her fingers through her hair. When she emerged from the rest room, David was waiting for her.

"You okay?" he asked without much doubt she was. Her

color was back, and the spark of shrewd intelligence had returned to her gold eyes.

"Fine, thanks." The fog lifted now that she was upright and moving, but she knew she could not face going back into the morgue. "Listen, I appreciate all the info, David. I'll—I'll . . . call or come by the office in a day or two and ask you some more questions if you don't mind."

"Sure, anytime. It's *always* dead around here."

The main entrance of the Lake Street Apartments smelled of mothballs and frying butter. She avoided breathing through her nose as she checked the names on the mailboxes with the one she'd written in her notebook. Dr. Brian Macy lived in apartment 206.

She found 206 and knocked, pressing an ear against the brass 0. There was nothing but silence from the other side of the door.

She knocked again, and tried the door. Locked.

She was placing a note under the edge of the 2 when the door of 203 was flung open to reveal the backlit figure of a circus gnome.

"What's yer business here, girlie?" The four-foot-ten elf charged into the hall with all the ferociousness of a pit bull, though it was the outfit that got Adele's attention: White blouse hung unevenly over one huge, deformed shoulder and one nonexistent one, the waist of the black-and-white checked skirt was cinched by a red patent leather belt an inch below the armpits. The hem ended three inches above amazingly wide ankles covered in red nubby socks. Fuzzy white rabbit-skin slippers completed the image.

"I'm looking for Dr. Brian Macy?" Adele bit her lip in lieu of collapsing in a fit of crazy-woman laughter.

A bit of the old lady's fierceness subsided. She looked Adele over. "What do you want with him?"

"Well, may I ask who *you* are?"—*and say, didn't I see you in* The Wizard of Oz? she silently added.

"I'm Ophelia Duggan. I own the building. My son Raymond helps me out now that I've got arthritis so bad in the shoulder. . . ." She rubbed her hump.

Adele bit her lip harder. Her thoughts strayed toward unearthly, Fellini-like scenes in which she imagined the father of the woman's child to have a hump on the opposing shoulder and wondered what chances the child of two hunchbacks had for being humpless.

". . . eight apartments," the woman was saying through clicking, ill-fitting dentures.

"Hi," Adele interrupted and stuck out her hand. "I'm Adele Monsarrat and I need to talk to Mr. Macy about a mutual acquaintance. Do you know if he's home?"

"He's not home," Ophelia Duggan said, warily shaking the amazon's hand. She noticed Adele's gold eyes, dropped the woman's hand, and stepped back. Wasn't she telling Ray just the other day that she thought people were getting stranger-looking all the time, even for San Francisco?

"Do you know where he works? Maybe I can catch him at . . ."

"He doesn't work anymore."

"Oh." Adele hesitated. "Well, do you know what time he'll be back? Maybe I can wait downstairs."

"You're going to wait a long time," the gnome said flatly. "He's dead, God rest him. Poor soul laid all night on the toilet floor there with a cracked noggin. It was a mess, I can tell you!"

The woman's words caused Adele to catch her breath. "Oh my God. Listen, Mrs. Duggan, was Dr. Macy tall, sort of fat, with black hair and buggy eyes?"

The landlady held her chin to think. "Well, I don't know about the bug eyes, but he was a big one. Wouldn't call him fat; he was healthy is all. He ate good. "

"How . . . who found him?"

"His boss from the laboratory come by to check on him 'cause he never showed up to work. Couldn't get him to answer his phone neither.

"A hard worker, that boy. Never late with the rent check. The boss knew something weren't right. He come right to my door there and tells me something's wrong, so I let him into the apartment. We found him laying right out on the toilet floor. Cracked his head wide-open on the rim of the john."

The woman made a horrible face and held her nose. "Ugh, I can't tell you what a stinking mess. I don't want to see nothing like that again for all the days I got left, which probably ain't too long now."

After her olfactory experience in the morgue, Adele could relate. "Dr. Macy worked in a laboratory?"

"Down in that Silicon [she pronounced it Silly Cone] Valley," she said. "He makes chemicals for pill companies and things like that there."

"Did you get the boss's name by any chance?"

Mrs. Duggan nodded. "You bet. His phone number, too. Dr. Cornelius." She walked back into her apartment muttering.

Adele, unsure as to whether she should follow, let curiosity be her guide, and stepped into the sunny apartment that initially smelled of cabbage and onions. Then, another stronger smell overpowered her before she went another inch.

Cat stink. The place was alive with cats of every color and size. She guessed there were fifty or more. Seeing her, they began to converge, several of them already sniffing cautiously at her shoes and purse. Just the sheer number of the feline creatures brought up uncomfortable thoughts of rat packs swarming over garbage heaps.

"Here it is," said the tiny woman as she shuffled back into the room. "You copy it down. I can't write anymore." She held up hands badly misshapen by the ravages of arthritis.

Fighting a kitten for control of the pen, Adele wrote the name and number down in her notebook. When she picked up the kitten and put it on the floor, it made a noise like a pterodactyl.

"Did Dr. Macy have any family?"

"Oh sure. His mother. The woman was just plain tore up. Her only child, you know. She hasn't made it over to clean out the apartment there, but the police told me I can't let no one in there anyway. You know, they're making sure there weren't no foul plays."

Adele shook her head in unison with the old lady and even clucked her tongue.

"Now, there *was* the girlfriend." Mrs. Duggan wrinkled her upper lip until, amazingly, it touched the end of her nose. "No good. I could tell she was no good."

"Do you know her name?" With her foot, Adele pushed away an orange tabby attempting to sharpen his claws on the side of her purse.

"Rosie Mastrelli or Mastrioni or some eyetie name like that." The woman snickered and lowered her voice, as if not to be overheard by the cats. "Sounds like a hooker name, if you ask me."

"Do you have her number or address?"

Mrs. Duggan shook her head. "Nah. That one was a gold digger; put on airs. She weren't going to stay around long. I could tell that the first time I laid eyes on her. Thought she was better than everybody."

"Do you remember when you saw Dr. Macy last?"

"I just told ya," she huffed. "Lying on the toilet floor dead as a salmon."

"No." Adele shook her head. "I mean alive. When was the last time you saw him alive?"

The landlady thought hard, screwing up her face as she did so. "Tuesday night just after "Mad About You" went off. He come over and ask me if I had the newspaper. I ask him what happened to his paper and he told me it got put in the garbage by mistake, so I give him my paper.

"Full of bad news. Don't hardly read it myself. I use it to line the cat pans." The old lady looked at her with rheumy eyes. "Absorbent, you know."

The phone rang and the woman shuffled off in the direction of the kitchen. As soon as their mistress left the room, the cats started closing in again, sniffing and rubbing against her. She felt like a stalk of catnip.

"I'm a dog person," she hissed through clenched teeth. "Go away!"

Being cats, of course, not one of them paid the slightest bit of attention.

The voice coming through the receiver was prerecorded. Adele hated voice mail, especially in places of business—like insurance companies and banks. She hated having to press in legions of numbers and letters, then having to wait forever to be scolded by some tinny-voiced, bitchy machine for not entering the correct digits. She especially hated the ones that did not give an option to speak to a living person. And more than anything, she hated using public phones whose locations had to have been chosen by that little-known group who worked for Pacific Bell—The Profoundly Deaf Practical Jokers Club. It was the only explanation for why the boothless phone would be placed on a heavily traf-ficked intersection, right outside the entrance of a busy parking garage.

Luckily, Mrs. Duggan had provided her with Dr. Cor-nelius's extension, because the message gave no other menu choices . . . either put in the extension number of the party you are calling or get hung up on.

Using vile language to explain to the voice mail an-nouncer how she felt, she punched in the extension number and waited for the second round of prerecorded messages.

"Hello, this is Dr. Cornelius."

Adele said, "Oh balls," and waited for the recorded message.

"Ah, hello? Larry Cornelius here."

There was an embarrassed pause while Adele decided whether to hang up or speak. "Oh my God, I'm sorry. I thought it was another recorded message. Well, never mind. Hello. My name is Adele Monsarrat and I'm—I'm—"

She absolutely did not want to say she was a nurse; she

wanted to lie. "I'm a deputy detective with Marin County PD." There was no such thing as a Marin County PD, but it sounded good.

From the other end came a faint intake of breath. "Wow, that sure didn't take long," he said in a low, discouraged voice.

Puzzled, she waited a beat and tried to lead him on. "Excuse me?"

"I said it didn't take you people long to track me down."

"Well, now that we have, I was wondering when you might be available to answer a few questions. I need to . . ."

"I don't care," he said. "I'd assume you'd want to meet as soon as possible."

"You're right about that," she agreed, not entirely sure what he was talking about. "From the phone prefix, I gather you're somewhere down in Silicon Valley . . . Stanford?"

"Close enough," he said, more guarded.

"Well, I'm in San Francisco now. I could . . ." She glanced at her watch and groaned. It was already five o'clock. Peter Chernin was picking her up in an hour. ". . . meet you at your office tomorrow?"

He practically choked. "Oh right," he said dramatically. "That's all I need." He lowered his voice. "There's already enough gossip going around here about Brian's death. How about if I meet you at Nicki's Cafe in Stanford Shopping Center tomorrow lunchtime?"

"Fine. How will I know you?"

"I'm balding on top and I wear glasses. I'll look just like every other computer-scientist nerd in there."

"I'm tall and have black hair," she said. "I'll be the only woman wearing handcuffs and a billy club off my belt."

"Obviously," he said dryly, "you haven't met any of the women who hang out in Stanford."

This remark was followed by a disconnecting click.

"Anybody," she said to the chrome front of the pay phone in which she could see a distorted image of her face with a keyhole for a nose, ". . . with a sense of humor like that, can't be all nerdy."

She counted out the last of her change and made another call to David Takamoto to verify that the name of the San Francisco corpse with the "cracked noggin" was the same as Mrs. Duggan's ex-tenant in apartment 206.

It was. Dr. Brian Macy, chemist.

Adele had trouble with parking garages. Other than the expense, which she usually found to be exorbitant (considering one was only renting a very small space for a relatively short time for one's car), she always felt that if and when "The Big Quake" happened, it would be either when she was in an elevator going to the fifty-seventh floor of a structurally unsafe building, or when she was in a parking garage on the bottom floor.

And the bottom floor of a large parking garage was exactly where she was right then, running to the Beast at full speed. That most apartment buildings did not provide parking except in the form of a public garage, was one of the reasons she didn't like city dwelling. In the city, one always had to worry about one's car—how long before it was stolen? Would only essential parts of it be stolen, like the steering wheel? Did it have the right stickers? How much would all the parking tickets add up to? Were they tax deductible? Could one maintain a savings account after repeated towings and increases in insurance premiums?

She had the key in the ignition, ready to start the Beast's pacemaker, when it occurred to her that Brian Macy's car might still be in the garage.

Employing her favorite motivational saying of "Just do it," she found the courage to not only run the length of the bottom floor of the garage, but to take the elevator three stories up to the street-level garage office.

She entered the five-by-eight plexiglass office and almost gagged from the smell of exhaust fumes and rubber. A

young Chinese-American man sat at a desk, working an outdated adding machine. Adele's mouth fell open as she took
in a sharp breath.

The man pulled down the handle of the adding machine
and looked up. "Help you?" he asked, in the choppy Chinese-
American accent that she had never been able to get a
handle on.

"Where did you get that?" she whispered, pointing at her
rhinestone denim jacket. It was too small for him, the cuffs
riding the middle of his forearm.

He stared at her as though she were speaking Greek and
didn't answer. Being slow to understand accents was a two-
way street.

"That's my jacket," she said more slowly. "It was stolen
out of the back of my car."

"It my jacket," the young man said rapidly, pointing to
the lapel of the garment. Pinned there was a brass name tag
that read "Chang." He smiled a very toothy smile. "Finders
creepers, losers keepers."

Adele didn't laugh at the mangled rhyme, but narrowed
her eyes and thought as quickly as she could, considering
that the exhaust fumes were destroying countless brain cells
with each breath she took. She *couldn't* give up the jacket
now that she'd found it—it was as if fate had willed her to
have it.

Adele had rescued the garment from the Mt. Carmel
Thrift Shop in Mill Valley when she was still in high school.
Because of the unusual softness of the denim and the large,
drapey arms and small waist, Adele guessed it had been
custom-made for one of the plethora of rock stars who lived
in Marin. From the multitude of tiny burn holes all over the
front and sleeves, she also concluded that its original owner
smoked a lot of dope.

Wherever there had been a burn hole, she'd fastened a
rhinestone. The clear and light blue stones ended up arranged
in an odd, random pattern that, according to those on drugs,
was claimed to be a message from the macrocosm.

"I want my jacket back," she said firmly.

The Chinese man narrowed his eyes back at her. "How I know it your jacket?"

"Inside, on the lining over the heart, are the initials A.M. in rhinestone." She'd put them there to use as extras in the event she incurred more burn holes.

Despite himself, he pulled the jacket out and glanced inside. Then he shook his head and stared at her with cold eyes. "I find it in garbage can in rest room. It my jacket now."

She was thinking about pulling out the deputy badge Tim had given her as a joke, when Chang said, "How much you pay?" He ran a hand over the rhinestones on the front, then rubbed his fingers together. "Nice jacket. I make you deal. Twenty dollar, I give you jacket. Twenty dollar. Cheap. Twenty dollar."

"I bought that jacket for three dollars. I'll give you three dollars for saving it from the trash."

The Chinese man made an expression that was the epitome of surprise and agony. "Ohhhhh, nooooo. You give twenty dollar. Nice jacket."

"Okay, ten," she said. "*And*, free parking for today."

He shook his head vehemently. "No can do. Fifteen dollar and you pay parking."

"Twelve dollar and free parking," she said, picking up his manner of speaking.

"I get into trouble with boss. No free parking and thirteen dollar for jacket."

"Look, pal," she began, then stopped. She still needed to find out about Brian Macy's car. "Okay, I'll tell you what, Chang. I'll give you twelve dollars for my jacket, and five dollars for parking, and three dollars for a little information."

Chang cocked his head to the side and raised his eyebrows. "Twenty dollar?"

Adele reached into her change purse and pulled out a crisp twenty. The man held it up to the fluorescent lights, took off the jacket, then held out his hand.

"What?" she barked. "I already gave you the twenty . . ."

"The ticket," he said. "Give me ticket for parking."

Rummaging around the purse for a minute or two, the panic that she'd lost her ticket was just settling into her temples when she remembered she'd put it in her shoe.

He grimaced when she handed the ticket to him, and held his nose. "Stinky shoe," he said as he stamped it "paid."

She ignored this little touch of vaudeville and pulled out the soft, black leather case that held her sheriff's deputy badge. She'd never shown it to anyone before, and flushed with embarrassment as she tried to flip it open the way she'd seen cops do in the movies.

Except it didn't flip open—instead, it flew out of her hand and hit the plexiglass wall behind her. Adele curbed the crazy-woman laughter by biting down on her tongue.

She retrieved the black case and opened it carefully. Chang stared at the badge and her picture ID and then back at her. "You cop?" he asked with a flicker of surprise.

She ignored his question, and asked one of her own. "Do you have a car here that belonged to a Brian Macy? He lived around the corner. He probably rented a space month to month."

Without a word, the man stood and went to a two-drawer filing cabinet shoved in the corner. On top was a coffee-maker that looked like it was fifty years old and had never been cleaned.

"How you spell last name?" Chang asked without turning around.

Adele spelled out the last name and was starting to spell Brian when Chang asked, "Brian Macy? A Porsche?"

She nodded. "Is it still here?"

Chang looked past her, pointing with the hand that still held Brian Macy's rental card. "Space A twenty-three. One floor down, on end."

"Do you have a spare key?"

"No room for key." He indicated the small space. "Too many renter."

"One more question, Chang." She smiled, but he did not return the expression. Perhaps, she thought, he was having second thoughts about the jacket. "Did you ever see Mr. Macy with a woman?"

Chang shook his head and sat down at his adding machine. "I see nobody. I work in office. I don't look at car come in and out."

"But surely he came in here to pay the rent on his space."

Again, Chang shook his head. "Drop box only." He indicated the wide slot in a portion of the wall. Under it hung a wire bicycle basket on brackets fastened to the wall.

Adele put on her jacket, feeling as if she were welcoming back a long-lost friend. Chang looked at it with a slight longing in his eyes.

"You sell jacket?" he asked somewhat sheepishly. "I give you twenty dollar. You park free."

Adele pulled the Beast up behind space A23, parked, and got out. The black 1974 911 Targa Porsche was locked, but she was prepared for that. From the Beast's duffle bag, she found, among several other tools, her slim Jim.

Praying that Brian Macy was not anal-retentive about his car, she pushed the instrument down inside the window, then pulled up. The lock released. Her prayers were answered when she opened the door and no sirens, computerized voices ("Move away from the car!"), bells or whistles went off.

She found several outdated *Thomas Guides* to San Francisco, a single loafer, a Starbucks' coffee mug, a giant nest of Jack in the Box wrappers, an ugly silk tie stained with catsup, and an empty McDonald's bag strewn about the car like so much flotsam and jetsam. Using several of the many paper napkins that littered the seats and floor, she opened the glove box. Except for a moldy owner's manual, it was empty.

Under the passenger seat, however, was the jackpot—a notepad that was mounted on a plastic board with a suction cup on the back. She'd bought one just like it at a rummage sale, and ended up throwing it away because it wouldn't stay stuck to the inside of the windshield. Apparently, Brian Macy hadn't had any better luck than she with the device.

On the top sheet was a license plate number written in jerky, uneven letters and numbers; on the next sheet down were the handwritten notations: *Rent to Mrs. D.—milk— wire @ Ace—Rosie—Tues. morn.* Then there was a line drawn across the page, and under that was *Miller Ave, 2nd flr., Belvedere Hotel 6 p. Mon.—banquet kitchen. Under microwave west wall.*

Adele checked her watch and swore, considered calling Detective Chernin and telling him the date was off, felt guilty, and got out of the Porsche, leaving the notes where she'd found them. The police would find them soon enough. Taking down his license plate number, she got back into the Beast singing "Onward Christian Soldiers."

Pete Chernin took her to the dollar movies—an inauspicious beginning, not because of the cheap admission, nor because of the movie he chose—*Seven*. Rather, it was Peter Chernin's strange repertoire of reactions to the film that kept her nervously peering at him from the corner of her eye.

The first "incident" came during the gluttony scene where Morgan Freeman (*"Ooooh don't you just love him?"*) and Brad Pitt (*"God, I hate that guy!"*) are scoping out the murder scene in the victim's kitchen—with the victim still sitting at the table.

Chernin's initial moan came out like a long, low dog growl, and her eyes shifted to the corners of their sockets for a gander at what might be ailing the man. His face was virtually alive with expressions which changed as rapidly as the scenes on the screen.

Horror—he actually shrank back in his seat and gasped when they showed that the victim's legs were chained together.

Disgust—he made a gagging sound and mocked sticking

his finger down his throat when Brad Pitt finds the bucket of vomit.

Humor—he laughed inappropriately and loudly, slapping his knee while he guffawed at Morgan Freeman's obvious disdain of Brad Pitt.

It didn't stop for the entire film, either. It got worse.

When the corpse of the sloth victim, skinned alive by the psychotic John Doe psycho murderer, unexpectedly sits up and screams, Detective Chernin jumped out of his seat and screamed like a hysterical woman. By the time the head in the box scene rolled around, he had chewed through the tab of his collar and was openly weeping, murmuring under his breath. "Oh dear God, not *her!*"

In the light of the lobby, she noticed his shirt was soaked through and he looked as though he'd just come off night-shift in a mine shaft. She debated whether or not to call 911 and the crisis unit.

"Really got into the film, didn't you?" she asked, hoping the sarcasm wouldn't come through.

He wiped away the sweat covering the pouches under his eyes and directed her to his car. "Yeah, I guess so. God, I love movies! I've seen *Ocean's 11* a hundred and six times. Can you believe that?"

"Really?" she said, having a blurry cinema flashback of a boozy Dean Martin and a repulsively slimy Frank Sinatra. "You must have been a prisoner of war during Vietnam or something."

He paused. "I, ah . . . don't understand."

"You know, as in torture methods?"

He laboriously mulled the comment over, trying his best to understand her meaning. Torture methods? Was she getting kinky, checking to see if he was into S and M or something?

"It was a joke." She smiled finally, watching the divider lines on the freeway. She was glad that she'd grown out of feeling uncomfortable when there were long pauses in the conversation, because she was sure there were going to be a few.

He broke the silence by asking her if there was any special place she wanted to go, or if there was anything she wanted to do. Was she hungry? How about grabbing a beer, bowling a game, or playing some pool?

She answered simply and directly, "No thanks," and silence again covered them like a king-size down quilt.

Not quite sure what might have triggered the streak of self-cruelty, a mile from her front door she asked the most fatal of questions: "So, what *are* your favorite movies, Peter?"

She could never be sure what had prompted her to do such a disastrous and abusive thing, but she paid dearly for it for the next three hours that they sat in his Yugo listening to him go on, nonstop, euphorically describing scenes from old, bad films that he loved.

Alfie. ("Really?" she'd asked, innocently.) *Valley of the Dolls.* ("Christ on a bicycle!" she said, mortified.) *Cleopatra.* (She looked more closely to make sure he wasn't putting her on.) *Erik the Viking.* (Huh?)

When her bladder couldn't hold out any longer, and she thought she would go insane if she heard him say "JESUS that was a GREAT damned movie, wasn't it?" or "What a CLASSIC piece of film!" one more time, she interrupted his glowing review of the 1951 hit, *Superman and the Mole Men*, to say she had to feed her dog and get some sleep. It was a lovely (So, she lied.) evening. Thanks. Goodnight. No, no no. Don't bother to walk me to the door. I can handle it.

"Don't worry, Nels, it was another date from purgatory," she told the Labrador when she got inside and found him pouting on his Mickey Rug. "You're still number one with me."

Peter Chernin felt like a teenager, even though he'd never really experienced what it was like to be one. His pimple years had been spent entirely in the dark of Rowland Movie Theater—rather like a mole, or a mushroom.

He drove home on the wings of brand new love. This woman really liked him—aw hell, she was downright *wild* about him, there was no mistaking that. He had a special sense about women.

Exuberant, the detective broke into an off-key rendition of "Singin' in the Rain," which he sang first note to last.

Wait until I tell Ritmann, he thought, whistling the little-remembered melody from *House of Evil. This'll stick his "a little old for her" right up his smart, young butt.*

NINETEEN

TIMOTHY RITMANN STOPPED READING THE
sports page (Goddamned A's!) and glanced over at the floor
of the stall next door. The hand-knitted red and tan argyle
socks belonged to the only person he knew who was clue-
less enough to wear them because they'd been made by his
mother. He guessed it took a mind as small as all indoors.

He went back to the sports page, moving on to the hockey
scores, when the whistling began. "Three Coins in the Fountain." He had to go back and reread the scores from the beginning. Halfway through, "Three Coins in the Fountain" turned
into a syncopated hum of "Some Enchanted Evening." The
happy-go-lucky sound of it grated on him like nails across a
blackboard.

"Jesus, Chernin, can't a guy take a crap without having to
listen to best loved overtures from Broadway?"

"What's a matter, Ritmann? A guy can't sing a few
tunes in the shitter? Maybe now we gotta post a 'Quiet—
Crapping Zone' sign in here?"

"Eat me, Chernin."

Both men did the masculine equivalent of giggling—they
each made a soft snuffling noise.

"I'm happy," said the older detective after a few minutes.
"A guy needs to sing a little when he's happy."

Tim felt his balls automatically tighten and rise. "Oh
yeah? What's to be so happy about? We got a county full of
corruption, the cost of living is on the rise, and radiation
levels from the bay are gonna kill every last one of us."

Detective Peter Chernin was smiling widely. He only wished he could see the facial expressions in the next stall. He wondered if Ritmann's balls were up to his neck yet.

"She's a real nice woman, that Adele. Nice, nice lady."

"Oh yeah?" *She might be nice, but where the hell was her taste?*

"Oh yeah! We had a great time. Hit it off like Bogie and Bacall, Tracy and Hepburn, Young and Luhan."

Young and Luhan? "Yeah? What'd you do?"

"Saw a movie then went to her house and talked half the night."

He could feel the diarrhea cramps start. At least he was in the right place for it. "Oh yeah?" *How could she? She didn't have time for me, but she can waste half the night with a . . . a . . . geek?* "Well, great. When are you guys going out again?" *Let's see, when's the next Be Kind to Clowns Day?*

"I'm thinking I'd ask her out again for tonight. Strike while the iron's hot. What do you think?"

"I think . . ." He silently snickered. ". . . a guy your age who spends half the night talking to a younger woman should probably catch up on his sleep before trying again. Wouldn't be too cool to stroke out while wolfing down a tofuburger or trying to keep up with her walking to the car."

"You and yo mama, Ritmann." Chernin laughed. "Like I said, she's smart. She knows quality when she sees it."

Tim folded the paper slowly while willing his guts to stop their imitation of a high-speed blender. Chernin wasn't *that* much older than he was, and maybe he was right about younger women wanting security. And Chernin really wasn't a bad-looking guy. If Liz Taylor could fall for Richard Burton, it was a good guess Adele could fall for a guy who looked like him. Why else would she spend half the night talking to him?

From the stall next door came the sound of the flush of success. With that, every sphincter on his body closed up tighter than a can of okra.

*   *   *

A few minutes after Adele passed the airport she went through a chain of thoughts that started with the safety of airplane food and ended with how she always made it to the gate as they were closing the door of the plane because airport security had picked her to hassle. Then she realized she had no idea what time lunchtime was to Lawrence Cornelius.

To some normal people, lunchtime meant noon—which gave her only twenty minutes to get to Nicki's. People who lived on the planet California, however, "did lunch" anywhere between 10:00 A.M. and 4:00 P.M.

She supposed it didn't matter what time he showed up; if she was early, she could spend the time balancing her checkbook—the truest of mathematical nightmares. If she was late, she'd apologize profusely and offer to jump off the nearest bridge.

Stanford Shopping Center was a place where the Upwardly Mobile and Beyond did their shopping. The stores ran a long and distinguished gamut from Neiman Marcus to Rolex. It was its own universe of pretension and overpricing run amuck.

There were certain rules one had to follow when shopping at Stanford Shopping Center. Like the fact that one did not shop in sweats; one *dressed* to the teeth. If one didn't follow the dress code and dress appropriately, one could expect to be tailed by security people for the length of one's entire visit.

Such was the case with Adele, who was dressed in black cotton sweatpants, running shoes, and a sweatshirt that read DANNY'S BALDHEADED BAR B QUE HOT SAUCE—A TWIST ON THE NORM printed under a picture of a bald man with a beard and twinkling blue eyes.

The security person approached her immediately after she'd entered the main thoroughfare of shops, eyeing first her sweatshirt and then her huge, oversize purse.

"May I help you find something?" asked the man in the blue uniform.

Adele looked at him like an afterthought. "Do I look like I've lost something?"

He did not smile. "What store are you looking for?" he asked, walking alongside her. He was having a time of it keeping up.

She stopped and sighed. She seemed to be a magnet for these people. "Are you a rapist?"

He didn't flinch. "No."

"Well I'm not a shoplifter, so if you don't stop harassing me, I'll start screaming rape."

"I'm going to have to ask you to check your bag in at security, ma'am."

Adele gaped first and then turned angry. "I refuse," she said as she turned her back on the man and continued walking. It was a risky thing to do. Most security guards were short-egoed, poorly trained men who loved the sense of power they got out of scaring people. They also liked shooting people. It was the ultimate in control, especially since they were almost never convicted.

The back of her head prickled right around where she guessed the bullet might enter. The guard caught up with her. He was speaking into his walkie-talkie, requesting emergency police backup.

She rolled her eyes, then tried to ignore him and the people turning to stare at them. The more attention they drew, the more excited the guard got. Adele glanced down, and saw that he had the beginning of an erection.

In the distance, a siren wailed. Momentarily distracted, the guard clipped his walkie-talkie to his belt.

It seemed like a good time to run.

Hiding out in the dressing room of Victoria's Secret, Adele struggled into the cupless bra appropriately named "Nipples and Nice." Other than a jogbra and the occasional brassiere under thin blouses, she hadn't worn underwear since the age of fifteen, when she decided bras and panties were unnatural devices designed for women by men who hated them.

She looked at her reflection in the mirror—broad shoulders, visible ribs, and two big nipples sticking up over the white lace rim—like eyes looking over bifocals. How anyone could think the look was sexually arousing was so far beyond her, she thought the bra might have been a joke item.

In any event, it wasn't something she'd wear in six million years, but it happened to be the first thing her hand landed on after running into the store. She was pretty sure she'd ditched both the cop and the security guard somewhere in the boys' sportswear section of Nordstrom's, but it was better to be safe than arrested. When she thought she'd waited long enough, she slipped out and joined the hordes of shopping-crazed California yuppies.

Lawrence Cornelius was already waiting at the door of Nicki's Cafe. The scientist was of medium height, had medium brown hair that was to the advanced side of thin on top, and wore glasses that hid nice eyes. He didn't smile often, but when he did, she thought him attractive in an L. L. Bean catalog kind of way.

He walked directly up to her with a confident, "Hello, Ms. Monsarrat," and led her to a table at the rear of the restaurant, away from the windows.

"How did you know it was me?" she asked after they'd ordered coffee. She was still nervous about the security guard and looked around to make sure she had a clear line to an escape route should she need one.

"I've been cursed with a photographic memory," he said in a pleasant, drawling manner. "I followed the serial murder cases in the *Chronicle* last year. You're much more attractive in person than your photos."

Adele blushed; not over the compliment, but that he knew she lied about being a detective.

Then, as if he'd read her mind: "So, you've gone from nurse to investigations?" It was tongue-in-cheek.

"I was given an honorary title of deputy detective at the height of the publicity," she said lamely, avoiding his eyes. The certificate was hidden in her "Other" file at home, along with her Outstanding Cookie Sales Award from the Girl Scouts of America. "I do investigations every once in a while for the Marin Sheriff's Department." She was lying freely, and doing a not so bad job of it. "I've been sent to inquire about Dr. Macy and . . ."

"And you want to know what I took out of Macy's apartment and if it had something to do with this plague thing in Marin."

She nodded, letting him take the lead. "That and everything else you know in connection with his death."

"All I can tell you is that Brian called my voice mail at work sometime after midnight on Wednesday. He left a barely coherent message, which I didn't get until I got to the lab about ten. When he didn't show up for work by noon, I called his apartment two or three times. I wasn't too panicked, but I *was* concerned. I mean, Brian was an obsessive-compulsive when it came to his work. The atmosphere around the lab is pretty laid-back, but he still showed up in shirt and tie at nine sharp every morning and never left much before five. He wouldn't think of not coming in unless he was . . . well, really sick or something.

"At first I thought he might still be at the hospital, but . . ."

"Hospital?"

"In his message he said that he was going to take a shower and go to the ER to be checked because he was sick."

The waitress, coffeepot in hand, interrupted to take their order. He ordered a jumbo mango iced tea and tuna salad sandwich on triple-seeded, extra-sour sourdough rye, hold the black olives and capers. Adele said she'd stick with coffee.

After a moment or two of internal debate, Dr. Cornelius lowered his voice to the point where she had to strain to hear him over the noise of the lunch crowd.

"I'll start at the beginning," he began hesitantly. "Otherwise none of this is going to make sense. About ten months ago, a government agency requested a meeting with the owner and CEO of our company. He'd been briefed that the meeting was about the development of a certain biochemical, so he invited Brian and me to be present.

"In the meeting, the agency expressed an interest in the development of a toxic agent that, once inside the human body, couldn't be traced. They wanted something that would mimic the symptomology of a naturally occurring illness, and, after an expected, familiar course, cause death.

"Our CEO is a born-again Christian; so he basically said, 'Get thee behind me Satan' and threw them out on their ears."

The scientist let his eyes wander away from hers. "A quarter of a million dollars is a lot of money, Ms. Monsarrat. Brian and I rationalized away the ethics and secretly pitched the agency on our own. Brian was a brilliant chemist, and my biochemical and toxicology background is vast, so we sold them and took on the project."

Lawrence Cornelius's sandwich arrived on a plate that took up a third of the table. The elaborate three-inch-high creation was surrounded by several types of salads, pickles, and a scoop of cottage cheese. He removed the sandwich and pushed the plate to the middle of the table, inviting her to help herself to the rest.

"So where did you develop the agent?"

"At the lab after hours," the scientist said, lifting the top piece of bread from his sandwich and sprinkling on a liberal amount of salt. "Mostly on weekends and holidays. We couldn't risk keeping the formula in the lab, so Brian kept it in a special refrigerator in his apartment, and would transport it on the days we worked on it."

Throwing his tie over his shoulder, he took a bite so huge that Adele marveled over how it would make it down his esophagus without choking him. In her mind she reviewed the Heimlich maneuver, and checked out what silverware would be available in case a cricothyrotomy was necessary.

When his mouth was cleared, he continued. "We'd just begun first round trials with mice. In another couple of months we would have turned over the D-seven to the agency so they could run the final trials."

"Why wouldn't you and Dr. Macy conduct the final trials?"

The scientist shook his head. "Documented use of primates is so tightly regulated at company and academic labs, that we could never get away with it. We'd have to answer to someone. The government agency we're dealing with answers to no one.

"But we had to put off the first round trials anyway because Brian was assigned to a big project for the company and couldn't afford the extra time."

Lawrence Cornelius drank off his iced tea and wiped his mouth. "I didn't get worried until Wednesday evening after I'd called his mom and a few of the guys at the lab. Nobody had heard from him. My wife insisted I drive up to San Francisco. To be honest, I went to his apartment not so much to check on Brian as to check on the supply of D-seven."

"Why was that?"

"His message—the part that I could understand—said that he thought someone had stolen some of the batch and used it to poison a lot of people. I'd read the *Intelligencer* article about what happened at the Hersh fund-raiser and the thought actually crossed my mind that the symptomology and course of illness sounded like D-seven."

He paused and snorted. "The most bizarre part of it was that Bri hated Hersh with an absolute passion. He even named the test mice Gordon or Hershy or Gordo."

Dr. Cornelius went after the other half of his sandwich, chewing like a man crazed with hunger. Sense of humor or not, her dislike for him grew steadily, in part because of his willingness to develop such a destructive weapon for money, and partly because he seemed to be missing an essential human quality; he might have been a genius in the lab, but he was a cretin in genuine human emotion or consciousness. In short, she figured him as the man who, in a sinking ship, would yell, "Every man for himself" as he pushed women and children out of his way and lowered the last lifeboat.

"But I don't understand why you didn't go to his apartment as soon as you got the message, or at least call the police after you read the *Pacific Intelligencer* article. I mean, didn't you believe what Dr. Macy told you in his message?"

He shrugged. "Certainly not. And I still don't. Besides even if those deaths *were* caused by D-seven, why would I want to draw attention to the situation? The agency we're working for wouldn't exactly have appreciated the publicity."

He saw her expression, put his sandwich down, and faced her. "You have to understand, Ms. Monsarrat, that Brian had a reputation for blowing things out of proportion. If it rained hard, he'd call the National Guard to report a flooding disaster. If he went over a speed bump, his car was totaled. If anyone even slightly crossed him or his mother, they became public enemy number one—like Dr. Hersh."

Adele cocked her head.

"Brian's mother was a former patient of Hersh's. He apparently didn't treat Mrs. Macy with kid gloves, and Brian went after the man. He threatened to kill him at one point."

He held up a hand before she could open her mouth. "Brian talked mean, but believe me, he wouldn't hurt a fly."

No flies, thought Adele, he was just going to develop a toxin that could kill a few human beings.

"The more I thought about the whole thing, the more preposterous it seemed, so I let it go." He noticed her expression of horrified incredulity had not changed and added: "Another thing about Brian you should know is that he had a minor biochemical flaw—he was allergic to alcohol.

Whenever he took a glass of wine, it was like a normal person drinking a pint of vodka.

"Tuesdays were his day off, and every Tuesday he'd get together with his girlfriend, Rose. For some perverted reason, she got off on getting him drunk. When I picked up his call about the missing stock and how he thought those people's deaths were caused by it, I figured he was drunk, and he'd read the *Intelligencer* article, overreacted, miscounted the stock and left a hysterical, drunken message." He held out his hands and scrunched his shoulders up. "Even when I found him dead, I still thought the same thing."

He attacked what remained of his sandwich with no lessening of zeal.

"*Was* the supply missing?" she asked. "I'm sure you checked it."

Unable to answer, he nodded, finishing his mouthful. "Of course, it wasn't missing," he said, then glanced away. "I took the samples and his lab notes before the police got there. That's why I wasn't surprised when you called. I expected the police would want to question me."

He started to take another bite, but she reached over and pulled the hand holding the sandwich away from his mouth. "I don't get it. Explain."

"The landlady? Mrs. Duggan? I figured she'd get around to telling the cops that I'd taken some things off the premises before their arrival. The first question they asked when they arrived was if anything had been touched. I said absolutely not, and the old woman went along with it. Surprised the hell out of me that she did.

"I think she was afraid I was going to come back and kill her or something if she ratted on me. Anyway, I didn't think she'd keep quiet about it for long."

"And you're sure no part of the samples was missing?"

"Not according to Brian's notes, and believe me, Brian was more fastidious about his formulas than I am about my research. He had that stuff measured down to the microgram."

"Would he have made more D-seven and not told you about it?"

"I seriously doubt it." He fluttered his eyes. "It made him nervous to have the measly four test tubes of it that we did have. He knew its potential and hated having it around. If it weren't for the money, he never would have agreed to help develop the thing. As it was, I thought a couple of times that he might be thinking of backing out of the deal."

Probably because he had a conscience, she thought, nodding and pursing her lips.

"Did you ever meet his girlfriend, Rose?"

"No. My wife and I invited them down a few times for dinner, but she always had something else going on. I never said anything, but I don't think she was really all that interested in him. She treated him like shit. Like I said, Brian had a tendency to blow things out of proportion."

His tie had fallen back into place. Instead of throwing it over his shoulder, he tucked it between the top two buttons on his shirt.

"Brian's mother was the type who got a choke hold on her kid and never let go. The man was desperate to get his own life. I think Rose was the first woman who ever paid any attention to him." He snickered. "They'd only met a few months ago, and the guy was already talking marriage and how many kids they were going to have."

"Do you know her last name or where she lived?" Adele asked, making notes.

He shook his head. "Not really. She had an Italian last name. Martinelli I think—something like that. I know she lived in the city somewhere on California Street, but I don't think Brian had ever been to her house. I remember him griping about that and the fact that she had a nasty temper."

"Nasty temper?"

He did a one-shoulder shrug. "Yeah," he said, a little disconcerted. "Brian said she'd haul off and hit him when her temper blew. That was another thing that he said on his message—that Rosie was going to kill him."

"Did he ever describe her to you?"

"No. He just said she was a real dish. I'm assuming with an Italian name she was probably dark. Brian liked brunettes, but he would have liked any woman who looked at him twice."

"Do you still have that message on your answering machine?" Adele asked.

"Doubt it. My machine automatically rewinds and gets recorded over. I'll check though."

"If any part of Dr. Macy's message is on that tape, save it. The cops . . . we're going to need it."

He nodded and stuffed the last bit of the sandwich in his mouth.

"Did you ever hear Dr. Macy mention a Hannah Sandell?"

"No," he said, chewing thoughtfully. "The name doesn't ring a bell."

She tapped her pen against the back of her hand and studied what she'd written. When she glanced up, he was looking at her uneasily—as if he were afraid she might cuff him and take him off to jail.

"Okay, so how does this D-seven work?" she asked. "I mean, how does it actually kill someone?"

He picked a dill seed from between his teeth with his little finger and burped. "First of all, you have to know that the base toxin for D-seven is extremely rare. It begins as an algae that grows on a particular marine plant that grows only in a particular body of water. There is one type of fish that eats this plant and metabolizes it in such a way that the base toxin ends up in its liver.

"Not only will there not be a laboratory in the world that will have a test for this toxin, but it would take a long, hard search to find a lab that has any documentation on it at all."

He waved a hand in the air. "Oh, there might be some informal medical report somewhere about a fisherman or a sailor who got sick after eating a certain fish, but mostly the real documentation about this particular fish will be in the form of local folklore.

"On top of that, Brian chemically altered the original toxin so that it behaved slightly differently. The original toxin attacked all organs, but wasn't as deadly, so that the victims had a fairly good survival rate.

"Brian's modified toxin targets fewer organs, but it's a thousand times more deadly."

"Brain, lungs, kidneys, and liver?"

"Very good." He nodded. "You've done your postmortem homework.

"Anyway, once it's metabolized, it binds specific cellular receptors with resultant necrosis of the organs."

"But why only certain organs?" she asked. "How does it know to attack only those and not others?"

"Couldn't tell you the exact specifics, but receptor antagonists often show exquisite specificity for the receptors of certain tissues." He shrugged. "I know Brian was doing some research with liposomes, but I'm not sure where he'd gone with it. It's fascinating stuff."

Adele thought for a minute. "If this toxin is so rare, how did you get a hold of it?"

The scientist smiled and held a finger to his lips. "Trade secret."

"Oh give it up," she said, sounding more curt than she meant to.

He shook his head. "Ms. Monsarrat, I've traveled all over the world, including some very desolate and exotic places, collecting toxins for my research. You can't expect that I would have limited myself to those toxins that were common?"

She guessed not; his ego would never allow it. "Have you done any tests with the samples you recovered from Dr. Macy's apartment?"

"Not yet. First round trials had just started and I . . ."

"Tell you what, Dr. Cornelius." She wrote her number on the back of a bank deposit slip and handed it to him along with three dollars to cover her cup of coffee. Remembering that she was in the land of overpricing, she threw down another single.

"Why don't you run whatever is in those four test tubes by a few mice as soon as you can, and call me with the results."

"Mind if I ask you a few questions?" Detective Ritmann asked.

She did not open her eyes, and he was glad—he remembered they were the same milky blue as those of the vicious dog in the condo next door to his—scary color, scary eyes, scary lady.

The effort it took to speak coherently, let alone speak well, was almost more than she could stand. "I—I'm sick. Later."

"To be blunt, Miss Sandell, you may not be able to talk later; I say let's give this a try now. We missed our appointment yesterday and I've got questions that need answering."

He could be a bastard when he needed to be. She didn't answer, but he was a good observer—she'd tightened up, and her heart rate on the monitor went from 90 to 120.

Hannah tried not to move her head. It was the headache-nausea part of the illness—the poisoning—that was unbearable.

"What's going on here, Miss Sandell?"

Hannah very slowly opened her eyes. "I'm sick. The plague . . ."

"Now you know I'm not talking about that, don't you?"

For the first time, she grew actively frightened. Trying to rationalize around the pain was difficult; the sickness had affected the way she thought—things began to take on strange proportions and get tangled.

"Do you recognize this?" In front of her eyes he dangled a ziplock bag containing one of her linen hankies. "It was found on Dr. Hersh's person when he came into emergency after his accident."

"I . . . don't know what it is."

"It's a handkerchief monogrammed with your initials."

"No."

"Do you know how or when it might have found its way to his pocket?"

"No."

"Miss Sandell . . ."

"No." She licked her lips. Her tongue was coated with grayish fur.

"If you cooperate now, Miss San . . ."

"No."

The nurse had told him not to upset the woman; that the plague victims were "fragile" at this stage. Personally, he didn't see anything fragile about the woman, who now looked more like a tall, angular man. With the proper haircut and clothes, she could pass for a Minnesota farmer. Minnesota farmers were tough.

"I need to know what your relationship with Mr. Fromer was, Ms. Sandell. Was he blackmailing you?"

"He was a little man," Hannah said, her lip curling. "Like you."

"Can you tell me what the nature of your relationship with Mrs. Hersh is?"

Hannah remained silent, her expression indecipherable. He checked the tracing on the heart monitor. It was going wild. The nurse out at the station looked up and frowned.

"What time did you visit Dr. Hersh at his office yesterday, Ms. Sandell?"

"No." She opened her eyes and stared through him.

It gave him the willies. "We have an eyewitness who says that you . . ."

"No," she said louder, then again, "No!"

"When was the last time you saw Tony Saludo?"

She was up on her elbow fixing him with those eyes. "Get out!" she growled. "Get—"

"When was the last time you saw your mother?"

Hannah's eyes widened and then narrowed. "You fucking prick. Get the hell out of here!" Her voice rose into a hysterical scream.

The nurse stood up, craning her neck to see what was going on.

"Okay, Miss Sandell, I'm leaving."

"Good."

"But I'll be back." He walked to the door and opened it feeling those crazy eyes following him. Untying his mask, he turned around and put a hand to his chin—just like Peter Falk in "Columbo." All he needed was to exchange the isolation gown for a raincoat.

"By the way, did Dr. Ingram give you the latest on the M. Plague?"

Silence. Her throat worked.

Jesus Christ. She has an Adam's apple! he thought.

"I guess you knew that our local labs finally sent all the blood and tissue specimens from all the victims to the lab in Atlanta?"

The monitor alarmed. Out at the nurses' station, the nurse motioned for him to come out. It seemed to him Hannah's color went more gray. He removed his isolation gown and discarded it, as if to prove a point. "They've found that the Mystery Plague isn't a plague at all. It's a noninfectious toxin. You know, as in poison?"

He let his words sink in, then added, "Can you believe that?"

Over the years, Adele had seen San Francisco phone books put to various uses—doorstops, paper planes, origami, mulch, and as wadballs which, if thrown wet at the sides of buses, stuck forever, like so many perpetually frozen yellow snowballs. Once, she'd seen Ryan O'Neal use one to stand on during the filming of a scene in which his feet were not shown.

Today, Adele found the thick book of opaque paper pages particularly use*less*. There was no specific listing for Rose Martinelli on California Street. There were eighteen listings for Martinelli, however, and using her phone card, she'd called them all. She tracked down two Rose Martinellis,

and one Rosella Martinelli. Two of the three women spoke
English, and all of them sounded like they were a hundred
and thirty years old. None had heard of Dr. Brian Macy, although one of the Roses did ask if he was related to Macy's
downtown because she shopped there all the time.

TWENTY

IT WAS WITH SOME TREPIDATION THAT ADELE drove the Beast toward the San Francisco Library. The Pontiac did not like being driven in San Francisco. Probably because of the hills, although she couldn't be sure. Within minutes after taking the downtown exit, the station wagon's engine dozed, went into a deep sleep, and came to rest at a stoplight which was, by some miracle, red.

She kicked the Beast in its solar plexus and hissed between clenched teeth. Behind her was a San Francisco black-and-white with the red and blue bar lights on top.

"If you don't shape up by the time the light turns," she growled, "I'll pour honey into all your parts and kill your damned ass."

The couple in a large red convertible next to her were watching her talk to herself and snickering. The man driving was dark and attractive in a New York Italian 1950's-"yo babe" sort of way. His companion was an older peroxide blonde with a mantel that reached halfway to the dash. A cigarette hung from her wet, red, collagen-filled lips, while her false eyelashes batted constantly to keep the smoke away from her violet-colored contacts.

Using language peppered with verbal bullets, Adele shouted the suggestion that they mind their own business. When the macho moron at the wheel gave her a left-handed one finger salute, his powder blue silk sports jacket rode up on his wrist, revealing three gaudy gold wristwatches.

As soon as the light turned green, she nudged the Beast,

who, after a refreshing nap, woke up with a start—no pun intended—and a loud belch of black exhaust.

Fully expecting to be pulled over for the disgraceful, illegal condition of her shandrydan, she looked in her rearview mirror only to find that the cops' attention had been wrested away from the Beast by the three wristwatches.

She parked in a high crime neighborhood, considered leaving the keys dangling from the ignition, but after a short debate with one of her more practical invisible friends, went to the side of loyalty. The eight-hundred-dollar investment in steel and plastic had faithfully, although not always safely, taken her where she wanted to go. If the aged heap needed to throw tantrums in the form of its sleep trick once in a while, she supposed it was entitled.

Remembering the library was a high security building, she purchased a *Pacific Intelligencer* and tucked it under her arm before entering. Two armed security people immediately approached and asked to see inside her oversize purse.

While one guard ran a detecting device over her body, the other went through her purse. She wasn't sure why the security was so strict at a public library, and wondered if someone had tried to get out of paying their fines by shooting the librarian.

The squat guard shook her head at the purse contents. "Why you carry all this junk, girl? Don't it hurt your back haulin' all this crap around with you?"

"I need and use everything in that bag on a daily basis," she sniffed.

Dubious, the guard pulled a sarong, a jog bra, and an old, flaccid carrot with black spots from Adele's purse. She looked to Adele as if for explanation.

"You never know," Adele said defensively, stuffing them back into the bag.

She found Tuesday's *Pacific Intelligencer* and almost cried with relief, until she discovered the section she wanted was missing. It was her library jinx at work—no matter what library she frequented, the books she wanted were always checked out, misshelved, or missing.

She found the section she needed shielding the face of a sleeping patron who appeared to have been there since the library was built. Looking at the clock, she decided she didn't have the time to wait until he finished his snooze. At his next sonorous inhale, she removed the section and replaced it with the current paper. Folding the newspaper under her arm, she sailed through her exit-inspection with the guards and went on her way.

"You change your mind about taking one of the cats?" Mrs. Duggan asked hopefully. She'd donned a red sweater and exchanged her fuzzy slippers for red patent leather flats.

Not wanting to disappoint the old lady, Adele said she was still thinking about it. (Like, in her dreams.)

"The reason I stopped by was to ask if you recognize this person?" She held out the newspaper and pointed to the photo of Gordon Hersh and Hannah Sandell.

Mrs. Duggan took the paper and walked inside her apartment.

Not wanting to deal with any more cat stench, Adele held back for a second, took a deep breath of stale apartment hallway air, and entered Cat Stink Hell.

"I'm practically blind, you know," Ophelia Duggan said as if in warning. Adele wondered if she should make a joke about bad eyesight being caused by cat dander, and vetoed the idea.

The old woman was climbing up on a step stool to check the top of the refrigerator for her glasses, when Adele pointed to the pair hanging from her neck.

With a Ruth Gordonian shrug, the old lady slid the bifocals onto her nose and then held out her free hand toward Adele for the paper.

"It's in your other hand," Adele reminded her, making a

mental note to check with her doctor about early prophylactic estrogen replacement for failing memory.

The old woman did the bifocal head bob for a minute or two, then handed back the newspaper. "Lord, look at that neckline there!" she said, shaking her head. "No decent woman would wear her chest out like that with men around."

Adele looked at Hannah's neckline. It was low, she had to give the old lady that much.

"But," sighed Mrs. Duggan, "what else would you expect from a girl named Rosie Martelloni?"

Miserable in her grief, Iris padded over to Cynthia's bed and put a hand on her double's shoulder.

"What's up, girlfriend?" Cynthia croaked after she'd opened her eyes and swallowed some saliva to put out the fire in her throat.

"Do you have time to talk?"

Cynthia laughed, pushed herself over to one side of the bed, and patted the empty space. "I've got some important meetings lined up with the President today, but I can probably spare you a few hours."

Iris grabbed a pillow off her bed and put it next to Cynthia's. They lay side by side, IV to IV, both staring at the acoustic squares that covered the ceiling.

"Did you ever try to count all the holes in one of those squares?" Cynthia asked in a voice that could have belonged to Louis Armstrong or Froggie.

"Did you?"

"Uhn huh. Four hundred and twelve. I counted them when I had this stroke patient who took *forever* to swallow her pills."

The teen burst out laughing, accidentally passing wind as she did so.

"Well!" Cynthia said, feigning indignation. "At least we know there's something alive and well in the south forty!" That set them off laughing again until the nurse came in and admonished them for setting off the monitor alarms. After they calmed down, they listened to the ward sounds that filtered into the room: call lights going off, monitor alarms, phones ringing.

They both felt a warming comfort in each other's presence. A bond had been formed that was stronger than any blood tie. Without having to say it, they were bound through being survivors.

"So," Cynthia said, at last, "why don't you start at the beginning and tell me your life's story?"

Unsure whether or not the nurse was kidding, Iris glanced over to check out the expression on her companion's face. "Okay." She began in all seriousness, nervously flicking her fingernails. "I was born at Children's Hospital fifteen years ago to parents who were the hapless victims of a shotgun wedding. . . . "

Both of them smiled, happy that it was going to be a long story.

Mimi sat at the back of her closet—it was all hers now, no more sharing space with Gordon—and played with the revolver. She was careful not to put her finger too close to the trigger; she didn't want it going off by accident the way it had when she checked Sam's pockets for her letter. If she was going to kill herself, she wanted to at least be in control of the trigger.

Twice she held the gun to her temple, and once put it in her mouth, but gagged and had to take it right out. The metal of the barrel had a funny taste, like the heads of matches mixed with kerosene . . . something she remembered from her first few attempts at camping with Hannah.

She had nothing to live for anymore. Her daughter hated her—with good reason. She had no friends—not real friends. Her parents were dead. Her husband was dead. She had no talents, no skills. With no one to steer, she was useless. She'd been shoved behind the wheel of her life for the first time and told to drive the advanced course at racing speed. It was too much. Her eyes blurred with tears, and she began to rock back and forth.

While she was disconnecting all the phones in the house, the idea came to her to simply put herself to sleep so she wouldn't *have* to drive. Iris would be better off without her. There'd be plenty of money to assure she'd be comfortable for the rest of her life. Gordon's Aunt Shirley would be glad to be Iris's guardian until she reached the age of eighteen.

Miriam lifted the revolver in earnest and her elbow hit something cold and metal. Her fingers found the object. A belt buckle. How many times had she told Gordon not to hang up his pants without first removing the belt?

Irked, she pulled the belt out of the loops and didn't know what to do with it. She didn't want to get up and hang it on the belt wheel, but she didn't want them to find her with it in her hand ... she wouldn't want anyone to think she had done this out of some stupid sentimental grief over Gordon.

How Esther could have chosen such a putz to hand her over to, she'd never know. Still, it was a nice leather belt. A Coach belt. Gordon bought the best. It would be a shame to get it bloody. Someone could get a lot of use out of it still. Some disadvantaged person rummaging around Goodwill would be thrilled to have it. Or maybe her cousin Mel's boys could use it. They were struggling to put the two boys through college—nice things were appreciated by people who didn't have much.

Carefully, she rolled up the belt and set it outside the closet door. When she got back inside, she picked up the revolver again, but her eyes were drawn to the collection of Gordon's shoes.

Expensive shoes. Bruno Magli. Nothing too good for O.J. or Gordon Hersh. "Gordon O.J. Marcos," she said and giggled in spite of herself. She stopped immediately. Gordon always did and said and bought what he wanted. He never consulted with her about anything. Even with Iris, he never asked what she thought was best for their daughter, he made all the decisions and acted on them—what house to buy, what car she'd drive, where they went on vacations, what school Iris would attend—even what washer and dryer the maid would use.

She never said a word, going along with everything without so much as a peep. Esther had done her job well, raising her to be a submissive subordinate. She'd done the same to her father, pushing him shamelessly until he would cower when she entered a room.

At the thought of Esther, guilt, that ever-present lump, expanded like rising bread dough in her throat. Her mother had never stopped guilt-tripping her about loving Hannah—scaring her with predictions of how her child would be born mentally defective because of her "unnatural" longings.

She'd threatened her with telling Gordon what kind of relationship they'd had and that he would do what any self-respecting mensch would do—disgrace her, then abandon them. Esther loved to describe how her perversion would someday result in her finding herself working in a laundry and starving to death along with her retarded child.

Long after Iris had shown herself to be a child of promise, and Gordon had prospered beyond anyone's dreams, Esther continued to harp on the subject, ending with the question, *"Think about it, Miriam, how many Jewish queer girls ever made good?"*

She hadn't dared mention Jackie Goldberg, Barbara Stanwyck, Edith Head, or any of the hundred or so other names that Esther would have recognized.

Powerless, she'd allowed her mother and Gordon to dictate what track her life would take. Now Hannah would be taking over the driving. Hannah always on the periphery, lying in wait for Gordon to vacate; as if she naturally assumed she'd be the next one in line to own her and pick out what was best for her for the rest of her life.

Miriam cringed at the thought of how much she'd jeopardized for the sake of her sexual passion with Hannah. *Like an animal,* she thought, shuddering at all the stupid chances she'd taken for the sake of . . . what? A moment's pleasure? A sexual fantasy? To squelch the needy, hollow feeling that never went away no matter what she did?

Where had her mind been to have written such a disgusting, adolescent letter to Hannah? She should have had her head examined. Then, to have carelessly misplaced it in a notebook . . . where Gordon, or . . . Mimi closed her eyes, God forbid—Iris—could have easily found it.

That Samuel Fromer was the one who did stumble on it seemed almost a just punishment for her carelessness.

Mimi closed her eyes and grimaced. Samuel Fromer. The world's sleaziest piece of human garbage. He claimed to have been looking for a blank piece of paper on which to list the guests he wanted to invite to Iris and Gordon's birthday party. He'd waited until Gordon left the house before he called her into the study. The moment she saw his self-satisfied sneer, the dread crept into her stomach.

He'd recited the letter, word for word, watching her as she panicked. Considering who Sam was, she had to give him credit for not outright blackmailing her right then and there. He could have had anything. Instead, he preferred to hold on to it as a sort of insurance against her getting out of line. The only bit of consolation she had was that despite his constant threats, he never did ascertain to whom the letter was written.

She had risked so much—breaking into Samuel's apartment and then the office. She recalled how she'd stood a few feet from his body just seconds after the killer had knocked her over, then calmly, almost casually, going through the files searching for her letter.

"I must have been mad," she whispered and buried her head in her hands.

There'd been other careless gambles as well—like the night they'd made love with Iris in the very next room and Gordon and Samuel right downstairs? And the day she'd lost her head and made a fool of herself attacking the male nurse after Samuel told her Hannah had been flirting with him in the cafeteria. How many people had overheard that confrontation?

Hannah had grown strange in the last few months. Her lover's obsession with possessing her was erotic, yes, but also unhealthy and frightening at the same time. What would happen, Mimi wondered, when the bloom was off the sexual flower? She was already tired of the way Hannah hovered over her, watching her every move. And besides a couple of years at college, did they really have so much in common?

Mimi picked up the pair of Bruno Magli loafers and impulsively threw them out the closet door. One hit the wall with a clunk. She wondered who would be in charge of disposing of the rest of Gordon's and her clothes. There were things of hers that she definitely did not want strangers to have.

She opened the closet door wider to let in more light. The orchid silk suit from Gianni Versace would fit Iris, but the white and black Chanel should be sold; Nancy Payne would give her at least a thousand for it.

Standing, she took down one of Gordon's Armani suits. It was a two-thousand-dollar suit and if he'd worn it once, she would have been surprised. She could probably put an ad in the classifieds.

Or, she could have an exclusive estate sale. There were so many things she could sell. Things that Gordon or Hannah had chosen for her. She ripped the three-thousand-dollar pink Marc Jacobs dress that Hannah had given her from its hanger. People always put her in pink. She hated pink. Pink was for little girls and blond bimbo waitresses.

She thought for a minute. She'd ask a thousand for it and settle for five hundred. The same with the Galliano silk dress.

Her Mercedes had to go, too. She hated the thing. It was always in the shop. Too big, too slow. A black Mercedes was a car for old, fat people. If she sold it, she could buy one of those Honda vans or a camper, maybe even take Iris out of school for a year and go traveling. Get to know her daughter. Tutor her; make sure she never allowed someone else to take over her life.

She'd buy clothes off the rack at Loehmann's: long dresses, leggings, and baggy overblouses, clothes everyone insisted she was too short to wear—clothes she'd longed to wear her whole life.

When the closet was cleared of everything except a few blouses, a couple of sweaters, and one skirt she'd hidden away years ago, she went downstairs, made herself a martini, and began demolishing the newly redecorated study.

They were sitting on the side of the bed dangling their feet and chewing Aspergum for the lingering aches and pains. Linda had left them alone, wisely making the choice that the healing going on between them was worth more than a few sets of vital signs.

Iris talked for two hours, crying and laughing alternately, once in a while simultaneously. When the teen was done, Cynthia took the platform, transforming the dreadful details of her life into an hour of sit-down comedy. Iris laughed, but understood the pain behind the events that the nurse made so light of.

"I wish you were my mother," the girl said sadly, and allowed herself to lean into the curve of Cynthia's body.

Cynthia gave the girl a nervous, sidelong glance. No one had ever said such a thing to her before. For once, she was at a loss for a snappy comeback.

"What's wrong with the one you've got?" Cynthia asked finally.

"My mother's a weak person," Iris said more grimly than before. "She lets people rule her life. My grandma, and then my dad and now her . . . girlfriend."

"You mean Amazon Woman?"

Iris blinked, peering at her cautiously. "You know about her?"

"Sure," Cynthia said calmly, not entirely clear of the girl's meaning. She had an inkling, though.

"I mean about what she is."

"What? That she's gay?"

The teen gawked with an expression not even the most talented of actresses could have imitated. "How did you know *that*?"

"It's no big deal, Iris. Hell girl, you grew up in the gay capital of the world. I'm surprised you'd even give it a second thought."

"If it was *your* mother she was doing it with, you'd be upset, too."

Cynthia started to say that nothing her own mother did would have surprised her, then changed her mind. "Are you sure they're lovers?"

"Oh yeah," Iris answered, her voice laced with disgust. "The night I got sick? After I went to bed, Mr. Fromer and my father were downstairs and my mother and Hannah came upstairs. At first I thought they were going to go through my mother's evening clothes, but they were talking in whispers and laughing, so I thought they were telling each other their secrets." Iris looked up at her, embarrassed. "You know, like about their old boyfriends or about sex . . . or something like that?"

"Sure." Cynthia nodded, hoping her understanding expression would put the girl at ease.

"I don't know very much about my mother's life." Iris fidgeted. "I mean, she never talks to me about herself or what she was like when she was my age. She never told me anything personal about her and my father, or . . . ." Abruptly, Iris began to cry. "I hate her! She—"

Cynthia pulled the girl close and let her cry. "You don't really hate her, Iris. You wanted to be close to her, but for some reason, your mom couldn't do that."

"Sometimes," Iris said finally, "I think she wanted to, but I think she was afraid that I wouldn't like her or something?

It's like she was so desperately lonely, and so insecure, she never really let anybody in, you know?"

Cynthia said she understood, and held the girl's hand, not saying anything more.

"That night?" Iris continued, "I got out of bed and was going to spy on them by listening through the wall with a glass? They started making these noises like they were working out or something, and I didn't know what was going on. So I went out into the hall and the bedroom door was open a little bit, and then . . . I looked in and they were, you know, doing it."

The teenager covered her face. "Oh God, it was repulsive."

Cynthia nodded, noncommittally.

"In my father's bed, too," Iris added miserably. "I mean, they didn't even have the sense to close the door all the way. It was so rude!"

After a few moments, Cynthia set her jaw and held Iris out at arm's length. "Okay, so that's all about your mother, Iris, not you."

The teenager's body stiffened. She pulled out of Cynthia's grasp and stared coldly at her. Behind the expression of accusation was a desire to be convinced. "But my father . . . she betrayed him. She . . ."

"It's still none of your business. It was too bad you had to witness that, but what went on between your mother and Hannah and your father is between them, not you."

"But it *is* my business," Iris insisted.

"Okay. Tell me why."

"It's my business because . . . because . . ."

Cynthia quietly marveled over the rate at which the girl's carotid artery was pumping. It was probably driving the monitor tech buggy. "What? Come on. Spill."

"Because I love my father and . . ." The girl started to cry again. ". . . they killed him. They plotted to kill him the night I got sick. They tried to give him poison, but I got it instead. It was in his coffee."

* * *

Hannah couldn't move. In her delirium, she imagined there was a guard posted outside her door. She could hear him breathing; the noise of it hurt her head. The worst part was that she knew he was listening to everything. They were all listening and watching, waiting for her to make a move.

A nurse walked by the window and looked in, shading her eyes against the glare of the fluorescent lights. Hannah felt for her pendant. She squeezed it tight until the edges of it cut into her fingertips. Goddamn it! Where was Mimi? Grieving over her dead husband? That was a joke. Hannah stiffened. Someone outside her room coughed, causing a spear of pain in her head. She gagged and heaved up nothing.

Mimi hadn't come to see her—she'd shied away, choosing to stay with Gordon and the brat. Things between them were slipping sideways, out of her control. Mimi had changed—she'd felt it the last time they'd made love—as if the magic was fading out and she was no longer interested . . .

The unnamed sensation, framed in fear, spread into her temples and down the back of her neck. Instantly, she clawed at her temples to make it stop. Wobbling around such an unsteady reality frightened her, but she would not let anything get in the way now, not after sixteen years of waiting.

She was furious with herself; it was elementary logic that a second dose of the toxin would act faster and be more devastating than the first. Dosing herself with the same amount of the D-7 as she'd ingested at the Belvedere Hotel, was unforgivable stupidity. She simply had not thought of the combined effects on her ability to think and act. She could not afford to make any more mistakes. Above all, she had to be careful of the flashbacks.

Hannah took a deep breath and then another. The flashbacks were so real, she'd come out of them confused as to where she was. The last one had been calamitous. Believing she was still in Brian Macy's apartment, she'd called the male nurse Brian and asked him, in Rosie's southern accent, why he was still alive after all that polenta.

Again, the unnerving panic rose at the back of her throat. She fought it down, running her fingers over the finely chiseled edges of the coin pendant. Workmanship. Precise thought and logic. It momentarily reassured her.

Taking a deep breath, she thought through the rubble of her plans, mentally listing each mistake and each success.

That the girl came home with a cold seemed like a gift of fate. As she had hoped, everyone in contact with her began coming down with the same thing. Had things gone according to plan, it would have appeared to everyone as though the girl had picked up some mystery virus on the plane and had passed it on to her father. No investigation, no suspicions. A bad virus from Europe. A virus his immune system couldn't fight off.

When the stupid, willful girl drank the coffee meant for her father, she'd at first thought everything was ruined, but the one thing Tony Saludo had taught her was that there were no such things as mistakes; it was simply a slight change in plans, and as it turned out, it had plenty of benefits.

In her grief, Mimi turned to her, once again leaning on her unshakable rock of Gibraltar. Gordon began to take serious note of her as a trustworthy force. Even Samuel Fromer had seen her as a valuable asset to Gordon's campaign. The Swan was the one who would help Gordon win the election, and keep the family together through thick and thin. Super-Swan come to save the day.

There was also an advantage to the girl's death—it would save Mimi the heartache of having to choose between them later, after the brat figured out their relationship and rebelled. The future emotional tug-of-war games that would most certainly go on over Mimi would get ugly.

It would be a dream come true to have Mimi all to herself to look after. People would nod and say what a good friend she was for sticking by poor Miriam through the tragic loss of her daughter and her husband. No one would even raise an eyebrow when she moved in and they became permanent companions. "Like spinster sisters," they'd say. "Oldest of friends." Their combined finances would set them up for a life of leisure and pleasure.

Mimi's vehement protests against leaving Gordon and thus destroying his political career still made her smile. Mimi was, under the childlike exterior, a very clever and practical woman—her allegiance to her husband's political advancement boiled down to the basics: money, prestige, and a secure, luxurious lifestyle. As long as Gordon could provide those things for her and Iris, she would never leave him. Which was why, of course, Gordon hadn't had a chance.

She tried to feel some remorse about the others, but she couldn't convince herself she hadn't simply aided the natural selection process with weeding out inferiors, or the ones—like Samuel Fromer—who were trouble. Their deaths and the illnesses of the others had been necessary to promote the M. Plague theory until all principal players were dead.

Confusing the two male nurses had been the closest she came to regret. It had been a perfect opportunity missed.

She never dreamed the medical and law enforcement establishments would be bright enough to pick up on the selective immunity factor so soon. Still, it would be all right; she'd planned ahead. Brian would once again be the invaluable link to her and Mimi's final salvation. As soon as the police found the makings of the bomb in his apartment, along with the schedule of Gordon's appearances that Fromer had provided her, it would be enough to implicate the inventor of the D-7 toxin as the person behind the murders. A case of revenge. The match of his handwriting on the office walls and the handwritten death threats, along with the record of the phone calls to Hersh's office, cinched it. And if none of that was enough to convince the police, there were always the catering people who couldn't have missed seeing the six-foot-four blubber barrel wandering around the confusion in the Belvedere Hotel kitchen on the night of the fund-raiser, looking around for something and—knowing him as well as she did—stopping to salivate over the trays of hors d'oeuvres.

Hannah marveled at how easy it had been. People were so predictable. Rosie had fueled Brian's hatred of Gordon Hersh. Once she had the chemist under her thumb, her tearful confession of how Dr. Hersh had brutally raped her while she lay helpless under anesthesia, had sent him into a murderous rage. Soon after, Rosie began planting seeds about how he could make Hersh's life miserable by phoning in death threats. The stink bomb and mailed hate messages were his own idea.

Other than the half-blind old landlady, no one associated with Brian Macy had actually seen Rosie Martinelli, nor would the cops find any trace of her—including fingerprints—in his apartment.

How and why Mimi had been meeting Samuel at the office toting a gun was something she would find out sooner or later. She doubted it would matter very much. The fool was dead, and whatever threat or attraction he'd held for Mimi was done. All that mattered now was to destroy every last bit of evidence that linked her to the murders.

But first, she had to pull herself together.

No sooner had the resolution been made than Hannah Sandell took a deep breath and slipped into a flashback.

Despite the dizziness and the pain behind her eyes, Hannah sat still, feeling for the hole on the inside hem of her skirt. Every second counted now, and time was running out.

It was the nurses' busiest time of the day shift. The rhythms of their activity in and around the patients' rooms, and sending Mimi to the cafeteria for more iced tea, allowed her a fifteen-minute window in which to do what she needed without interference.

With Brian dead and soon to be discovered, she was hav-

ing to choose priorities. Gordon would have to be dosed first. Then, if she could hold out that long, Iris and Cynthia. Relapses.

The thick layers of foundation and rouge weren't going to cover her pallor much longer. In the last hour, she'd vomited four times, and soaked her clothes with perspiration. Mimi would soon notice, and insist she be checked by Dr. Ingram.

Mimi, her little bird. Hannah closed her eyes until the room stopped spinning and the nausea passed. When it came down to it, she could not bring herself to put the powder into Mimi's coffee. She'd been afraid that Mimi wouldn't be strong enough to fight the toxin no matter how small a dose she gave. And if Mimi died, everything would be lost.

They'd been making love when Ingram called to say they needed to come to the hospital right away. She went prepared this time. No more mistakes with Gordon Hersh. He'd been too lucky—giving his coffee to Iris, not eating the poisoned hors d'oeuvres, and then she had to take the chance in the midst of a thousand people to dump powder into his drink—only to have it be "denatured." The coffee she'd brought to his office contained enough D-7 to kill a horse.

But still, Gordon had survived. A modern-day Rasputin. This time, she was determined he would die. In spite of the pain ripping her head in two, she smiled. All that Russian history in college had finally come to use: The idea of using the hem of her skirt to hide the prepared syringe (ironic that she'd stolen it from Gordon's own medical kit) and two of the three remaining test tubes of D-7 came from Czarina Alexandra Romanoff, who, when she knew the Bolsheviks were coming, had her daughters sew their jewels into the hems of their dresses.

Hooking the syringe with her fingernail, Hannah slid it into her palm and up her sleeve. She'd already pulled down a loop of plastic intravenous line so that it almost touched the floor. The rubber port where the nurses injected medications was level with her knee.

With a constant eye on the door, she reached for it, missed, tried again and snagged it. She worked the needle cap off the syringe. A drop of sweat rolled into one eye and stung like acid.

Bile rose in her throat. She blinked several times and steadied her hand. The tip of the needle did not go through the rubber port easily. She pushed with the rest of her strength until she felt it pierce the membrane. When she could see the needle tip safely on the inside of the tubing, she shoved down the plunger.

In an awkward movement, she tried to stand, fell back in the chair, stood again, grabbed for the side rail, fell heavily to her knees and vomited. Backing away from the small, round puddle of bile, she pulled herself up. At the top of the mattress, she came face-to-face with Gordon Hersh.

Eyes wide, he stared at her accusingly and began beating the side rails as best he could with his hands restrained at the wrists.

She forced herself to put one foot in front of the other. The red box. She had to make it to the red box next to the sink before someone came in.

Gordon banged louder. It would be a matter of seconds before he found the call light or a nurse heard the racket.

The opening flaps on the hard plastic box were whimsically marked with red and white concentric circles.

The call light over the door lit up and flashed.

She let the syringe drop through the bull's-eye of the target, and grabbed the edge of the sink. Holding herself upright for a half a second, she pushed off and fell backward into space.

It was getting dark when Adele let herself into the house. Nelson greeted her as usual by laying his Mickey Mouse rug on her feet for a few seconds before he took it back. It was as if he were saying . . . *I like you just this much.* On the days he was really glad to see her, he'd leave the slobbery rag lying on her feet for a few extra seconds.

"Honey, I'm home," she whispered in his ear and kissed the top of his head. "But not for very long."

Nelson whined.

"Because," she explained, "Nancy Drew's hot to trot."

"Hey." It was Cynthia whispering in her frog voice.

Adele had to turn up the volume on the answering machine to understand what she was saying.

"You're up to something, Del. I can smell it. Add this to the notebook: The kid says her mom and the White Swan killed her father. Says she heard them goin' at it in the bedroom the night she got sick. She claims she got sick from drinking the coffee that Hannah and her mother made for her father.

"Remember Hannah making sure she brought us coffee the day I got sick? She saw me slip and contaminate myself with Iris's secretions, so maybe she thought I should be the most logical one to go."

Marcus and Gordon, too, Adele silently added.

"Tim's been in talking to the Swan. By the way, he stopped in to say hello, and ended up asking me about *you!* He thinks you know something he doesn't. Do you? Sorry I couldn't be in on this, but I've been too busy playing one of the victims.

"He asked Iris some questions, but I told him to back off. She's too raw for that yet. He's acting weird, too. Can't put my finger on it. It's almost like he's— Oh-oh. Here comes Linda with my meds. Gotta go."

Adele listened for the disconnect and heard instead: "Oh yeah—Skip told me about Marcus. How the hell did *he* come down with the plague? You think he was getting it on with Gordon? Or, maybe Hannah really is a man, and he and Marcus were getting it on?"

After the next beep, Tim's message was brief and to the point: "Hey. The plague isn't a plague. It's a toxin manufactured by a psycho named Brian Macy—who apparently killed himself by taking a dose of the stuff. Takamoto called and gave me the lowdown so I contacted SFPD. They found evidence in his apartment linking him to the bomb. I'm heading over there. I think we got ourselves a revenge crime.

"If you want more details, call me as soon as you get in. I notice you didn't mention that you weren't coming in to work today, which means you're out there getting into trouble."

There was a silent pause in which she thought perhaps he'd hung up, except his voice came up again, tight and edgy.

"Hear you and old Richard Burton, I mean Peter, really hit it off last night. Did he take you to see *Hawaii*, or did you see *PT 109*?" He snickered. "Page me or else I torture the rabbit."

Adele rewound the tape and checked her wig in the mirror. What a jerk. He sets her up with a guy whose hair screamed squeebe, and then rubs her nose in it? "Sure, I'll call you, Uncle Timmy, when you catch up."

The phone rang as she was getting into the Beast. Rushing back to the house, her foot got tangled in the Mickey Mouse rug and she sprawled on top of Nelson, her two legs getting entwined with his four. The message was already in progress, so she left the receiver where it was and listened.

"Larry Cornelius here." He was panting as if he'd been running. "Not only are the amounts in the tubes all off, but I've got four test tubes full of baking powder and four viable mice with serious cases of gas. Three detectives from three different law enforcement agencies are on their way to question me about Brian's involvement in the deaths.

"Would you give me a call as soon . . ."

Nelson listened to the rest of the message by himself. By the time it was ended, she and the Beast were on their way to Ross Commons.

TWENTY-ONE

THE KEY CLICKED IN THE ALARM BOX, SHUT-
ting off the security system. Adele flipped on the lights, put
her hands on her hips, and decided to begin at the beginning.
In the foyer, she ran gloved hands under the plinths, then
down inside the two alabaster vases. Going to her knees, she
started at one corner of the hardwood floor, knocking, tap-
ping, listening for a false, hollow sound in the wood.

It was a big house, she thought, but she would not leave
until she'd searched every drawer, every nook, book, and
carrot.

Detective Ritmann ducked as a seventeen-pound persian
cat jumped from the top of the bookshelf onto his shoulder.
Prying its claws out of his suit jacket, he let it fall to the
floor where it bounced once, rolled over and scattered away
like a fat butterscotch pudding.

"Miss Monsarrat was here?" he asked, disbelieving.
"Today?"

The lady dwarf nodded. "Yesterday, too. She comes in
here and shows me this photograph of that Jezebel Brian
went around with, and I tells her 'Sure, you betcha, that's
Rose' and she runs outta here like she's got ants in her
pants."

"Do you have the photograph Miss Monsarrat showed
you?" the detective asked politely, although he was twitching with impatience.

Wordlessly, the old woman pulled the paper out of the

pocket of her red plastic apron, unfolded it, and pointed to the photo of Hannah Sandell.

Tim studied the photograph for a second, then looked back at Mrs. Duggan, who was scratching her head. The gray hair moved back and forth on her scalp like a wig.

"Say, you think she and this Rosie are in on something together? This Adele, you know, had gold eyes like one of these damned cats. Didn't trust her far as I could throw her."

She rubbed her hump and looked off into the distance. "This kinda thing makes me wish me and Fred had stayed in Parachute. People there was normal."

"Adele is okay," he said, and pushed a gray tabby off his shoe. "She works on our side." He sighed and moved to the door. "She just works a lot faster than the rest of us."

The unmarked video had been taped to the lining of a suede jacket. Adele snapped it into the VCR and sat on the end of the bed, watching the TV screen.

Video snow. Nothing but squiggly lines and black and gray snow. She popped the tape out and was taping it back to the lining of the coat when Sam Spade, with his hat pulled down low over one eye, tapped her on the brain.

Why would she keep a blank video taped to the inside of a jacket, Adele? he asked, fingering the gold pocket watch hanging from the chain attached to his vest.

"For video emergencies?" she asked.

Remember the Moore case in eighty-nine? Halfway through The Maltese Falcon *tape, the guy had filmed himself murdering those two gals?*

She put the tape back in and kept her thumb pressed to the fast forward. Sure enough, in the middle of the tape a flicker of recorded film came on the screen.

Aerial view. Hannah Sandell having sex with a very young and very drunk blonde—the emotionally injured Sandy, Adele guessed.

Aerial view. Hannah Sandell and an enthusiastic, contor-

tionistic redheaded woman. An interesting demonstration of
the sex toys under her bed.

Aerial view. Hannah Sandell and Mimi Hersh.

Seeing her from so many angles, especially when her hair
was pulled back from her face, it was amazing just how
much Hannah Sandell really did resemble Mick Jagger.

Lying back, Adele studied the ceiling fan over the bed.
The base was decorated with circles of black glass. She
picked out the one that was loaded, certain that, had she not
known what she was looking for, even she would have
missed it.

She rewound the tape and put it back where it came from.

Good find, Adele, but no cigar, said the panel of imaginary
sleuthing judges who were critiquing her search techniques.

Grimly, she set about checking every inch of the furniture, then headed for the library.

Halfway around the first shelf, she ran into the cookbook
section. Searching was quickly reduced to browsing, and
halfway through a book of gourmet hors d'oeuvres, she was
as ravenous as she'd ever been in her life.

"Do you really think she'd miss one or two carrots?" she
asked the bronze bust acting as a bookend. It might have
been Marie Curie or maybe Camille Claudel.

*She wanted to hand over thousands of dollars' worth of
clothes and jewelry to you at the drop of a clever line,* said
the bust. *Two carrots ain't gonna break her, babe.*

Permission granted, Adele hurried to the kitchen and
opened the refrigerator. Carbohydrate-loading hormones shot
into the food center of her brain, causing her hand to jerk
away from the carrots and grab the sourdough rye bread instead. Immediately, sodium and fat-loading hormones rushed
to hop on the food craving bandwagon.

The capers and mayonnaise jars were on the marble
countertop and opened before she knew what was happening, although she wasn't so transported that she wouldn't
have given the mole on her left cheek for a Vidalia onion.

Adele sprinkled a slice of bread with capers, reading the propaganda on the label of the mayonnaise jar while she did so. It said it was "low fat" mayonnaise—an oxymoron if there ever was one. She found a knife and spread the other slice of rye with the tiniest bit of mayonnaise.

At first bite, Adele groaned, momentarily lost in taste pleasure. Caper and mayo sandwiches were added to her list of gastronomical favorite combo sandwiches—right up there with peanut butter and mayo, and cottage cheese with catsup on burnt bread.

"Maybe just a bit more mayo, huh? To make up for the onion?"

Fat makes cellulite! shouted her slender, muscular thighs.

"Pffft. I can afford it." She plunged the knife into the middle of the jar. It hit something solid.

Fishing around, she pushed a cylindrical object halfway out of the cellulite-making muck. The hairs on the back of her neck danced.

A plastic test tube three-quarters filled with white powder. The screw top was carefully marked No.3 in black ballpoint.

"Christ on a bike." She spit the half-masticated mouthful of sandwich into the garbage disposal and washed out her mouth.

From the side of the mayonnaise jar she peeled off the grocery receipt. "TJ's LF Mayo" was the only item at $1.79. It had been purchased ten days before.

"Okay, so where the hell are tubes one and two?"

Or four for that matter, said the food processor.

She held the tube up to the light, shook it once, and carefully put it back inside the mayonnaise. Then she ran through the house returning everything to its original place. It would all be untouched and newly discovered when Tim followed her psychic revelations as to the whereabouts of the evidence.

* * *

On the short run back to the Beast, odd snippets of information caused Adele's senses to go to red alert and her brain to break open. Her body tensed with the resulting gush of adrenaline. Test tube number three left her desperate to know where one, two, and four were. Hannah must have had some with her at the hospital when she poisoned Gordon and herself.

And who else would she want to do in? asked the phantom detective, brushing off a speck of dust from his immaculate white gloves.

"Iris?" Sure. Her father had had a relapse, so why not the daughter? It would serve to get the girl out of the way. *Good. Who else?* asked one of the sleuth judges who looked like Winston Churchill.

"Cynthia? For good measure. Leave no wounded."

Her hand explored the top of the Beast's rear passenger-side tire and grasped the ignition key. When she turned it, the Beast did not so much as grunt. She hit its chest dash and tried again. It was the car's way of telling her to slow down—relax—think things over for a minute.

"Okay," she said, settling into the overstuffed seat. "What else?"

She recalled the threads and the sewing scissors on the bed.

Linda's comment about how desperate Hannah was to get dressed left no doubt that she had some or all of the rest of the tubes hidden in her clothes.

She tried the Beast, and it jerked forward, full of energy. A half mile later, the vehicle, in a viciously cruel mood, went to sleep. Using all her strength, she steered the napping car into the College of Marin parking lot, letting it smash into the No Parking Without Permit sign. Emerging from the vehicle, she slammed the door, kicked the tire, took a swing at the CB antenna, and went in search of a phone.

"Do you know where he is, Peter? I need to talk to him right away."

"He stopped back in the office after he questioned the Sandell woman." Detective Chernin's voice changed to a more intimate timbre. "Hey—how about we take in an early movie tonight? I think *Braveheart*'s playing at the Grand for a buck fifty. Maybe we could grab a beer down at the alleys afterward?"

Adele gripped the metal edge of the phone booth shelf, wanting to scream. "Ah, I don't think I'm going to be done here for quite a while, Pete. Do you know where Tim is now? This is urgent. I really need to speak to him."

"Isn't this something I can help you with? I mean, I know Tim's a good-looking buck, but I'm just as . . ."

"Do you know where he is now?"

He didn't miss the Don't-fuck-with-me tone. "I don't. Sure I can't help?"

She read him the number on the phone. "Radio his car. Tell him to call me at that number stat. I'll wait here for five minutes, then I'm headed to Ellis." She hung up and did stretches, watching her watch. Two minutes later she remembered Tim's pager. It was part guess, part vague memory of something Cynthia had told her a long time ago that led her to add the numeric code NOW to the end of the phone booth's number. When her watch indicated she'd been waiting eight minutes, she headed back to the Beast. A block from the booth, she was sure she heard ringing and sprinted back at a pace that would have won her an Olympic gold medal.

"Hey buddy," said Peter Chernin, sounding irritated. "Adele is waiting at a public phone for you to call. You got about three minutes left to get her." Chernin read off the number she'd given him and hung up.

Tim guessed the detective had waited till the last minute to call him. Cursing, he checked the number with the one that he now read off his pager—it was the same with the exception of the addition of his emergency code. He dialed from the car phone, at the same time pulling off the highway and into one of the most infamous rest stops in all of San Francisco Bay Area. He groaned, extremely glad he was an officer of the law and had a badge to flash—it would keep the pariahs at bay.

She answered on the tenth ring.

"Why do you always push it right to the wall before you decide to call?" he asked before she'd even had a chance to say hello.

"Because I want to be absolutely sure of my facts," she said, sucking air. "It's like people who wait until they're at death's door before they call the doctor. And who says this is the wall?"

"It is as of thirty-six minutes ago."

"Explain."

"At first it looked like Macy was our man. Then the lab called about the syringe you pulled out of Gordon Hersh's sharps box. I brought the chemical component readout down to Cornelius, who confirmed that what was clinging to the sides of the inside of that syringe was D-seven."

He paused briefly, then added wryly, "I can't believe you flashed him that fake deputy sheriff's badge, Adele. That's stooping kind of low, don't you think?"

"Hey," she said defiantly, to cover her humiliation, "whatever works."

"The lab also dusted for fingerprints on the barrel."

"Hannah Sandell," she said.

Like a cross or a wreath of garlic, Tim held up his badge against the window as two obviously gay men approached his car. Their salacious smiles faded into expressions of alarm as they fled in the direction of the men's room. "Congratulations, Miss Monsarrat, you've just won the Maytag washer and dryer."

The mass exodus of fifteen or twenty gay men from the men's bathroom was instantaneous.

"Care to spin for the new car?" he asked.

"Turn the letters, Vanna."

"They dusted Macy's apartment and . . ."

". . . and they found none of Sandell's fingerprints. You did, however, find something as obscure as a strand of blond hair that will test out to be hers. You also have Mrs. Duggan as a witness, *and* you will find some pretty interesting phone calls on Dr. Macy's final bill."

The woman needs to be in business, Tim thought, trying to control his desire. Her capability and her brains excited him more than any woman he'd ever known. What amazed him was that he'd never even kissed her—except in a brotherly manner. "She's won the Ford Fiesta, ladies and gentlemen!

"Atlanta also did some fancy footwork and came up with a stain that when applied to the tissues of the victims, revealed that it was taken up by crystals that were concentrated in the brain, lungs, kidneys, and liver. D-seven crystals."

"I've got to go," she said abruptly. "All of this is old news to me."

"Adele!" he shouted.

She brought the phone back to her ear. "What? Hurry up, I've gotta go."

"Talk to me. Now!"

Adele had lived with a Green Beret long enough to know the sound of irrefutable command when she heard it. "Okay, okay. My guess is that she's got at least two vials with her at the hospital. At some point she'll try to re-dose Iris for sure, and Cynthia, too, if she can. Her house is loaded with evidence . . ."

She heard him open his mouth and hurried on." . . . that is exactly where she left it, untouched. Sounds to me like you followed the trail of bread crumbs, so I don't need to waste any more time telling you the rest . . ."

"Wait . . ."

"I'm about ten minutes away from Ellis. The Beast is being temperamental, so I'm going to run. How far away in time are you?"

He checked his watch. It was late enough in the evening for most of the dinner crowds and night schoolers to be off the streets. "Twenty-five minutes to Ellis if I use the stick-on bubble gum machine and siren. I'll radio Cini or Chernin to get over there with a squad car. . . . "

"Don't you dare!" she snapped. "I'll be over there before either one of those guys have their fannies off the chair. I know what and who I'm dealing with—they don't."

She paused, then added in a much softer tone: "Tim. I know what I'm doing. You just get there as fast as you can. I'll handle it until then, okay?"

He hesitated. He didn't want to take away her chance to land the marlin by herself. Yet, if something happened to her or anyone else . . .

"Okay, Monsarrat. I'm probably committing professional suicide but it's yours."

"I'm gone," she said, already judging time, distance, and pace.

Tim reached around to the backseat and pulled out the battery-operated blue flashing light. Putting it on the roof, he hit the siren.

Seven of the fifteen gay men who were rushing to their cars simultaneously stopped and put their hands up over their heads.

The hazy, unreal world that came with pain and drugs had not robbed Hannah of her faculties, at least not enough that the PA system announcement escaped her notice. The time she'd spent with Mimi at the brat's bedside had not been wasted; she'd made note of every detail of hospital routine from where the bedpans were kept, to how to inject IV lines and silence monitor and ventilator alarms.

She knew the pandemonium that always followed the announcement: "ATTENTION ALL PERSONNEL. CODE BLUE." Code blue was impending death, code red for fire, and code yellow for a psychiatric crisis. Every time a code blue occurred, the patients were left completely on their own for anywhere from five to thirty minutes while the staff responded.

She struggled to lift herself onto her elbows. Through the viewing window, she could see the empty nurses' station and deserted hall. The sight motivated her into a sitting position, and then off the end of the bed. She tested her feet. Her sense of balance was off, and it was hard to hold her head upright. She closed her eyes and took some steps in place until the dizziness passed. Holding onto the mattress, she walked around the bed to where the monitor was and pressed the yellow button with the word "hold" printed in bold letters.

It lit up and flashed. Two at a time, she peeled the electrodes off her torso, watching as the squiggly pattern on the screen went to a flat line. In the corner of the screen, a message flashed:

CAUTION! ALARMS SILENCED!

The IV catheter came out on its own as soon as the tape was loosened. She used the corner of her gown to stop the flow of blood and stumbled to the closet. The transfer of the two test tubes and the extra syringe from her skirt hem to her purse required a certain amount of dexterity. That she managed the task within a minute or so, boosted her confidence.

She dressed quickly, glad for the ease of the pullover blouse and elastic waistband on the skirt. Pulling her hair back into a short ponytail, she glanced at herself in the mirror. The image wasn't exactly the White Swan, but she would pass on the street as a regular harried housewife.

The layout of the ward gave her a straight shot to the lighted exit sign at the end of the hall. From there, the back stairwell led to the parking lot. She inched into the hall. Between where she stood and the exit sign was Iris's room. A stainless steel kitchen cart and a chart rack had been left unattended in the middle of the hall, just a few feet from the exit.

A nurse—her nurse—ran to the station and picked up the phone. Hannah pulled back behind the curtain and froze. Her mind whirled, and for a minute the room swam away in a haze of white fog. Heart pounding in her throat, she bit her lip until the taste of blood filled her mouth. It woke her up, and cleared the haze.

She peeked out. The nurse was gone and the station was once again deserted. Still, she had to hurry—it wouldn't be long before they began to filter back and discovered she was no longer on monitor. She had gone only a few yards when a noise behind her caused her to turn on her heel. Running toward her at full speed was the med tech. She stepped against the wall, and pushed the sheath off the syringe. The needle was only two inches long, but jammed into an eye or neck, it would be enough to slow him down. She readied herself for the impact, her hand closed around the barrel, moving out of her purse.

He ran by her without so much as a glance in her direction. At the station, he rooted among the papers, picked up a chart, and hurried back toward the commotion.

Sagging against the wall, she felt one of the acute room viewing windows at her back. It was Gordon's old room, but the lights were out, making it impossible to see if it was empty or not. She stepped inside.

As her eyes adjusted to the dim light, she listened carefully to the mechanical sound of an IV pump. *A new patient already?*

"Mommy, is that you?" The voice came out of the dark. It was old and weak. Hannah peered around the corner of the bathroom door and saw a wisp of white hair surrounding a face that was a Death Valley of wrinkles.

"Shh!" She went closer, finger to her lips.

"Mommy?" The feeble voice rose.

She leaned close to the elderly man's ear and hissed.

"Shut up you old fool and go to sleep or I'll smother you with the pillow."

"Yes, Mama." He closed his eyes and faked sleep.

Through the window between the rooms, Hannah could see that Iris was reading. Cynthia appeared to be asleep, but she couldn't be sure.

Too risky. She'd scream at the sight of me and then Cynthia might wake up and . . . no. It isn't going to work. Hannah rested her head against the wall and concentrated. In her line of vision, three things jumped out at her: the exit sign, the portable charting rack, and the kitchen cart filled with nighttime snacks. She studied the trays holding milk, tea, hot cocoa, bananas, and graham crackers. What had Linda called them? HS snacks. Hour of sleep snacks. She managed to laugh even though it hurt her head.

HS snacks. That was good. Very funny. Hannah Sandell snacks.

She removed one of the test tubes. The powder in the vial marked No.2 was almost gone; she'd not wanted to make any mistake with Brian—his dose used up almost the whole vial. The rest had gone to Gordon—to be done with him once and for all. She didn't want any more survivors. The No.1 vial was full. It would be more than enough.

She opened both of the vials and looked for the name and room number tags on the sides of the trays. 802B O'NEIL— Jell-O and apple juice. On tray 802A was the brat's cocoa, banana, and packaged graham crackers.

"A treat for everyone," Hannah murmured, pulling out the two trays. She felt someone coming, and without turning to look in the direction of the intruder, dumped the powder into the beverages and fixed her sights on the exit sign, stumbling toward it as fast as she could go.

Her skirt flapped against her legs. It was damp. For a moment she was distracted, trying to remember what she had spilled on herself, or if it had been raining when she came into the hospital.

But that was hours ago. Wasn't it?

Behind her, someone shouted.

She dropped the two tubes into the outside pockets of her purse as if they were burning her hands. She would have to get rid of them along with the other.

Then there would be nothing left except Mimi.

Linda yawned and checked the time again. 2015 hours. Mrs. Turina had tried to escape her earthly body at 1901 and had been detained by the code team. The code itself had taken an hour out of all their schedules.

She'd have to skimp on checking the IV's. Meds would be late and HS snacks weren't even worth bothering with. Except she couldn't send a full cart back to the kitchen; the supervisor and the dietician would both be down her throat . . . and with her luck, someone would go into insulin shock because they didn't have their " 'nana and Jell-O."

"Okay, Junior Trainees," she said, addressing her entire evening staff of unlicensed, nonmedical personnel. She sighed. There wasn't one R.N. or L.V.N. in the bunch.

"Give the nineteen hundred and twenty hundred meds with the HS snacks. Do quick vitals, then leave them alone to feed and sleep."

The excitement of the code was still coursing through Mirek, uprooting emotions and imparting a curious energy that made him feel joyous. He had watched carefully as the code team performed like the workings of a fine clock; it was precision for the sole purpose of saving a life. For the first time he'd experienced the rush of adrenaline instead of fear. For the first time, he, Miroslav Dvorak, had laid hands upon the sick and dying. He had made a difference in bringing one of God's creations back to life.

Working in unison with the doctor who was attempting to intubate, he'd held the tube ready, and turned on the overhead lights when needed. Then, the charge nurse had picked him out of the crowd and placed him at the patient's side to do the chest compressions of CPR.

Remembering the doctor's praise, his eyes welled with tears. "Good compressions, son. Keep it up," he whispered to himself. "Me, Dvorak. I do good compressions!"

He smiled and then knit his eyebrows. The big, pale woman who was in the hallway during the code . . . the one who seemed afraid of him, was in front of the kitchen cart, hovering over the food trays. Upon hearing him approach, she started, and without turning, hurried down the hall toward the stairway exit.

Ah, that was why she seemed fearful, he thought. The woman was hungry and had been trying to steal food. He himself had done that many times in the markets of Pizen.

"Wait!" he shouted. "I will give you food. Don't run away."

But the woman did not stop. He saw her stuffing something into the front of her purse. Mirek prayed it would be enough food to sustain her for the night.

Cynthia picked up her book and tried to read, but the shifting of her eyes threatened to bring back the pain and nausea. Lying back, she took comfort from watching Iris, who was engrossed in a tattered tome.

"What are you reading, Iris?"

"A book of international fairy tales."

"Does it help?"

Iris thought for a moment, smashing her lips together with her fingers as she did so. "It lets me escape for a while. When I was little, my parents used to read to me all the time, except the books they'd read came right off the *Times* bestsellers lists? I fell asleep listening to things like *The Road Less Traveled*, and biographies of American politicians and businessmen.

"Every school I attended focused more on computer science and things like that, so I never heard of Little Red Riding Hood until recently. I decided I'd better catch up on my childhood reading before I get too old."

Cynthia nodded, recalling that her course had gone in just

the opposite direction. At the age of nine she'd grown sick of the insipid choice of reading material in the "children's" section of her school library. She found the biggest, most adult-looking book she could. It had taken her a full year to finish Ayn Rand's *The Fountainhead*, but when she'd tried to give a book report, her teacher called her parents to suggest their child needed psychiatric attention.

"Just keep reading fairy tales, Iris. They keep you young."

The med tech whom Iris thought was interesting because of his accent came into the room with their snack trays. As was the unconscious habit of teens and young adults, Mirek and Iris eyed each other briefly, appraising the physical attractiveness of the other. They silently gave each other a grade of A+, and smiled.

After the aide left, Iris gave her banana a curled lip, but hungrily eyed the cocoa and two packages of graham crackers.

Cynthia looked at her tray and wondered why anyone with half a brain could ever think for one moment that orange Jell-O and apple juice were the things to serve sick people. Sickeningly sweet, both Jell-O and apple juice were by far the two most commonly vomited items on the food chain. She reached for her Jell-O anyway—if she hoped to get out of this dump, she had to get her peristaltic waves in order.

"Are the natives restless in here again?" Linda asked, giving the lump in the bed a sideways glance. "You're off the scope."

The yellow hold button flashing at the bottom of the bedside monitor caught her immediate attention. Then, looking more closely, she realized the lump was distorted. A corner of a pillow stuck out where the head should have been.

Linda's eyes automatically went to the closet, which was devoid of clothes. Still, she poked the lump anyway, hoping against hope that her finger would meet the solid resistance of flesh and bone.

Hannah crouched down next to the Mercedes and opened her purse. She ran her hand over the contents, then let her fingers search along the sides and bottom for the familiar tangle of keys. Panic crept into her temples. Her heart raced as she tore the purse apart, throwing everything except the test tubes and her wallet to the ground. They'd taken away her keys.

A white car with a flashing blue light squealed and skidded around a curve in the drive leading to the emergency entrance to the hospital.

For a measure of time, Hannah was motionless as stone. She felt cold and powerfully sick. Slowly, she became aware that she must move, but to where? The idea of going back to her room momentarily appealed to her. Except she was so close. She had to remember the purpose of what she was doing; remember the reward for following through.

Her fingers, still searching for her keys, brushed against one of the test tubes. She pulled it out. First and foremost the order of business was to destroy the remaining three vials in the same manner as the one she'd used at the dinner. As soon as she accomplished that vital task, then she would readmit herself to the hospital, saying she was delirious when she left and hadn't known what she was doing.

Hannah closed her eyes, thinking of the relief she would feel when there was no more evidence that could be used against her.

TWENTY-TWO

FOR THE FIRST FIVE MINUTES OF THE RUN, ADELE was short of breath, which was the way it went for her in any high-stress situation. It was her worst drawback in competition running. By the time she entered the back stairwell of Ellis Hospital, her legs were shaking with adrenaline. She made it to Ward 8 without ever feeling the stairs beneath her feet.

Flying into the hallway, she collided with two people who both looked the way she felt.

"Where did you see her?" Linda yelled.

Frightened, Mirek stammered. It was like the time the VB had raided his grandfather's home demanding to know where the "American propaganda literature"—a long outdated *Time* magazine—was hidden.

Adele grabbed the front of his scrub top and pulled him off his feet. Their noses touched. "Goddamn it, Mirek, talk! Where did you see her and how long ago?"

"She is by the kitchen cart. I—I think she takes some food. I . . . ten minutes ago. She . . ."

"Where did she go?"

Mirek pointed to the back stairwell exit.

Adele set him down. "Why do you think she was taking food?"

"She takes the trays out and then runs away very scared when she see me. I think she steals. . . ."

"Hey! Everybody!" Adele yelled, already making her

way toward room 802. "Retrieve all the snacks from the patients, STAT! Don't worry about isolation technique . . . just get those trays. Write down every detail of what each patient ate or drank!

"Linda—get on the intercom and announce that the patients are not to touch their snacks. Then call pharmacy and get a supply of ipecac sent up stat."

She entered Cynthia and Iris's room, assessing the situation as she went. Graham cracker held in hand, Iris was chewing. Cynthia had just put a spoonful of orange Jell-O in her mouth.

Adele lunged for Cynthia, grabbing her by the chin. "Spit it out!" she yelled, holding the Jell-O bowl to her mouth. "Everything is poisoned. Wash your mouth out with water from the tap and gargle for five minutes with mouthwash."

Bewildered, Cynthia did as she was commanded. Iris had already spit out the graham cracker onto her tray.

"How much Jell-O did you swallow?"

In the nanosecond between the question and the answer, Adele's heart skipped.

"None," Cynthia said, letting water dribble out the side of her mouth. "That was my first bite."

"What about the apple juice?"

In answer, Cynthia curled her lip. "You know I hate the stuff."

"What about you, Iris? Did you drink any of that cocoa yet?"

Frightened, Iris started to whimper. "No, no cocoa. I ate a whole graham cracker, though."

"Was the package opened or ripped in any way?"

Iris shook her head and drank mouthwash straight from the bottle.

Adele gave the girl a quick hug of relief. "It's all right. You should be okay."

The ward's intercom crackled to life and a staticky, underwater version of Linda's voice boomed into the rooms. "If you have been served a snack, do not—I repeat—do not eat or drink anything from your trays. A nurse will be around immediately to collect your snack. If you have already eaten food or drunk any beverage that was on your tray, tell the nurse immediately."

"Keep rinsing," Adele instructed. "I'll be right back."

Adele worked alongside the aides and nurses running in and out of rooms collecting trays—most of which were untouched. Silently, Adele sent a word of thanks to the network airing a "60 Minutes" special on the contaminated food served in fast-food joints. The majority of patients were so involved in watching it, they had not yet begun their snacks. The rest of the patients were already asleep and hadn't touched their trays.

Adele entered the last room to be checked, just as the middle-aged son of the patient picked up a cup of cocoa off his mother's snack tray and lifted the Styrofoam rim to his lips.

Without taking her eyes off the cup, she tensed the muscles of her legs. The cup tipped slightly and she sprang, catlike, diving outward, stretching toward the cup—an Olympic broadjump finalist going for the gold. In the back of her mind, she thanked Gavin for his combat training.

The man's arm jerked upward, and the cup flew into the wall where it exploded, spraying hot chocolate everywhere. He crashed to the floor, taking Adele with him.

Dazed, he gaped at her, cocoa dripping off the end of his nose. The patient's two other visitors stared down at them, their jaws all uniformly unhinged.

The sight was too much for her. Adele broke into her crazy woman laughter, wheezing with it even as she got to her feet. It wasn't until she concentrated on horrible, morbid thoughts, that she managed to bring the wild laughter under control.

"Didn't you hear the announcement?" she asked.

In silence, the visitors and the patient looked at one another, all eyes and open mouths.

She helped the man to his feet. "Did you drink any of the cocoa?"

All at once, everyone raised their hands and began to sign rapidly. She wondered if it was as confusing to them as when hearing people all talked at once.

She got a few signs here and there, having studied a rudimentary form of sign language—one usually taught to young children. Signing in exact English, she asked, "Did you drink . . ."

She couldn't remember the sign for cocoa, and had to improvise. ". . . sweet, brown milk?"

They looked at her like she was from another planet.

Adele resorted to fingerspelling. "Did you swallow c-o-c-o-a?"

The son signed "No. You hit me!" wearing an accusatory, indignant expression.

"Good!" she signed with happy enthusiasm.

Now they really gaped.

"Drink bad! Poison!" she signed. "Wait for your nurse to tell you more."

She left them signing like mad, and ran into the next room where a pale Mirek was checking the gathered snack trays with meticulous care. Linda stood next to him going over the lists the aide handed her.

"We've got two patients who drank some of their cocoa," she said. "Nobody ate the Jell-O or the bananas, and no one took any juice or tea. The graham crackers were all the packaged kind."

"Ipecac the cocoa patients immediately." Adele moved swiftly toward room 802. "I doubt any trays other than Room 802's were touched, but I don't want to take chances. Don't worry about getting a doctor's order . . . Ingram will be glad to cover anything we do."

As soon as Cynthia saw her, she made a comic, protective gesture over her Jell-O.

"Very funny," Adele said, more casually than she felt.

They stared at each other for a beat. Then, Cynthia put

her hands on her hips. "So! What's the problem? The food budget get cut again, or what?"

They collided in the middle of the stairs between the third and fourth landings. To the casual observer, it might have appeared that they held onto each other longer than was necessary after the collision.

"The charge nurse told me she escaped," he panted. "You were busy picking up trays, so I checked the parking lot for her car. It's still here, but no sign of her. I've got Chernin on his way to her house. Cini will cover the hospital grounds. I'm checking the other floors."

"Where's the car?"

"Visitor lot in the back. Gray Mercedes. I disconnected the distributor. Even if she got to it, she couldn't drive it."

Adele raised her eyebrows. *Even if she got to it, she couldn't drive it because I have her keys.*

"Is everybody okay upstairs?"

She nodded. "One of the aides saw her tampering with the snack trays. I'm sure the lab will find Iris and Cyn's snacks loaded with the rest of the D-seven." She paused. "That is, with the exception of what she's got tucked away in the mayonnaise jar in her fridge."

"A mayonnaise jar in her refrigerator? How the hell did you find that?"

"Oh my darling," she said, tweaking his nose, "don't you know that devious minds work alike?"

"You sure you're okay, lady?" The cabbie, whose real name was Richard Nixon, kept his eyes shifting nervously between the rearview mirror and the road. He recognized the woman in his backseat as a hospital runaway; they were easy to spot. She'd flagged him down outside the main parking lot, her hospital ID band still attached to her wrist. She looked like death and smelled like puke—all sure signs.

"I had a lady 'bout a year ago? Gave birth to a baby right

there in the backseat while I was drivin'." He chuckled. "Scared the hell right outta' me. Gee, I mean all that yellin' ?

"You aren't havin' a baby or nothin' are you, lady?"

Hannah shook her head. "Migraine," she said, barely above a whisper.

"Oh, yeah. I know about those. My sister's kid gets them. They're bad. Makes the kid throw up for days. She's gotta go in a dark room and . . ."

"Just drive," Hannah said wearily. "And keep your eyes on the road in front of you."

He stole a peek at her from time to time, and once, when she'd rolled down the window, he watched her throw something out. Looked like a small glass bottle—probably a single swigger of vodka or gin.

He slowed when he came to Shady Lane. "Which house, lady?" he asked in a loud voice. The woman looked like she might be asleep.

She answered at once, and opened eyes that looked like clear marbles. "On the left. The one with the tall hedges. You can pull in right—"

The woman bolted forward. "Keep going!" she shouted in his ear.

The cabbie jerked the wheel. "You said . . ."

"Drive, goddamn it! Don't stop. Step on it! Go! Go! Go!"

Richard Nixon, aka Tommy Smith, swerved back onto the road and gunned it. He'd taken a good look around first, though. To see what had spooked her. The house, as far as he could see, was deserted and dark. But his headlights had caught the reflectors of a car that was parked by the gate of the house next door. The vehicle was hidden almost entirely by a row of juniper bushes. He wouldn't have thought a thing of it, except for the glimpse of the back of a balding head sticking up over the headrest.

"Where to now, lady?" He was getting nervous; he didn't want any part of the woman's troubles. For all he knew she could be mixed up with the Mafia or be some kind of drug kingpin. He just wanted the broad out of his cab. He wanted regular fares—old ladies coming home from bridge club meetings in Greenbrae, or an uncomplicated drunk from Arthur's.

"Sausalito," she said. "Spencer Drive."

"So much for sitting Shiva," Mimi said, looking herself over in the mirror. She cocked her head and smiled at the image. The long, black gauze skirt and the matching black top contrasted with her skin, and matched her hair. The tiny bells on the earrings that dangled all the way to her collarbone made a happy sound as she twirled across the bedroom.

She took another sip of wine. Hannah would reprimand her for choosing to wear silver jewelry with black. Esther would have said she looked like an old crow and that it wasn't appropriate to wear black at such a young age. Gordon wouldn't have approved of any of it. He would have criticized her for looking like a hippie. He would have further made her feel guilty by saying she would corrupt Iris by appearing to uphold the radical, unstable ideals of their misguided generation rather than being embarrassed by the "peace/love" mentality.

She imagined Gordon lecturing her, shaking his finger the way Esther had. "Next, you'll start smoking marijuana!" he'd say.

"Yes!" She laughed, already digging through the "junk" closet. At the very back, under the stack of ancient board games, she pulled out a gray shoe box in which she saved bits and pieces of memorabilia. At the bottom lay a perfectly rolled joint that was fifteen years old. Hannah had given it to her for her twenty-second birthday.

With matches from The Brown Derby, she lit up and—unlike Bill Clinton—inhaled deeply. She'd held it for a full five seconds when the sound of the front doorbell knocked the smoke out of her as if she'd been hit. In the panic of being caught, she frantically waved at the air, though she did have the presence of mind to carefully snuff out the end of the joint—no sense in wasting vintage grass.

Halfway down the staircase, her foot caught in the hem of her skirt. Hanging onto the railing, she slid down to the bottom on her behind. As she tried to untangle her feet, Mimi gave in to a fit of giggles.

She answered the door bent double with wheezing laughter.

Tim and Adele rode in the unmarked car listening to Detective Chernin's report of the Sandell residence.

"Nothing going on here," he said cheerfully. "Place as dark as the haunted house in *The Haunting*. Not even the trees are stirring."

"Push him," Adele instructed. "What about traffic . . . foot or vehicular?"

"Chernin? Give me a stat on traffic by the house."

"This is one dead neighborhood. Not so much as a raccoon unless you want to count the taxi that pulled in by mistake and then beat it."

"That's her!" Adele hissed. "She saw him and ran. How long ago?"

Chernin guessed it had been just about twelve minutes give or take a second.

Tim opened his mouth, but she cut him off. "Get out your blue bubble and head for Spencer Drive in Sausalito," she demanded. "She's going for Mimi."

Tim stuck the bubble on top of the roof. "She's not going to go there, Adele. She'd be stupid to do that. She's probably headed for the airport."

The nurse rolled her eyes and looked at him unbelieving. "Christ on a bike, Ritmann, how can you possibly say that? She doesn't have a clue about what we have on her . . . except a stupid hanky in Gordon's pocket."

He swerved to avoid a double-parked truck, then gave her a quick look. "How do you know any of this? How did you figure out that she . . . that . . ."

"Love and sex, Tim," she said, as if to explain everything. "Two prime motivating factors. Love and sex is what this is all about."

Hannah pushed past her lover and went to the couch in the study. She fell onto it and covered her face.

Mimi could not stop laughing.

The sound of Mimi's laughter grated on her until the pain in her head was exploding. "You're ridiculous," she whispered. "Look at yourself."

The petite woman sobered at once. "What do you mean? I was just having fun. I found that joint you gave me on my birthday. Remember?" Mimi's smile returned, and she giggled. "Remember that night that you and me and Marty DeLaney went to Lena's Cafe and got caught with fake IDs by that jerk of a bouncer who made us . . ."

"You look like the wicked witch of Oz," Hannah said mockingly. "Those earrings are something I'd expect to see on a gypsy. What have you done with the gold and pearl pair I gave you?"

"Upstairs," Mimi muttered as a deep flush of shame settled over her. "I thought I'd wear something *I* liked for once."

"Well, it didn't work. You have less taste now than when you were in college."

"Why aren't you in the hospital?" Mimi asked, taking notice of Hannah's gray coloring. "You don't look well."

"I wanted to see what was so important that you couldn't be bothered to come and see me, Mimi. I couldn't imagine you pulling the grieving widow routine.

"The nurses told me you haven't even called to ask how I was."

"I'm sorry, Hannah." Mimi hung her head. The scared, helpless feeling had kicked up again in the pit of her stomach. "Please don't be mad at me. I needed some time alone. It's been so long since I've . . ."

Hannah snorted. "Oh please, Mimi, spare me. *You* needed

time alone? Who do you think you're talking to? You can barely go to the bathroom alone."

"Scared little rabbit—can't even go to the toilet by herself!" How many times had Esther used those same words to shame her in front of family and strangers? Miriam plunged down the hole of the memory, and all the landmark ones like it. Esther picking out her prom dresses . . . always too frilly and sexless and old-fashioned. Esther choosing the passages for her bas mitzvah, and the vows she'd recite at her wedding. Gordon choosing her clothes and her friends. She hadn't even been allowed to name her own child—Gordon and Esther had taken care of that.

The same rage she felt while cleaning out the bedroom closet again filled her. She drew up, clenching her fists. "Oh, fuck you," she said. Then louder, "FUCK YOU!"

Incredulous, Hannah stared at her. "What the hell has come over you, Mimi?"

"You aren't going to run my life. Do you think I don't see what you're trying to do? Did you think spineless Mimi was going to turn her life over to you once Gordon was out of the way?"

Hannah sat up. "Mimi, I . . ."

"I don't want to hear it! I've made some decisions, Hannah. I made them the day Iris got ill. I don't think this is a good idea. I don't want to be with you anymore. It's costing me too much."

Hannah smiled uncertainly. "Why are you doing this?" she asked. "Are you making a joke?"

"No. I've decided I want to be on my own with Iris. I don't want to be divided between you; there isn't room for you both. To be honest, Hannah, my daughter needs me more than I need you."

Hannah got slowly to her feet, folding her arms against her stomach. *It was the gesture of an old woman,* Mimi thought. Then, for the first time, she noticed how Hannah's mouth had an odd, sunken look. There were wrinkles around her lips.

"I'll make some tea, and then drive you back to Ellis," she said harshly. "You—you need medical attention."

Hannah's mouth went dry until her tongue felt like a piece of tree bark. "You're dumping me?" She forced herself to sound amused by the very idea. "Don't be so dramatic, Mimi. You can't do this—not after what I've done to make a future for us. For God's sake, I've . . ." She stopped before she could say ". . . *killed for you.*"

Mimi went rigid, a terrible cold sensation creeping into the pit of her stomach. "What? What have you done?"

"Waited," Hannah finished. "I've waited a long time for you."

"Maybe that's the problem." Mimi sighed, relieved. "I didn't wait for you. I got on with my life . . . such as it was.

"I'm so tired of following everybody else, Han. For once in my life I want to lead."

"Is that all?" Hannah reached out for her, running a hand over her breasts and down her arms. "Baby girl, you can lead. You can lead me anywhere." She leaned over to kiss her.

Mimi's stomach clenched at the smell of Hannah's fetid breath. Pushing her away, she hurried into the kitchen. "That isn't what I mean, Hannah," she said, glad not to have the intense blue eyes boring into her anymore. "I don't want to lead anybody except my daughter. Maybe in a few years I'll be ready for something different. You filled a need, but it was only temporary. You have to move on now, Hannah."

Only when she placed the cup in front of Hannah, did she have the courage to look her in the eyes. In them she read a curious mixture of horrified fascination, hatred, and fear. Pity and guilt caused her to take Hannah's icy hand and chafe it warm.

"Drink your tea, Han," she said with the kindness of a Jewish mother. "It'll make you feel better."

"Oh, I don't think so, Mimi," Hannah said in a voice that was dry and hard.

Mimi thought only that Hannah was sick and unhappy. She didn't realize she was listening to the voice of doom.

"No dog?" Tim whispered. "I heard Hersh had a shar-pei that he used to show his patients what face lifts . . ."

Adele gave him a look. "No dog. Gordon was allergic to pet dander."

"Security system?"

"Disabled or broken."

"How do you know?"

Adele shot him another sharp look. "Oh, please. I was Miss Security System of the 1986 Marin Home Show, remember?"

He held up a hand. "Okay, okay. Just checking."

"You check the front of the house, I'll do the back." She nodded to the gun in his hand. "You're not going to need that."

"You do things your way, Monsarrat, I'll do them mine." He smiled broadly, which had the desired effect of stopping the rush of her irritation.

Adele peered in the study windows, creeping from bush to bush. She couldn't believe anyone with as much money as the Hershes hadn't been told of the security risks of so much dense foliage against the house. The kitchen windows were too high off the ground for her to see anything, but she could hear women's voices.

She headed for the rear of the house, where there was a patio between the kitchen and the pool. Inching her way to the end of the house, she peered through the oleander to the patio windows.

From her vantage point all she could see were the bottoms of two long skirts. Off the back of a high stool hung a purse—Hannah's purse. A pair of tiny feet in Birkenstocks were barely visible from under the black skirt. Mimi.

The women's voices were low. Adele moved closer to hear them.

". . . feel different now." It was Mimi's voice. "For all

those years, Han, I was infatuated, crazed with that sexual energy. I needed you . . . or I thought I did. Please Hannah, try to understand, I want a normal life with Iris. We've been given a second chance. I'm just not ready to have a relationship with you. Maybe sometime in the future we can be friends, but for right now . . ."

"It's okay, Mimi. I understand. Drink your tea and then . . ."

Adele made a sudden, noiseless leap through the oleander bush in alarm. Mimi was pouring hot water into the cups that sat in front of them. Completely out in the open, Adele inched closer to the house, keeping her eyes on Hannah's lower half.

Within a few seconds, one hand snaked down to the purse and opened the flap. It disappeared inside and pulled out an object. Adele squinted.

"May I . . . some Equal?" Hannah asked. ". . . can't drink this without it."

"I've . . . somewhere . . . the maid puts . . ." The black skirt turned and the Birkenstocks disappeared from view. The hand also disappeared for a moment, then returned whatever it had held to her purse.

Adele swiveled on the balls of her shoes, stood up, and ran like the Devil himself was chasing her. At the front door, she rang the bell and banged the brass lion head knocker at the same time. Tim rushed around the corner of the house, but did not step onto the porch.

"What the hell are you doing?" he whispered.

"She's dosing Mimi!"

"She's wha—?"

At that instant, the door opened. Before her, Mimi stood holding a cup of steaming liquid. "Why Adele! What a nice surprise to see you. Won't you come in and have some tea?" she asked, half lifting her cup.

Without hesitation, Adele took the cup out of her hand. "Do you mind?"

Astonished by the sudden gesture, Mimi's mouth flapped.

"Ah, no. I, ah . . . I was just having . . . tea with . . . it's ah, herbal?

"Come into the kitchen. Hannah's here and . . . Won't you come and join . . ."

Adele ran past her to the kitchen, which was empty. The patio door stood open. Adele put Mimi's tea down on the counter. "Don't touch that or Hannah's tea!" she warned, running for the open door. "They might both be poisoned."

Mimi looked at her own cup, then at the nurse's retreating back. The chill that had started in her stomach returned, bringing with it the full realization of something she'd suspected, but did not want to think about.

She caught up with Adele on the far side of the pool.

"Go back inside," Adele demanded.

Mimi ignored her. "I know the way she has to go to get off the grounds," she said. "There's only one gate in the wall."

Adele was starting to say that she knew the layout when the petite woman took off in an astounding sprint that made her feel like a slug. She made a mental note to invite Mimi on a challenge run.

As the lights from the San Francisco skyline came into view, Adele saw two people in silhouette approach them.

"Tim?"

He was out of breath. Hannah was struggling with the handcuffs.

"I got halfway through Ms. Sandell's Miranda rights when she decided she needed exercise."

"You have no right to do this!" Hannah yelled.

"There are ten innocent people who, if they were still alive, would disagree with you, Ms. Sandell."

"You don't know what you're talking about!" The icy eyes darted around, straining to see the detective. "I haven't done anything. I'll hire the best lawyer in the country to sue you for wrongful arrest. I'll . . ."

Adele stopped listening to the woman's rantings, and paid

attention to the more subtle things going on—things that Hannah didn't want them to notice, such as how the muscles of her body were beginning to tighten. The fine, involuntary movements were almost imperceptible, but Gavin had taught her well how to interpret such movements.

Within a second of the thought, Hannah made a lightning fast move, breaking out of Tim's grip, knocking him off balance and jamming her knee into his face as he went down. She had turned to run, but Adele was ready.

Raising her leg, Adele snapped the heel of her left foot into Hannah's knee. The joint gave like a piece of rotten wood. On Hannah's way down, Adele snapped her arm out straight against the woman's neck in a move she knew as a clothesliner.

Hannah thought she'd been hit with a volley of bullets as concurrent flashes of white pain jolted through her body. Spinning around, the last thing she saw before the detective fell on her was Mimi's triumphant smile.

TWENTY-THREE

IRIS SAT ON THE WINDOW SEAT NEXT TO THE pale, sleeping woman.

"Is she okay?" the teenager whispered to Adele, "She looks so skinny and . . . and like she's still sick."

"She *is* still sick." Adele moved her feet into the path of a shaft of sunlight running across Cynthia's living room and studied her sleeping friend. Bringing the nurse home from the hospital had been a happy occasion for everyone—her, the patient, and most certainly for the staff sentenced to caring for her.

"She isn't as young as you are, and I think she probably got a larger dose of the D-seven than you did. You were actually lucky to be the first victim; Hannah didn't know how much to give at that point. You probably got about half of what she gave everybody else."

"Oh yeah, I'm so lucky," Iris said bitterly. "She turns my mother into a lesbian, then she murders my father. The next thing she'll do is get the papers to broadcast every disgusting detail of her relationship with my mother. We'll all be in some awful magazine. I'll never be able to go anywhere without people pointing at me or whispering behind my back."

Nelson nuzzled his head under Iris's hand, silently demanding to be petted. Despite the sudden well of tears, she ran both hands gently over the dog's head, stopping to scratch behind his ears.

Adele let the girl have her misery for a moment, then

leaned back in the beanbag chair, studying the ceiling. "Do you know who Patty Hearst is?"

Iris shook her head.

"How about Jean Harris or Squeaky Fromme?"

"No."

"Heidi Fleiss?"

"Oh yeah," Iris said with the absolute conviction of a teenager who knows everything. "I read about her. She won the Nobel Prize for literature."

Adele speculated on whether or not Ms. Fleiss's address books could be considered literature and decided not.

"Uh, no she didn't, but the point I'm trying to make is that all these women did things that made them infamous characters. But if you and I fell over them today, we wouldn't know them.

"My friend Kitch believed that people's main interest is in themselves. Unless you are a true Hitler, most people who make the news—no matter how scandalous—are forgotten quickly. Or, to use his exact words, 'In a few years, who'll give a rosy red rat's ass who you are or what you did?' "

Iris smiled.

"The only people who are going to remember what went on will be the survivors of the victims and Hannah—if she's still alive.

"Your real friends won't give . . ."

". . . a rosy red rat's ass?"

"Exactly. Hey, look at it as an opportunity to see who your friends really are."

Nelson whined for more attention. Not getting it as fast as he thought he should, he climbed onto Adele's lap and licked Her face. It wasn't something he normally did, but Nelson wasn't a normal dog.

Adele pushed him off, wiping her face with the hem of her skirt. "Remember that fire in Oakland when all those houses burned down?"

Iris nodded. "My father and I watched it from the top of

Mount Tam. I remember because he taught me how to say conflagration."

"Well, I had some friends who lost everything they had . . . antique furniture from her grandmother, a superb music collection, cars, irreplaceable old photographs—things that take a lifetime to collect.

"When they were allowed to go back to where their house used to stand, they sifted through the ashes looking for anything that might have been spared. Out of a whole houseful of possessions, they came away with a silver picture frame, an antique vase, and a bracelet.

"Those things that had previously been minor items in the scheme of all their valuable possessions, suddenly became priceless."

Iris silently stroked Nelson, listening intently.

"I know how much you loved your father, and I hope you'll go on loving him for a long time. You can't bring him back to life, just like you can't change anything that's already done and said. All you can do now is sift through the ashes, rescue what's left and go from there."

"In other words," Cynthia spoke without opening her eyes, "if you step in shit, use it to fertilize the rest of the garden."

"Hi, Sicko." Adele got up and made room for herself on the window seat. Cynthia opened her eyes and gave them each a pinch on whatever limb was closest at hand.

"How do you feel?" Iris asked. Apprehensive about losing any more people close to her, she gingerly patted Cynthia's leg.

"Like a million bucks . . . have stampeded over me wearing spiked heels attached to their hooves." She sat up and ran a hand over her face. "Man, I'll tell you one thing for certain—never, for the rest of my life will I ever let anybody buy me another cup of coffee."

Adele and Iris laughed. At the sound of merriment, Nelson wagged his tail and jumped up onto the window seat. Pushing the ninety-pound dog off her lap, Cynthia crossed her legs in order to make more room for her two sickbed over-seers. "What's the latest from the Blue Roof Motel?"

The Blue Roof Motel was the popular name for the Marin County Civic Center—a monstrosity of a Frank Lloyd Wright building which indeed sported a bright blue tiled roof. Housed under that roof were the county jail and the sheriff's department.

"You'll be glad to know that Hannah is wearing one of the county's most elegant orange jumpsuits and some matching ankle bracelets," said Adele. "She's awaiting arraignment. She hired the illustrious Mr. Jack Desmond to defend her."

"What does Tim say?" Cynthia asked, yawning. Immediately the two other women and the dog followed suit.

"He said not to worry—there's no way she can get out on bail. The evidence is too overwhelming. It's a capital murder case."

"You know, he called me at the hospital last night to see how I was and when I was going home. Then he just flapped at the mouth for about forty minutes about nothing. What's with him?"

Adele cocked her head. "What do you mean?"

"He was so weird. Like he's in love or on drugs."

Adele shrugged. "Who knows? Maybe he's distracted with work . . . you know how anal he gets about work." She paused while her insides quietly did flip-flops over broken bottles. "You don't think he's in love, do you?" She hoped her voice was casual. "He didn't say anything to *me* about it."

"Are you talking about Detective Ritmann?" Iris asked innocently.

They nodded.

"Oh, I know for sure he's in love," she said with decisive certainty.

"How do you know?" asked Cynthia.

Adele sat poised, expectant and freaked-out.

"Because he wears too much aftershave and he walks funny."

"Walks funny?"

"Yeah. Like his balls are swollen? You know—blue balls?"

Adele and Cynthia howled until Cynthia thought she was going to throw up.

"Timmy's balls aside, what's up with you, my little twin?" Cynthia wiped away the laugh-tears. "What are you going to do for the rest of the summer?"

Iris concentrated on her thumbnail. "My mom wants us to take a trip together across the United States. In a camper." She looked up to gauge what the nurses' reactions were. Both nodded, trying to gauge *her* reaction.

"Sounds good to me," Cynthia ventured.

"Yeah? Well, see, my mom traded in the Mercedes for this really cool camper that's got beds and a kitchen and shower in it? She said we could camp out anywhere we wanted to go. New Mexico and Yosemite? Go all the way to Maine and then down to Key West. You know, like make a circle around the whole country?

"We're thinking about moving, too. Mom said that if we find a place we like while we're on the road, we'd check it out. And the best part?"

Carried on the young woman's mood, Adele and Cynthia both raised their eyebrows, grinning.

"I can go to a school close to where we live if I want. I don't have to go to boarding school anymore."

"So I take it you and your mom are talking again?" Adele asked, remembering how set Iris was on believing that her mother had been in on the plot to kill her father. As it turned out, the only person who could convince her of her mother's innocence was Detective Ritmann. It took him a hellish two-hour private session with the girl.

"Yeah. She's changed a lot since my dad died. We've been talking more, and she has a sense of humor all of a sudden."

Iris paused. "You know, she's actually kind of smart?"

"I bet you'll find even more than that in the ashes," Cynthia said, thinking of the inner strength Mimi must have had to face the initial scandal.

"What about you?" Iris asked. "What did you find in your ashes, Cyn?"

Cynthia thought for a minute. "Well, I met you, and I got a few weeks off from work, and I now know how it feels to be intubated, so I'll never again lose my patience with an intubated patient who's fighting the ventilator.

"But my best find is that from now on, anytime I get into trouble, Adele has to take care of it for me." She beamed.

"How do you figure that?" asked Adele.

"You saved my life—twice. There are many cultures that believe that if someone saves your life, they're responsible for everything you do until you die; good ..." Cynthia smiled a nasty smile. ". . . and bad."

Adele groaned, lowering her head in her hands. "Does this mean I have to find myself a good lawyer?"

"Forget the lawyer," Cynthia said. "I suggest you start looking for a good shrink."

TWENTY-FOUR

THE MAN SEARCHED HIS INSIDE JACKET POCKET
for a handkerchief.

"I suggest we find a couple of good shrinks first thing."
He unfolded the square of cloth with "JD" embroidered in
one corner and dabbed at his upper lip. "Men who are
respected in their field, used to giving expert testimony."

Hannah paused in her study of the cheap weave of the orange denim jumpsuit to glance across the table at the notori-
ous Jack Desmond, attorney-at-law. He was pudgy, soft as
dough, and wore a gold pinky ring. She found him repellent.

"A psychiatrist?" She frowned, not understanding. "For
what? I'm not crazy."

Loosening his tie, the man leaned back in his chair and
chuckled contemptuously. Christ, what had he eaten for
breakfast that made him sick? The sausage? Maybe the
eggs. He belched. Probably the bacon—it had been too
soggy.

"Don't play dumb, Ms. Sandell. Murder by poison is, by
definition, premeditated murder. It's also one of the first-
degree murders that is punishable by death.

"There isn't a jury in the world who is going to sit and listen to months of testimony about a rich, successful woman,
also a lesbian—though definitely not an equal opportunity
employer—who deliberately poisoned twenty-eight innocent
people, ten of whom died a horrible death—and not want to
hang you personally."

He rubbed his eyes and drank off the last of his tea, which

had turned cold. He slowly walked across the attorney-client interview room and stood close to the barred window, hoping for some fresh air.

"Christ, the prosecution will have them weeping in their hankies with photos and personal profiles of the vital young victims who died, and the sweet old people who were robbed of their golden years.

"Then just when they're nice and vulnerable, they'll bring in your personal X-rated videos and photos of the box of sadomasochistic sex toys under your bed. They'll bring in your employees to testify that you were a Simone LeGree . . . a—a—" He searched among the papers in his briefcase, picked up one and read from it: ". . . an 'abusive monster to work for.' That was from your receptionist."

He picked up another sheet. "Your firm's manager reports: 'Ms. Sandell continually harassed the female employees, sexually and emotionally, threatening termination if her demands weren't met.' "

He looked at her. His upper lip turned up into a sneer. "Ms. Sandell, by the time the prosecution and the press get done with you, nothing less than the death penalty will seem adequate. You'll be portrayed as a perverse, cunning, scheming fiend, worse than Susan Smith, Jeffrey Dahmer, and Timothy McVeigh put together. You won't even be safe with the other inmates."

The lawyer shook out his handkerchief and wiped his neck.

"At the arraignment we'll need to enter a plea of not guilty by reason of insanity. It's the only defense you have, Ms. Sandell. I know several psychiatrists—'hired guns' we call them—in Sacramento and L.A. who specialize in . . ."

"I'm not crazy," Hannah insisted. The voice of the man who had raped her ricocheted through the years until the voice of her mother drowned it out.

Greta Nyquist. The woman materialized behind the attorney's shoulder. Hannah shuddered with hatred. When the aging prostitute had had enough of the streets, she'd tracked

her down and threatened—like Fromer—to go to the papers
with the lowdown on the White Swan. What the boozed-up
old cow demanded by way of hush money was staggering—
a million dollars and fifty percent of Sandell Designs.

Hannah knew it wouldn't stop there. No matter what
she gave the despicable waste of flesh, the extortion would
go on forever.

The deal she made with Tony Saludo to rid herself of
Greta was simple, his price modest.

Tony Saludo suddenly materialized across the table
where the attorney sat. Surprised, she gazed at him with af-
fection. He had been the only person who cared about her.
She often thought of him as the true craftsman behind the
creation of the White Swan.

Reaching out to touch him, her hand met with a dirty
plastic ashtray instead. Hannah blinked and glanced away,
trying to get a grip on herself. She couldn't afford to have
another flashback—not now.

Mr. Desmond was still talking. "With a viable insanity
defense we can bargain with the DA's office for something
less than the death penalty. Without the insanity defense, we
won't be able to negotiate. You'll be convicted and sentenced to death.

"Ms. Sandell, I'm not exaggerating when I say that in all
my years of criminal defense work, I've never seen a case
that calls out for the temporary insanity defense more than
this one."

His shirt was soaked with perspiration, and a headache
had started behind his eyes. He'd wasted three hours of his
time with the dyke going around and around the mulberry,
and now she was going to pull the "But I'm not crazy" stunt?

She was completely off the tracks. All anybody had to
do—if they could stand it—was to look into those eyes and
see how crazy she was.

"I said I am *not* crazy, Mr. Desmond, and I won't have
anyone else saying so either."

"Well, okay, sure. You and I know you aren't crazy *now*,

but we have to enter a plea that at the time of the murders you were insane. See, if the shrinks examine you and render the opinion that you were insane at the time the acts were committed, but that presently you're sane enough to stand trial. . . ."

"May I see your pen, Mr. Desmond?"

Reluctantly he handed it to her, then watched in fascination as she fondled the barrel with her fingers.

"A gold Flèche, isn't it?"

"Uh huh. Ms. Sandell, you're facing ten counts of first-degree murder and eighteen counts of attempted murder. If you're convicted and sentenced to death—which you will be unless you enter an insanity plea—under the new expedited criminal appellate system, you'll be executed within a year and a half." He stared at her, looking for some sign of fear or panic.

"Do you understand how serious the situation is? Do you understand that you're facing almost certain execution unless we . . ."

"It's a beautiful piece of workmanship." She held the gold pen up to the light. The half smile that appeared on Hannah's face was mean for its size.

A thought crossed Desmond's mind that his client had definitely vacated the attic by way of the back stairs—as they said in the shrink business.

"It's been said that it takes a Swiss craftsman a total of forty hours to make one of these pens." Hannah put the pen against her face and slid it down over her mouth and throat. Her voice was low and almost gentle when she said: "Great care is taken that each instrument be flawless. Did you know that, Mr. Desmond?"

The lawyer shook his head in spite of the growing nausea. He smiled nervously. The interview had taken on the gallows humor of the secret code scenes between Mandrake and the psychotic General Jack Ripper in *Dr. Strangelove*. Hannah might as well have been talking about precious bodily fluids or purity of essence.

"Uhn huh." He gave what he thought might be a tight, Peter Sellers kind of smile. "Okay, well, let's put some focus on what we're going to enter as a plea." He tried pulling the writing instrument from her grip. There wasn't much of a struggle; although he was strong, he couldn't budge the thing out of her fingers.

"Pens are very functional objects, Mr. Desmond," Hannah said, her voice low and steady. The half smile was back.

"Ms. Sandell, please. We need to concentrate on building your defense before . . ."

"They record our innermost thoughts, they authorize, they put laws into effect, they make words that teach, create pain and happiness. They're small and very practical. For instance . . ."

"Ms. Sandell?" He glanced nervously at the locked door and wondered if he should motion or call for assistance. It wasn't the first time in his career that he'd thought about how long it might take for a deputy to reach him, but he couldn't remember ever feeling this threatened.

He felt in his jacket pocket, hoping against hope that he might find a stray Tylenol. The headache behind his eyes was turning into a migraine.

Fully aware of the uselessness of it, he walked to the door and looked through the glass window for a deputy. It might be a good idea to have a witness. It would add to the credibility of the insanity plea. That he hadn't brought along his assistant was an oversight on his part; one he wouldn't make again.

". . . slit open the windpipe, you can use a part of the barrel to hold the hole open so the person can breathe through it . . . it keeps the airway open, you see?"

"Ms. Sandell, please, I need your attention, here. This is your life we're talking abo—"

"Did you also know that most pens are a perfect place to conceal small amounts of cocaine or . . ." She looked up at him with a wicked, evil smile. ". . . other illegal drugs? Take even the most common of plastic pens." She held up the one she had brought with her. "They actually hold more than the heavier metal pens."

Her smile turned into a grin, her eyes not moving from his.

He swallowed bile and sat down hard. It hadn't dawned on him earlier; how did she get a hold of a pen? She was maximum security. Nothing like that would have gotten past the guards . . . unless she'd concealed it in her vagina or rectum.

"You are a pig, Mr. Desmond, or is the politically correct term 'reptile' for lawyers these days? Do you really believe that I would let you hire anyone—especially some asshole man—to make me look crazy?

"Did you ever meet Gordon Hersh, Mr. Desmond?"

He shook his head, mesmerized by the intense blue eyes. Wasn't that how Charles Manson got his followers to do his bidding? Mesmerized them with his eyes?

"Both of you have a similar need to dominate and control. The physical resemblance is almost uncanny, you know. You and Gordon would have admired each other."

"Ms. Sandell, why don't we stop now?" He began to gather his things. It was an effort. He felt dizzy and weak. "I can come back later when you're feeling better. You seem tired and . . ."

Her eyes turned hard. "*I'm* feeling fine, Mr. Desmond, how are *you* feeling? You look pale."

He felt far away, and he had this peculiar sense of being smaller.

"How was that tea, Mr. Desmond? Was it strong enough? Did it have enough sugar?"

He gripped the edge of the table. Perspiring heavily, he attempted to raise his arm to motion for the guard, but didn't have the strength to get it off the table.

Hannah was suddenly very close to him, robbing him of air.

In the dark of her shadow, his lips parted as his throat worked, trying to scream without breath.

PARADOX

The third Adele Monsarrat thriller by Echo Heron

For an excerpt of this riveting novel, please read on . . .

The three year old sucked her thumb and stared out the car window. For as far as she could see, there was nothing but thick, white fog—fertile ground for bogeymen.

"Mommy?" It came out a whimpery mumble.

As if startled by the presence of the child, the woman's gray eyes snapped to the rearview mirror. Her grave expression did not change. "What?"

"Where's Daddy and Butchie?"

"Butchie should be back there with you, and Daddy is asleep."

Erin returned her gaze to the road in time to see the side of the mountain coming at her. Reflexively tugging at the wheel, the car jumped back onto the black pavement but not before a jutting rock scraped the side. Erin searched beyond the headlights for some break in the fog. The child tugged at the too-tight seat belt and began to whine in earnest, her voice climbing the decibel scale.

"Where's my daddy and Butchie?"

"They're in sleepyman's land, baby," Erin said as tenderly as she could. The front right tire went off the narrow road and her eyes again returned to the rearview mirror, searching for something behind them. "Just like you should be. Now lay your head back and make believe you're inside a big bowl of whipped cream. Make believe we're . . ."

"I want my daddy!" the child's voice quivered and rose.

"Baby, you need to relax now. Try to . . ."

"I waaant my daaaadddy!" The high-pitched wail cut through Erin's head like a knife; there was no shriek in the world like that of an agitated three year old. To emphasize her point, the child kicked the back of the seat and pushed on the seat belt button so that the veins in her forehead stuck out, blue and pulsing.

Erin's hands tightened on the steering wheel. "We're going to Daddy right now, darling. Stay quiet and we'll . . ."

"No! I want my daddy NOW!" The ear-piercing scream that followed pulled Erin's eyes to the rearview mirror in time to see the head of curly light brown hair slide under the shoulder strap, toward the floor.

"I WANT MY . . ."

Erin reached back to make a blind grab at the child when a sharp set of baby teeth attached themselves to her pinky and sank in with all the tenacity of a pit bull. A shard of white pain shot up her arm and exploded in the back of her neck.

A slight pull in the wheel forced her attention back to the road—except the road had turned to white nothingness, and the nose of the car was at an odd angle to where the road should have been. They hung, as if suspended, in midair. Erin let go of the wheel and relaxed; the realization that she was going to die came as a relief. No fear. No remorse.

In the split second before the huge white mouth swallowed them whole, she hoped she would be forgiven.

PARADOX
by Echo Heron
Published by Ivy Books.
Available in bookstores October 1998.

INTENSIVE CARE
The Story of a Nurse

As a veteran of coronary care and emergency room nursing, author Echo Heron provides a compelling insider's look into the workings of a hospital. Here is one nurse's true story, filled with all the tragedy, drama, and triumph experienced in a life dedicated to healing.

CONDITION CRITICAL
The Story of a Nurse Continues

Echo Heron continues her engrossing chronicle of the high-pressured life of a nurse. The convict who must recover in time for his own execution and the young woman, paralyzed in a tragic accident, who vows to walk out of the hospital are just two of the remarkable people you will meet in these pages. This unforgettable account of medicine from the trenches will stay with you long after the last page has been turned.

by Echo Heron

Now, at a time when the spotlight is turned on health care and what goes on in hospitals,

Echo Heron

has written

TENDING LIVES
Nurses
on the Medical Front

a compelling collection of real-life medical dramas experienced by nurses throughout the country.

Each nurse has a chapter, every chapter written in his or her own voice. Their experiences range from inspiring to tragic to downright funny. And the stories are charged with the issues that affect nursing care today.

TENDING LIVES

is a moving, inspiring book about a noble profession.

Published by Ivy Books.
Available in bookstores everywhere.